CRITICS RAVE
FOR MINDA WEBBER AND
THE REMARKABLE MISS FRANKENSTEIN!

"[A] clever, laugh-out-loud, madness-and-mayhem romp through vampire-, werewolf- and ghost-ridden London. Webber does for vampires what Sandra Hill did for Vikings!"

—*RT BOOKclub*

"This wacky satirical paranormal romance will have readers howling in laughter...action-packed and amusing."

—*The Midwest Book Review*

THE LADY & THE VAMP

Asher lay his hand over his heart, pretending to be wounded. "You think so little of me." He held up his fingers, one by one counting off her complaints. "Let me see, I'm puffed up with my own consequence. I'm so vain I can't put on a hat. I don't know my Milton. I'm a womanizer and a rogue," he said. "And I'm also nosy. Did I get them all?"

"Don't forget rude," Jane said politely, her eyes twinkling.

Asher was encouraged. Bowing to her, he remarked, "In spite of my faults, I think you would like me to kiss you. If only to compare to those fifty or sixty other gentlemen."

"A lady would be foolish indeed to admit to such."

Reaching over, Asher lifted her chin with his fingers. "We know what I think about you being a lady."

Other *Love Spell* books by Minda Webber:

THE REMARKABLE MISS FRANKENSTEIN

The Reluctant Miss Van Helsing

Minda Webber

LOVE SPELL

NEW YORK CITY

To my father, George Webber,
who always believed that I could reach the stars,
and to my mother, Maxine Webber, who picked me back up
when I didn't quite reach them. I miss you, Dad, but I know
you are smiling down on me from Heaven.

LOVE SPELL®

January 2006

Published by

Dorchester Publishing Co., Inc.
200 Madison Avenue
New York, NY 10016

ISBN 0-505-52638-7

Printed in the United States of America.

Visit us on the web at www.dorchesterpub.com.

ACKNOWLEDGMENTS

To my sister, Marilyn Webber, for being the best sister a gal can have, and to my son, Jake Bohannon, for being the best son in the world, with no prejudice attached; Christopher K., my humorous editor, and Helen B., my agent, with great taste in humor; Ryan Faltisek for being the great guy that he is; Karla, Mary Alice, Tony and Esther for their help and comments; Yolanda, Marilyn and Karla for their always enthusiastic help and being the world's best bosses— or at least San Antonio's; Terry for being the computer whiz she is and helping me, the computer dummy that I am; the corner gang—Ron, Diann, Bill, Angie and Israel; Dan for being a great guy in spite of his stuffed-cat-abusing dog, Waggs; Mary, Christine and Missy— the cover girls; Louise and Dale, for going beyond the call of friendship, along with Shirley, for the car thing, and Alice. Debbie Lorz, my old high school chum, who drove over a hundred miles in the blistering heat of summer to pick up six copies of my book—what a friend. And for T.J.—I miss you very much, too. No one brings me police line-up tapes or stuffed animals anymore.

AUTHOR'S NOTE

No good vampires were actually staked, no good werewolves were shot with silver bullets, and no good or bad ostriches were plucked of their feathers during the writing of this book, although I'm not sure about the soiled doves. However, many enormous liberties were taken with historical dates, events and people, making this book a hardcore fiction of the quirky, fun kind. Forgive me and I'll do it again for the third book in the series.

The Mask

The trouble with being a Van Helsing was that one was expected to be a vampire hunter whether male or female, and whether or not one was up to the job. This message was drummed into all little Van Helsings from the cradle. When other children were out playing marbles and hopscotch, Van Helsings were playing hide-and-seek in crypts, pin the stake into the vampire, and "Tag, you're bit." Where other young children were frightened of monsters under the bed, in the wardrobe or in the cellars, the Van Helsing progeny were told that not only were there monsters under the bed, but behind doors, in crypts and in the shadows of the night. And it was the Van Helsing family duty to stake those blood-sipping fiends known in the ancient language as the Nosferatu.

"At least tonight I won't get blood on my gown," Jane muttered to herself, her mood dark.

It didn't matter that she, Ethel Jane Van Helsing, daughter of Major Edward Van Helsing, got nauseated at the sight of blood. It didn't matter that a life of dig-

ging up graves and dodging drops of gore was forever
ruining her gowns. It didn't matter that she had heart
palpitations over hairy-legged, beady-eyed spiders—
most especially those tricky web-spinning little monsters that crawled all over her while she was out hunting
the undead in the dead of night, and in the cold black
hearts of various crypts and mausoleums. No, none of
her feelings mattered in the day-is-night world of the
Van Helsing clan; Jane was expected to do her duty in
the most splendid and spectacular manner that befitted
her grand heritage.

Worse, no one in the Van Helsing clan besides Jane's
brother, Brandon, could understand her reluctance at
hunting vampires and then driving a Van Helsing–brand
stake through their cold-blooded hearts. Unfortunately,
Brandon was away right now in the Carpathian Mountains. She could use her brother's help right now in putting an end to an amoral immortal vampire.

Instead Jane was left to do the despised deed alone,
which was why she was standing here with her grandfather at the top of the stairs at the Stewart Masquerade
Ball, her stomach in knots.

In the foyer below Jane and her grandfather lay a
magical, sparkling kingdom, with large marble columns
decorated by large gold masks and brightly colored ribbons. Candles in Venetian chandeliers illuminated the
alabaster columns, their light reflected from large gilt-
framed mirrors hanging on cream pin-striped walls.
Servants dressed in blue livery scurried back and forth
between the jewel-bedecked and costumed guests in the
ballroom.

"Why wasn't I born a Smith or Doe?" Jane sighed
quietly as she observed flirtatious young ladies and gentlemen of the *ton* dancing their mating dance, jewels
glittering brightly from costumes re-created from days
of old. She clearly understood that tonight many a

young lady was setting her cap for a member of the aristocracy, marriage her only goal. Jane herself was not so fortunate. She was doffing her cap and taking up her holy water. While others were enjoying the night and its promise of young love, Jane was dreading it.

"Heh? What was that about a doe? This isn't a hunting party, Jane—is it?" Colonel Ebenezer Van Helsing asked. "I thought we were in London and not the country, girl."

"Nothing, Grandfather, just wishful thinking," Jane replied, patting the man's arm and staring up at him. Her grandfather was a tall, thin specimen with a long face. It was not a handsome face, for Van Helsings were rarely attractive people. Yet it was a kind face, filled with the wrinkles and lines of a long and well-lived life.

"Fishing, who's fishing? I thought we were going to a ball!"

Jane couldn't help but smile. Her crusty old grandfather was seventy-two and a little hard of hearing. What he heard was oftentimes erroneous, and sometimes rather funny.

"We are at a masquerade ball." Normally Jane loved balls, routs and musicals—any kind of social gathering. She loved London's massive residences, with their glittering decors, and the exquisite clothes worn by the Peers of the realm. Jane even enjoyed the insipid conversations about the weather and about who was seeing whom (or what). Although the *ton*'s gossip could be malicious or trivial, it was still a nice change from her usual family conversation, which was generally about saving the world from the undead.

"Of all social events, I think masquerades are my favorite," she related to her grandfather. In such a glittering world of make-believe, the green could pretend experience beyond their years; the more mature could regain a portion of their lost youth for a few precious hours, and the less fortunate in looks could cater to their lovers' fondest wishes.

For Jane, whose face was remarkable in its unremarkability, masquerading as someone else was a dream come true. She was an astute and intelligent female, and thus well knew her faults. Her skin was marred with freckles, her nose was too snub and her hair was a shade of brown that reflected neither gold nor red highlights. But at a masquerade ball, anything could happen. Even an ugly ducking could be a swan until the stroke of midnight.

"And yet, tonight I wish we were anywhere else in the world—even a dusty old mausoleum," she told her grandfather. For she had been reluctantly recruited—a dainty, bird-loving lady made to masquerade as a vampire hunter, as a temptress.

"Duty is duty, my child," her grandfather commented gruffly. "You have your marching orders from your father. Remember Operation Petticoat. It's a grand scheme. I never would have thought to use your mother's last name as a disguise, as well as this masked costume. Of course, you've been in the country so long that I doubt anyone besides your friends the Frankensteins would recognize you."

Jane frowned, her brow creased with worry. "I hope so. Father will be quite displeased if anything goes wrong." At his command, she was attending this ball as Miss Paine. The subterfuge was to help her stalk the Earl of Wolverton, a surprising powerful member of the nefarious Nosferatu. With all her previous failed attempts at vampire-slaying, she knew she needed all the help she could get, for the earl was an intelligent predator and the kind of man capable of silencing a room full of people by simply walking through the door.

"You'll do fine, Jane. You are a Van Helsing," her grandfather reminded her proudly, patting her arm. "Just don't forget the holy water," he added.

She nodded, going over her father's grand scheme in her mind. After attracting the Earl of Wolverton's attention, she was to maneuver him into an empty room, where she would attack. She was then to pool her resources: pouring holy water on him and liquidating the earl. Jane shuddered. She would have to remember to step back so that the melting pieces of vampire wouldn't splash her costume. In the murderous schools of nineteenth-century real estate and vampire hunting, Jane had learned that location was everything.

These thoughts churning in her head, Jane grudgingly made her way down the stairs with her grandfather. On the last few steps, Ebenezer Van Helsing finally noticed where they were, the ladies and gentlemen swaying and whirling before them, adorned in everything from Louis XV costumes to demon garb.

"Why are all these people dressed so queerly?" he asked, perplexed.

"It's a masquerade ball, Grandfather. Remember? That's why I'm dressed like Cleopatra and you're the Grim Reaper," Jane reminded him calmly. She knew how he hated a fuss when he forgot things, or when he went off into one of his many flights of fancy. And despite the embarrassing things her grandfather did and said at times, Jane loved the crusty old man. Sometimes she adored him more for his imperfections. To her, the slightly off-center septuagenarian was a breath of fresh air in the live-and-let-vampires-die atmosphere of her home.

"Yes, I am the Grim Reaper. Quite appropriate for me. If I were one of those sneaky vampires, I would be running scared right now," Ebenezer bragged. "Yes, *quite* appropriate."

"Quite," Jane agreed, patting his arm again. He had been quite the vampire hunter in his day, slaying the infamous Nosferatn, Lugosi, Lee and Langella. However, age had taken its toll, and the sun had set on his glorious nighttime heroics. Which was another reminder that Jane was on her own tonight. She could not count on her grandfather for help, for she did not want to endanger him; and her brother was in Austria, and her father was at home with a raging case of gout.

Her grandfather, monocle in hand, surveyed the guests, as he pointed out a colorful costume here and there. Many of the outfits looked authentic, with a few demonic exceptions.

Ebenezer shook his head. "Humbug!" he said.

Jane, curious as to what had made him use his favorite epithet, glanced over at her grandfather. He was looking at two young bucks dressed as devils.

"Ignorance is never pretty, even if it is not their fault," he said.

Jane knew only too well that in the real-life world of vampires and shape-shifters, there was an unwritten law that the less said by those in the know to the rest of the world, the better. What mortal person in his right mind would want to learn the truth of many otherworldly creatures? Who wanted to know that the big bad werewolf really had eaten Little Red Riding Hood's grandma, and that Sleeping Beauty's prince was a vampire? Run-of-the-mill mortals were just too insecure to react with any sanity about the supernatural world. And thus you saw problems like the one capturing her grandfather's attention now. Obviously these two young men attired like demons, with their scruffy-looking tails and red pitchforks, knew nothing about Lucifer's strict rules.

"Hell might be sulphurous, and it might be unbearably hot, but a dress code is still a dress code," Jane agreed with her grandfather's unspoken criticism. "King Lucifer can't abide disheveled subjects. And these young bucks know nothing about Hell. Where are the ink stains on their devilish little fingers? Devils always have an ink stain or two on their index fingers from drawing up all those contracts!"

Her grandfather nodded wisely. "And I'll be deuced. Demons never carry pitchforks anymore. Lucifer certainly wouldn't call these the Devil's own. He would burn them to a crisp if he saw them dressed as such pitiful little beggars."

"I know. Lucifer would never accept such an . . . agricultural mode of dress. And no self-respecting devil would ever have a tail so unattended-looking." Jane shook her head. "Alas, they're tails we can never tell."

Ebenezer sighed. Then, spotting one of his old vampire-hunting cronies entering the card room, he said, "There's Gellar Buffyton!" And with those words he was off, hurrying to catch up with his old friend and leaving Jane alone to review her options.

After careful consideration, she recognized that she had none. Not with recent developments. Two days ago, her father had found out that the diabolical Dracul, who had used an alias since his infamy spread across the world, was none other than the celebrated rake Neil Asher, the very stylish Earl of Wolverton—the man Jane was now after. It was amazing that he'd hidden in London for as many years as he had, especially with the Van Helsings, the scourge of vampire-kind living there as well.

Gleefully, her father's network of spies had told the major of their astounding discovery. They had been so excited by their sleuthing, Jane was surprised they hadn't shouted their discovery from the rooftops of London. The celebrating spies had even written a poem for the occasion, which Jane could recite by heart now, since her father had made her memorize each and every word. She whispered it, prepping herself for her mission like a good officer prepping his troops before war:

"Oh, you better watch out. You better not die. You better not doubt, I'm telling you why. Dracul is coming to Town! He's making a list, and who knows who'll be first? He's going to find out whose blood will slake his thirst. Dracul is coming to Town: He bites you when you're sleeping. He knows when you're awake. So hang the garlic in your bedchamber, get a cross for goodness' sake. Dracul is coming to Town!"

She sighed. "It's not Shakespeare," she admitted. But she would give credit where credit was due. Finding Dracul was the most sought-after honor her father's employees could hope to achieve. Besides dispatching the monster, of course.

Yes, everyone who was anyone in the field of vampire-slaying wanted to be the one to put an end to this most heinous and debauched undead of all time. He was a creature so perverted and deranged, he'd let his three brides feed on children while he himself feasted on young virgins, terrorizing them before he took their life's blood and their maidenheads. He was evil to the core, a vampire who had never run tame, and who knew nothing of the quality of mercy.

And Jane was to dissolve the dissolute Dracul tonight, or so her father had ordered. It would be a major achievement, and would place Jane in the gloriously elite ranks of all the other Van Helsings. This was what her father sought: his daughter's destruction of the Prince of Supreme Evil. But Jane only wanted a cup of hot chocolate, a good novel to read and her trusted dog, Spot, by her side.

Sighing softly, she regretted again that life was never quite what one expected. But then, death probably wasn't either, she decided as she watched a guest stroll by in a black robe and with a sickle in his hand.

Taking a deep breath, she forced her chin up and straightened her back, pushing her gloomy thoughts away. She was about to put her father's strategy, Operation Petticoat, into effect.

Actually, she thought as she glanced down at herself, it was a bad name for the operation, as she had no petticoats at all. In fact, she felt almost naked as she inspected her Cleopatra costume, tailored by Miss Elizabeth Burton. The gown's material was a shimmering green that clung to Jane's body while baring her right shoulder and arm. The left side of the garment had a rich golden wrap attached, hiding the deep pocket where Jane had stashed her flask of holy water. It was a costume designed to entice, yet to hide what needed to be hidden. The outfit had been specified by the major, her father, after he'd reviewed military tactics and decided to use holy water as the instrument of destruction for the Prince of Darkness. That decision had been reached after the major had painstakingly discussed in vivid detail with Jane the mis-*stakes* of her last two vampire slayings, and how this time everything would go just right.

To complete the outfit, Jane wore on her upper arm two golden serpentine bracelets. A dark golden mask covered most of her face and, to her relief, her freckles. A long black wig hung silkily down her back. In truth she looked like another woman, which gave her confidence. But, she reminded herself, "Though a daffodil may want to be a rose, it will be a daffodil even if it can somehow change its petals."

Still, she was in fine looks tonight. Earlier, when she had inspected her reflection like a general inspects his troops, she had decided she did look rather enticing. She felt almost mysterious, and attractive enough to be a seducer of Anthonys and Caesars. She hoped the subterfuge would work, and that she would be able to lure the lusty Earl of Wolverton into a secluded room. Once there, she would then do her duty, hoping not to actually have her virtue or life compromised by the earl's legendary appetites.

Jane took a deep breath. It was going to be quite a messy night. Especially for Count Dracul, alias the Prince of Darkness, alias the Earl of Wolverton.

Every Vampire Tells a Story

"Impatience is the hobgoblin of little minds," Jane reminded herself, scanning the crowded ballroom. As of yet, the Earl of Wolverton had not put in an appearance. This left Jane to ponder if the posthumous prince was out having a midnight snack while she was stuck pretending to be the Queen of the Nile. At the rate the night was going, she would have been better off having herself rolled up and delivered to the earl in a carpet, as the real Cleopatra had done with Julius Caesar. After all, Jane just wanted this whole unpleasant business over and done with as quickly as possible. Then she could go home and be privately sick.

"Humbug!" she groused. "Can't a vampire be counted on to cooperate just a tad? All he has to do is show up and be wooed. I'm the one who has to do the hard part—playing a wanton woman." It would not be an easy role for a lady who'd never even seen her brother's mistress.

Playing with the pocket of her gown, Jane continued to scan the ballroom. She noticed a tall man dressed in a

11

knight's costume. His mask hid his face and hair, but the chilling blue of his eyes struck her strangely, with both menace and an air of foreboding. The knight was whispering to Lady Veronique—a French widow with few morals, or so it was said. The lady was wearing a half-mask of gold with a gypsy costume.

Jane shuddered, wondering who the black knight was, and at her strange reaction to him. But a few seconds later both he and Lady Veronique were gone, the black knight escorting the notorious French widow from the room, and Jane felt relieved that they were gone.

Again she scanned the room, and suddenly her face lit up in a smile. It appeared that Clair Frankenstein Huntsley had arrived in London a day earlier than expected!

In spite of her apprehension and dread of the messy task ahead, Jane knew that the new Mrs. Huntsley was bound to improve her humor. Clair was one of her few close friends, since friendships were hard to form and maintain as one of those mortals living on the boundaries of the supernatural world. It was a hard life when one couldn't tell others much about oneself, unless one's friends were also familiar with familiars, werewolves and vampires. Even now, from her bosom friend, Jane still had many secrets bound by Van Helsing blood oaths that couldn't be repeated to another living soul unless they too were vampire slayers.

Yes, without Clair, Jane's life would have been much lonelier. Fortunately for her, her friend had burst into her life like a raging thunderstorm. Blithely and in her very unique manner, Clair Frankenstein had mischievously opened Jane's eyes to the absurdity of English society and their part in it. From early childhood the two girls had shared laughter and—in later, more mature years—light despair at the various eccentricities of both their families. Clair didn't care that Jane wasn't a beauty of the two. Clair didn't care that Jane was a round peg trying to fit into a square hole. Clair didn't care that Jane had yet to live up to her family motto; *A vampire a day is the Van Helsing way.*

Of course, the girls were very different in some ways. Clair was a Frankenstein, and Frankensteins rarely cared about anything not directly related to their studies of supernatural monsters. Jane's family just staked them, make no mistake about it. Clair would say, "Every vampire tells a story." Jane would say, "Watch where you stand if you don't want to ruin your gown."

And now too, Clair Frankenstein was a Huntsley, since she had recently married Baron Harold Ian Huntsley, whom she called Harry whenever she was angry or very merry. Quite appropriate, the Harry bit, Jane mused, since Clair's husband was sometimes the hairiest thing in London.

Jane giggled, watching Clair converse with two gentlemen who were dressed as a sheik of Arabia and a Roman centurion. Clair herself wore a shepherdess costume, complete with crook.

Jane laughed louder, saying to herself, "Only Clair would be outrageous enough to dress as a shepherd when she is married to one of the biggest wolves around." But then, Clair had seen the sheep in wolf's clothing that was the baron's good nature and kind heart after he'd fallen in love. Jane had heard many a rumor that Baron Huntsley was one of the biggest rakes in London before he met Clair, but he'd fallen head over paws for her. Now his wolfish tendencies were reserved for full moons.

As Jane strolled toward Clair, she couldn't help but feel a twinge of the green-eyed monster, jealousy. Less than a year ago her friend had been involved in one of her usual supernatural research projects, trying to prove scientifically the presence of vampires and werewolves in London. Clair had not known with any certainty if monsters were lurking in the city's graveyards and doorways, but had set about proving it. And Clair's comedy-of-errors experiments had yielded results she hadn't expected: marriage to the man of her dreams. Well, to the werewolf of her dreams. And Jane was jealous of her friend's happiness.

It was lucky, for Jane and Clair's friendship that the Van Helsings only hunted vampires and occasionally, demons. Werewolves and other hairy shape-shifting creatures were off-limits. Not one of Jane's antecedents had ever harmed a shape-shifter—not with the skeletons in the Van Helsing closet. A fact her mortal-purist father discouraged having disclosed was that the great monster-hunting Van Helsings had werelionesses for both a great-grandmother and a great-aunt. This ancestry Jane took great pride in. Just as she was proud that neither of her feline relatives had ever run tame, and that they lived their lives exactly as they wanted, walking on the wild side of life with their mates.

As Jane approached Clair and the two gentlemen, she craned her neck trying to spy Frederick, the Frankenstein monster. Freddie was Clair's adopted cousin, and he loved masquerade balls. He always dressed up in the most outlandish costumes. Since he was well over six feet tall, he always stuck out like a sore thumb, and was about as attractive.

Glancing about her, Jane could see several of the usual Frederick impersonators, with their green face paint and shoes the size of Derbyshire, but not the real thing. A pity. Jane enjoyed Frederick's polite, childlike manners, and was never afraid of being alone with him. Even if he did have a face that would launch a thousand ships—all running away from him, of course. But, then, his mismatched looks weren't his fault. No, that blame lay at Dr. Victor Frankenstein's feet, since he was the one who'd created Frederick out of odd body parts. The doctor really should have been more selective in his selection of a nose and chin for his monster, and not so caught up in the reanimation of dead flesh that he overlooked looks in favor of graveyard-robbing expediency. Or so Jane had thought on one or two occasions.

As she approached her close friend, Jane noted how beautiful Clair looked tonight, what with her shining golden hair and large gray eyes. "Clair, you arrived early! I thought you wouldn't be in Town until tomorrow," she said.

Clair bent her head, her tawny curls bouncing. She studied Jane's costume, listening to the voice and finally smiling as pleased recognition lit her eyes. "Jane Van—"

Jane interrupted before her friend could finish, looking at the two gentlemen standing nearby. "Paine. That's right, Clair. Jane Paine." Pulling her friend aside, she whispered dolefully, "Father is having me use my mother's maiden name for the time being."

Clair Huntsley, née Frankenstein, arched a brow but kept her expression stoic. "Major Van Helsing is at it again, with some harum-scarum scheme, isn't he?" she asked. "A stratagem most assuredly designed to deliver some poor unsuspecting dead man walking right into a permanent coffin?" Poor Jane, she thought, born a Van Helsing when she fainted at the drop of blood. The situation was so bloody unfair.

Her friend shrugged philosophically. "You know how eccentric he is, and how thoroughly dedicated to his vampire-slaying duty."

"Eccentric?" Clair almost snorted. "*My* family is eccentric. Your father and cousins are unhinged—like Frederick's wrist gets at times. Always running around in their black capes, muttering rubbish, carrying huge black bags, planning some mysterious cloak-and-dagger business stuff . . ." Clair laughed wryly. "And don't forget your cousin's fetish for crypts." How Jane, with her love of birds and her artistic temperament, had ever come from that deranged clan was a question she had asked more than once. Jane, who was made up of fairy dreams and hopes as light as gossamer wings, and who was just as fragile—she was definitely a bird of a different feather.

Seeing her friend's tense expression, Clair decided to change the subject. She smiled, holding out both hands, genuinely glad to see Jane. "Ian decided to return to Town a bit early. I meant to get in touch, and was going to call on you tomorrow if you weren't here tonight at the Stewart Ball. Now I feel like some wooly-headed female. Come, let's talk."

Actually, Clair had meant to send Jane a note saying she had arrived in London at noon. However, her adorable husband had had other ideas, distracting her with his wolfish appetites. And what a fine distraction it had been, Clair mused dreamily—love in the afternoon with a hot-blooded husband who took her to the wild side.

Waving goodbye to the sheik and centurion, Clair took Jane's arm and strolled her toward the punch bowls. "You look grand tonight and quite mysterious," she remarked, pleased. In her green Egyptian creation, Jane seemed right in line with Clair's great-aunt Abby's tarot-card prediction.

Only last night, Clair had asked her great-aunt if her friend Asher, the Earl of Wolverton, was destined to find true love. In the back of Clair's mind, Jane had popped up as a possible bride for the vampire, who himself had a few months ago popped up from his coffin and into Clair's life like a vainglorious jack-in-the-box. Since that time, Asher had saved her beloved husband's life as well as Clair's own, creating a lasting bond between them all.

Clair had been delighted when her great-aunt predicted, "A queen in green will be the means. He lives by night, his bride-to-be by daylight. She hunts his kind, but love she will find."

Clair had seen the threads of the two lives spinning themselves together, and she had wanted to laugh aloud with glee. Life was oftentimes filled with ironies, and what sweet irony that a Van Helsing vampire hunter would be destined for the Master Vampire of all London. Oh, how the fates would laugh when Clair's newest plan—Plan Z, Against all Odds—was finished and done. She didn't care one whit that the objects of her plan were mortal enemies; she had never cared for bigotry, and wouldn't stand for it now.

"Clair?" Jane called curiously.

Clair started, then smiled looking sheepishly, adorable in her shepherdess costume. "Sorry, I was woolgathering," she said.

"How is the wedded state treating you? You've certainly got a sparkle in your eye tonight. Married life seems to agree with you," Jane remarked.

Clair grinned. She had speculated and suspected much about the things that went bump in the night before marriage. Now she knew exactly what that bumping was and how delicious it could be. Well, all's *were* that ends *were*, she thought saucily.

"Married life is intense, interesting and infinitely wonderful," she replied at last, chewing on her bottom lip. But that was the understatement of the year. Marriage to a werewolf was a course that never ran smoothly. From the first moment she awoke to watch her husband of less than a day transform from mortal to wolf, the fur had flown. All of it his. It would have been awe inspiring, if Clair hadn't been so furious to find out the truth.

Why hadn't he told her he was a werewolf, when she was knee-deep in scientific research into shape-shifters and vampires? After his startling but spectacular revelation, Clair had of course tried to yell at him in an intelligent manner—but it had been next to impossible with him howling at the moon and running around sniffing all the furniture.

"We've resolved all our differences admirably," she told her friend cheerfully. "I now have a full-time lab specimen to explore to my heart's content." And explore she had—on many very interesting, although not so scientific, occasions. The scientific method had been forgotten in the search for primal passion's release.

"I'm just wild about Harry Ian," she confided happily, glad her close friend was in London so that they could share confidences once again. "He is the most remarkable man I have ever met. A jack-of-all-trades, he is strong yet gentle, tender yet passionate, intelligent yet fun to be around. He makes every day a holiday." She loved him all sleek and muscled in his human form, and she loved him all furry-faced with his big white fangs. Her husband was like many beasts in one, especially in bed on nights close to the full moon, when he answered the call of the wild. To say their love life was passionate and wild was an understatement. "These days, my only complaint is waking up after a full moon to find fur or muddy footprints in our bed."

"Yes, well, sheets are sheets, even if they are silk. But love is love." Jane hugged her and smiled. "I am glad you are so well content with wedded bliss. You deserve as much."

"As do you," Clair responded.

Jane shrugged slightly. "Happiness isn't easily found when one's duty is slaying vampires," she complained.

Noting her friend's somber expression, Clair quickly changed the subject again. Glancing down, she remarked, "I do so admire your costume. And I imagine you are much cooler than I am in this costume."

Jane laughed self-consciously. "I know it is not in my usual style, but I decided to be adventuresome tonight."

Clair was surprised. This was too good to be true. "Are you perchance husband-hunting?" She knew just how deeply Jane had been hurt by two would-be suitors when both gentlemen defected. Having desired something and failed not once but twice, Jane would be beyond timid to try again.

Although she lived in her own little world, where reality changed day to day and monster to monster, Clair was astute enough to recognize that Jane was too aware of self-perceived flaws. She was not a beauty in the traditional sense of the world of 1828 London; Jane didn't have fair skin and hair, or eyes the color of the sky. Still, she was a wonderful person and needed to know it.

"Jane, you would make anyone a grand wife. Your soul speaks from your remarkable-colored eyes, and you have a very fine character and caring disposition. There is none better," Clair complimented.

"I'm certainly no beauty. We all know that," her friend replied morosely.

"Ha! Beauty is in the eye of the beholder. Look at Frederick. Many people find him hideous to look at, but I think he is a fine specimen of many men."

Jane Van Helsing looked at her friend and laughed. Clair was indeed good and kind. "Yes, Frederick is as fine a men as any. And I'm hunting all right," she added. Was that an understatement! Then, realizing what she'd said, Jane resisted kicking herself. The Earl of Wolverton, whom her friend had once mistakenly believed to be a werewolf, was Clair's confidant now. And Jane's blood oath prescribed saying any more about her mission.

Clair clapped her hands together. "I can't believe it!

You always told me you would never get married. I'm so happy you decided to give matrimony another chance. It can truly be wonderful if you find the one you love." She looked delighted, scheming even.

Jane shook her head. Clair always saw the silver lining in every storm cloud. She was always hopeful. But the silver was often tucked away or absent. Jane's own hopes had long been dead on the vine, dying a withering death as she contemplated the long years ahead. Those years were decorated in bleak shades of gray, were shadow years, spent in darkness, her precious youth wasted in haunting cemetery after cemetery, always on the prowl for those monsters who feast on blood. She would spend her life reluctantly queasy at her stomach and casting up her accounts, fending off hairy little spiders and ruining fashionable gown after fashionable gown. All to be a Van Helsing.

"I was teasing about husband-hunting, Clair," she said when she noticed her friend's expression. "You know I am close to becoming an ape-leader at my advanced age of twenty-three. Besides, you must remember how my only season in Town went. It was a disaster of the first order." Jane needed to throw her friend off the trail; if Clair caught even a hint of the scent of intrigue, she might as well go home now, empty-handed except for a full flask of holy water.

"Your first season wasn't *that* terrible."

Jane gave a short bark of laughter with a hint of resignation mixed in. "Yes, it was. I was extremely plump, and my father insisted on those out-of-date sausage curls and gowns better suited for a dowager."

"Exactly. I always thought your father sabotaged your chances. Although I never understood why. But, then, Major Van Helsing is not a man easily understood—unless it is his love of the hunt," Clair remarked thoughtfully.

"Indeed! Truer words were never spoken. The major lives for that thrill. Foxes, birds and his prey of choice—the undead," Jane affirmed. "My father can ride the hounds to within an inch of his life and stake a vampire to the last inch of his."

Clair nodded thoughtfully, suddenly realizing the truth: The major probably wanted Jane to remain unmarried so that she could continue to hunt vampires and carry on the glory of the family name. Well, the major could just cry in his brandy 'til the cows came home. Marriage was heavenly bliss, and Jane was going to get married and so was Asher. To each other. Just, neither one of them knew about it yet.

Despite Jane's lineage, Clair knew very well that Jane would never be a danger to Asher. The girl was too softhearted. When Jane was nine, she had pulled the tail off a lizard. Clair had caught her trying to put the tail back on, woebegone and crying that she was sorry. She had only stopped weeping when Clair explained that lizards' tails grew back automatically—and sometimes their heads, if Uncle Victor was around. Later that same day, Clair and Jane had buried the tail, complete with eulogy. Clair had been quite proud of herself, using knowledge gained from her aunt Mary's work as a pet-funeral director and taxidermist to conduct the service.

Jane gave Clair a let-us-not-discuss-this-subject-further face, pursing her lips and furrowing her forehead. Clair did what all good friends do at one time or another and ignored her.

"Fiddle-faddle. Rome wasn't built in a day, and love doesn't grow on trees." Although it might hang from them, she mused wryly. "If you'll recall, I was a wallflower for many seasons. I didn't think there was anyone for me. I thought I would die an old maid aunt. Although . . . Uncle Victor did promise that he would create a husband for me if I hadn't found one by the time I was thirty," Clair admitted.

Jane couldn't help but shudder at the image.

Clair laughed. "I know! As much as I love my adopted cousin, Frederick, I wouldn't want to be married to so many different men, even if they were all sewn together. Needless to say, it wasn't one of my uncle's better ideas."

Jane agreed.

"Anyway, Jane, I am twenty-five years old and only recently fell in love and married."

"Clair, you would have had more than an offer or two if your head hadn't been up in the clouds. What with your supernatural studies and your bluestocking conversation, you ran most poor gents off."

Clair smiled shrewdly. "It's a good thing I did, or I would have missed my Ian. Speaking of him," she said, glancing around the ballroom, "where, oh where, has my little *were* gone? Where, oh where, can he be?" Perhaps her husband was in the gardens, getting a breath of fresh air since the full moon was still two nights away. She shivered, anticipating the nights to come. Call it moon glow, being moonstruck or moon-mad, but Ian was an animal in the bedchamber, taking her to unheard of heights of pure pleasure. Every night was a howl.

Since her friend was ignoring her wishes, Jane took it upon herself to change the subject. "Speaking of Frederick, I don't see him here tonight," she said, slyly peeking through the crowd in hopes of seeing that polished Peer of the Realm, the Earl of Wolverton.

"No, he's still with Uncle Victor in Germany. They're researching mushrooms. Something to do with seeing forty-foot pachyderms and twenty-foot daffodils after eating them."

Personally, to Jane, most of Dr. Frankenstein's research sounded like a big white elephant. Who really cared either way—except maybe really large mice? Next, the dumbo would be trying to prove elephants could fly. But Jane smiled faintly at Clair and nodded her head in what she hoped was an approving manner.

Out of the corner of her eye, she caught a glimpse of something happening. Turning slightly, Jane spotted him: Neil Asher, the Earl of Wolverton, alias the Prince of Darkness, alias Dracul. He was entering the ballroom.

Jane couldn't help but notice him at once, his vital, youthful energy seeming to pulsate in the air. He had an Old World charm; but, then, upon reflection, Jane remembered that he was from the oldest world there was. In mortal years the earl, Dracul, appeared to be in his mid-thirties. But appearances were deceiving, especially when dealing with vampires, who were the unholy guardians of the fountain of youth. Neil Asher, the Earl of Wolverton, was likely older than Methuselah.

Clair's attention was still absorbed in scanning the ballroom and looking for her wayward werewolf spouse, but Jane heard two young ladies remark behind her, "What a handsome devil that Earl of Wolverton is, quite the man-about-town."

As Jane studiously regarded the earl, she agreed, appreciating his devil-may-care attitude and swagger. Asher, it appeared, was never discomposed—or decomposed, she was happy to note—facing the world with great decorum. Yes, the haughty undead earl was known for not giving a fig for anyone's good opinion. But then he had a whole fig tree of regard for himself.

The women's remarks continued, and Jane eavesdropped shamelessly. "I hear the earl can't abide anything less than perfection in his life. Everything he owns is of the first scratch."

Just like Old Scratch, the Devil himself, Jane mused, noting the earl's costume. The vampire also had a devilish glint in his eye, adding to his diabolical charm. Jane found herself amused. The earl was a vampire pretending to be a man pretending to be Lucifer himself, the King of Demons.

Yes, the Earl of Wolverton dressed all in black, just as the Devil did, which meant the two probably had more than a passing acquaintance. The earl's black jacket fit him perfectly, outlining his massive shoulders and broad chest. His long legs were encased in tight black breeches, and his mask hid only his eyes and the top of his aristocratic nose, leaving the rest of his perfect countenance for inspection. His burnished chestnut hair showed gold and copper under the light of the Venetian chandeliers and glinted along with the two golden horns set atop his head. He was truly temptation on the hoof, since he affected her Van Helsing sense and sensibilities.

She sighed. It was a shame that he was a vampire. It was even more of a shame that she was a plain Jane, vampire-hunting Van Helsing and could never attract a man of Neil Asher's ilk. The earl was a connoisseur of all things bright and beauteous, all things lush and lucre-ful. Asher couldn't abide anything less than perfection in his well ordered, beautiful and hedonistic life. That shouldn't surprise her. That was a long-standing character trait of the forces of Darkness. And of men in general.

Once again, the two young ladies behind Jane made comments. "I hear Asher delights in all things great, though rarely small. Especially in the bosom area."

The other woman gasped in shock. "Charlotte, how could you know that?"

The first young lady lowered her voice, making it

hard for Jane to catch her words. "My brother told me. It's whispered among the demimonde of London."

Clair Huntsley finally spotted her husband, waved, then turned back to Jane, noting her friend was once again eavesdropping—a deplorable habit that Clair herself had proudly taught her. Observing Jane's distraction, Clair turned in the direction her friend was staring, watching the Earl of Wolverton's grand entrance. Jane was apparently captivated by the handsome vampire, which was very good for Plan Z. Clair wondered if Jane had guessed that the earl was one of the Nosferatu. She didn't think so. And Clair hadn't yet confided in her about it. She would leave that little detail for later.

Studying Asher's face, Clair frowned. "Asher is paler than usual." She remarked. She truly valued the man's friendship, in spite of his high-handed arrogance. She owed him a debt that would take a great deal to repay.

"Perhaps he's overextended himself," Jane commented thoughtfully. Being Dracul would put a drain on anyone's energy—all that debauching, drinking and despoiling virgins, she thought to herself.

"Perhaps," Clair conceded worriedly. She harbored a deep guilt over Asher's unrequited feelings for her. She knew she had hurt him deeply by not returning his affection. But how could she when Ian was the love of her life?

It didn't matter that reanimated dead flesh fascinated all Frankensteins. It didn't matter that Asher was an alluring, intelligent vampire, a shade made up of the cold touch of the grave, the call of night breezes and twilight hours. She hadn't fallen for him. Her love was Ian alone.

Asher was mystery, mist and predator. He was filled with ghosts of the wind, memories of royal courtiers with elaborate lace cuffs, finely dressed ladies in wigs and loose court morals. He was of a people long gone, people who had worn shiny armor, held swords lifted high as their battle cries filled the air. Honor and the bonds of blood had bound him then as they bound him now. Asher was centuries old and aging, though he looked forever young. But while for many years the urbane Asher was sharp of both tongue and teeth, lately his razor wit had borne a venomous twist that Clair disliked.

"I don't know," she hedged. "Asher's eyes seem rather more haunted than usual." They were stark, sad eyes, all laughter appearing to have fled into some murky darkness in the depths of his soul. That was why, in her typical Frankenstein fashion, Clair had decided to do something special for Asher to cheer him up. Something most wondrous, like finding him a wife: someone with a nice figure and wonderful silver-green eyes. Someone who was both compassionate and feisty when roused—a trait Asher would definitely need in a mate, especially with his own toplofty view of himself. And who could be feistier than a vampire hunter? Never mind that Asher wouldn't want a wife, and most assuredly not a vampire-slaying Van Helsing.

"Jane dear, Ian and I are having a house party at Ian's estate in Wales next weekend. I would so like you to come."

"I . . . I," Jane hedged. Her attention was on the earl. How could she melt such a handsome visage with holy water? But regret was a four-letter word—well, six— with which spinsters were quite familiar. She could certainly use a cup of cocoa right now to settle her nerves.

"I have invited a party of around twenty ladies and gentlemen, with guests such as Lord Graystroke and the Earl of Wolverton," Clair continued slyly, pleased to see her friend's face pinken.

Yes, she thought smugly, her matchmaking plan would be a smashing success. The old Frankenstein genes, which her aunt Mary Frankenstein swore included matchmaking, were pulsing within her. Just wait until she told Ian her plan! Clair chewed her lip. On second thought, she would keep mum about the new scheme. Ian still hadn't recuperated completely from the last one.

"A house party? How, um . . . nice." Jane nodded halfhearted, having a strong and strange urge to stick her head in the sand like her favorite ostrich, Orville, did when he got upset. She felt guilt crushing down on her chest. How could she accept Clair's honorable invitation, knowing that the earl's life was limited if her father's scheme unfolded as planned? Knowing that she intended to melt Clair's friend's face off tonight?

Rubbing her head, which had started to ache, Jane felt a dreadful coldness seep inside her. She was betraying Clair's friendship by harming this devastating earl. Yet, if he were Dracul, how could she not? But if he was the unprincipled Prince of Darkness, then why had he saved Clair and her husband's lives, at risk to his own? Where were the debauchery and depravity in that demonic deed?

"Jane you haven't answered my question," Clair said as she noted her friend's tense stance and lack of attention.

"House . . . party . . . nice," Jane replied, trying to keep her face sphinxlike. Almost against her will, her eyes were drawn back to the dashing earl, who was flirting with a bevy of beauties.

Clair laughed. "Asher knows his worth, and he makes sure everyone else does too. Come, let me introduce you."

Jane shook her head. "I need to refresh myself in the ladies' room. Later, perhaps."

Clair studied Jane closely, noticing her extreme agitation. "Is this more than nerves at meeting such a devilishly handsome man?" she asked.

"Of course not!" Jane said, looking anywhere else.

Her friend was hiding something, Clair decided. "Of course not," she agreed, giving a warm smile. Jane had a secret, and she would find out what it was. After all, she was a Frankenstein and a Huntsley now—a practically invincible combination. Oh, to what heights she could aspire, and Ian would pick her up if she ever slipped and fell. "All right then, Jane. I will introduce you later. May I remind you that Asher's not an ogre?"

"No, just a devil," Jane replied. She well knew that Asher was no ogre. He was worse. He was the fang-faced vilest of villainous vampires, Count Dracul, who wasn't even a count at all, but an earl. The liar.

Clair arched a brow.

Jane smiled. "The Devil made me say it," she joked.

Clair laughed. "Well, if you'll excuse me, I see that my husband is motioning me over to him. But I will see you later on and make your introduction to Asher. I just know that when you get to know the Earl of Wolverton, you will find him . . . most intriguing. He can be a bit overweening at times, but after all, he is Asher. Besides, my dear friend, he is someone you will never forget. I'll stake my life on it."

Jane nodded and then quickly strolled away, whispering softly to herself, "No, Clair you are staking the earl's."

Who Was that Masked Woman?

Lord Asher, Earl of Wolverton, stood alone dressed in black, his gaze riveted on the Huntsleys. He almost smiled at Clair's foolish shepherdess costume and the joke it implied: Clair protecting her flocks from the big bad wolf. The big bad wolf in question would be her husband, Ian.

Asher grimaced, uttering disgustedly, "Well, they say love is blind. It would have to be for Clair to prefer Huntsley to my own renowned personage." He shook his head and wondered: How could she prefer a lycanthrope to a vampire? After all, everyone who was anyone knew his species was superior.

For over three hundred years, Asher had been looking for a nameless face in the night, was always searching out souls and places. Suffering long, dreamless days of sleep, awakening at night, he longed for something more, some warmth lacking from his exalted world. Peers of the Realm and vampire princesses, nothing meant anything. Then, less than six months ago, Asher had almost grasped his dream. Regrettably, she had fallen in love with Ian Huntsley. And even more sadly, wolves mated for life. Asher clenched his fists and watched Ian Huntsley protectively usher his wife out of the ballroom.

Watching Asher, Jane Van Helsing stood across the room in an alcove surrounded by ferns. She was for all purposes invisible to the other members of the *ton* where she stood, and she studied Asher watching Clair and Ian exit. The earl, unaware that he was being observed, let down his guard and briefly revealed his broken and bleeding heart.

An student of both human and vampire natures, Jane was surprised. Vampires were notorious for their deadpan expressions. That the earl had revealed emotion meant that what he felt was intense. Clair had told Jane that Asher had some misplaced affection for her, but . . .

"Clair's wrong. This is no misplaced affection. Asher is in love with her," Jane realized, suddenly filled with disquiet. "But how can Dracul love anything? He's too mean. Yet, I can't blame him for loving Clair. She's adorable."

As she spoke, a slight twinge of jealously pricked Jane's heart, surprising her. She knew the earl was a handsome man—only an idiot would fail to see that. But as her mother always said, handsome is as handsome does. Sucking someone dry of all his or her life's fluid was not her idea of polite society. And even if the earl weren't in love with Clair, he wouldn't be interested in someone as mousy as herself.

Besides, Jane had a scheme to bring to fruition, just like all the other Van Helsings marching through history. They all stopped to the beat of a different drum. It didn't matter that she preferred the flute.

It was time to firm up her resolve. In spite of her many years of practice on vampire dummies, Jane had never made a true vampire kill, even though she was twenty-three years of age. This galling fact was an unheard-of and shameful precedent in Van Helsing history. It was why her father was so annoyed with her. Still, Jane couldn't help her squeamishness. She got sick when she saw little dogs run over by carriages. She felt nauseated when she saw burns on the little boys who were chimney cleaners, and she had stolen one away from his master. Now Timmy worked in the stables at her family's country home.

Shaking her head dolefully, Jane remembered her first staking. She'd been sixteen and scared. She had closed her eyes and staked the pillow in the coffin instead of the vampire. Her father had finished the task with one quick stroke, using the Van Helsing–brand, #4 mallet. Blood had sprayed everywhere. Jane had gotten sick all over the major's favorite hunting jacket. To say her father was not pleased was a major understatement. It had been a day to live in family infamy. Especially since her uncle Jakob and six male cousins had also witnessed her deplorable lack of killer breeding. She had also learned the lesson that day: Everything in life is location. A lady just needed to know where to stand.

Her disastrous and humiliating second attempt at staking had occurred at age twenty, with even less success than her first. This vampire, a newly made fledgling, quite muscular and attractive, had definitely not been an old bag of bones like the first. When Jane had opened the coffin, she'd got much more than she bargained for. The fledgling was naked as the day he was born (or made), and in full splendor, decked out in all his glory, his erection was rampant. Behind her, Steven Ray, the fourth oldest of her male cousins, had commented drolly that he'd known the vampire was going to pop out of his coffin, but not quite in such a way.

It had all been too much for Jane; she had run screaming from the crypt, her face beet red, her

cousins' taunts ringing in her ears. As she ran, she'd berated herself. Instead of striking at the vampire—or in
the very least, her cousins—she had turned tail and fled.
To this day, she was still living down that fiasco. Her
cousins called her the Streak, making sly comments like,
"Don't look now, Ethel Jane!"

After the awkward naked-vampire debacle, Jane had
been sent home in disgrace to the family estate in
Dorchester. Now, almost three years later, her father
had called her back. Unfortunately, it had been shortly
after her arrival that the spies announced Dracul had
come to Town. And that abysmal revelation had led her
to tonight, which had her reaching for the flask of
brandy she had cleverly hidden beside the holy water in
her gown's deep pocket. The strong liquor was concealed in a silver flask, which she only used in case of an
emergency—a *vampire* emergency.

Sneaking a quick peek about, Jane took a sip of
brandy. The fiery liquid traced a burning pathway to
her stomach, imbuing her momentarily with courage.
"Tonight I will just stalk up and strike with my holy water and no stake." She took another sip. "I won't have to
worry about blood splattering my gown tonight. And
that's something," she coached herself. "No bloody
mess, just a bit of watery goo."

Frown lines creased her brow as Jane tried to remember the section on the corrosiveness of holy water in the
family manual on methods of vampire extermination.
Her father had said that the earl's flesh would melt.
Nervously, she gulped more brandy. Maybe melting
flesh would be worse than pounding a stake through the
chest cavity.

Glancing over at the polished earl, Jane shuddered.
"How can I melt those exquisite looks?" She mused
again. "Maybe I can find a good reason why this job
must be done. Or maybe I can make the job a game."

Well, either way, she would have just one more sip of brandy to help the medicine of her heritage go down. Taking a long swallow, she closed her eyes. She wished she was finished and on her merry way, feeding some birds.

"A vampire a day is the Van Helsing way," she muttered to herself. Her words begin to slur slightly as she gathered her fortified resolve. Slowly she would put her plan into action. She would casually walk the earl's way and introduce herself. That would be shocking in itself, since she and the earl hadn't been formally introduced.

"Manners be damned. I have a world to save in spite of the earl's—alias *Dracul's*—good looks and my friend's misguided loyalty."

Somehow she would manage to flatter and cajole Count Dracul, getting him to walk with her into the conservatory. There she would do her wicked deed.

"This time, I won't fail. Finally the major will see me succeed." She only hoped she wouldn't be sick in the puddle that Count Dracul was about to become.

"The die is cast," she told herself firmly. "There is no retreat for a Van Helsing." And so saying, she lurched several steps forward, feeling as graceful as a swan. She felt beautiful and seductive, a siren to be reckoned with. How amazing, she thought. I can conquer the world! If only her obnoxious cousins could see her now.

She tracked the earl through the ballroom, silent and graceful as a cat, idly wondering if Cleopatra the First had been a tippler of brandy. She must have been, to have let herself be rolled up naked in a carpet and delivered to her suitor that way. Had Caesar immediately seized her? It seemed only likely after seeing Cleopatra au naturel.

A short distance away, Lord Asher paced, trying to destroy the feelings that he felt in his heart for Clair. Somewhere, men and women were locked in fiery embraces. Somewhere under the blue-black skies, lovers were kissing. Somewhere in the world, romantic words being written were shared by lovers. "But not for me," Asher moaned. To wait so long for love to arrive, only to discover that his love was fruitless—it was a hard burden to bear.

"I'm becoming morbid. I feel like somebody's walked over my grave, and maybe it's me," he complained as he restlessly stalked toward the balcony. There, the open doors were an invitation to the cool breezes of the night he so cherished. But before he could reach the door, a lady in a Cleopatra costume clumsily barged into him.

He caught her around the waist before she fell flat on her face. She had nice, lush breasts, which felt very nice pressed against him. He did so love large, plump breasts. They were so fun to bite and suck. Although he was still an old-fashioned vampire, the neck being the most erogenous zone for him, breasts were a definite second.

Examining her neck, Asher found it to be very pale and elegant, like a swan's. He'd bet she was good to the last drop. This female was definitely worth a closer look, a taste, a prime bit of blood.

He straightened, then leaned back slightly, his eyes running over her figure. The woman in his arms was small in stature—probably five foot two—but not in form. Her hips were wide, her breasts plump. Her waist, though not tiny, was also not large. His nostrils twitched. The lady had been tippling at the brandy bottle. He almost laughed as she tried to gaze haughtily at him. Her incredible silver-green eyes reminded him of moonlit mist through a wet, lush forest. Although right now they were slightly unfocused.

"I'm so sorry. It wasn't supposed to happen this way at all," she announced firmly, then hiccuped.

Asher hid his grin. "What wasn't supposed to happen?"

"I meant to dazzle you, not fall over you," she explained. Her tone was condescending, as if she spoke to a half-wit. "Don't you know anything? Pay attention!"

The little lady was a tartar, and saucy, Asher mused. "Apparently not. I don't even know your name," he admitted, wondering what the face looked like beneath her mask. Was it as remarkable as her eyes?

"I would never give my name to the Devil," she said pertly, staring at the mask he wore.

In the back of her mind, Jane thought her voice sounded a tad bit slurred. Was she tipsy? Heavens, surely not. A lady never became tipsy—most especially not in public.

The earl grinned lasciviously. "Better the devil you know." He trailed off. "And we could get to know each other oh-so-well."

Jane shook her head. Didn't she appear the epitome of English virtue? In her hazy cloud of overindulgence, she forgot she was supposed to be a siren bent on seduction.

But her prim image was ruined when she hiccuped again, quite loudly.

She remembered her task as Asher chortled. "The vicar at our church always said the Devil would try to tempt mortal man and woman. I can see what he meant. You *are* a temptation," she said, a small smile playing at her lips. This seductress demeanor was easier to assume than she'd thought. With her woman's intuition, she could tell the earl was falling victim to her charms.

"So, you have to admit you must give the Devil his due," he bantered. His blue eyes were mesmerizing. But Jane fought that off.

"Only if you like extremely hot and sulphurous places to spend eternity," she replied. She almost added that he should be particularly worried about spending an eternity in hell at the moment, because he was an immortal creature and by all accounts quite amoral too. The earl reputedly had more than three mistresses in his keeping, not to mention his three brides. Not only morally corrupt, the vampire must also be exhausted, Jane mused, making another black mark in her head against the earl. Add gluttony to the list for all his bloodsucking.

And yet, Jane's eyes welled with tears. This lovely creature was immortal now, but by tomorrow he would be dust in the wind. All he'd be was dust in the wind. The thought saddened her tremendously.

"Poor, wicked, devilish earl," she said, gazing up at him sadly. Who would cry over his coffin? He would be buried in—or swept into—unconsecrated ground. After tonight, she would never see those handsome features again for as long as she lived.

She wondered if the earl was tired of being undead, and if maybe would like to be permanently un-undead? That would be a good thing. Really, what did one do for surprises in life after one had lived for centuries? It had probably been decades since he'd walked in the bright golden daylight, watched green things grow or birds taking majestic flight, the sun glittering off their wings. The enigmatic earl was probably bored silly, and would quite likely welcome the grave. Well, maybe. If he did, it would certainly ease her guilt, she decided. Her nose became stuffy. Poor, poor, wicked earl. He would soon be a slushy spot on the terrace.

My, it was hot here, she realized suddenly. As hot as Hades. It would melt her chocolate, if she had brought any. How clever of her to have left her bonbons at home. Delicately, she wiped her brow.

Lord Asher watched in amusement as the tiny woman in his arms clumsily mopped her brow. He wondered if she was more affected by the brandy she'd consumed or by his presence. It would not be the first time or the last he had made a lady swoon, his fiery glance sending their senses and passions spiraling heatedly out of control.

"What need have I to fear hell?" he asked. "I, my dear, have been there so many times that I could make my way out blindfolded," he went on smoothly.

Jane laughed. "How delightful! We could all play a game of blindman's bluff and skip merrily to the Devil. And when you felt like it, you could lead us back." My goodness! What was she saying? The vicar at her church would be appalled.

Asher smiled. This mysterious lady in green, besides being slightly bosky, also had a sense of humor. "Maybe we should start a little slower. I could introduce you to the music of the night. That in itself is daring enough."

Staring into the earl's eyes, Jane wanted to fall into those icy blue orbs. Desire swept through her, catching her by surprise with its fearsome strength. She wanted to run into the night with him, to let him show her the heights of the underworld.

Mopping her brow again, Jane fought her attraction. Where had those thoughts come from? Must be his vampiric powers, she decided foggily. But being the Van Helsing that she was, she wouldn't let it show.

"I'd like to introduce myself," he said.

"I know who you are. The Earl of Wolverton." Jane hiccuped delicately, pondering her strange feelings for this fickle fiend of forever. Perhaps she had sipped a bit too much brandy.

The earl bowed elegantly, a gesture that was second nature. "Neil Asher, but you may call me Asher. And who are you?"

"That's for me to know and you to never find out," she responded, wondering why there suddenly seemed to be two earls standing in front of her. "Er, you don't have a twin, do you?" she asked.

"Pardon?" Asher said, looking surprised.

"It's nothing," she managed, waving her hand in the air. "I am *not* going to tell you my name. You could burn me with fire, cast me into a lake, hang me from ceiling rafters—"

Asher interrupted. "I get the picture." And he did. Ceiling rafters, what fun! She would be naked, of course, and he would kiss every inch of her delectable body before he had his midnight snack.

The woman continued, "You could drag me behind runaway horses, or carry me into the bushes—"

Asher grinned wickedly. "I could?"

Jane nodded solemnly, standing unsteadily, hoping the room would quit spinning. What vampire magic was this? Still, the crafty, devious undead earl must not find out her real name. That would be a total disaster.

Grabbing her arm, he hurried her out and down the terrace stairway, into the night where the soft glow of the moon had turned the formal gardens into a beautiful fairyland.

As she stumbled down the stone steps after him, Jane realized that her father's plan might yet be a smashing success—if only the earl would slow down. And the sooner the better. Her stomach was reacting strangely, and she felt very sleepy.

For once, fortune seemed to be smiling on her; she and the earl were alone. All she had to do now was throw the holy water in his face. Well, maybe not his face. After all, he had those remarkable blue eyes. They reminded her of the ice caps, so pure a blue as to be almost white, with a darker hue encircling the pupils. And his smile . . . Well, that smile could easily speed up a heartbeat—like it was doing now.

She debated whether throwing the holy water on his chest would still dispatch him. Face or chest, face or chest? she asked silently. The decision had to be made.

And soon, from the way things were advancing. The earl had stopped and was pulling her toward him. If only she knew which image before her was the true Lord Asher.

Squeezing her eyes shut, she opened them again to find one of the faces a bit vaguer than the other. The second must be the true earl. "If only the world would stop spinning," she commented dizzily.

Taken aback, Asher stared at the woman in his arms. "I think you've had a bit too much to drink, my queen." Perhaps the night was not going to end as he'd anticipated, with him pumping hard into this sweet Cleopatra's hot, lush valley of the Nile. It seemed he'd ended up with a sphinx.

Anxiety and guilt ridden, and quite inebriated, Jane jerked the first thing out of her pocket that she could find. Unstoppering it, she closed her eyes and prepared herself to do her father's task. She flung the contents at the earl. It splashed onto his chest, saturating his superfine jacket.

"Hi-ho!" she exclaimed. Then, opening her eyes and glancing down at the flask in her hand, she gasped in horror when she saw that the container was silver. Her wits befuddled, Jane still knew something was wrong. The holy water was in a brown bottle, not a silver flask. The thing in the silver flask was brandy. Mortified, Jane gaped at the earl as alcohol fumes hit the air. Dark liquid trailed down her foe's chest.

Astonished, Asher stared down at his ruined coat. Renfield, his valet, would be quite up in arms. His mysterious Queen of the Nile was potty in the head. Just his luck. Dryly, he remarked, "By deuce, if you didn't like my costume, you could have just told me!"

Taking one long look at her brandy-drenched earl, Jane shook her fist in the air, tears in her eyes. "Curses! Foiled again! I'll never live down the embarrassment."

Not if any of her kin heard of the night's fiasco, not to mention that the handsome earl was now thinking her the Queen of Fools. Some vampire slayer she was.

And yet, she could not but be a bit relieved he was alive. He and his beautiful blue eyes. Without further ado or fanfare, Jane turned, her dignity in tatters, and teetered off into the dark, cold night.

Lord Asher cocked his head, raised an aristocratic brow and studied the small figure hurrying unsteadily away. His mind sought out the lone stranger. "Bloody hell! Who was that masked woman, anyway?"

The Best Laid Plans of
Van Helsings on Vampires

Morning came, a gray, rainy, dismal day as Jane walked into her father's study. She found the major standing by the ornately crafted fireplace, on the moss green Persian carpet that once again she was being called onto.

"Not the old failure-is-not-an-option speech again," she mumbled under breath, praying to escape it.

Major Van Helsing was dressed with his usual military precision in a green hunting jacket, forest green waistcoat and doeskin breeches. Jane wanted to cringe at his foreboding expression as she stood and faced his steely-eyed glare.

The major made Jane feel ten again, back when she had traded her silver cross for a beautiful blue hair ribbon. The major had lectured her quite severely, throwing the brightly colored ribbon into the fireplace. Jane's other punishment had been to have her hair shorn just below the ears. It had taken years to grow out, and the incident had been traumatic for her, who at ten had only just started noticing her looks. Even then, she had known that her freckles weren't very attractive and her lips were a bit too full. So her straight hair, which hung to her knees, was her crowning glory. The shade a dark blond, her locks were her mother's pride and joy as well as her own. Her mother hadn't spoken to her father for four months after the incident, and neither had Jane.

"Your conduct is unbecoming, Jane! You are a disgrace to the Van Helsing name. This is a grave new disappointment in a long line of disappointments, I might add," the major pronounced harshly, his round face rigid with disdain.

"Chin up," Jane whispered. Dejectedly she stared at her overweight, overwrought father, wondering if he cared that his grave disappointment could have resulted in his daughter being gravely disposed—in a real grave, that was, if Dracul had retaliated.

"Jane, what am I to do with you?" he asked. "Don't you know that you don't make holy water out of wine? And whiskey? You could have been badly bitten. You must take more care. Our work is the work of angels. Last night you came home reeking of brandy, your dress a mess, babbling about ruined jackets and handsome devils. And to make matters worse, the Earl of Wolverton is alive and well." The major shook his head and grumbled, "Well, as alive as the undead can be. He wasn't a spot. I was to see the spot, Jane. To see the spot. Don't you see, Jane?"

Jane remained stoic as her father berated her. Once again, she had besmirched the Van Helsing name. She was a twenty-three-year-old family member who had never executed a bloodsucker. She was a complete washout. And there was nothing to be done about it.

As usual whenever Jane got rattled, her mind began operating on two or three different levels, leading her to blurt out comments that were unrelated. "Where's Spot?" Was her faithful dog around? "Are there any chocolate bonbons in the study?" Chocolate was her comfort food.

"Bonbons, at a time like this? Get hold of yourself soldier!" the major demanded, giving her a withering glance. "Failure is not an option when we are the last thing between the world and the dastardly undead."

Yes, here it came: the old failure-is-not-an-option speech. Jane silently groaned and rubbed her forehead, massaging the ache there. Never again would she consume so much brandy. Courage was one thing, a headache the size of the Tower of London was quite another. How her brother and cousins could literally and physically stand the mornings after their many indulgences, she couldn't conceive.

"I'm sorry, Papa. But I am no longer a girl in the nursery." She thought she might defend herself a tad.

"I didn't raise you to get bosky! And your mother raised you to be a lady!" he ranted.

"You only remember me being a lady when it's convenient. I am sorry that I failed you. That is all."

All in all, last night had been a disastrous farce, with her in the lead role. The earl was a worthy foe, and she had made a complete ninny of herself. Never had she been so gauche. Never had she sucked down so much courage-replenishing brandy. But, then, never had she tried to melt the face off of the most breathtaking man—make that vampire—she had ever seen. As she recalled the features of the tall, elegant earl, it was hard to believe he was undead. He looked very human, even in his demon mask.

"Are you absolutely sure the Earl of Wolverton is what you think he is? Who you think he is? I have never seen a vampire look so human," she said nervously, wondering if vampire bats were cute. She had never seen one. What would a vampire do for clothing when he changed from a bat into human form again? Would he run around in the altogether, exposing himself to whomever happened to be unfortunate enough to be passing by? Or perhaps, in the earl's case, *fortunate* enough to be passing by.

The thought made Jane blush, and she tried to discover where the odd feeling had come from. Was there some corner deep within her heart that hid such naughty, carnal thoughts? Feeling wanton, she quickly glanced up at her father, suddenly glad that Van Helsings didn't have mind reading abilities along with their innate stalking ability.

The major glowered at her in disgruntled silence. His look boded ill. Jane wondered what complaints and tirades she had missed while dreaming of the earl's post-bat physique.

Her father's stiff disapproval made Jane wonder if he was going to order her to polish all the silver crosses and chains used to bind vampires in their dungeons? It was an all day affair and one of her least favorite punishments, what with all the slimy silver polish getting on her clothes and hands.

"The earl just looks so . . . human," Jane explained, feeling meek and stifled and oppressed.

Her father gestured wildly, knocking a small porcelain figurine onto the floor. It was of a slayer raising a coffin lid. "Sometimes, Jane, you are as dim-witted as those birds you watch! Sometimes I fear that in spite of your remarkable breeding, you wouldn't know a vampire when he bit you on the neck. You don't think the Prince of Darkness, the Count of Contempt and Corruption, could fool you with illusions? Of course he looks human! Have you lost your senses? Have you forgotten your lessons? The more powerful the vampire, the more human he looks."

Jane shook her head wearily, walking over to pick the broken porcelain up off the floor, noting that the figure's stake had been broken along with his neck. She shivered, wondering if it was a prophetic sign. Putting the pieces on the fireplace mantel, she arranged them as the raised coffin lid, the mallet, the man and the stake. The major was a stickler for order. A place for everything and everything in its place. All was in alphabetical order here, from the books in the library to the food in the pantry.

"Then let Uncle Jakob hunt him," she said. "I haven't the experience or courage for such a task."

"Tut, tut. Any Van Helsing alive is superior to the undead, just by degree of breathing. You simply need to try harder. Put your heart into it, Jane!"

Just once, Jane wished her father would look upon her and see a lady of gentle breeding who loved music, dancing and bird-watching, a daughter who wished to make her father proud, to do her family duty, yet who desperately longed to be free to be who she truly was, not a reflection of what someone else saw or wanted.

"Sir, you thrill at the hunt of the undead. I merely love to hunt rare species of birds—and just to observe them. You enjoy hanging about in mausoleums, while I prefer museums of natural history and art. You love the blood sport of staking vampires. I love walking the hills and eating blood pudding," Jane said patiently. "Although, I must say that I despise the name." Cook had been tricky when she was little and called it fairy pudding.

The major shook his head. "I never should have married into your mother's side of the family. The Paines haven't the backbone of the Van Helsings. And your mother, God rest her soul, had her head in the clouds or the trees—wherever those bloody damn birds were nesting! Of course, it was such a pretty head and such a sweet smile she had."

Yes, Jane's mother's smile had been sweet, and in spite of the major's gruffness and harsh ways, he had loved her deeply. Jane knew she had inherited her mother's love of bird-watching. She had spent many happy years trailing beside the woman, drawing and discussing the species in the trees. "Mother was always proud of me, despite my lack of slayer talents," she replied stiffly. Her mother had never made her feel ashamed to be herself. Rather, she had made Jane feel special, like a princess in an old story.

Tears welled in her eyes. She missed the gentle influence of her mother, who had been dead these past twelve years. Though Jane had been made to study the vampire-slaying way before her mother's death, the road had been greatly eased by the woman's unflinching love—and there had been many fewer hours of Van Helsing lessons. After she passed away, Jane's life had become more rigid and structured, her days filled with training and more training.

For many years, her mornings had begun with instructions on vampire etiquette. For example, they never belched in public after draining someone dry. She also learned that a seven-course meal to the Nosferatu meant seven different victims, all of various ages. That way, the vampires got a smorgasbord of flavor.

The major ignored his daughter's furrowed brow and wounded dignity. "Do you remember any of what you were taught?" he asked.

Jane nodded dutifully, although she could only come up with two things on such short notice. "Don't charge until you see the red in their eyes, and a rolling Van Helsing gathers no bites."

"Quite. Rules two and five. Never forget that vampires are vile, vicious and vulgar, each dying to drain you dry. They all suck. No, never forget your lessons, Jane, for they will save your life."

"Yes, sir." Her training was flooding back. Jane had learned how to walk among the living dead quietly and keep living. She could shoot an arrow over eighty yards and hit a target, but only if the bull's-eye was inanimate and painted yellow. If the target was alive, such as a deer, Jane always missed. Perhaps, she thought dryly, she could ask the earl to wear a yellow waistcoat and stand very still. After all, he was an inanimate object, was true dead weight.

"Bloody gout! If only I could have gone last night, I would have struck, splashed and succeeded. I can't have my brother Jakob driving the first stake! Not this time. I would never live down the ignominy. Ever since he gave Vlad the Impaler a taste of his own medicine, he has crowed like a cock. This time, I will be the cock. Dracul, grandson to Vlad, is mine." The major stared at her, his fists striking the chair. "The earl won't escape my clutches!"

Jane pursed her lips, her eyebrows beetling. A pox on her father and his imbecilic competition with his brother. Their sibling rivalry was a competition that had begun in their childhood. First the Van Helsing brothers had struggled against each other to see who could carry the most coffins. Next had come seeing who could lob garlic cloves the farthest. Later it had been a fierce race to see which brother could invent the newest stake technology. As they'd reached adulthood, Jakob had married Edward's childhood sweetheart. And to put the icing on the cake, he had snuffed Vlad the Impaler when only in his twenties. The heroic feat had made him the more renowned Van Helsing in supernatural circles, forever garnering Jane's father's dislike and envy.

"It's not *your* clutches that hold the stake," Jane retorted incautiously. Her father's contemptuous glare caused her to wince.

"I am ashamed of you, Jane. Deeply ashamed. You know I would proudly lead the charge if it weren't for this damn gout! As my daughter, it is your duty to do what I cannot. You have Van Helsing blood flowing through your veins. Get hold of yourself, girl!"

Jane sniffed once and looked away. To the major, all other forms of human endeavor shrank in significance compared to war with the undead.

"We must develop a new strategy," the major went on. "I won't let that degenerate Dracul get away. My daughter will be the one that does the demented monster in. Jane, you will just have to keep a stiff upper lip and all that. Go once more into the breach. Once more. Imitate the action of the tiger and summon up the blood."

"Great, just great," Jane mumbled. Her father was misquoting Shakespeare again, not to mention speaking of blood. A subject that had pretty much been drained dry.

She listened listlessly as her father formed a new plan which she would be expected to execute. In her head she objected quite loudly, but on the outside she remained the perfect picture of the well-bred lady, listening politely.

Her dog, Spot—a cross between a mongrel and a mutt, with one black circle around his right eye—wandered into the room, sniffing at Jane's skirts. Jane tenderly patted his head. Spot loved her unconditionally, as her mother had done. There was no feeling quite like being loved like that, she realized.

Her father went on, "This new strategy is brilliant, and you will execute it brilliantly. You will sneak up on the earl, and he will never know what struck him."

Jane doubted that. She couldn't resist pointing out, "I imagine having a four-foot stake in the heart would be pretty obvious, most especially to the devious undead."

Her father glared at her, and Spot laid his head on her shoe. Jane sighed. Life as a Van Helsing was never easy.

Although, she could say, it was also never dull. Her family was the life of any party—of course, they mostly hung out with the undead.

Sneaking a glance out the room's large bay windows, Jane noticed a skylark feeding at her brass-plated bird feeder. What a delicate little eater the bird was. Jane smiled, wondering abstractedly if man would ever fly the skies as freely. Probably not; even her ostrich, with his large feathers, couldn't get his massive weight off the ground. No, man would never fly. Only vampires who turned into bats in the dead of the night were delegated that privilege.

More movement outside the window caught Jane's eye. "Oh my goodness," she whispered. It was the yellow-bellied sapsucker again. What a marvelous bird he was, with all his golden plumage. If only she had her drawing materials. Could she match that vivid hue? She spent hours detailing her birds.

"Jane, pay attention," her father ordered gruffly.

Again she sighed, and the bird flew away. Another day, another duty, another mission. She only hoped that this one she'd achieve.

"Troop alert, Ethel Jane! Our new strategy is a bloody fine one. Your treacherous target will never know what hit him."

"Perfect," she agreed resolutely. Curses! What had she missed by daydreaming?

Missing his daughter's peevish expression, the major raised his brandy glass in a regimental salute, saying brusquely, "Tally ho! Jane, you can do this. I *know* you can. Be all the Van Helsing you can be—and that is quite a lot. No bloodsucker will ever get the best of one of us, not even a female. Remember, the only thing you have to fear is fear itself."

"Well . . . let's not forget the big bad vampire with his

big white fangs," Jane muttered, resisting the urge to give a military bow. Annoyed, she cocked her head and glared at her father's back as he turned. Her faithful dog, Spot, did the same. Picking up on Jane's agitation, he growled.

The major scowled. He had heard Jane's quietly whispered blasphemy. From leading and training men for a number of years, the major understood how bad it was when the troops were unhappy. He could tell that Jane was angry. He could hear that Spot was too. But it couldn't be helped.

"The world must be saved, and the Van Helsings are the only ones who can accomplish that objective," he reminded his daughter gruffly, hiding his disgust. To think, the world needed saving, and all he had to offer was his angry, calamity-ridden daughter!

"Remember, Jane, the early Van Helsing gets the vampire," he advised over his shoulder. "If only your brother, Brandon, were here, instead of off chasing vampires in Transylvania. Transylvania, of all places! I told him not to go there. No self-respecting vampire I know would be caught dead in that country. It's too backward."

"Dead, who's dead?" Jane's grandfather shouted as he tottered into the room, a bony hand to his ear.

Jane smiled slightly at him. He was a dear man, if a handful. "No one yet, Grandfather," she said loudly. "We were talking about the next vict—vampire to be slain."

"Capital, capital. The only good vampire is a dead vampire," her grandfather agreed. He then went about preparing several mousetraps with cheese and blood pudding.

Rubbing her forehead, Jane tried to ignore the insistent stirrings of a headache. Seven years ago, her grandfather had gotten it into his head that the ghost of Christmas present visited him on a regular basis, asking his advice on who was naughty and nice. But the ghost of Christmas present Jane could live with; after all, he only visited three times a year. What truly annoyed her was that four years ago Ebenezer had become fixated on the idea that vampire mice had invaded the house. It didn't matter that there wasn't any such thing: her grandfather was convinced. He had set about building a better mousetrap to catch the devious little suckers. In the country with Jane last year, he had even invented the coffin trap. A marvel of nineteenth-century ingenuity it would have been—if it had worked. Instead, the coffin lid, which was supposed to snap shut once its quarry laid down to rest, generally fired late and only caught the tail. As far as Jane knew, the Van Helsing properties had the best-fed mice in London—and they were all en*tailed*.

Things that Go
Bump in the Night

The purple hue of twilight filled the heavens as stars climbed higher in the sky, while Jane Van Helsing trudged sadly toward her dismal duty. The wind whipped through the trees, blowing several dead leaves westward where they caught, crackling, in the tall wrought iron fence to her right.

"My father is having partridge pie with lemon tarts tonight, and I'm having to stake for dinner," Jane grumbled to herself. Then, rhetorically she asked, "Brandon, where are you? Oh, brother, what am I to do?"

Despite Jane's abysmal record at staking vampires, the major felt too much was at stake for a staking to be postponed, so Jane was to strike immediately—make no mistake. In the process she'd be taking a life and breaking her friendship with Clair. All to make her father and dead ancestors proud. She'd rather jump in a lake.

"How I hate the smell of burning vampires in the night, and the metallic smell of spilled blood," Jane muttered, recalling the earl's attractive countenance the evening before. She recalled arriving at the masquerade ball and meeting the handsome vampire, but later in the night was all blurred. Jane felt a shiver run through her—a shiver not related to fear, but to something more primal. She almost gasped aloud, finally realizing that the feeling was desire. When she and Clair were younger, they had secretly read about certain things men and women did at night. The books had been forbidden them due to their explicit nature: their use of the word *leg* instead of *limb*.

The thought slowed Jane down, her trot subsiding to a fast walk. "No, it's too absurd. I don't desire the Prince of the Profane, the Fiend of Forever. I couldn't. Not really."

She shuddered again as the truth bored into her. She had wanted the earl to kiss her last night. She had longed to feel his cold lips upon hers. She had longed for the touch of— "It must have been the brandy," she told herself, cutting off further thought.

Humbug! What would her mother say about a daughter who felt desire, especially after all those lessons in ladylike constraint? Ladies didn't think about kissing or anything that went on in the dark of night. And while Van Helsings did, they were primarily concerned with four-foot pieces of wood and the hearty placement of them. Also, a true Van Helsing would never desire a creature who sucked down his food. Not only was that evil, it was bad for dinner parties! What would her ancestors say? They were probably turning over in their graves right now.

Worse, she began to consider what her father would say. "Court-martial, definitely," Jane remarked to herself. "With no Van Helsing honors and no French horns playing taps." He had really become quite the bear after her mother died.

Now he was autocratic, fanatical and would be permanently disturbed to know that his daughter was fan-

tasizing about the Earl of Wolverton, aka Dracul—
most especially since the major was patting himself on
the back over his newest plan. He called it Out on a
Limb. The point being to penetrate the six-foot-two
vampire from above, in a tree. The strategy had been
adopted due to Jane's being too short to stake accurately
any six-foot-something creature, even standing on tip-
toe. And this would give her momentum, diving down
from above.

Yes, like the name implied, to accomplish her mission
Jane would have to climb a tree and go out on a limb. It
was not a bad plan, really, Jane told herself halfheart-
edly, trying to be fair to her zealot father as she approached the large oak at the end of Berkeley Square.
She'd attempted worse. She was simply branching out.

"Maybe if I were a monkey," she mused. "Or what if
I were an acrobat at the circus—or that attractive
though rather apish Tars, Lord Graystroke, fellow? The
major's plan might just be perfect." But Jane was all too
aware that she hadn't climbed a tree since she'd left the
schoolroom. This was bound to end in disaster.

Stopping at the massive oak and glancing about, she
noted that only fog filled the night. No one was around.
That's one good thing, she thought as she stared up, up,
up the huge trunk. But she couldn't think of any other
good things.

Jane sighed in resignation. It didn't matter that she
was rusty at climbing trees; she could just as well forget
her insecurities and fears. "Tonight's the night. It has
just got to be all right." She had to have a reason to believe that. She knew the rules. The first cut must be the
deepest, and must be true to destroy that which was
forever young. Her father's vampire-assault trainer,
Mr. Stewart, had cautioned her that to spare the rod
was to spoil the sneak attack. Then Mr. Stewart had

patiently gone over the rules again and again, despite her telling him that she didn't wish to talk about them anymore.

"There had better not be any spiders or cobwebs in that oak tree," she called out dramatically, hoping those things would take it as a warning and flee. She could really use a nice piece of chocolate about now. That was her cure-all for feeling overwhelmed.

"Bah! Humbug!" Disgruntled, she tucked her skirt ends under her belt. Mr. Stewart had suggested she wear breeches like a boy. Horsefeathers to that! She would be a very old maid before she let herself appear in public in pants. Vampire-hunting might be a messy, dirty job, but she would still be the same dignified lady she'd always been. Or that she'd tried to be.

No, just because she was a slayer, that didn't mean she had to ignore fashion. She wouldn't. Thus her silk gown of pale peach had lace at the neckline and sleeves. The dress was of the first water, meaning the design had only recently arrived off the boat from Paris. Her one concession to practicality had been to wear her hair in a single long braid, rather than atop her head as usual.

"All dressed up and no place to go but up a tree. Humph!" she muttered.

Checking once more to see if she was alone in the square, Jane unslung the black bag of tools on her shoulder and set it on the ground, then removed a rope. As she began fastening the rope to both her body and the bag, she pursed her lips, her expression one of supreme irritation.

"There is *another* problem with being a well-dressed vampire hunter," she realized, preparing to climb the tree. "I bet I chip my nails or bark my shin."

She stifled the mad urge to kick her black bag, for it held all of her work tools: silver crosses, chains, holy water vials, garlic, all manner of stakes. She had so many different kinds of stakes, all made by her family. Each was specialized.

Jane began to climb the tree, her gown tucked between her knees. After several awkward starts, she finally reached a limb she felt reasonably certain would be a good perch: She would have a bird's-eye view of her hapless victim's approach. Unluckily, she not only chipped her nails in the effort, but also skinned her knees and tore her gown. Muttering unladylike curses, she vowed this time her father would outfit her with three new silk dresses for the one she'd ruined on his stupid, stupid plan.

"That is, if I live to see the dawn and Madame Burton's dressmaking shop again," she admitted.

Cautiously, Jane settled back against the harsh bark of the tree, wishing she was home in her big soft bed with its plump pillows. She would so much rather be there with a good novel and a nice cup of cocoa. Or she could be working on her drawings of the yellow-bellied sapsucker to add to her beloved collection.

Realistically, Jane knew she lived with her head in the clouds, but it was so much prettier up there. There, life was beautiful, filled with light, laughter, dignity and serenity. Make-believe was much dreamier than her cold, bleak life of cemeteries and walking corpses. Well, Lord Asher was somewhat dreamy, but she had to kill him.

Leaning her head against the oak, Jane decided that if she survived this night, she could have a treat. She would have *both* cocoa *and* chocolate bonbons. Imagining the rich taste of the chocolate on her tongue enabled Jane to forget her circumstances momentarily, until a realization called out for immediate attention. She'd forgotten her bag on the ground.

Swearing and slapping her hand against her head, she leaned over and struggled with great effort to haul the tools up to the limb where she was perched. Once she and the bag were securely settled, she began to check the supplies. Her father had warned her time and again that her tools must be kept clean, in mint condition and in alphabetical order. She hoped she'd been listening the last time she used them.

Opening her case, she winced at the smell of garlic wafting forth. That was another downside to being a vampire slayer—she absolutely hated garlic: the smell, the taste, the way the ugly little plant was shaped. Jane rummaged quickly through her bag, noting that she was short a stake or two.

"Curses!" she exclaimed. She didn't have Van Helsing models #3 or #4. She didn't think that was a good thing. The #2 was thinner, generally used for staking extremely thin or short vampires. The #1 was an economy model, was not particularly sharp and was used only to stake mummies, who were often very ancient vampires in disguise.

Jane knew the #1 was definitely out, and the #2 wasn't much better. She could only hope it would work on such a big, healthy specimen as the earl without a wooden mallet, since she had also neglected to pack those. She supposed her nosedive attack would be enough. She hoped.

Staring dejectedly at her two small stakes, Jane felt cords of apprehension tighten the muscles in her neck, and she admitted that the odds of her mission's success had just been greatly reduced. Still, jumping from a tree and attacking from behind might give her the leverage she needed. "I can only hope that gravity will do the trick," she said.

Jane's brow wrinkled as she tried to recall her Staking

101 class for any other tricks, but it was useless; her mind was a blank. Not surprising, since Staking 101 had been held in the long-ago spring, when the red-breasted robin was first spotted bob, bob, bobbing along through Hyde Park. Jane's mind had been on its rocking, not on her studies.

Shrugging, she pulled out the Van Helsing model #2 and closed her bag. The smell of garlic thankfully faded, and Jane breathed easier.

"Sometimes, I can be such a ninny," she despaired. Not often—well, not as often as her cousins accused her of—but sometimes. She should have checked her bag before leaving home. But there had been that yellow-bellied sapsucker outside the window, and Cook had brought those delicious apricot tarts. . . .

"Well, no use harping on missed stakes," she decreed fatalistically. She would have to stick the great big, very handsome Earl of Wolverton with a very short, very thin weapon. If she was lucky, she would succeed. If she was even luckier, she would be carried away by a giant yellow-bellied sapsucker to live with him in the clouds.

Time passed, and Jane grew restless squatting on her tree limb. She began to feel like that Tars fellow, Lord Graystroke, who had lived in a hut with baboons for many years. Only recently had he returned to England, forced by his father to reluctantly do his familial duty. Lord Graystroke had come back with incredibly bad manners, such as scratching himself in public and gulping down bananas. Still, the man had a nice smile and good looks that had many women pining for him. Jane had felt an instant kinship with him for having to live a life solely for the benefit of others and never himself.

Some members of polite society complained that Lord Graystroke had a chimp on his shoulder. To Jane, this made perfect sense. The titled nobleman had lived among apes most of his life; if he wanted to carry one around, who was she to judge? Besides, Jane understood exactly how Lord Graystroke felt with a monkey on his back, as she herself felt the quite cumbersome weight of her ancestors frowning down at her from above—or, it could very well be possible, frowning up from down below.

Jane pictured the generations upon generations of Van Helsings. The portraits situated in the family galley always stared down at her, their hawklike features judging, waiting for her to make a mistake. And they never had to wait long, she had to admit.

The distant sound of a horse's hooves on the cobblestones drew Jane from her thoughts. The Earl of Wolverton was on his way to the home of his yellow-ribboned mistress. He was taking this route along Berkeley Square, under the old oak tree, just as her father's spies had predicted, and at the right time of night.

"'By the pricking of my thumbs, something wicked this way comes,'" she quoted in a near whisper, recalling from vampire physiology that the Nosferatu could hear remarkably well for being dead.

Jane herself could distinctly hear the coming horse on the cobblestone street. Closer and closer the man and his horse came, and Jane peered into the inky blackness. Squinting hard, at last she could just make out the earl and his stallion. Asher was riding his favorite steed, an impressive dappled-gray brute with a solid white mane and tail. The horse was almost as impressive as his owner.

Lord Asher was on his way to his latest paramour's house to give her an emerald necklace—his way of apologizing for running off to Paris a few months back. He had fled in order to escape having to watch Baron Ian Huntsley marry Clair Frankenstein.

"Clair," he muttered to himself. "How can that silly woman be happy in her marriage to that nodcock?" The whole conundrum disturbed his sense of order in the universe. "Has the woman no sense of good taste?" Patting his dappled stallion's neck, he added, "I'm much more handsome, wealthier, more fashionable, and my title is greater than Huntsley's!"

He shook his head, thinking that if he were not quite so self-assured of his own superiority, he would be downcast. But when someone had looks like his—he shrugged philosophically—it was hard to be too Friday-faced.

"Clair Frankenstein Huntsley will end me in Bedlam," he remarked crossly to his horse. "I'm even reduced to talking to you."

The stallion lifted his head and snorted.

"My sentiments exactly." Kneeing the beast slightly to increase its stride, Asher added, "Perhaps a good roll with my latest mistress will drive the doldrums away."

Up ahead and high above, Jane waited. Her heart rate was increasing. There was now no time for a reprieve. The earl was dead in her sights. She crouched, feeling a deadening of her heart. Clair would never forgive her. Jane would never forgive herself, she realized darkly as she prepared to leap. But as she threw one leg over the limb, her head jerked back. It took her a frightened moment to determine that her waist-length braid was caught on several branches of the oak.

"Horsefeathers! Will nothing go right this night?" she murmured, yanking at her hair and finally managing to free it. But approaching the massive oak, Neil Asher, the Earl of Wolverton, was in innocent bliss of his impending doom. So that was going well.

Heat surged into Lord Asher's groin, his mind ignoring the slightly strange ambient sounds as he focused on reaching his paramour. Once there, he would coax her into kissing him all over, soothing his battered heart. His mind involved with such racy delights, he dismissed the noisy thump behind him, never looking back to see the spread-eagle figure leaping from the tree above, her skirts flying and her eyes closed, clutching a Van Helsing model #2 stake; nor did he see her hit the ground.

Yes, hurrying his horse along, the Earl of Wolverton was oblivious to all that went on behind him—a rare occurrence. And he missed one major thing go bump in the night.

The Battlefield Is Earth

"Vampires, vampires everywhere, and not one dropped. To think!" the major accused, his tone full of anger.

Oh no, Jane thought. Her father was getting worse. He was always seeing vampires here, there and everywhere, but lately his obsession had gotten so bad that the manor halls were decked with boughs of garlic.

"You rushed, daughter. And once again you fell flat!" the major growled.

Yes, she had failed at her task of destroying the Earl of Wolverton. But really, did her father have to get so red faced about the whole affair? She was the one who'd taken the plunge.

"It may not have been one of my finer moments. In fact, it might be considered one of my lowest moments," Jane conceded ruefully. Still, *she* was the one whose labors had borne no fruit after risking her life to go literally out on a limb. *She* was the one with the broken fingernails and bruised hip and elbows. And not forgotten was yet another gown ruined in her trek through danger.

"If I keep ruining gowns like this, I shall soon have nothing to wear," she complained.

"Gowns! Who cares about gowns at a time like this? Dracul is in town, Jane, and you speak of clothes?"

"I feel rather like that nursery rhyme—Humpty Dumpty." And all the prince vampires and all the major's men couldn't put her back together again.

"Nursery rhymes and vampires don't mix, Jane," her father retorted curtly.

Jane nodded. She was heartily sick of everything. She was tired of feeling less important than the clueless humanity amongst whom she lived. She was sick of not being pretty enough for society, a duckling in a world of swans. She was bored of never being clever enough or enough of a Van Helsing to suit her father's staunch convictions of what she was and should be. If only women had more rights: the right to decide their own futures, the right to be heard. Well, Jane amended, she could be heard, but the men in her life rarely listened—except for her brother Brandon and Frederick Frankenstein.

Sometimes she really hated being under her father's thumb, just like all good daughters and wives everywhere. She was tired of treading water, close to drowning at all times. If people could only accept her for who she was. But, then, who was she if not her father's disappointment, the butt of her cousins' jokes?

To the gentlemen of the *ton* she was a wallflower. She was Clair's dear friend, Brandon's sweet sister and Spot and Orville's beloved mistress. It was strange, she thought ruefully, that she could see the reflection of herself in other people's eyes, but never quite clearly in her own.

"Now pay attention, Jane. The whole art of war with the undead consists of getting at what is buried on the other side of the graveyard," the major insisted. Jane knew that he had stolen the quote from the Duke of Wellington, giving it a slight revision.

"So, we had a slight setback, Papa," she admitted softly. "I am sorry. It's just that my braid got entwined in the tree limbs, and I lost my timing. It could have happened to anyone."

Bitterly resigned and in a foul humor, the major barked, "No, Jane, it could only happen to you."

"I made a mistake, Papa. It's not the end of the world," Jane said, her back still aching from her ignominious leap. She knew that, in spite of all his harshness, her father cared for her. Perhaps not as much as he did for Brandon, but he did care—although he rarely acknowledged it.

She would pay for her incautiousness. Outraged, the major's face turned even redder under his silver-brown hair. "Not the end of the world? Not the end of the world! It very well could be if that dastardly Prince of Darkness decides to suck the human race dry!" the major spluttered.

"Don't you think that's a bit melodramatic? Even Dracul couldn't drink England dry. No one has that big an appetite."

The major shook his head. "Jane, Jane, where did I go wrong with you? I took you to the crypts when you were still in swaddling. I lined your nursery with garlic, gave you padded stakes and dolls that bit, yet you choose to look out the window at birds. *Birds!* I gave you the best education a vampire hunter could buy. What do I get for my troubles? A calamity, Jane!"

"I did my best."

"Then do better," the major retorted coldly. He rested his arm on the fireplace mantel and lowered his head.

Jane stared into space, somber. Her normally stoic father looked defeated. She hated the expression he was wearing, making her feel crushing guilt once again. She hated disappointing him as she was always doing, over and over. She was the only daughter in the Van Helsing family for over three generations, which had made growing up with her brother and cousins—all male, *tallyho!* vampire executioners—extremely difficult. She was never as strong or courageous as they. Where her cousins longed for more slaying, more sport, more gambling and other less gentlemanly pursuits, she longed for a family and children, or to fly free like her beloved birds. The major was proud of his son and ashamed of her. That fact rankled and hurt with equal intensity. Yet, Jane loved her father in spite of his cruelty to her. She loved and wanted to be loved by her family.

"You will go to the Huntsley house party you told me about," the major ordered. "There you will be able to get the earl alone and strike."

"That would be disloyal to Clair. One doesn't stake one's host's guests," Jane replied icily, her silver-green eyes shooting sparks. "It just isn't done in polite society."

Major Van Helsing sighed. His daughter looked petite and dainty, but she was a little devil when riled: a regrettable character failing that came from her mother's side of the family. The girl was being silly—no doubt due to her foolish womanly constitution.

"Loyalty is a fine thing, but saving the world is more important. That diabolic, devious Dracul must be stopped. And you must be the one to do the deed! Clair will get over your bad manners when she realizes what a viper she has brought to her bosom."

Jane scowled at her father. His assurances were hardly reassuring. "The house party will have many guests. Count Dracul will be surrounded."

"You can get him alone, Jane. I know you can. You must act the mysterious seductress—without the seduction, of course," the major clarified. "It's the same plan as at the ball, but with no brandy."

Jane arched her eyebrow. She had never been one to turn gentlemen's heads, and this time she'd have no mask to hide behind. "Sir, you know well I hold little interest for gentlemen. I am almost twenty-three years of age, and in that time I have only received two gentlemen callers—and they didn't really want me." One was an author looking to write a book about the Van Helsings and vampires. Fiction, of course, since no one outside the business truly believed in such matters.

Her second suitor had family connections to several lumber mills. He had only been interested in a contract for producing Van Helsing stakes and mallets at a tidy profit. He had even wanted to introduce a new line of Van Helsing mallets called hammers, and to put them on sale to the great unwashed public. Her father had quickly vetoed both the idea and the suitor.

"You will do as I command, and I will have no shilly-shallying due to 'female sensibilities.' Van Helsings do not have female sensibilities," he assured her.

Jane shook her head. Seduction by a virgin? No. Make that seduction by a spinster virgin who was not a beauty. As a strategy, it was quite daring—and quite imbecilic. Once again, Jane would be made to play the fool, not to mention made to betray her best friend. She felt her eyes well with unshed tears, and her nose became stuffy.

"I don't think I can," she said.

"You will, or Spot will be turned out in the streets, and that infernal bird of yours will be sent to the butcher."

"No." Jane gasped in horror.

"Yes!" Absorbed in his scheming, the major began to pace. "This is war, Jane. And war is hell."

Jane's sniffles vanished. Oh no, she thought. Not the old war-is-hell speech. If she'd heard it once, she'd heard it a thousand times. Make that a thousand and one times, she accepted silently. Now her father would march up and down, limping slightly with his gout, gesturing into the air. He would get so carried away that he would go back to his earlier training days. Jane could almost hear "The Battle Hymn of the Van Helsings" playing in the background.

Restlessly, she picked up a training manual on the effects of silver chains on vampire flesh. Pretending to thumb through it, she instead looked at the catalogue of fashions for young ladies she had inserted inside. The colorful images were from the fashion magazine *La Belle Assemble*.

As her father continued his tirade, Jane would take a glance at the pictures and then at him as she pretended to listen and read. The major never noticed, caught up in his fervor.

"I know it's not easy for you young men"—the major stopped and rephrased—"you young ladies—young lady—but you must go forth and battle the enemy. It takes stern courage, and keeping your senses sharp and your wits keen. But you can do it. For this war, this hellish war, is a necessary evil to stop a truer evil from spreading across the world. When you look in your mirror tonight, think brave thoughts. Know that you fight for the souls of the living. Know that you fight a war for the world, with our battlefield, the earth. I know there will be casualties—"

You can say that again, Jane thought sarcastically. Her father's wars *were* hell. She'd already lost her peach gown to a tree, and her Cleopatra costume to a mud puddle. She'd endured a horrid headache from overindulgence in brandy, and she was bruised and sore from her fall from the tree. Yes, there had been casualties. She reluctantly turned her attention back to her father.

"—But fear cannot keep you from doing your duty. I know you will succeed. So, tallyho, men. Tallyho!" the major voiced gustily and listened to the echo of his own voice.

"Yes, war is hell, men," he continued, "but somebody has to fight it. Why, I remember a vampire hunt in 1795, when I was just a young man. I had gotten accidentally locked in a crypt with seven bloodsuckers. Seven, and I had only three stakes to my name. Luckily, I carried my model six with me that night."

Jane rolled her eyes. The 1795 vampire story again? She wanted to giggle at the thought of her father trying to stake a vampire with a model six stake. The #6 was huge and difficult to wield, though it could take down an elephant. Happily, there were no such things as vampire elephants. However, there were vampire demons, which were what the model six had been designed to slay. But to use the #6 required two men to shove it into the demon's gut area where the demon's heart was located.

Jane knew the ending of this tale. Her father had exposed most of his foes to sunlight. Still, she raised a brow. The last time she had heard the 1795 hunt story, there were five vampires. The time before, there had been four. The story kept getting fishier and fishier. The number of vampires grew bigger. It was a whale of a tale her father was telling now, with more vampires than he could fry.

Suddenly she heard a loud *thwack* to her right. A small arrow-stake was embedded in the wall next to a painting.

She gasped, her eyes searching around for the shooter. Her grandfather, Ebenezer, was squatted down behind the green divan, his bow in hand. She shook her head. He had almost shot a Van Dyck! Like a governess reprimanding her wayward ward, Jane held out her hand, determinedly demanding that her grandfather surrender his bow. The wiry old gentlemen glared at her fiercely, a look of wounded dignity on his face and at odds with his silver hair, which was sticking straight up.

Jane sighed, feeling like she was standing before a dike, trying to plug up all its leaks with her fingers. But the more she tried, the more holes opened. Soon she wouldn't have enough digits. Of course, she could always go to Clair's uncle Victor and ask that he add a sixth finger to her hand.

Jane's grandfather, watching her warily, shuffled backward, still in his crouch.

"Give me the bow, Grandfather," she said.

"Humbug, Jane. I almost got the sneaky devil, but the clever little imp ran in here. So, you see why you can't have it, my dear—I have to get the nasty little bloodsucker."

Her grandfather must mean some vampiric mouse he was chasing. Fortunately she knew there were no such things as vampire mice, just as there were no such things as vampire elephants. "I can't have you shooting up the house," she said. Her headache was growing worse. She wanted to scream.

Her father stopped reminiscing about the good old staking days, and brusquely ordered, "Come now, Father. Let us put up the bow and arrows. It's still too light for the little buggers to be out of their tiny little coffins." He beckoned pompously to his sire.

Ebenezer stood, unrolling his long form and shaking his head side to side. "While Van Helsing's away, the mice will play."

"If you will give me the bow, Grandfather, I will take a watch for you. I know you're tired and you need your rest," Jane cajoled.

The old man smiled, at last handing her the tiny bow and arrows. Then he followed his son, the major, out of the room. Briskly he turned and saluted, confirming what Jane knew to be true: "I shall return."

Jane went over to the wall where the Van Dyck hung and yanked the arrow out. She wasn't even plugging the holes in the dike any longer; she was already drowning.

The Lady Is a Trap

Jane arrived late in the afternoon at the Huntsley manor, in a state of high anxiety. This ill-conceived plan of her father's to hunt the Earl of Wolverton at her friend's house party was a huge mistake. At the very least, it would likely ruin another of her gowns.

Jane felt like a traitor, wondering how she could betray Clair by staking the handsome earl in her home. Yet how could she devastate her father? She had to do one or the other.

Peering out the carriage window, Jane was the picture of a forlorn miss. Wearily, she sighed and looked around. It wasn't easy being a Van Helsing, spending your nights in cemeteries, searching for red-gold eyes in every darkening sky.

"Can I do what I've set out to do?" she asked herself. She was almost tired of asking. "It's all so confusing," she went on, knowing that with the Earl of Wolverton, she had bitten off more than she could chew. She only hoped she was more than he could chew, too.

She sighed. Would she ever be able to do things *her*

71

way? These questions twisted round and round in her mind while the carriage bumped along, driving her to distraction. Not to mention giving her another slight headache. Her maid, Lucy, hadn't helped matters by continually complaining of road sickness on the journey. Fortunately for Jane, Lucy was now asleep.

As they neared their final destination, the Huntsley country estate, Jane could feel the carriage slowing down and turning up the dirt lane to the large manor house. Her maid moaned.

"We're almost there, Lucy. Just another moment or two," Jane consoled her grimly. Yet how could the maid complain? She wasn't the one with death and betrayal to face. Jane wasn't even sure how exactly she would dispatch the devastatingly handsome Prince of Darkness.

As they approached the manor, Jane surveyed everything with an artistic eye. The sun was slowly sinking behind the rolling hills, casting warm shadows on the estate's massive manor, which had twining vines of ivy curling against its sides. Lush green gardens and dark forested wood lay tangled beyond, boasting flowers of every hue and birds of every manner. On the way up the long and winding drive, Jane spotted a hawk circling high in the clouds, and several peacocks strutting about the lawn, magnificent in their finery. Swans dotted the distant lakeshore, and several brown wrens flew above. Huntsley Manor was a beautiful spot, a wild estate, barely tamed and thus fitting for a werewolf and his bride.

Disembarking her carriage, Jane dusted herself off and walked up the long front staircase, her nerves stretched taut. Fear sat heavy in her stomach. She was announced by the butler and, after a brief coze with Clair, was shown to her room where she could dress for dinner and thankfully compose herself.

For dinner Jane chose a pale green gown of shimmering silk with tiny beads at the hem and a rounded neck-line. The color brought out the greenish highlights in her eyes. Studying the mirror, she sighed. "I just look like me," she complained. Just once she would like to look in the mirror and see a ravishing beauty.

Making a face at herself, Jane accepted defeat. She was what she was, and tonight she would set in motion her father's plan to stake the earl. Lucky for her, the earl wasn't aware of her repeated attempts on his un-life. She even felt fairly certain he wouldn't recognize her as the demented, tipsy woman in the Cleopatra mask at the ball, so all she had to overcome was her own plainness.

Shaking her head, she closed the door to her guest room and said, "I can't fail again." The sly jeers of her cousins about the vampire with the erection would be peanuts compared to the big white goober of another bungled attempt—and her father had promised to tell them.

Putting on a patently false smile, Jane went to the green salon, where the other guests of the house party were having a drink before dinner. "Et tu, Brutes," she murmured as she entered, feeling already like a traitor. She had been a puppet, a bird watcher, a poet, a pawn and the queen of fools, but never had she really been a back-stabber or a bad friend. Yet, what choice did she have?

She could hear bits of scattered conversation. It appeared that Lady Veronique had disappeared. How strange. Perhaps she had run away with some lover. Jane nodded. Yes, that was probably what had happened to the merry-making widow.

Clair hurried over to greet Jane, causing Jane's guilt to run amok. "You look divine," Jane said sincerely.

Her friend's tawny hair shone gold in the soft glow of the chandeliers. Her gown was a deep violet with a square bodice, cut rather high and definitely de trop.

Clair noticed Jane's glance at the bodice's unfashionable neckline, and said, "Ian won't let me wear anything lower." She laughed. "He seems to have some mad annoyance with men staring at my breasts."

Jane giggled. "Well, the dress is lovely, even with its high neckline."

Clair shook her head. "If Ian had his way, I would be running around with material up to my chin." She smiled a secret smile, clearly thinking about her husband. The couple were clearly in love.

"Let me return the compliment, Jane," she said. "You too look lovely."

"And you were always a bad liar, but the thought is well meant," Jane replied.

"Jane, Jane—what shall I do with you? You are in fine looks tonight. Come, let's meet our guests. Tell me whom you don't know."

As Clair introduced Jane to various members of the party, Jane kept her eyes open and her senses alert. Where was the earl?

"Jane, you must meet one of Ian's cronies—Mr. Warner," Clair said as she tapped a man on his rather stout arm and subsequently introduced Jane to both him and the woman next to him. "And this is his fair wife, Mrs. Warner."

Jane noted Mr. Warner, a tall but portly man, whose clothes, though fashionable, seemed to be in need of considerable attention. She couldn't help but wonder if his valet had indulged in one glass too many of the claret.

His wife, his bride of only a few weeks, was a stout woman with raven black hair, and she was her husband's direct opposite in manner and dress. Still, she clearly adored her porcine spouse.

Before the introductions, Clair had confided happily

that she'd gotten the lucky couple together. What she hadn't confided was that Mr. Warner was a wereboar. But, then, Clair didn't need to tell Jane what Jane could figure out for herself. Shape-shifters gave off a heat energy that Jane could usually pick up. Despite her father's views against the mixing of species by marriage, most Van Helsings could spot a were creature a foot away. It was due to shape-shifter blood. Although the major pretended the family line was pure, their small amount of werelioness blood sensitized Van Helsings to the supernatural creatures around them.

Jane was next reintroduced to Lord Graystroke and his bosom companion, a Mr. George, whose diminutive appearance and curiosity were legendary among the *ton*. In Jane's opinion, Lord Graystroke remained the most interesting person she'd ever met. His dark brown hair had been lightened by his many years in the sun to the color of wet sand. And his massive shoulders were impressive. Jane decided they were probably due to all that swinging around in trees he reputedly did.

She suddenly wondered if Lord Graystroke was a wereape, and if that was why he'd lived among the primates of Africa for two decades. It certainly would explain all that monkey business. Yet, she didn't get the tingly, heated feeling she usually experienced around a shape-shifter. At last she decided Lord Graystroke was not one of the members of the supernatural world—at least, not by birth.

Lord Graystroke was polite to Jane; yet his eyes were distant and there was restlessness about his person, as if he would rather be hanging around in the jungle than standing stoically, sipping bourbon here, Jane decided. He was the epitome of the well dressed and polite English gentleman, and had slipped only once in the introductions. He had almost said, "I am Tars."

Jane had gently interrupted, saying, "I am *Miss* Jane."

Before further introductions were made, Clair confided to Jane that Lord Graystroke was going through a difficult time. Tonight he had a chip of respectability and familial duty on his shoulder, rather than his orange chimp, Cheetah. It was an adjustment.

Jane understood only too well. As she'd noted before, Lord Graystroke was having to pretend to be something he was not.

Suddenly Clair grabbed Jane's arm and turned her toward the door. Neil Asher, Earl of Wolverton, had just entered the room. "See there, Jane?" Clair asked, tilting her head in the man's direction. "The earl has arrived."

Jane's breathing deepened. "He's very handsome," she admitted softly. Tonight the earl was wearing a deep blue velvet coat with a pale blue waistcoat. The color brought out the vampire's marvelous eyes, which appeared to glow with an icy blue fire as he made his way toward her.

Staring at Clair Huntsley, Asher twitched his lip up in a semblance of a smile. As always, she was breathtaking. His cold, dead heart beat warmer. He wanted to share the moonlight with her and hear her pulse pounding like a drum as it pumped rich blood throughout her marvelously decadent body— which Ian Huntsley, lucky wolf that he was, owned lock, stock and smoking hot barrel.

As he made his way toward her, the highlight of this provincial house party, Asher thought back over the centuries. When he'd been a hundred and seventeen, it had been a very good year—for female fledgling vampires. They had hunted together in the soft summer nights, and hidden in fine mausoleums in the daylight.

When he was a mere two hundred and twenty-one, it had been another good year—for Parisian courtesans with their perfumed hair and their white flesh bare.

When he was two hundred and eighty-nine, it had

been a very good year—for blue-blooded aristocrats with their elaborate wigs and their carriages so fine.

So many good years he had spent a-roving, walking alone. He had lived decades upon decades, traveling a hundred roadways, never quite finding a true home. Then he had met Clair, and he had believed the world would be a different place, an exciting world filled with laughter and love for him once again. Alas, he had been most foully mistaken. As the Earl of Wolverton seldom was.

Still, he thought wryly as he approached Clair, he would survive this heartbreak, just as he had survived having his heart stopped when he'd become a vampire. Yes, he thought smugly, he had once been a human, a vampire, a pauper, a pirate, a poet, a pawn and a king. But each time he had found himself flat in his coffin, he had picked himself up and Renfield had dusted off his jacket.

Yes, the world would keep spinning 'round, the nights would still be lovely and long, and Asher would continue to try and live the vampire creed, forgetting that tomorrow ever comes. And he would survive this thwarted love affair and survive it in the grand style his rank demanded.

"Ah, the remarkable Clair Frankenstein," he said, his eyes drinking her in as he took her hand in his. Swiftly he lifted it to his lips, and with his usual savoir faire, he curbed the primal instinct to bite down. He smiled at her with a hint of devilment in his eyes, hoping Huntsley was watching and eating his heart out. Werewolves were known to literally do that.

As usual whenever Clair was near, Asher found himself ignoring everyone else. He barely noticed the lady next to the new Mrs. Huntsley.

"How is your room? All is satisfactory?" Clair asked.

Asher nodded haughtily, knowing what she was asking. Although her guest list included quite a number of shape-shifters and two vampires, many of the guests were mortals. The coffin she had prepared for him in a hidden chamber in the cellar was perfect. She had even lined the coffin with lavender. "Most appropriate. My thanks to my considerate host." Placing a second lingering kiss upon her hand, he regretfully released it. "The way you look tonight . . . Well, where do I begin? You are enchanting."

Blushing, Clair drew away and asked, "Asher, have you met my dear friend Miss Paine?"

Jane watched her friend interact with the earl, and her heart beat a furious *pit-pat* in her chest as Asher turned his fabulous blue eyes in her direction. Would he recognize her? she wondered. Please, anything but that.

She blushed furiously, making her freckles stand out. Silently she begged fate to not let the Earl of Wolverton know that she was the one who'd splashed him with brandy.

For a second, Asher froze; then he politely bowed, and Jane curtsied gracefully in spite of her knees knocking together.

Clair made formal introductions. Lord Asher raked his eyes from Jane's head to her neck to her toes to her neck again.

Clair excused herself with a sly smile. She saw icy fires in Asher's eyes, and Jane's blush. Wedding bells were ringing in her head, and she wished her arms were four inches longer so that she could pat herself on the back. Hiding a self-satisfied chuckle, she silently bragged that she was getting this matchmaking business down to an art. And with that, she left the odd couple alone.

Asher turned to Jane and hissed, "It is you." His lips curved into a slight sneer as he inspected her. At the masquerade ball, they had been strangers in the night exchanging glances. Then Asher had wondered about the chances of, before the night was through, passionately partaking of her blood. Tonight his mysterious Cleopatra was revealed in all her unsplendor. The fairy tale was false. The swan had become a rather ordinary duckling. What were the chances that the insane, mysterious maid of the masquerade would be a friend of Clair's?

"I never thought to see you again after you doused me with booze," he remarked curtly, pulling out his monocle and continuing to examine her. He felt strangely disappointed and irritated that she wasn't the temptress he had imagined. Nor would he forget that she had ruined one of his favorite jackets, causing his longtime servant Renfield to pitch a fit about the sordid state of his wardrobe when he had arrived home. "Why did you do that?"

"A mistake, my lord," Jane managed to choke out. So much for hoping he wouldn't recognize her! Oh, if only she could stick her head in the sand like her ostrich.

"So, what ill wind blew you to the Huntsleys'?" Asher questioned, disgusted to realize that he had thought about this maid from the masquerade more than once, twice or even thrice since the farcical incident.

"Clair and I have been friends since nursery days," Jane explained. "Quite good friends, really."

"Then I must express my condolences to her. Did you ruin her pelisse, too?"

Jane narrowed her eyes. "You might try, my lord. However, if you knew Clair well, then you would know that she is fiercely loyal—to those she loves." She saw him flinch and knew she had scored a hit. "How did you know it was I you met that night? My mask covered my face."

"I am no fool," Asher snapped. He had noted her freckles, tiny brown dots that covered her cheeks and her nose, and danced at the edge of her bodice. He wondered if they covered her breasts, those milky, plump orbs that were surprisingly outstanding. He wondered what those breasts would taste like.

Bloody hell! Asher shook his head. Where had that thought come from? This lunatic female was certainly not his style. He was one for the best and the beautiful alone.

"You have freckles," he said bluntly, again staring down at her impressive chest. "How not the fashion." He preferred his women to be a whiter shade of pale, nothing like blemishes or freckles marring their skin.

"I didn't know it was the fashion to be insulting." She had meant to give an apology, regretting what she had twice tried to do to the earl. But now she found herself fighting back tears. She hated her freckles. "No *gentleman* would make reference to them."

"My manners can be deplorable at times," Asher agreed contemptuously, shrugging his shoulders. "But then, I have never claimed to be a gentleman, just an earl."

Jane lifted her chin. "No, you would never let anyone forget your consequence."

Asher narrowed his eyes. "I didn't know it was fashionable for a young *lady*," he accused, stressing the word, "to throw brandy all over her acquaintances." Disdainfully he watched Jane's blush deepen. He had seen demons of that same deep crimson.

"Touché," Jane replied coldly. Yes, this rude earl just might be the conceited Count Dracul after all. "I meant to apologize immediately once seeing you again, as any lady should do. I suppose I was overwhelmed by your exalted presence and lost my head, both tonight and on the night of the masquerade," she finished sardonically.

"You were drunk as a lord that night," he accused.

Jane answered tightly, gritting her teeth, anger flooding her system like electrical current. "A gentleman would never point that out. And I must remind you that I did not overindulge that night. I couldn't have. Ladies never do." She couldn't remember much, but her mother had trained her too well in ladylike carriage.

"The ladies I know certainly do," Asher replied, sneering slightly. The ladies and not so ladylike ladies of the bar he had courted and discarded had indulged in many things; most were quite debauched.

Jane lifted her chin a degree higher, glaring up at the arrogant vampire. "I'm sure most of the *ladies*"—she stressed the word just as he had done— "that you have known are quite beyond the pale. Although, what they see in you besides your own puffed-up consequence is beyond me. It appears that a Peer of the Realm's impressive title is no indicator of sterling character or good manners."

Asher arched an aristocratic brow and lifted an elegant hand to shoo her away. Frankly, he didn't care if her feelings were tromped upon; he was too old a vampire to learn new tricks such as kindheartedness. And he had never been one to cater to the masses. He had seen too many abuses of conformity. Just take the French Revolution, for one—people lost their heads over that!

"I am what I am and proud of it. My lineage goes back to William the Conqueror. Can you say the same?" he snapped. "Which makes me wonder why I am wasting my time in having a conversation with you."

Jane clenched her fists, resisting a strong impulse to punch the odious earl in his arrogant though beautiful face. Have one drink too many, once in her life, and see how it got thrown back in her face, and in a public setting! She was really going to have to find false courage someplace else from now on.

"Bloody buffoon!" she swore, glaring at Asher. She longed to say more, to tell him exactly what she thought of his remarks, but she was too angry to do anything other than fight back tears. This pompous bloodsucking fiend thought he owned the world!

Asher's chuckle deepened as he glanced down at her tightly clenched fists. "Really, Miss Paine, despite your friendship with Clair, I begin to see that you are no lady at all. Perhaps you could try to imitate your dear friend and seek out at least a bit of charm. Gentlemen don't attend to shrews unless they're beautiful—a claim you certainly can't make." And with those words, he casually strolled away.

"Oh, if I only had my model four stake!" Jane seethed, anger overcoming her wounded feelings. "I'd know just where to stick it, you rotten vampire."

Time Waits for No Man, But a Vampire Can Hold It Hostage

He'd kill that scamp Clair Frankenstein Huntsley. Asher swore silently, sitting up straighter. And he'd throw in her husband for fun.

The blue of his eyes glowed with glacial flames as he stared disdainfully at her, showing Clair his displeasure. Of all the guests at this house party, he was seated next to the very irritating and ordinary Miss Paine. What an insult to him, a connoisseur of great beauty. Not to mention the fact that Miss Paine was touched in the head. Why had Clair chosen her for his dinner partner? Surely she didn't think he would find Miss Paine of interest. Asher pondered as he glanced sideways at the object of his pique.

He supposed Miss Paine did have a graceful swanlike neck, pale and elegant. And her eyes were very large, slightly tilted and of a silverish green hue he had never seen on a human being before. But her nose was definitely too snub, her hair of a plain brown color, and she had all those tiny little freckles.

Humph, he thought, turning his steely gaze back in the direction of his hostess.

Clair winked at him, then looked at her husband, who was seated on her left. She ignored Asher's aristocratic huff and, with an expression of utter innocence, gazed into her spouse's dark green eyes.

Ian Huntsley almost laughed. He knew his wife's look well. Leaning closer to avoid being overheard, he asked, "My love, what are you up to?"

"*Moi?*" she said.

Ian arched a brow.

Clair laughed. "You know me so well."

Ian waggled his brows. It wasn't the pale moon that excited him anymore—it was the thrill of his wife. Just the nearness of her had him panting, wanting to howl with delight. "Shall I describe in detail that mole you have on your very cute, very luscious—"

She slapped a hand over his mouth. "Harry Ian!"

He nipped at her fingers. He knew he was in trouble when she called him Harry. "*Elbow*. You have the most luscious elbows I know."

Clair withdrew her hand. She knew exactly what her husband had truly been going to say. But that was the trouble with Harry Ian: He really was a wolf—and not only every full moon, but in bed, out of bed, on the table, on his desk in the study, in the stables and even on the blue Persian rug in their bedroom. Or at least wolfishly hungry for her. Yes, love and passion definitely burned brightly in their bedchamber, enough to keep them warm on even the frostiest winter night.

Ian chuckled and Clair blushed. "What are you up to?" he repeated.

Clair glanced down the table at the scowling Asher and frowning Jane. Ian followed her gaze.

"Well?" he asked, frowning as well. "What? Asher? As much as I hate to admit it, the vampire saved us both from a vicious blood feud." It had formed a blood bond of sorts between them. But that didn't mean he had to like the bloody pompous bastard.

"Asher needs a wife, and Jane needs a husband," Clair explained. Her eyes were all innocent and wide.

Ian groaned. "No. No, you are not matchmaking again. Please tell me you aren't. Besides, Asher eats females like Miss Paine for breakfast. Literally."

Clair smiled her secret smile. Her husband knew that she was a friend of the famous Van Helsings; she just hadn't told him that Jane was one, having introduced her as Miss Paine. Clair knew that Ian might have one or two tiny objections to her matchmaking a master vampire and a vampire hunter. However, Clair also knew that once the pair fell in love, her slight omission would be a sweet deceit, and Ian would forget all about it . . . she hoped.

Ian glanced back at the pair, who were busily ignoring each other, and shook his head. "I don't exactly think it's a match made in heaven. But then, with a vampire for the intended, I don't think it could be!"

"Very funny," Clair remarked. "I think it's a fine match. Asher is very lonely, and so is Jane. Jane is loyal and intelligent. Also, she's very clever when she's not nervous. Asher is loyal in his own way, and his wit is piercing."

"Along with his fangs." Ian shook his head. "Clair, they don't even appear to like each other."

"Nonsense! Great-aunt Abby predicted a match for the two of them with her tarot cards."

Ian rolled his eyes. He knew Clair believed in her great-aunt's fortune-telling abilities. He even knew that sometimes Great-aunt Abby was correct. But it was clearly the luck of the draw and not any true clairvoyant ability.

Ignoring him, Clair continued. "I believe they are

right for each other, and if I put them into each other's orbits enough, they will feel the gravitational pull."

"And will be satellites for life."

"Exactly," Clair stated. "We'll see them married before the holiday season.

Ian snorted.

As Clair and her husband were arguing, Jane was silently fuming, thinking that if her friend were a vampire, she just might happily stake her too. How could she have been placed in such close proximity to the earl on her first night here? Jane wondered begrudgingly. She needed time to come to grips with what she had to do. She needed time to gather up her self-esteem, for the earl had greatly battered it earlier in the evening.

Jane cursed silently, fidgeting in her chair and knowing that she should not. But Asher was sitting so close, his frosty scent teasing her nostrils, and that made her uncomfortable. How could Clair have placed the most handsome man in the room right by her side? She felt as though everyone were staring at Beauty and the Beast. Of course, in this house of a werewolf, that might mean Clair and Ian.

To make matters worse, Neil Asher's mere presence was causing her heart to beat more quickly and her breathing to speed up. She was scared, and not of being attacked at the dinner table. Even such a debaucher as Count Dracul wouldn't slurp on her in public, not with all twenty-odd guests watching.

She was frightened not of the earl but of herself. She was once again feeling a resurgence of the earl's magnetic sensuality, like she'd felt on the night of the ill-fated masquerade ball. The strange urge was something she hadn't felt since her first suitor, the author, courted her. He had been a handsome young gentleman, and had kissed her three times. The third kiss had involved something scary with his tongue, but it had stirred something deep within her. Not long afterward, her suitor's deceit had been revealed.

Yes, that had been a dismal, heartbreaking discovery: that the man was wooing her only for her family connection to the supernatural in the hope that it might help his career. It had scarred Jane deeply, making her wonder if anyone could ever love her for who she was. She was no beauty, but couldn't someone see past that to the warm, loving person inside who had so much to give?

Since the earl had spoken to her only twice, and both times briefly, Jane turned to her other neighbor, Mr. Warner. The man was rooting about in his food as if he were looking for truffles. His cravat was stained with oyster sauce, or perhaps it was the lentil soup. After two attempts at conversation, and getting mere grunts in return, Jane gave up. Mr. Warner really was a were*boor*.

Turning back to the earl and trying hard not be obvious, Jane studied him from the corner of her eye. She watched as he took a small bite of duck. She had never been this up close and personal before with the undead. She had also never seen a vampire eat real food, but due to her lessons, she knew one could. Vampires could eat small amounts of meat and drain certain types of liquor without problem. Much more was not tolerated. Of course, they could bespell a person to believe they'd eaten an eight-course dinner and consumed everything served.

The earl continued to eat in silence, for the moment ignoring everyone else as well as Jane.

Enough was enough, Jane decided firmly. She had a duty to do, in spite of the strange urgings this pompous bloodsucker stirred in her. She had to get him alone with her.

"My lord, I believe you are ignoring me," she said. There, she had taken the bull by the horns, or rather the vampire by the fangs.

Asher turned toward her, his sneer spoiling his aristocratic beauty. Jane couldn't help but smile, wondering if all the blue blood he'd drunk had gone to his toplofty head.

"Madame, are you perchance speaking to me?" he asked. "Are you speaking to me?"

"It appears that I am," she said, batting her eyelashes in what she hoped was a flirtatious manner.

Asher cocked his head, studying her. "Do you have something in your eye?" he asked.

Jane could feel the heat of a blush start in her cheeks. "No, I do not."

Asher gave her a look that was clearly a dismissal, then turned back to his other dinner companion.

Well, that went well, Jane thought in embarrassment. Stabbing at a piece of squab with her fork, she watched in horrified amazement as it flipped off her plate and struck the earl's immaculate jacket. The vampire looked down, slowly shook his head and glared at her.

"Are you intending to ruin another of my jackets?"

Jane groaned, longing to put her head in her hands and weep. But the earl calmly removed the squab from his coat.

"I'm sorry. It just slipped," she said.

"My valet will be quite upset." Asher was about to go on when he noticed that Miss Paine's embarrassed flush had spread to her lovely bosom. It was such a bounteous bosom—slightly marred by the freckles, it was true, but so pale and kissable. But the woman really was a clumsy puss.

"Somehow, when I am around you I seem to do the most foolish things," she remarked.

He shrugged. "I am an earl. People are always toad-eating, doing the most remarkably silly things to gain my attention."

"It's not that you are an earl that had me flustered," Jane remarked.

Asher smiled. "Oh. Well, my looks have been known to distract women and send them to their knees as well."

Jane shook her head. "Such conceit."

Asher shrugged. "Why should I be modest? I'm a grand personage, and well know it."

"Indeed," Jane retorted. "You poor man, having women dropping at your feet like flies. You must be honey laced with vinegar."

He snorted, surprised to find Miss Paine had a clever bone in her body. He wondered which it was. "I must admit, of all the females I have had dropping around me recently, you left the most lasting impression."

"I did?" Jane asked, taken aback. Had she made headway?

"Yes, you left a lasting impression on my jacket. Renfield was quite upset." He gave a short cackle. So much for making an impression.

"I take it Renfield is your valet?" she said.

Asher nodded, noting Miss Paine-in-the-Neck's lips. They were wide and too full, but they were definitely delicious-looking. A stark image hit him squarely between the eyes as he envisioned those too-full lips causing him to ripen and swell as they took him into her mouth and sucked upon him. His rambunctious rod hardened, and Asher shifted uncomfortably in his seat. Had the world run mad? What was he thinking?

"You must think me the most graceless female you have ever met," the woman conceded, both graciously and regretfully. "Please forgive any disquiet I have caused."

Asher remained silent, arching a brow.

Jane's embarrassment began to fade somewhat, her temper beginning to simmer instead. The earl could be easier in his acceptance of her apology, she thought. "Thank you for making me feel so much better about my clumsy nature. I must compliment you on your gift of charm."

Her sarcasm caught Asher's attention. Once again, this little odd duck was acting the shrew. Strange, because most women bent over backwards to please him— and managed some rather interesting positions too.

"You aren't the most clumsy," he admitted. He recalled Ann Boleyn, who used to trip over her slippers constantly. That's how she fell in love with Henry VIII and lost her head.

Cocking his head, he studied Miss Paine more closely, noticing the faint blue lines in her throat, which made him unusually curious whether her blood was sweet or tart, or perhaps a combination of the two. Maybe he would sneak a sip for an aperitif. She was certainly more attractive when her blood was up. So he would anger her some more.

Looking pointedly at the wineglass in her hand, he remarked, "I see you are tippling again."

Her eyes flashed green fire. "Only this glass of wine," she remarked. "I was foolish that first night I met you. But I learned my lesson."

Asher waited, his glass raised to his lips. "Go on. This lesson was . . . ?"

"You could say that the night of the ball was a first-time experience in overindulgence for me. Most definitely, it was a mistake that will never be repeated," she replied. She shuddered in memory. "I don't know how you gentlemen can drink like that night after night without stopping. I felt like elephants were dancing in my skull the morning after."

"Yes, the aftereffects of overindulgence do not a fine morning make," Asher agreed, thinking of the few times he had drunk shape-shifter blood chased by the blood of warlocks. His preternatural hangover had lasted two nights, and he'd felt as if he were staked out and left to dry. Since then, he'd sworn off the more exotic victims.

"Yes, the morning after is so unpleasant. I wonder why gentlemen so often indulge," she mused.

"Men must have their sport." In agreement with his words, Asher's gaze again took in the modest display of Miss Paine's most outstanding assets. He wondered if her breasts would spill over his large, long-fingered hands? True, he'd been right in earlier thinking she was not his usual style, but maybe a change of pace would help his ennui. Life had lately become too much the same.

With both people and vampires acting the same way century after century, lately Asher's life had begun to stream into one long, endless night. Little children grew old and died. Centuries passed. His dreams as a fledgling had already been fulfilled or changed, leaving him agitated and restless, searching for something or someone to elevate his night-to-night existence. Lately he'd been asking himself: Was this all there was to undeath?

Jane shifted nervously, her blood humming. The look in the earl's eyes was electric. She knew why women fell at his feet when he looked at them.

Asher watched her, his expression thoughtful. Miss Paine was indeed a breath of fresh air, and he was a sporting vampire always on the lookout for new adventures. Perhaps he would give her the thrill of her spinsterish life and woo her a little. Enough to get a taste of that intriguing blood and see if those breasts and elegant neck tasted as good as they looked.

He would court her only slightly—enough to stir interest, but not so much that he would be in danger of offering for the plain Miss Paine. Since she was definitely not a diamond of the first water, the guests would be intrigued and gossip, and Asher did so enjoy good gossip. He could also show Clair Frankenstein Huntsley and her fur-faced husband that his love for her was dying a quick death.

He would be very careful, as he always was. He was too wily a foe to be caught by the parson's mousetrap. For too many years he had steered clear of marriage-minded females and virgins. The elevated and titled debutantes of polite society were a danger to bachelors like himself. They could be compromised. And compromised meant married in almost every case, due to honor and society's conventions.

Yes, he decided, as he smiled at his intended victim, he would use Miss Paine and use her very well indeed. It was a shame he couldn't use her completely. But he would leave Miss Paine's virginity intact, since to do as his instincts strongly urged would only result in a hasty and repugnant marriage.

He turned on his most seductive smile, the one that had seduced queens. He had just found a way to liven up the next few nights. Imagine, a master vampire wooing a spinster. The gossips would have a field day!

Seeing the earl's glorious smile turned on her, Jane swallowed hard. "My lord?"

His smile showed perfect white teeth. "Call me Asher," he said quietly. "All my friends do."

Jane swallowed again. She felt as if she were drowning in the blue depths of his eyes. What was this strange feeling that seemed to be eating her? Was this how his victims ended up eaten?

"Asher," she said softly, her lips trembling. When he smiled like that, she wanted to kiss him silly. Her heart beat faster. She wondered if he could hear it.

He leaned closer, almost brushing her ear. "And I may call you . . . ?" He looked as if he would kiss her.

The force of his magnetism nearly left her breathless.

Silently, she repeated what she knew to be true: Asher was a bloodsucking vampire. In point of fact, he was the prince of bloodsucking vampires. He was also the enemy, and a lady wasn't supposed to want to kiss anyone, much less the enemy.

Jane leaned back in her chair, as far from temptation as she could get. Even though she was an intelligent female, a Van Helsing and almost on the shelf, she was no match for this hot-blooded rake who also happened to be a cold-blooded killer.

"I'm Jane," she answered, repeating silently to herself that this was Dracul, the Prince of Darkness, and that she was a Van Helsing, destroyer of vampires.

He leaned in close, his breath cold on her neck, and she could smell a scent like autumn apples and woodsmoke in winter.

Jane shivered. Her plan was working—although she still couldn't figure out why the about-face on the earl's part. He was clearly planning something. All night he had insulted her, and now he was trying to charm her? Jane knew that she didn't stand a chance figuring out his motives if she couldn't think clearly, and she couldn't think clearly with him smiling at her like that. Caution being the better part of valor, she hastily remarked, "I'm sorry, I have a headache." And with those words she practically leapt out of her chair and went to make her good night to Clair.

Asher shook his head. No one had ever gotten a headache before when he was bedazzling her. Maybe he was losing his charm, getting too long in the fang for this sort of thing.

Glancing at the six-foot mirror situated across the room and directly above the buffet table, he observed himself. My, what a handsome devil, he mused. Staring hard at his reflection, he smiled. He didn't look a day over two hundred.

No, Asher reasoned, he wasn't getting older; he was just getting better. He was in his prime. After all, he hadn't even reached his three-hundred-and-ninety-fourth birthday yet. No, the strange Miss Jane Paine must really have a headache.

To Build a Better Vampire Trap

Jane spent the next day looking for Asher's coffin, putting garlic in his bed and avoiding being caught. Not your typical day at a house party.

She ran into Clair twice and even had a nice luncheon with her, which only increased her guilt. But no matter her friendship with Clair, her guestly duty or attraction to the vampire, Jane's destiny had been mapped out long before she was even born.

Besides, she owed the Prince of Death absolutely nothing. He was the unprincipled sovereign of darkness, and she was certainly no minion of his. He was a blood-guzzling creature of the night, and she got violently ill at the sight of blood. He slept in a coffin. She slept with five pillows. He bit people when he was hungry. She bit her nails when she was nervous. The only things they really had in common were their deep affections for Clair and their distaste for garlic.

No, she had no right to feel anything but revulsion for the devastatingly handsome earl. Jane knew that clearly. Asher had to be destroyed, and by her, with no mistakes.

Yet she also knew that perpetrating the damning deed would damage something inside her irrevocably.

Finally, dusty and exhausted as she was, Jane's knack for solving puzzles came through. She had searched everywhere else, leaving only the large cellar. It had to be right. And she'd made her discovery not a moment too soon, she thought, the late afternoon rays of the sun flitting through the thick glass windows of the cellar hallway; soon the earl would be rising for the night.

Ignoring her guilt and the ugly little gargoyle that decorated the archway of the room's large wooden door, Jane took out the large flask she'd hidden in her handbag and poured some holy water from it into a bucket. Carefully she placed the metal bucket above the partially open door, balancing it upon the perch. Jane reasoned that when Asher pushed on the door, it would spring open and cause the bucket to fall. The blessed water would then cascade down over the master vampire, melting him.

Regret flowed from her like a steady stream out to sea, and Jane fervently wished she weren't feeling so wishy-washy about this whole watered-down affair. She was really something of a watering pot.

Already she could feel the tears in her eyes, and she was only waiting for Asher to appear. She didn't want to view his demise, but it was only fitting. She herself should be the one to clean up the mess, not leave parts of a waterlogged vampire for Clair to deal with. Jane knew it was the least she could do after so grossly insulting her friend's hospitality.

Hearing a noise in the other room, Jane bit her lip. Her heart pounded furiously. She hated this! She felt like a wicked witch. In her mind she could hear him screaming, "I'm melting! I'm melting!"

Hearing the slight scratching noise again, Jane called out, "Stop!"

Scurrying into the adjacent room, she quickly scanned

the floor and then the door. No saturated pieces of Lord Asher were disintegrating into a pool of holy water; there was only a small mouse sniffing at some spilled crumbs along the floor. Jane was so relieved, she began to giggle like a schoolgirl. Her laughter was slightly hysterical as she glanced up at the trap still precariously perched upon the doorsill. But no, Asher hadn't yet kicked the bucket.

Happiness filled her being. Jane felt as light as air. She hadn't betrayed either Asher or Clair.

A noise from behind startled Jane, causing her to spin and back up. An orange-furred tomcat had sprung into the room. Unfortunately, the slight bump Jane gave the door was enough to send the holy water tumbling down, bucket and all, drenching her.

So, with a look of pure disbelief on her face, Jane stood in the doorway sopping wet, an empty bucket at her feet and a slight bump on the top of her head where the bucket had struck.

"Curses. Foiled again," she muttered.

If she didn't know better, Jane would swear that she had been cursed, for all the bad luck that she'd had in trying to get rid of the earl. Or maybe it was good luck. Maybe Asher had a guardian angel at his side—if vampires could have guardian angels. Could they? She rubbed her aching head. Another thing to puzzle out. When would she ever find time to answer all the questions she'd stored away for a rainy day?

Picking up the empty bucket, Jane quickly made her way to the servants' stairs in the back of the house. She wanted no one to see her looking like a drowned cat. But just as she reached the landing, she heard the sound of footsteps behind her.

"Oh no! Please let it be anybody but him," Jane muttered in disbelief. She turned slowly, for she was sure she recognized the booted step. Humiliated, she saw the one vampire she did not wish to see. He was handsome, dry, and most assuredly had some pact with the Devil. How else could he look so good and remain so safe?

Asher stifled a smile, his lips twitching only slightly as he took in the very bedraggled Jane and her bucket. She must have been fishing and fallen into the pond.

"Why, Miss Jane, what calamity has befallen you now? You appear to be all wet."

"Your powers of observation are truly remarkable," Jane snapped. Once again, the earl had caught her at her worst. She lifted her chin and ground her teeth. "And I grow excessively tired of know-it-all males."

Then, gathering what little dignity she had left, she picked up her waterlogged skirts and carried them proudly up the steps, tiny drops of water following in her wake—along with Asher's chortles.

If the Coffin Fits, Bury It

"What a wet blanket," Asher remarked, still chuckling as he walked through the door to the guest suite he'd been given. Seeing Jane resemble a drowned cat had cheered him immensely. He was in a much better mood than when he'd previously awakened.

He was never a morning person—rather, a late sunset person. But today he had awakened with a fierce hunger, both physically and spiritually. And it was due to a spinsterish virgin with only passable looks, even if she did have a neck to die for.

As he entered his guestroom, he spied his valet, Renfield—a gaunt older man with slightly graying hair—setting out his evening clothes. The human had been in his service for over sixty years and was the perfect valet and servant. The lines on his face were a testimony to his age, experience and exasperation with Asher's decided lack of concern regarding clothing.

Asher's nose twitched. "Bloody hell! What's that smell?" he asked.

"Garlic, sir," Renfield answered. He wore an expression of disgust.

"What the hell is garlic doing in my room?" Asher grimaced. Garlic was one of the old antivampire wives' tales that didn't hold water. Sometimes at early sunset his kind would gather in a crowded pub for myth hour, laughing at the fallacies of vampire legends and lore. Mirrors, garlic and turning into bats were a few of the most misguided notions. But it was best to keep the legends speckled with lies. That gave vampires a leg up and out of the grave, so to speak.

Glaring at his valet, Asher raised a brow. Garlic wouldn't hurt him, but he really couldn't abide the herb's smell—or even the way the silly plant looked.

"It was spread in the sheets, my lord. I took the liberty of having them replaced, but I'm afraid that, with your sense of smell, a trace remains." Renfield helped Asher out of his coat. "Do you think someone is on to us, master?"

Asher shook his head. "No. I doubt it. This party is mainly weres and humans who are in league with them. No vampire hunter would come here."

"Then who, my lord? Who would play such a smelly trick?"

Yanking off his breeches, Asher ripped a seam. His blue eyes darkened. "Huntsley did this. It sounds just like him. One of his bizarre practical jests."

"Really, master!" Renfield's tone was sharp. "Those breeches you just ripped are brand new. I just received the bill from Weston the other day. My lord, I must protest. You are forever ruining your clothing. Only three weeks ago you came home with blood soaking your cravat. I had to throw it away!"

"Yes, well, we had a bit of an orgy at the Granville estate after the will was read. Besides, I have plenty of cravats."

Renfield stared stoically at his master. There was a long-suffering look on his homely face. "You are always splitting heirs, sir, as well you know."

"I am a wealthy vampire," Asher replied, stepping into a pair of midnight black pants. "What should buying clothes matter?"

Not to be discouraged, Renfield continued his tirade. "Last week you came home smelling like gypsy girls and drunken revels. Your brand-new jacket of superfine reeked. It smelled like a winery. It took four days to air it out properly."

Asher cocked his brow at his valet, who was now fully enraged and looked like a bantam rooster flapping his wings. "The brandy-soaked jacket was not my fault," he argued. "In fact, the lady who did the deed, a Miss Paine in the Royal Ass, is here at the party."

"She should be boiled in oil, sir," Renfield said. "You only wore that black superfine once."

"My, my, Renfield. You are becoming a bloodthirsty little monster, aren't you."

"It must be your influence, master," the valet replied. He helped Asher into a forest green coat that brought out the copper and gold highlights in his master's collar-length hair. "But I quite despair that you will reach the grand old age of four hundred with any proper attire left at all."

Asher had to agree. For centuries people had been trying to sneak up and stake him. It was quite tedious. And not only was it ruinous to his jackets, but especially trying to his undead soul, always having to watch his back against people like those fanatical nuts the Van Helsings. No vampire wanted to have to watch his back against someone trying to stick him, but most especially was it inconvenient when that vampire was at the sticking point with his mistress, which was when the Van Helsings he'd encountered invariably tried to stake him.

When the hunter became the hunted, things could get downright nasty.

"Have no fear, Renfield, I have the Midas touch in business."

"If only you were as concerned about your wardrobe, my job would be much simpler. And I am a simple man," his valet protested modestly.

"You, simple? Ha! Why, you're quite the old tartar—always ringing a peal over my head and searching out exotic hiding places for my coffin away from home."

"As I said before, sir, your influence must be rubbing off on me," the valet replied, handing over a comb.

Glancing in the mirror, Asher cocked his head to one side to study himself, glad that the myths of vampires lacking reflections were just that. It would be such a shame to waste reflective surfaces on other people's beauty and not his own. Brushing a hand through his hair, he reminded himself that he wasn't getting older, just better.

"I promise I will be careful of my clothing tonight, Renfield," he told the valet. "After all, I promised Clair that I would take only a small snack per night, not a full meal. And only with the snack's permission. Which leaves me only shape-shifters to choose from, which shouldn't be messy. Although why Clair is worrying about *me* hurting her guests is beyond me. I would only take a drink or two from them, while the werewolves here would eat them whole."

Renfield shook his head, remaining silent as he finished tying the oriental, a new knot, for Asher's cravat. "Done, my lord."

"You are quite the artiste," Asher acknowledged, stepping closer to the mirror and studying himself. He shuddered momentarily at what he glimpsed in the mirror. Was that a gray hair?

Examining the thick curl by his ear, he noted it was

merely very light blond. He shook his head. He was way too young, barely out of his fledgling years, to be set upon by the signs of aging.

"You don't think I am getting wrinkles, do you?" he asked. Asher examined his eyes and forehead.

"Wrinkles on *your* face, my lord? Why, they wouldn't dare," Reinfield replied benignly.

Asher gave a curt nod. "Then, how do I look? I want to impress Clair and irritate Huntsley," he added slyly.

"Like a god. Zeus come down from Olympus," the stiff-necked valet answered.

"Of course I do," Asher agreed thoughtfully. But a hint of worry filled his words. That wasn't a silver hair, was it?

Duty, Honor, Dracul

"Behave yourself, Asher," Clair admonished gently as she watched him watch her guests—or, more to the point, or points, the pulses beating in their necks. Some guests were dancing to the gentle strains of a waltz, while others formed colorful groups in conversation. Asher was avidly attending the latter, his predatory instincts clear.

"Don't I always?" he asked, a wicked gleam in his eyes.

Clair shook her head, then switched her attention to her husband. Ian stood off to the right talking with Mr. Warner, the wereboar. Her husband and Mr. Warner were old friends, often running wild together under the full moon. Ian hunted rabbits, while the wereboar generally searched out truffles. The chocolate kind. And he'd break into Mr. Godiva's Chocolate Emporium to get them.

Clair gave her husband an adoring look, then returned to Asher. "You must behave, or I'll rethink my opinion of you," she warned.

Asher smiled. *"De mortuis nil nisi bonum."*

Clair stared at him blankly for a moment. "Hmm, let me think. My Latin is not quite what it used to be." Finger to chin, she thought for a few moments, then suddenly smiled. " 'Of the dead, say nothing but good.' " Pleased with herself, she laughed, the sound like tinkling bells. "My husband would say that with you, Asher, it's not always possible."

Asher grimaced. "What sort of whimsy is this? All these lovely beating pulses. All that lovely blue blood just beneath the surface, waiting to be tasted. And I'm available to offer my services," he teased, hungrily watching the delectable Lady Daffney waltz by, her pale neck beautiful, her low-cut gown revealing two of her ripest assets.

Clair struck him on the arm with her fan. "Only a little snack while you are here at Huntsley Manor—no feasting. And it must be done voluntarily on the part of the donor. With no vampire tricks like mesmerizing. Remember, you promised."

"It will present little difficulty. I usually have the women neck and neck, in line for my attentions." Asher smiled lasciviously.

Clair laughed again at his conceit. "I wonder if you will ever change your good opinion of yourself. How *do* you fit that monstrous ego of yours into your coffin?"

Lifting her hand to his lips, he gave her a quick kiss, savoring the taste of her skin. "Come share my coffin some dawn, and I'll show you just what fits into where," he teased.

Clair again slapped him briskly with her fan. His swaggering boasts were in character, and she couldn't help but be amused by them.

"Clair, you truly are a beautiful woman, inside and out, with a love of life that's contagious," the vampire remarked. She was a hard woman to forget. Asher found her to be a ghost in his mind that sometimes haunted the early hours of his mornings, especially when he lay cold and still, waiting for the sleep of the dead to overtake him.

"I am afraid you won't live to see another sunset if you keep flirting with me so outrageously," she warned, smiling at her husband, who was watching Asher grimly.

Asher shook his head, theatrically moaning. His teasing words must hide the longing in his heart and the deep ache that accompanied it, for he would have no pity from Clair, and most certainly not from the werewolf. Asher's cold heart might be breaking, but the Huntsleys could never know. "What you see in that big bag of fur is beyond me. Yes, love is surely blind."

"Perhaps you might pay attention to those who are single," Clair suggested. "No one likes to be a wallflower."

"And who is your soft heart concerned for?" ˥

"My dear friend Jane."

"Ah yes. Plain Jane Paine."

At the earl's tone, another, less formidable person might have been daunted by the task Clair set herself. But "Never say never" had been the bywords of the Frankenstein clan for years.

"Perhaps due to your advancing years, you can't see that Jane is not plain at all," Clair admonished gently, glancing across the room to note that Jane was speaking with Lord Graystroke. Her friend's face was animated. "Jane might not be a beauty in the traditional sense of the word, but she has her own quiet loveliness—and wondrous green eyes that are rarely unkind or watch idly as an injustice is done to those less fortunate."

Asher shrugged, his face expressionless. "I am not old," he said.

Clair hid a smile behind her fan. Her plan, Against All Odds, was still on course. Jane would drag this haughty vampire down a peg or two and make a man out of him. Well, as much of a man as she could, when the man in question was really a vampire.

Yes, Jane would soon have a husband who would cherish and delight her, give her a woman's confidence—rather like Sleeping Beauty, as, with the kiss of eternal love from a vampire, she would be brought to life. It would be a fairy tale come true, with Clair as the orchestrator. Perfectly brilliant, she decided cheerfully.

Unaware of Clair's Plan Z, Jane chose to get a breath of fresh air. The ballroom had grown slightly stuffy with so many people in attendance, and so she strolled out the large French doors to the stone terrace overlooking the gardens. Sighing, she focused her eyes on the people dancing inside, twirling in a kaleidoscope of colors. She felt completely alone.

"Couples. This is a world of pairs, and I'm solo. Even Noah paired animals on the ark!" She was standing outside the gaiety of life, alone again as usual.

"Humbug," she grumbled. Then, shaking herself loose from her self-imposed pity, she began to study the people inside.

Over the years, Jane had quite grown accustomed to sitting out more dances than she was asked to stand for. Gentlemen generally preferred to court great beauties or heiresses; since Jane was neither, she had developed a game to amuse herself at balls and routs while she was stranded alone or with the other less popular ladies. She called it the Who's Hoo Bird Game. Taking a gander at Lady Daffney, who was just then dancing past in the arms of a tall country squire, Jane instantaneously knew what fowl Lady Daffney resembled.

"With her wispy golden hair and bounteous backside, Lady Daffney looks like a plump duck. And her husband, Sir Donald, with his feathery brown hair and prodigious lips, can be a mallard." Jane stifled a laugh as an image came to mind, of Lady Daffney and her four children traipsing across the Huntsleys' lawn, all quacking.

The squire Lady Daffney was flirting with looked rather like a hawk with his fierce features and beaklike nose. Of course, at a ball with a house full of shapeshifters, it was possible that the squire truly was the bird in question.

"Hmm. Do werehawks feather their nests? And I wonder if Clair is serving poached eggs and kippers for breakfast?" Jane hoped so, since that was one of her favorite dishes.

Next her attention settled on Asher, and she observed him through the open balcony doors. He was watching Clair and Ian waltzing. For just a moment the earl's cold facade slipped, revealing a tiny glimmer of hidden pain. Jane felt a sharp jab of pity as she wondered how he could stand to watch his true love dance adoringly in another man's arms. "His unrequited love must prick him greatly. Maybe even through the heart."

It was strange how both humans and vampires could fall in love with the wrong person. How much simpler life would be if all men and women were born knowing just whom to love.

Scrupulously observing her foe, Jane felt surprise: She wouldn't have thought vampires had the hearts to love. The major would say she was being ridiculous, felled by ideas of sentimental claptrap and folly. But Jane knew that wasn't true, for she was watching Asher watching Clair.

And, monster that he was, Asher surprised Jane by doing nothing but standing and watching the happy Huntsleys together. This strange scenario did not fit with the callous Count Dracul's reputation. Perhaps the Earl of Wolverton, alias the Prince of Darkness, had devious plans for the happily wedded pair yet to be revealed. But if he did have rotten, foul plans, then why hadn't Baron Huntsley discovered them? Jane well knew that no one was better at sniffing things out than a werewolf . . . with the one exception of a weredog.

She found herself again bemoaning her situation: "How can I turn Asher to ashes? How can I not?" If Asher was Dracul, then Clair was in deadly danger—as were Orville and Spot—if Jane didn't do the major's burdensome bidding.

"This is all a grave humbug," she muttered, her conscience fighting her familial duty. She winced, the turmoil in her heart giving her a slight headache.

Deciding a walk along the cliffside below the house might relieve the ache between her eyes, Jane hurried down the stone steps and to it. A pathway had been cut into the dark gray stones, which rose in rocky four-foot walls on either side of her, with planted rosebushes scattered here and there. Their fragrance was sweet perfume added to the night's own brisk, salty scent.

Breathing deeply, Jane started down the path, thinking hard truths. Clair had two men who loved and worshipped her, while she herself had none. Pursing her lips tightly, Jane fought her envy of her best bosom friend, but the green-eyed monster tried to wrap icy tentacles around her heart. She felt a moment of pettiness and thought that, even though Clair had two men in love with her, the two men in question were really monsters. Of course, they were remarkably handsome monsters—and both looked at Clair as if she hung the moon, which was saying something for both werewolves and vampires.

Cocking her head, Jane wondered what special quality some women had that caused men to lose their heads. What magic did these mortal women possess in order to bespell males with a look or a smile? These seductive sirens caused men to fight for them, to lay the world at their feet and to chart new territories. These fortunate females drove men mad with desire, caused them to beat their chests, crash through balcony windows or howl at the moon. And Jane couldn't even get a gentleman to ask her to dance. Life was terribly unfair.

She frowned in frustration. Why couldn't she stir men in the same way? What was she lacking? Was it some flaw in her makeup, some lack of chemical reaction? Was it due more to her lack of looks, or was her personality somehow at fault? Why did it seem that all men had a failure to appreciate her? Why couldn't Asher look at her in the way he looked at Clair?

Jane sighed in resignation. Truth, though beautiful in itself, could be quite ugly. Even if Asher suddenly became insane with desire for her, it wouldn't matter; she had her marching orders. She could still hear her father's parting words: "You will fight on the beaches, you will fight in the fields, you will fight in the cemeteries, you will fight at the Huntsleys'. You will not quit! As that treacherous dog Bonaparte once said, 'Victory belongs to the most persevering.' You will persevere this time, Jane! Yes, you will, or my name isn't Major Edward Abraham Van Helsing!"

The major's words haunting her, Jane grimaced. She must do her deadly duty in the dead of night. She would make sure that the walking dead were soon truly dead, both to the worlds of both daylight and darkness, even if she must deaden her conscience until it died a final death. Poor Asher, he would not be dead just until dark anymore; he would just be dead. He'd join the pool of vampires whom the Van Helsings had proudly caused to swim in the sea of the dead. Asher would never see another sunset, nor smile another smile full of wicked promises of dark pleasures late in the night. His attractive countenance would no longer grace balls or routs, and he would join the ranks of the eternally and permanently dead.

As Jane woefully drew her dreaded conclusions, guilt eating holes in her soul, she stopped walking and rested under the branches of an oak tree. The gnarled and aging trunk was so large that it cast her in shadow. Deep in thought, she did not hear the approach of the intruder until it was too late to flee.

Cool Hand Neil

Asher grinned. He had needed to expend barely any effort in his seduction of the beautiful Lady Daffney. The woman had given him heated encouragement, her gaze flicking from the top of his breeches to the terrace and then beyond, and now here she was not ten minutes later standing among the dark gray, monolithic stones of the Huntsley property. Tonight, it seemed, he would have his drink on the rocks.

Suddenly the thick cloud, which had half hidden the crescent moon, shifted, revealing not Lady Daffney but Jane Paine in her pale green silk gown. Asher's grin faded. Miss Paine seemed to appear wherever he did, again and again, rather like the ten plagues of Egypt. He hated having his plans for a moonlight tryst with a skilled female interrupted, especially by a silly virgin. And especially when he was so thirsty.

Cocking his head to one side, he studied the forlorn figure, noting how her abundant cleavage was visible in the pale glow of the moon. After a moment he shrugged philosophically; it appeared fate had different ideas for him than he'd had for himself on this dark night. His stomach was beginning to growl, and that meant it was time for dinner.

Jane didn't hear his approach. She was quoting to herself, "'What in me is dark, yet from those flames, no light, but only darkness visible. The mind is its own place, and in itself can make a heaven of hell, a hell of heaven.'"

Asher stepped forward. "Dante."

Startled, Jane gasped. She quickly glanced up at the tall, formidable figure, but immediately she knew it was the earl, which eased her fears. Somewhat. Foolish, yet she really wasn't afraid of being alone here with the Prince of Darkness. Partly it was because she knew Clair would exterminate Asher if he exsanguinated her. Of course, Clair might also scotch Jane if she slayed Asher.

"It's Milton," she corrected.

Asher looked stung. "I beg to differ. I believe that particular quote is Dante," he remarked curtly.

Jane squared her jaw. "Milton," she repeated quite firmly, annoyed. She was something of a scholar, and knew her quotes backward and forward. And the earl was just a little bit too smug.

"No, it's Dante. I know it's Dante. And I'm never wrong," he argued.

"Well, this time you are!"

"No, I'm not," he replied tersely. Who did this country-bred chit think she was, Plato?

"Yes, you are," Jane said waspishly. Who did the toplofty earl think he was, Socrates?

"It's Dante."

"It's Milton—and we sound like two nursery children arguing over who gets to play with which toys."

"I am never childish. And it's Dante."

Jane snorted in disbelief. Then, very quietly, she muttered, "Milton."

Asher's patience was fraying fast. He said, "I am extremely well-read, Jane. And I recognize that quote from Dante." He growled, losing his last modicum of civility.

"Then you recognize it incorrectly," Jane repeated stubbornly, her smile fixed. The man might be an earl and a vampire, but his knowledge of the classics was a comedy. A divine one. "It's from *Paradise Lost*."

Asher's brow furrowed. The little Philistine was standing up to him, telling him that he was in the wrong! What was wrong with her? "Don't you realize that you're arguing with an earl?" He took a posture of extreme arrogance, his feet braced apart and his broad shoulders squared.

"Earl, shmearl. I have many faults, but timidity isn't one of them. When you are wrong, you are wrong. You can battle with me over the quotation for a decade and will still be in the wrong. And I would argue with the king himself if he were silly enough to say Milton was Dante, when anyone with half an education can tell the difference."

Asher's heart stopped. As much as an undead heart could. This chit was unbelievable! Didn't she recognize his august personage, and always-correct nature? He didn't think she did, not by the way she was glaring at him. Her green eyes sparkled like emeralds with silver fires inside. Miss Paine was a thorn in his side. No, make that a stake. Yet she was certainly pretty out here in the moonlight. There was much more to Miss Paine in the Neck than first met the eye, it seemed.

"My, my, a bluestocking—how intriguing."

Jane frowned. "I know it's not the thing to be: a woman with intelligence." She shrugged. "But I won't hide the fact."

"And well you shouldn't. Stupidity bores me greatly."

She smiled. "What an enlightened attitude."

"Of course. I'm an earl. What did you expect?" he asked, surprised that he had repeated his thought out loud.

She moved out of the shadows into the direct glow of the moon. "Pomposity does *not* become you."

He grimaced. "Bloody hell, did your mother teach you nothing of ladylike manners?"

"Did yours?" She returned, making a face at him.

He couldn't help it; he was so surprised that he laughed. "She tried," he admitted. "But . . ."

Jane smiled. "I take it you were an unwilling pupil."

"Very. I had my mind on other more . . . interesting subjects."

"Hmm. I see." And Jane did see. Neil Asher had been a rake from early in life. "Did you try and seduce your nurse from the cradle?"

He chuckled. "Only to get my rattle."

"Oh, you are incorrigible," she said. He reminded her of a peacock, what with his beautiful plumage and harem of ladybirds eagerly following him about.

"Can I help it if women find me irresistible?" he asked. "I would tell you about it, but you would think me vainer than I am."

Jane snorted. Asher had the face and fangs to suck in any woman. But he was as vain as they came. "How ever do you manage to get a hat on that swelled head of yours?" she asked.

This time, Asher snorted. Miss Paine was definitely a bird of a different feather. For a Plain Jane spinster, she had a wicked sense of humor and an honesty that amused him along with her antics. That was something he hadn't seen since Clair Frankenstein had haphazardly entered his life.

"Really, my lord, conceit is a bloody humbug," she said.

"Jane Paine, what a mouth you have on you." Asher remarked, half-irritated. He wasn't really conceited. He couldn't help it if he was close to perfection. "I wonder what I should do with it?"

He studied her plump pink lips. They were wide, and made for kissing. Nervously she licked them, her pink tongue sliding out and across.

He took a step closer, consciously.

She took a step closer, unconsciously.

He cocked his head and studied her. Moonlight became her.

"Have you ever been kissed?" he asked.

"Of course."

He arched a brow in disbelief, and she looked irritated.

"At least fifty times," she said.

He arched both brows in patent disbelief.

"Maybe sixty times," Jane lied again. "Besides, it's really none of your business."

Asher lay his hand over his heart, pretending to be wounded. "You think so little of me."

He held up his fingers, one by one counting off her complaints. "Let me see, I'm puffed up with my own consequence. I'm so vain I can't put on a hat. I don't know my Milton. I'm a womanizer and a rogue," he said. "And I'm also nosy. Did I get them all?"

"Don't forget rude," Jane said politely, her eyes twinkling.

Asher was encouraged. Bowing to her, he remarked, "In spite of my faults, I think you would like me to kiss you. If only to compare to those fifty or sixty other gentlemen."

"A lady would be foolish indeed to admit to such."

Reaching over, Asher lifted her chin with his fingers. "But then we know what I think about your being a lady."

Staring at his firm, sensuous mouth, Jane unconsciously licked her lips again. He was a toothsome temptation. His eyes were pure blue, drawing her in, almost drowning her in their glacial depths.

Her heart sped up, beating furiously. Asher's face was close to hers, his eyes bright with interest. If he moved a smidgen closer, he could kiss her. *Would* he kiss her? This was a heady experience—erotic, exciting and downright scary.

Asher took her in his arms and smoothed back a curl of hair that had somehow gotten loose from the braids piled upon her head. She was very pretty now, gazing up at him with a sense of wonder. Yes, there was definitely some fairy dust swirling around in the night wind.

"Shall I kiss you now?" he asked.

But before Jane could answer, she felt something crawling up the back of her neck.

Tiny little feet. Spider feet.

She shoved Asher away and began swiping at her neck and jumping up and down. "Oh, it's on me! It's on me!" she howled as if the hounds of hell were snapping at her heels. "Get off! Get off!"

"What the bloody hell are you doing?" Asher had heard of nervous virgins before, but this was ridiculous. He stepped back a cautious distance.

She continued to jump up and down like a demented frog, howling, "A spider's on me!"

"A spider?"

After one last swipe, she sighed in relief. "It's gone." Rubbing her neck, she shuddered. "I have a . . . slight aversion to them."

"Slight?" Asher asked, dumbstruck. His second impression of her had been right: The woman was touched in the head.

"Well, maybe a bit more than slight," Jane admitted,

117

glancing around nervously. "I do hope the horrid little thing isn't planning a second attack."

"Hmm," Asher said thoughtfully, feeling full of mischief. "I imagine the poor little fellow was a scout for a much larger army. This cliffside is notorious for spider armies."

Jane's face paled. "Spider armies? Here?"

"At least fifty or sixty of them," Asher continued mercilessly, his expression deadpan as he extended his arm. "Each with their own spider general. I think it's time I escorted you back inside—away from the battlefield."

"Fifty or sixty armies of tiny spiders?" Jane repeated belligerently, catching on and ignoring his extended arm. Asher was playing with her fears, just like her cousins did. Just like Count Dracul would do. He was dismissing another's concerns as if they were nothing more than dust in the wind.

"Your manners *are* truly appalling, to tease a lady about the slight aversion she might have to hairy little legs crawling all over her," she snapped, starting up the pathway without him. "So, sirrah, I will escort myself. And I also want to mention that I despise cobwebs and hard-hearted rakes."

Asher smiled reluctantly as he watched Jane stomp away. He would like to have his own hairy legs crawling all over her—and if that mad thought didn't beat all, he wondered what did.

Everything at Stake

"To stake or not to stake, that is the question," Jane said, sneaking down the stairway to the library. She wondered if Shakespeare ever had similar problems. "Here I am, a twenty-three-year-old ape-leader, and I'm at a house party with more than a few single gentlemen. Yet, instead of hunting a husband like any intelligent lady nearing the shelf would do, I'm hunting a vampire. A handsome, arrogant, mesmerizing vampire."

"I dislike it immensely," she went on, "creeping around in the dead of night trying to do what's best. Gee, thanks, Clair," she muttered to herself, wishing her friend hadn't told her what she had.

After spying Jane returning from her walk along the cliffside, Clair had mentioned that Asher had a habit of drinking brandy in the library after everyone else went to bed. That was why Jane was now tripping about in the dark, hoping no one would discover her. If Asher were there, Jane would pretend that she couldn't sleep and had come for a book. It was late, and Asher would be drinking, so perhaps she might be able to seduce him into kissing her. And then, after the kiss . . .

After the kiss was the part Jane was having concerns about. How far should she go in her enticement? How far was too far? She didn't really know what went on with overheated vampires, or if vampires even got overheated. No one had ever told her what to do with a wolf—not the werewolf kind, but the woman-devouring kind. Well, the woman-devouring kind of vampire with great sexual appetites.

She had changed into a different gown, one with a much higher neckline. It was off-white, with rows of lace at the bodice. (After seeing her reflection, Jane had unhappily decided that she looked like a big pillow. She really was going to have cut back on the chocolate.) It was not certainly evening wear designed to titillate. But it would do what it was designed for; hiding the Van Helsing model-four stake in its pocket.

Reaching the library, she hesitated briefly and took a deep breath. Then she pushed open the large, ornate door and stepped within, efficiently shutting it behind her.

Her target stood a little to the left of some floor-to-ceiling bookshelves. He was casually flipping through a volume of poetry. Briefly Jane wondered if he was checking out the quote from *Paradise Lost*.

Candlelight in the room gave golden tints to Asher's copper-colored hair. He wore no cravat, and his shirt was unbuttoned, exposing a large portion of strong, smooth chest of a whiter shade of pale. His aura of mystique and masculine beauty called to Jane, stunning her with its magnetism. Her body tingling in strange places, Jane couldn't take her eyes off this power and strength she had only guessed at. This was one dangerous vampire. Yet watching the muscles in his chest ripple slightly, she felt a happy fluttering in her stomach, as though a hundred butterflies were tickling her insides.

"Jane, what are you doing here?" the earl asked, observing her expression and wondering if she was still mad at him.

He watched the pinkish flush spread from her cheeks to her neck. Idly he wondered if her other cheeks would turn red when lightly spanked. And did she have freckles on her bum? It was an intriguing idea, and one he most definitely wished to explore. But regrettably he might never know what lay hidden under her skirt—virgin territory being priced as it was.

"I wanted to get a book. I wasn't sleepy," she explained sheepishly.

"Milton?" Asher asked, studying her. She didn't appear irritated with him. What was she *really* doing here? Did she want a kiss, or was it truly a book she was after? Could she not sleep because she was thinking of him—as he had been of her, much to his discontent.

"Dante."

She grinned impishly. He found himself grinning reluctantly back.

Asher stood up and walked over to the bookshelf, and pulled down a thick black volume. He strode over and handed it to her. "Dante," he said.

"Thank you."

Jane looked uncomfortable and out of her depth. Asher decided to admit something that had been plaguing him. "Oh, you were correct. I looked up that quote and it was Milton."

Her eyes widened in surprise. "I didn't know earls knew how to apologize."

He smiled at her wickedly. "I'll let you in on a little secret. We earls only apologize late at night, when we are alone with a lady who intrigues us."

"Then you must be saying it three hundred and sixty nights a year."

Asher laughed. "Touché."

The earl's warm laughter and the smile in his eyes disconcerted Jane. She immediately turned her attention to the floor, where she just happened to notice a piece of fur stuck on the front left foot of the green brocade settee. Absentmindedly she remarked, "It sure is hard to get good help these days."

"What?" Asher asked, looking confused.

Glancing up, she felt her blush deepen. "Nothing." Ninny! Birdbrain! she berated herself silently. She should be batting her eyelashes or hanging on his arm. She was a total disaster at seduction. She should have had some training in the amorous arts. Instead her lessons had consisted of learning how to kill two vampires with one stone, and to never attack two vampires with one stake—or was that to never attack one vampire with two stakes? Jane sometimes got the rules confused. There were so very many, and they were so very varied. Who would have thought that the training manual for undead-slaying was over twelve hundred pages of dead weight, all in small print?

"I take it you avoided any marching spider armies," Asher said, unable to resist.

Jane shook her head ruefully. Her temper fit had long passed. "I apologize for being such a . . . ninny."

He smiled. "I find you rather adorable."

She frowned slightly, silently begging, *Don't let him be charming now. No, not now!* She didn't want to hurt Asher; she'd rather kiss him silly and do those other things people did in the dark behind closed doors. But what choice did she have?

The earl moved closer, stopping but a few scant inches away. His nostrils flaring, he breathed in her unique scent—the scent of jasmine and misty woods in the rural mountains of Germany. He could hear the rapid beating of her heart, sense her blood pulsing just beneath the skin of her neck.

His hunger had grown ravenous. In point of fact, he thought of drinking from her with a growling anticipation, somehow sensing that she would be good to the last drop. Just like that Swiss miss he had sampled while touring the Alps several years ago. Perhaps even better, if his pulse rate was any indication.

He couldn't seem to take his eyes off her. The flickering flames in the nearby stone hearth highlighted her figure, revealing her rounded hips and full, rather remarkable breasts.

"When you were kissed before, by your legion of men, did you enjoy it?" he asked, his hunger changing slightly. He wanted her desperately. He *needed* her desperately. He was aching to sink himself into her—and not his teeth. He hadn't felt lust this strong since he was a mere stripling of a vampire, one hundred and one years of age.

"It was nice," Jane said shyly.

"Nice?" Asher repeated, shaking his head to clear away the lust. He scolded himself silently. He couldn't take her virginity—but he could take a taste of her breasts and neck.

"Oh, Jane, I can do so much better than nice," he boasted, pulling her swiftly into his arms, bending his head and kissing her passionately. Her lips were very soft, and he savored their sweetness.

He could hear the blood rushing through her veins. As a child his mother had scolded him not to play with his food. As a fully functional adult, playing with his food remained half the fun. And what fun this morsel would be!

He deepened the kiss, and she opened her mouth to him. He used his tongue to ravish it thoroughly. She tasted wonderful, like golden honey after the bees had feasted on orange blossoms in the late spring. Her smell was almost as good, reminding him of hot, sultry nights and sweet kisses beneath the moonlight.

He had always enjoyed kissing and extended foreplay. But kissing Jane was an elevation to a primal experience of raw lust that he had never before experienced. He wanted to rip off her clothes and plunge into her wet, hot body. Yet, at the same time, he wanted to simply wrap her in his arms and hold on tight.

Waiting to exhale, Jane savored her first kiss. She tasted the dark depths of the earl's mouth, the sweetness and the tart tang like apple cider wine. It was a heady experience, like a walk in the clouds. Asher's kiss was better than brandy, better than strawberries with fresh clotted cream, better than chocolate and even better than spotting the yellow-bellied sapsucker. She wrapped her hands around the back of his neck, running her fingers through the silky smoothness of his burnished hair as he yanked down her gown, revealing her breasts.

"Amazing," Asher mumbled. Awe-inspiring, he thought.

She was so lost to passion that she sighed wistfully into his mouth, and she felt her toes curl up in her slippers.

Hearing her sigh, Asher moved from licking her breasts to her neck, taking tiny nibbles as his muscles began to clench. Blood rushed to his groin, his cock growing heavy and hot. Jane's neck was glorious, was heaven on earth. This little virginal friend of Clair's had fired his blood to a feverish pitch. He didn't understand it, but at the moment he didn't really care.

The earl's cold breath on her neck drew Jane back to her senses. Regretfully she fingered the stake in her pocket. Still she hesitated, hating herself and her heritage. Her mind was screaming no, her heart was screaming no, but she could see her father in her mind's eye shouting, "Yes!" and berating her for un–Van Helsing-like hesitation.

Gathering resolve and duty around her like a cold, wet blanket, Jane removed the stake and lifted it high behind Asher's back. She would plunge it down and end his undead life on the count of three.

In her head, she counted: "One . . . two . . . four." No, three, she thought. I should say "three." Yet again she hesitated, for Asher continued to explore her neck with tiny, heavenly kisses.

She wouldn't do this—*couldn't* do this—to Asher, Clair or herself, she decided, starting to lower the stake. She didn't know what she would do about her father and his threats, but this just wasn't going to work. Maybe she could smuggle her stuff to Clair's. But on the next full moon, would Ian eat her birds? She could smuggle them to Dr. Frankenstein, but would he add unseemly appendages to them?

Her heart bruised, she lowered her stake a bit more. Deep in her heart she knew that the man savoring her neck couldn't be the depraved, drooling Count Dracul of legend.

At that precise moment, Jane felt a prick of fangs on her neck: the true kiss of a vampire on a Van Helsing! Curses, what sacrilege!

Frightened and guilt-ridden, her father's words flowing through her mind like a flash flood, Jane steeled herself. "One small stab for man, one giant stab for mankind," she gasped.

His fangs pierced her skin, gently breaking it, and apprehension gave way to panic. Instinctively she struck—and just in the nick of time to save herself from a wicked love bite.

Her stake caught Asher square in his left buttock, since she had lowered it from the center of his back. She could felt the sharpened point sinking through the taut flesh. Her stomach turned over, leaving her both queasy and breathless.

Carried away by his passion, Lord Asher was momentarily stunned by the burning in his backside. The pain became sharper as he threw back his head and roared in pain and rage.

Outraged as Jane's betrayal hit him full force, Asher roughly shoved her away. She crashed upon the carpet by the green brocade settee, legs sprawled wide. "I'll kill you for this!" he hissed.

In shock, on the floor, Jane said, "You can't kill me. What would Baron Huntsley say?" She wailed in abject misery.

"Do you think I give a bloody damn about Huntsley or you?" he growled.

"Clair would be upset if you sucked me dry," Jane suggested, her voice thick with misery. "I'm sorry. Really sorry. Really, really sorry," she blurted, staring in morbid fascination at the red glowing eyes of the enraged vampire before her. She remembered the words from the childhood song she'd sung with her brother: "Dracul, the red-eyed vampire (vampire!), had some very wicked teeth. And if ever you got near him (near him), you would find yourself deceased . . ."

Damn. She was going to go down in history as the Van Helsing who'd staked Dracul in his fanny. Her father would have it written on her headstone. For if looks could kill, her demise would come at any moment.

Jane knew she should be more frightened, but all she felt was numb. So numb that she forgot the state of her gown, her exposed pale breasts. If she raised a white flag, she wondered, would Asher call a truce? Staring at his glowering expression and deadly fangs, she guessed not.

"You bloodthirsty bitch!" Asher spat furiously. Ignoring the sight of Jane's marvelous breasts, he reached behind himself and touched the embedded stake. He winced in pain as he shook his head in disbelief. He was not going to go gently into this good night. He could feel his fangs extending, his eyes were blue flames. And he watched in further seething disbelief as Jane leaned over and threw up all over the carpet, splattering his boots.

"That really rips it," he snarled. His dignity was in tatters, his ass was aching and Renfield would gripe that he had another hole in his clothing. At this rate he'd be naked before April. What a scold the valet was going to give him.

Embarrassed and still nauseous, Jane sneaked a peak at Asher, wiping her mouth on her sleeve. She could feel his anger like the blast of a coal furnace. Yet the vampire's eyes were so glacial, she felt ice shards piercing her to the very center of her soul. He reached around again, gritted his teeth, and yanked out the stake. His eyes shut against the agony.

Jane turned her head, not wanting to see more of his blood spilling. She managed to shakily make it to her knees, sad that she was about to die and hadn't had her nightly chocolate. She hoped Brandon would avenge her. And what would Spot and Orville do? Orville would probably be served for dinner by her heartless father.

"I'm sorry you're hurt, but—," Jane began, swallowing against the tightness in her chest. She was cut off abruptly by her foe's next remark.

"You viperous witch!" Asher had never been angrier. This crackpot female was at the bottom of all his problems. He was outraged that she had tried to stake him. He was incensed that such a small, plain woman hadn't been more interested in his seduction. Her interest was not in winning his heart, but in removing it.

"Just who the bloody hell do you think you are?" he asked, clenching and unclenching his fists. If it weren't for Clair, he would have ripped out her throat. "No one stakes the Earl of Wolverton! Most certainly not some short, mousy chit!" Yet as incredible as it seemed, it appeared that the calumnious Jane had done just that. And to add insult to injury, he had ignominiously been staked in the arse!

Leaning down over her, the earl shook a finger in her face, which made Jane mad. The major was always doing that. And while she might owe her father familial duty, she didn't owe Asher anything. Surprisingly, she slapped his finger away, which only enraged the earl more. He leapt upon her, knocking her breath out as they fell to the floor, Asher on top and Jane on bottom.

Gasping for air, she fought his great weight, her fists striking his broad chest without result. Asher apparently felt nothing. Terrified and still in shock, Jane understood all too clearly that she was going to be dead before dawn, dead to the world. Yes, this path she'd taken definitely came to a dead end.

However, remarkable as it seemed, in some small part Jane felt a great relief, as though a heavy burden had been lifted from her shoulders. She had struck and failed. But in her failure, Asher retained his life. Which was the only truly good thing from this whole debacle, as it had been from her previous failures.

"Why did you stake me?" Asher growled, his fangs glistening in the candlelight. He glared down at her beneath him, his pulse beating in his temple as he waged a terrible battle to control his rage.

"Why?" She could hear the anger, pain and confusion all in that one word. "Why, Jane? Tell me before I spill your treacherous blood."

Trying to wither her with his gaze, Asher watched a tear trace a path down the woman's freckled cheek. Something deep within him stirred. If it were sympathy, he would rip it out by the root and force-feed it to the lunatic beneath him.

Glaring at her, Asher realized that she was one female he would never forget. But just what in the bloody hell did she want?

He felt like a jackass. Betrayed by a kiss? How utterly degrading. It was beneath him. He was an earl, for heaven's sake! A master vampire! And yet, plain Miss Paine in the Ass had stabbed him. And if other immortals found out the exact location of his humiliating wound, he'd never put it behind him. He'd stake all he owned that he'd go through eternity as the butt of their jests.

As Jane tried to answer, the door to the room burst open and people spilled inside. First in line were Ian and Clair, shock etched upon their faces. Asher leapt up, putting his back to the wall, resolutely hiding his blood-soaked arse and the hole in his breeches. But he was not quick enough to prevent Ian and Clair from seeing. Jane gasped and tried ineptly to right her gown.

His quick movement had caused him pain. Asher tried to stifle a groan, his behind feeling like a large stick had been stuck there. Scowling, he thought caustically: Sticks and stones may break my bones, but a stake in the ass is worse.

Behind Ian and Clair, Mr. Warner stumbled into the room. He was wearing only one slipper, his dressing gown half on and half off. Behind him stood Lady Daffney, the squire and his wife, and Lord Graystroke. All were stunned. Some had their mouths hanging open, but all were speechless—a first for any tonnish crowd this size.

The room gave a collective gasp of shock and titillation: One of the most elusive catches of any season had just been caught, compromising a female of enough pedigree and social standing to force him to do the correct thing and propose. There were three or four "ah-hah!"s and one or two, "The rakish Wolverton is caught at last."

Someone else crowed, "What entertainment! This is bloody swell."

His expression grim, Baron Huntsley studied the unbelievable scene before him, thinking Jane Paine had definitely pulled an asinine stunt. "Bloody hell. Wedding bells," he muttered to himself.

Asher glowered, his dignity in tatters, his lips twisted with ironic rage. His fists clenched tightly, he hid his backside. "Bloody witch, please don't snitch," he whispered.

Jane stood frozen like an ice statue. Shifting her gaze from the people in the doorway to Asher, she found herself hoping the scar on his backside wouldn't be too disfiguring. Then, spotting the blood running down his pant leg, she turned pale. "Oh, ick! I may be sick."

Surveying the scene, Clair was the only one who smiled calmly. Her Plan Z was a striking success.

Some Like It Not

The Huntsley manor house quieted down, the guests going back to bed after the startling sight of a very mussed Jane Paine and Asher alone in the library, but many were asking how a plain Jane had finally caught the elusive and debonair Earl of Wolverton. Pacing back and forth across his bedchamber, Ian Huntsley was wondering why Asher had been staked in the behind by an on-the-shelf old maid.

The answer to his question stared back at him with beautiful, guileless gray eyes. He knew that expression well. Clair was a delightful bundle of matchmaking female, mismanaging all of those around her with a cheerful passion and usually chaotic results. Crooking his finger, he motioned his wife to him.

"Clair, what do you know about this?" he asked.

Standing before her husband, Clair Frankenstein Huntsley averted her gaze, staring at the bed curtains, studying them as if her life depended upon it. "I do believe we need to air these out," she remarked evasively.

"Clair, why did Asher have a jagged hole in his posterior?" Ian pressed. He loved his redoubtable wife with a passion unmatched. She was everything wonderful and wondrous in life. He thought she was truly remarkable. But sometimes she was a bit eccentric, due no doubt to her heritage. And trouble seemed to follow her like a pig to its trough.

"Yes, that *was* unusual. I wasn't expecting that," she hedged, fingering the sleeves of his rust-colored dressing gown. She hid a grin. Leave it to Jane to turn everything on its end. Asher probably wouldn't be able to sit down for a night or two.

"I knew you were playing matchmaker. I didn't agree with it, but I know how you love your little projects. Trying to make Asher fall in love with that plain old maid . . . Well, to be honest I thought it was rather humorous. And that it would certainly get you in no trouble." Ian broke away from his wife, not wanting to be distracted. And she distracted him terribly just by breathing. Contact was impossible. He started pacing the room again.

"This matchmaking scheme has at least kept you out of climbing around crypts for glimpses of vampires, or haunting old castles in search of ghosts." He stopped pacing and looked at his wife. She was going to drive him insane—if he didn't love her to death first. In spite of all the mad things she had done, the foiled plots, her comedy-of-errors investigations and her truly bizarre family of Frederick the monster—a rather riveting fellow—and madman uncle, Ian wouldn't have traded one minute of his life with her. "But Asher is really going to have get hitched."

"So it would appear," Clair remarked cheerfully.

Ian frowned. "You know, I thought this matchmaking business would keep you safe."

"But it has, darling. *Asher's* the one who got staked,"

Clair remarked, a frown creasing her brow. "Although, I must admit I never intended for that to happen. But then the course of true love never runs smooth."

Ian shook his head. "Clair, I don't mind that your uncle Victor runs around robbing graves for spare body parts. I don't even mind that you are choosing the undead as potential husbands for spinsterish friends. But I do mind when our guest, particularly a guest who has saved both of our lives, is attacked. It reflects badly on both my hospitality, and on the debt of honor I owe to that confounded vampire."

"Asher will be fine," Clair replied. "You know his healing abilities are almost as remarkable as your own. He'll be sitting down in a night or two with his usual savoir faire."

Ian almost chuckled. The image of Asher's chagrined expression when he'd seen where the master vampire was staked was a sight Ian would never forget. But, glancing out the corner of his eye at Clair, he remained solemn. He didn't want to encourage his wife in any more shenanigans.

He held up his wrist, tugging back his robe and exposing two fresh fang marks.

"Ian!" Clair gasped, coming closer to inspect the wound as she knelt on the floor before her darkly handsome husband.

He raised a sardonic brow, his rugged features grim. "For Asher to heal fast, he needed to feed quickly and quietly. Since we didn't want him feeding off our guests, that left me. So not only has your meddling caused this compromising situation, but it left me as a midnight snack for the earl!"

Clair lovingly traced the bite marks. "I'm sorry, darling. I never intended for this to happen. It certainly wasn't in my plan."

Ian raised both eyebrows. The best-laid plans of Clair Frankenstein always went awry.

"Well, I didn't," she said. "I don't know what went wrong."

"Try the stake," Ian suggested wryly. "Then try explaining why Miss Paine wanted to stab Asher."

Clair rested her head on her husband's muscular thighs, wondering if she could hedge her bets. Wondering if Ian was going to get all red in the face and shout at her, or if he'd get all red other places and make love to her. She definitely voted for the latter. "Well, Jane has a few minor idiosyncrasies," she admitted.

"Minor idiosyncrasies? She could have killed him!" Ian snapped. "Wait. Let me rephrase that," he said as he ran his hands through his tousled locks. "Miss Jane could have killed him *again*."

He caressed his wife's face briefly, adding in a piqued tone, "You know, I hate the way he watches you. The bloody neck sucker is in love with you! But I can't have him dead again—not at our house party. It's just not done."

Clair nodded, keeping judiciously quiet.

Ian slumped into the plump cushions of his favorite chair, laying his head in his hand. "Clair, why would Miss Jane attack a guest in our home? Has Asher scorned her? Has she got a screw loose, like Frederick?"

Clair narrowed her eyes at her husband. "Frederick can't help having a few loose screws, and you know that. But Uncle Victor always tightens them."

Ian knew Clair was trying to throw him off the scent, which was ridiculous since he was a werewolf. "All right, my love. I know Jane is a dear friend, which means she's likely a bit of an odd duck like the rest of those you care for. But is she . . . more than odd? Does insanity run in her family?"

That was a hard question to answer. Major Van Helsing wasn't actually a madman, although he was frequently mad. Still, Clair shot her husband a smoldering look, and not the bedroom kind. "You think my friend belongs in a madhouse because she and I are bosom pals?"

Ian backtracked rapidly, almost tripping over his words in the process. He had plans for later on tonight, right after this discussion. Plans of a very naked Clair and her hot lips savoring him. Plans of his hot lips worshipping her. He didn't need Clair to have a fit of temper and foil his amorous mood.

"No . . . not that." Ian waved his hands in the air. "Forget about it. However, I would like to know what Jane thought she was doing tonight."

Clair thought about Ian's question. Then she thought for a moment longer. Then she sat on the bed and thought again, her expression one of intense reflection.

Ian knew his wife's delaying tactics when he saw them. "Clair?" he prompted.

Waving her hand in a dismissive gesture, she said, "There might have been one small thing—a tiny thing, really—that I forgot to tell you about Jane."

Ian nodded, worried. He wished it was a full moon and he could be a werewolf and howl, running free in the night, rather than hearing another comedy-of-errors confession from his wife. "And this tiny thing is . . . ?" He spoke carefully.

"Jane is using her mother's maiden name—Paine." Clair stood, deciding to put some distance between her hot-blooded husband and herself. She knew he would never hurt her, but an angry werewolf threw off tremendous body heat. She was warm as it was.

"Clair, give me the real name of the violent little vixen."

Clair bit her lower lip.

"Her last name is . . . ?" Ian's tone held harshness, his patience wearing to an end.

"Van Helsing," she answered.

The words were like hammer blows. Ian stood, rubbing his forehead. He definitely felt a headache coming on.

"Let me get this straight. Miss Jane Paine is really Miss Jane Van Helsing—of the Van Helsings, who are the foremost vampire hunters in the world. This daughter of the illustrious vampire-staking family you invited to our house party without telling me who she really is. Next, you invite the Master Vampire of London, to whom we owe our lives, to this same house party—"

Clair started to interrupt, but Ian tersely waved her silent.

"So, we now have a vampire hunter and a vampire between whom you are trying to play matchmaker. Bloody hell, Clair! This sounds like something your great-aunt Abby would do. Or your uncle Victor. Instead of wedding bells, we'll be playing funeral marches. And *this* is the tiny oversight you forgot to mention to me?"

Ian was furious; Clair could tell by the ticking of his jaw muscle. Besides, disapproval was written in his eyes. But she had been a Frankenstein before she was a Huntsley, and they were all a stubborn lot—from her grave-robbing, monster-making uncle Victor, to her eccentric great-aunt Abby, who thought she was various historical characters, to her aunt Mary, whose specialty was pet taxidermy. Clair knew beyond a shadow of a doubt that she was dead right about Asher and Jane being perfect for each other. And she intended to prove it, if they didn't kill each other first.

"I know what I'm doing," she stated firmly, unafraid of her husband's ire. "Truly."

"I am overjoyed to know that. Perhaps you can explain to Asher. I am supposed to meet with him in the next hour to discuss his upcoming proposal of marriage. As a man . . . as a vampire—bloody hell, whatever! His honor and life are at stake, not his heart. And I must tell him that his bride-to-be slays his kind for a living, a hobby and a crusade. What a delightful turn of events!" he snapped angrily.

Clair was taken aback. She watched her husband start pacing again, back and forth, his dark hair gleaming like black silk in the glow of the candles. "Ian, my love, I just want Asher to be happy. I just want my good friend Jane to be happy too. Jane will make him so. And Asher will make Jane happy when he realizes he wants to—which will make Jane happy to know that Asher desires her to be happy. I owe Asher your life. I wanted to do something special for him. As a thank-you."

Ian halted, stared hard at her, shook his head and resumed pacing. "Happy? Happy! Oh, happy days in the old Wolverton mansion! I can see it now. Jane will be off lurking in the shadows with a stake in her hand, while Asher's off haunting mausoleums, trying to find new resting places for his coffin—places his wife can't find! And I imagine keeping his backside to the wall. Asher won't be able to rest in peace for years and years." Ian added sardonically, "Perhaps I can loan him some armor. Do you think there's a butt-plate to be had in the armory?"

Her husband's unreasonable attitude finally made Clair lose her temper. Stamping her foot, she glared just as fiercely at him as her husband was glaring at her. "Jane is perfect for Asher. She is well-read, though not as well-read as he is, but give her another hundred years and she would be. She is loyal—you know all Van Helsings are loyal. She is witty and has a gentle nature."

"Gentle nature?" Ian scoffed. "She stuffed his arse with a four-foot stake!"

Clair shrugged. "I full well know that Jane hates that

part of her duty. She gets sick at the sight of the blood. Didn't you see the spot on the carpet?"

Ian said nothing, only glared at her, so she determinedly continued her defense. "I remember when Jane was around eight and I was ten, I fell and cut my leg. It bled badly, and we were a mile or so from home, Jane bound up my leg with her stocking, gagging the whole time."

Ian arched a brow, unmoved.

"She is loyal and sweet, and I wager that in three or four months Asher will lose his heart to her."

Ian arched both brows. His eyes widened.

Waving a hand in front of her face, Clair explained haughtily, "I mean that in the romantic sense, not the slaying sense."

Ian dropped wearily back into his favorite chair and shook his head. "I don't know why I care. I don't know why I'm worried. I don't even know why I donated my blood. I don't like the bloody bloodsucking fiend."

Seeing her husband's slumped shoulders, Clair went to him. She touched his arm gently and planted a tender kiss on his brow. "I know it looks bad now, but things will work out." Patting his arm, she stepped back and headed for the door. "I'm just going to talk to Jane now. I'm sure she must be a trifle upset."

"A trifle? I'm sure she's on the point of total hysteria. She is supposed to hunt vampires, not marry them."

"Tsk, tsk. You worrywart. You just wait and see. They *will* be perfect for each other. And someday they will both get down on their knees and thank us."

As Clair opened the door, Ian called out to her, "Clair, you do realize she tried to end his unlife."

Clair shrugged. Then, with her perfect Frankensteinian logic, she added, "No one's perfect."

Much I-Do's about Nothing

"To be a vampire bride or not to be a vampire bride," Clair remarked. That was the question she knew was rolling through her friend's mind. Anxious, she made her way down the hallway on the third floor where all the party guests were staying.

She knocked softly at Jane's door, not wanting to disturb any of the guests who were actually trying to sleep. She knew Jane wouldn't be, not with her future swinging in the balance like a pendulum gone awry. There was too much at stake, no pun intended. Besides, there were questions Clair needed to ask in order to satisfy her Frankensteinian curiosity. She well knew that Asher's ego could use a prick or two, but really, in the butt? That was a bit much. And why on earth was Jane trying to stake the man of Clair's dreams for her? How could Clair get the two of them together if Jane ran around assaulting Asher with her family's ridiculously ornate stakes?

Jane opened the door, her eyes red and swollen, her hair a mess of tangles, and her robe buttoned unevenly.

Clair had never seen her looking so woebegone or in such a state of disarray. Jane stood out in stark contrast with the rest of the room, which was neat and tidy. Glancing at the vanity table, Clair noticed that all the items—brush, comb, face cream, ribbons and rice powder—were all placed neatly in a row, an inch from the bottom of the table and all in alphabetical order. The major's regimental training evidenced Jane's occupancy of the room. The major had trained his daughter well—but not well enough, or Asher would be dust on this old manor's library floor right now.

Clair held up her hand. "I just want to say three words: Wedded bliss is bliss."

Jane wearily shook her head. "Clair, that's *four* words."

Clair shrugged. "So it is. May I come in?"

Motioning her friend inside, Jane pushed at her hair then closed the door. "My hair's in shambles. I look a fright. I hate disarray, and my life is the biggest mess of all," she said, her eyes glittering with tears. She sat down mechanically, her nerves clearly raw.

What a midsummer's nightmare! she thought raggedly. In a span of mere moments her whole world had turned upside down. Her future was foreboding and frightening. Did Clair have any chocolate? "Can you ever forgive me? What a horrid friend you must think me. What a horrid guest."

Clair knew exactly what Jane was asking. A guest shouldn't try to stake another guest at a house party without expecting serious displeasure from the hostess.

"Why did you do it?" she said. But she had a pretty good idea why. That maniacal major must have been plotting his vampire-destroying schemes again. Still, Neil Asher had lived in London for years on and off, and the Van Helsings had never fixed their sights on him before. Why now?

No, it didn't make sense. Clair had carefully ex-

plained her mistake to Jane, it was true, in mistaking
Asher for a werewolf during the farce that occurred
when Clair was doing supernatural research for the
prestigious Scientific Discovery of the Decade Award.
But due to the debt she owed him for his role in it, Clair
had wisely kept quiet about Asher. Clair generally told
Jane most things, but she had kept quiet about the Earl
of Wolverton being a vampire, since Jane was, after all,
a Van Helsing, and a Van Helsing and her duty were not
soon parted.

Clair had only recently decided to reveal all to Jane
when she'd instead decided that Jane and Asher would
suit admirably. Clair frowned. Jane had almost ruined
her plan. Really, some people could be so inconsiderate!

Seeing Clair's frown, and taking her friend's silence
for appalled revulsion at had what she had done, Jane
sank wearily into the soft cushion of a pale blue chair
next to the small fireplace in the center of the room.
She gestured shakily for Clair to join her.

"I . . ." She tried to speak, then lowered her head. "I
can still see Lord Asher's face when I shoved that stake
in his backside. He looked so stunned, and for a
moment—I probably imagined it, but I thought I
caught a glimpse of true hurt in his eyes." That vulnerability had shaken Jane almost as much as anything
she'd ever seen. Her, ashamed of doing her duty!

"Jane?"

She glanced up at Clair. She had also hurt her friend
by the betrayal. "I am so ashamed," she said. "You've always been my closest friend, and to treat your hospitality like this . . . Please forgive me."

"I do."

Jane glanced up in surprise. What she saw on Clair's
face lightened her heart.

"You don't hate me?"

Clair shook her head. "We've been friends for far too

long to let a little vampire blood come between us. Although I must insist that you cease and desist in your attacks on Asher."

"Is the earl hurt . . ." Jane hesitated, trying not to cry. "Is Asher hurt badly? I wouldn't have killed him, really. Well, I tried . . . but I just couldn't bring myself to the sticking point. In fact, if he hadn't begun to bite me, I don't think I would have struck at all. . . ." Jane hesitated, guilt eating her worse than Asher ever could have. "Please tell me, is he in much pain?"

"He'll be fine. Neil heals remarkably fast," Clair said. "So . . . you know what he is." It really wasn't a question, since the answer was a jagged hole in the vampire's fanny.

Jane nodded woodenly.

"Why did you try and stake him now—at our house party?"

Jane looked away. "Actually, I have been trying to get rid of him for the past ten days. I'm a dismal failure as a Van Helsing. I'm the butt of all the family jokes. My cousins can be most cruel at times. Still, I didn't want to come here to do it, but my father insisted. I longed to tell you, but I took that horrid blood oath."

Clair nodded solemnly. She knew how important that was—and how sick Jane always got after taking the Van Helsing blood oath.

Jane continued speaking, tears sparkling on her eyelashes. "The major is fearful that my uncle Jakob will discover who Asher really is, stake him and steal all the glory. He made me an offer I couldn't refuse. He said that if I failed to come to your party and do my duty, he would give both Orville and Spot away—Orville to the butcher. All I could imagine was Orville lying on some great block with his head cut off."

Clair felt a little concerned. She knew that Major Van

Helsing was just mean enough to do what he said if Jane didn't follow his strict commands. He truly was an old stick in the mud.

"So I had to stop the evil from spreading. You *do* understand?" Jane begged, wringing her hands.

"You mean, Asher being a vampire?"

Jane shook her head. "Pay attention here, Clair. Asher is not only a vampire, but *Count Dracul*—the Prince of Darkness! He's a truly terrible monster of such nefarious evil that the world would be much better off with him not walking the face of it. Even if he is—or maybe especially because he is—dead."

Clair's mouth made a perfect O. "You think our Asher is Dracul?" She tried not to laugh. Last year she had accused Asher of being a werewolf. Now he was being confused with an evil vampire prince? What rotten luck. She said, "Asher may be a rake, behave rather pompously at times and have a certain reputation among the demimonde, but he is not this Dracul character. I know Asher. He has saved not only my life, but Ian's as well."

Jane sighed. "I truly didn't believe it. That was probably why, when the moment came, I got stuck and couldn't strike that place most vampires get staked."

Clair nodded. She understood perfectly. "Yes, you struck low, rather than strike the spot where vampires are staked to make sure they're struck dead."

Jane managed a faint smile, relieved to have a friend who understood her. "I didn't believe it about Asher," she repeated. "Especially tonight." Jane kept thinking of Asher's kisses. "Even though the major's spies were quite convinced that the Earl of Wolverton is Dracul."

Rubbing her forehead, she remembered the warmth she had glimpsed in Asher's eyes when he had kissed her—kissed her like she had dreamed of being kissed.

Well, actually it had been better. No dream could compare with the reality of Asher.

Yes, Jane had felt his hunger, but not evil. No, Asher might be many things, but he wasn't the malevolent force that was the legendary Count Dracul. She added thoughtfully "No, I don't believe Asher is the Prince of Darkness, but he is a vampire. The major compelled me strongly to remove the earl. What shall I do? You know the major hates Orville with a passion."

Clair wanted to roll her eyes. That bloody ostrich again! Jane needed to get her priorities straight. "Famous last names are hard to live up to. I should know. Take me, for example. After your uncle creates a human monster out of spare cadavers . . . well, how can I ever top that?"

Jane's face lightened. "Marry a werewolf, I presume."

Clair laughed.

"I have been meaning to ask, do you ever get fleas in your bed?"

Clair laughed even harder, holding her sides. "No! Only muddy footprints—in the most unusual places." She grinned mischievously, remembering one of her gowns with paw prints all over the bodice. Ian got a little frisky, especially in wolf form.

Jane sighed. "Sometimes I despise being a Van Helsing. I despise the sight of blood. I despise spiders, and I'm not very fond of dirt. And now I've been forced to attack an important member of the nobility in your home. I am so sorry, Clair."

Reaching over, Clair patted her hand. "Jane, of all people, I know too well the burden of family loyalty. I am a Frankenstein, so how could I not? We too haunt cemeteries at night and do odd things. Who am I to cast stones? Some of my earliest memories are of robbing graves or mixing potions in Uncle Victor's lab."

"But you enjoy the graveyard robbing and potion mixing."

Clair smiled. "True. One of my fondest memories is when Uncle Victor made Frederick and came running down the stairs screaming, 'It's alive! It's alive!'"

"A moment to live in history," Jane said sincerely.

"That it was," Clair agreed brightly. "As tonight will probably be. Asher will never live this down. Whatever else happens, Jane, you have my backing and Ian's."

Jane hung her head, placing a hand against her forehead. "What have I done? The major is going to be so disappointed in me. Not only did I not succeed with Asher, I have gotten myself compromised by him." She burst into tears again. "If Asher doesn't marry me, I'm ruined. If he does marry me, I'm ruined and probably dead, along with him. My father will get rid of both Asher and me—if Asher doesn't get rid of me first."

Jane sobbed, her nerves finally getting the better of her. "Maybe we can share the same coffin," she sniffled.

"Now, now, nobody is going to fit you for a casket. Instead we'll fit you for a wedding gown," Clair soothed Jane, holding both her friend's hands. "This will all work out."

"Impossible."

"There's no choice, and I am not one to beat about the bush. You are compromised. You have done what many a female set out to do and failed: bringing Asher to his knees. He will propose. You must accept, and your father must concede to the match for honor's sake." Clair hid her elation. Her Plan Z had changed dramatically, but the end result was the same. She would see these two married or her name wasn't Clair Elizabeth Frankenstein Huntsley.

Jane shook her head fiercely. "My father will never agree. He'd rather see me a corpse than married to one.

Besides, Asher hates me. I imagine he wants to suck me dry for this." Jane wailed, "I should just roll over and play dead now." A sense of dread began rolling over her.

"Now, now," Clair remonstrated, patting Jane's hands. "It's not as bad as all that."

"But it is," Jane argued, nodding vigorously. "Even your husband wants to kill me for this fiasco."

Clair stared in disbelief. "Ian said that?" Her husband was a puppy dog—when he wasn't a big, scary werewolf.

"No. But I can tell murder when I see it in someone's eyes. I have embarrassed you, your husband and his guests. I have abused his hospitality. So Ian will want me dead too." Wound up, Jane continued, big fat tears rolling down her cheeks. "Just what does that say about me—that everyone I know wants to murder me?"

She held on as though Clair's hands were a lifeline. "I'm not a bad person. Not really. I go to church. I feed my birds and take in stray dogs and cats, in spite of the major's many protests. Grandfather Ebenezer and I deliver Christmas gifts to the street urchins from the lists my grandfather makes all year. I even pull the weeds from neglected graves when we are hunting in the cemeteries," Jane said sadly. "But don't tell my cousins that last bit, especially Dwight. He's an odious toad."

"I know. You're a fine person, Jane. Why do you think you are my friend? I wouldn't have just anyone. And no one will touch a hair on my bosom friend's head," Clair asserted firmly.

Standing, Jane pulled away from the warmth of Clair's comfort and began to pace back and forth and back and forth across the thick Persian carpet. Watching her, Clair felt as if her eyes were crossing.

"No, I'm not a fine person," she said. "I am pulled in two different directions. I'm formed into a shape I don't even recognize at times. My Van Helsing duty lies one way, but my heart and dreams lie in another." Jane's features contorted with anguish. "I didn't want to stake Asher. I don't want to stake any vampires ever. Blood is just so . . . bloody! Dirt is just so dirty. And spiders—well, they have eight legs and crawl all over you. I think I want a large marble angel to decorate my headstone," she finished in another torrent of sobs.

Trying to commiserate and read between the lines was not an easy feat when Jane was upset. And Ian thought Clair was hard to follow! Ha! Still, Clair persevered. Her brilliant plan was not going to go awry. Determinedly she asked, "But most especially Asher. You wouldn't mind being married to Asher—although it is a little late to worry about that particular point now. Marrying Asher is the only solution for you after tonight."

Jane stared at Clair for a long moment, then quietly said, "Yes. But he loathes me now."

"All husbands hate their wives every now and then. It's just the nature of the beast. Nobody can be blissful all the time. If we were, we wouldn't know what true bliss is. And nobody can be likeable all the time. Not even Ian."

Jane stared hard at Clair, trying to reason out what her friend had just said. "Bliss isn't bliss, unless we are sometimes unhappy?"

"Yes. You've got it," Clair remarked happily. "Besides, between husbands and wives, making up after a jolly good fight is invigorating." Clair remembered Ian making love to her in the pantry after their most recent argument—one about serving the truffles that Mr. Warner had gathered on his last hunt.

"Who wants pig drool on one's food?"

Jane stopped pacing for a moment and looked at Clair, confused.

Undaunted, her friend went on. "Be thankful Asher is upset with you. If he wasn't, he'd be touched in the head. Imagine, not being upset with the person that stuck you in the fanny! I couldn't allow you to marry a raving lunatic, now, could I?"

In a bizarre way, that made sense. But there were so many problems with a match between Jane and Asher, such as their domestic arrangements—what time they would sleep and where. She certainly would never be caught dead in a coffin. (Or at least alive in one.) And her husband would never be able to take a walk in the sun with her, unless she wanted him to be a dried-up raisin. How could she want that? Her husband was a beauty if a beast, and a plain Jane like herself would never waste such a thing.

But then reality set in, and she said, "Asher is a great connoisseur of beauty. He buys only the finest things and courts the loveliest women. I'm no beauty. I can't believe he will offer for me."

Clair waggled her index finger at Jane, her brows arched. "Tut-tut. Never judge a vampire by his coffin." She went to stand before her friend, put her arms on her shoulders.

"Jane, you are pretty. You have just refused to see it all these years. You have the most remarkable greenish eyes I have ever seen, and a very good figure—a fine figure, indeed. Asher will be most impressed. But more importantly, you are intelligent, compassionate and have a core of iron. You also have a sense of the ridiculous, which you will need in dealing with our toplofty earl," she added with a laugh.

Jane shook her head. "But . . . how can I endure being married to a vampire when I am a Van Helsing? If I am torn by duty now, what will happen when I wed?"

"When you marry, your duty will be to your husband first and foremost. You can retire permanently from slaying."

Clair's words struck Jane like a #3 mallet. She was perfectly correct, and wasn't it marvelous? Wedding vows before God superceded family vows—at least Jane hoped that was so. No more midnight stakeouts!

"No more of this vampire cloak-and-dagger stuff. I can live a normal life. Well, as normal as anyone can whose husband has both feet in the grave." For the first time since Clair arrived, Jane smiled, a wistful smile of hope. Then reality intruded again, and her features darkened. "No, the major will never allow it. He will have me drawn and quartered. And he'll have Orville served for Christmas dinner."

Clair laughed, the sound light in the dismal room. "I think they quit doing that in Shakespeare's day," she said.

"Serving ostrich?"

"Drawing and quartering."

Jane's lips quirked. "And what a fine time the bard would have had with this. A vampire hunter married to a vampire! What a farce."

"Yes, your life is like a play! Rather like *Romeo and Juliet.*"

Jane pursed her lips, deflated. There were many problems with that analogy. "No. Romeo was in love with Juliet." She wondered what would have happened if Romeo hadn't died. Would he have ever loved again? Could she herself marry a vampire who was in love with her friend? No, even Shakespeare's plots weren't this convoluted.

Looking at her friend, Clair smiled a secret smile, thinking that with a little time and luck, the earl would fall deeply and forever in love with Jane. He might be sorely angry right now, as well as sore, but soon he would be focusing on a different bottom than his own: the pert one on his soon-to-be bride.

"Well then, Jane, what about *The Taming of the Shrew*?" she suggested. Clair shook her head. "No, you're no shrew. A shrew couldn't hold a stake," she teased. "Not with those mousy little paws."

Jane knew her friend was trying to cheer her up. She appreciated the effort and didn't want Clair to feel bad, so in a lighter manner she said, "All right, I have it. My life could be the play *Hamlet*—all of us doing our familial duty."

Clair waved the suggestion away. "No, too gloomy. Everyone dies in *Hamlet*. Your ending will be a happy ending."

" 'To sleep, perchance to dream,' " Jane quoted. And dream she did. Of a world where love reigned and she was queen. Of a father who adored his daughter, whose only duty was to love and be loved. Of a vampire with a rakish smile and a heart that beat just for her.

Clair grinned. Yes, Jane was perfect for Asher; she knew more than enough Shakespeare. "All's well that ends well," she joked. Now, if Ian would go have a talk with the piqued Asher and get quickly back to bed, she had a few dreams to come herself.

"Somehow I doubt it," Jane remarked. After a moment she added, "Well, at least Orville can be happy."

"Hmm?" Clair asked, distracted.

"He won't go to the butcher," Jane told her. "Just a vampire's lair." But then a look of horror crossed her face. "Good grief! Does Asher like pets? Vampires don't drink bird blood, do they?"

A Van Helsing by
Any Other Name . . .

Returning to the library, Ian found Asher, a study in icy reflection, staring silently out the large bay windows. Even with his world in turmoil, the Earl was still the best-dressed vampire about town. Yet, below that facade was a smoldering rage that was ready to burst into a white-hot inferno.

Ian wondered if Asher would suffer the slings and arrows of outrageous misfortune, or if he would take up fangs against his sea of troubles? He sincerely hoped not.

Warily Ian seated himself at his large mahogany desk. Asher glanced over at him. The vampire's face gave no indication of the violence of his feelings, but he stiffly raised a hand, growling, his eyes glowing with a strange bluish red light.

"Say nothing about where I was staked," he said. "In fact, a blood oath of secrecy might be best."

Ian stifled a grin. He was no fool. To get staked where he had must be mortifying for the arrogant earl. He couldn't resist a little ribbing. "Perhaps you're slipping, old man. You might want to practice your lovemaking techniques if this is what you get in the end."

Asher turned, his eyes ablaze. "You know better than that! Miss Jane is simply a pain—in the arse. She's a menace to polite society and clothing everywhere."

Ian nodded because he couldn't help but agree. Jane Van Helsing had certainly put a crimp in this party along with the stake in Asher's backside. "In this day and age, being found alone with an innocent unmarried female in a state of dishabille is asking for marriage. She's stuck you both in an unpleasant situation I'm afraid," he admitted.

Asher's rage flared, and he was clearly unamused. "Huntsley . . . take care where you step."

But Ian had no choice. As host of the house party, he was responsible not only for Asher's well-being but also Jane's. "Well . . . this wasn't well done, Asher. Miss Paine, besides being a bosom friend to Clair, is a young lady of family. An innocent, unmarried lady. How you two were found . . . Do I need to speak to you of honor?"

Asher remained silent, his jaw muscles clenched. He glared fiercely at Ian. He wanted to strangle Huntsley with his bare hands. The baron was second, right after Jane Paine.

The thought of Jane made Asher see red; the very idea of her made him cross. The fact that he had longed for the unhinged chit made him want to spout foul curses. She'd never know just how much he wanted to bite her neck and spank her bottom. He was living a nightmare, all courtesy of one crazy girl.

"She's a madwoman! Running about splashing people with brandy, rambling about spiders, sticking people in the ass with sharp objects! I tell you, Huntsley, she's just not natural."

Ian shook his head. Treading cautiously, he said, "Be

that as it may, Miss Paine has been severely compromised by you."

"I was the one who was injured!" Asher snarled. "Talk about ripped clothing, that femme fatale is hell on wheels. Renfield is already quite beside himself."

Ian arched a sardonic brow. "You speak of your wardrobe, but Miss Paine will be ruined. No man will want to marry her after this."

Asher snorted. "As if any wanted to before. Huntsley, that calamity-ridden female is safer on the shelf. Bloody damn! Nothing occurred between the two of us. We did not do the deed—and looking back now, I wonder why I was even tempted to tarry with such a demented mortal."

Ian shook his head. "The world of the living is not unlike the undead one. All society will know of Jane's ruin in less than a fortnight. It won't help your reputation any, either. Her family is well-known, and you know how the combined Councils of weres and vampires feel about bringing ourselves into public scrutiny. They will be livid unless you do the honorable thing and marry her." He reminded Asher, "It was not so long ago that we were all hunted nearly to extinction. We must blend in with society and live our lives like humans, or as humanly as possible. Besides, there is your duty. You have ruined an innocent—"

Asher interrupted harshly, running his fingers through his hair. He began to pace, wincing sharply from the wound in his backside. "She's no innocent. Potty, insane, deranged, but no innocent. Bah! No innocent wields a stake like that. Or kisses like that, either!"

Ian glared at him. "You know she's a virgin. And you were trying to get a little taste when you were caught. Honor demands and depends upon your marrying Jane. You were seen in a state of dishabille with her, a respectable lady of good breeding and background, her gown twisted, her breasts half revealed, her lips red and swollen, late at night. You have no choice, Asher, and well you know it. You could escape the scandal by going to the continent if you refuse to do the honorable thing, but the vampire council will hunt you down and imprison you for four hundred years for drawing attention to the otherworldly."

He waited patiently for Asher to gather his emotions. It was a rare opportunity to observe the earl's cool facade so crumbled.

"The woman is consistently inconsistent," Asher complained. "One minute she is kissing me madly, passionately—the next she is planting a foot of wood in my ass!" He banged his fists on Ian's massive walnut desk, and Ian held his breath, hoping it could withstand the vampire's wrath.

The Earl of Wolverton continued his tirade. "Her mind must be the size of a chestnut to do what she did. Besides, the feral female has a foul temper. I do not want to marry her.

"I don't even know her people," he raged on. "Her heritage. I am a bloody earl, for pity's sake. I am a master vampire with a lineage longer than all my titles. I am descended from kings both mortal and immortal." Asher roared, his fist clenched high in the air as he shook it. "I shall not marry beneath me. Most especially not a madwoman!"

Ian debated telling Asher of Jane's lineage, but decided to wait, knowing he would only be pouring fuel on the fire.

"Marriage is the only route," he said instead, hoping Asher would agree. If the arrogant vampire refused, then Major Van Helsing would surely call him out. The attention would be disastrous. The eyes of the *ton* would be focused on the supernatural world, and one mistake could mean a revelation that could result in full-scale panic. And mortals always tried to kill what they feared. It would be a war—costly, bloody and devastating to men and monsters alike. "There is no other option. Too many eyes saw you tonight."

Asher nodded, his expression brooding. He said, "I, who have spent hundreds of years as a connoisseur of the beautiful, will be shackled to a female only slightly above ordinary." In his anger, he forgot the sweet taste of her kiss and her mouthwatering breasts. No matter how lush, no tit was worth this tat. And her to-die-for neck was little added incentive.

Ian shrugged. "All cats are gray in the dark," he proposed.

Asher stopped pacing and dropped restlessly into the large Louis XIV chair in front of the desk. A loud groan escaped him. He had forgotten his injury. His pride and backside now smarting, he replied, "When I want to bed a cat, I'll let you know."

Then reality hit him smack-dab in the face. He wanted to scream to the heavens, for fate was quite unfair. As the wily werewolf said, honor was honor, and something no earl or master vampire could ignore. Especially with the Council watching. Being sentenced to a forced sleep for five hundred years wasn't something he wanted to experience. Besides, if he married Jane, with her mortal lifespan, she would only inconvenience his life temporarily.

Clenching his fists, Asher rested his forehead upon them. "I am going to marry a mousy madwoman—a back-staking shrew."

"Tame her," Ian suggested.

"She will cost me a fortune in clothing. And she's not right in the head. Or maybe she just has a morbid fear of kissing," Asher joked to himself sarcastically. Rubbing his backside, he continued following that train of thought. "I fear there's more to this story than meets the eye. She must know I am a vampire, else why use a wooden stake on me? It was the Van Helsing model four, by the way," he added, just to impress Baron Huntsley with his houseguest's perfidy.

Ian knew the time had come, and he was not looking forward to what he had to reveal. He only hoped Asher didn't believe in biting the messenger.

"Don't give me that look. What is it?" Asher asked.

Ian coughed slightly, trying to decide just how to repair Clair's omission. "I myself only recently discovered that Miss Jane knows what you are. She was *sent* here to destroy you."

Asher's fangs flashed in the candle light, giving his handsome face a devilish look. "Because I am the Master Vampire of London?" he asked.

Ian answered carefully, weighing his options. "It's not so much what you are at this point, but who they think you are." If Asher attacked, he would feint to the right and roll backward towards the hearth. Hanging above the fireplace was his Welsh ancestors' sword. He didn't think he would have to kill the vampire, merely threaten him.

"Who? The suspense is killing me," Asher retorted. "And I've had enough of people trying to kill me tonight."

Ian leaned back in his chair, still watchful. "Dracul. The Prince of Darkness."

Asher fought appalled surprise. "Dracul? Has he come to Town? Here to London? That would be a disaster of epic proportions, most especially for me."

"He holds no love for you, same clan or not," Ian agreed.

Asher took a deep breath. Count Dracul was debauched, deadly and a malignant presence to be avoided whenever possible. Asher and the count had been at odds for over a hundred years. "Yes. Our enmity is long standing. Who thinks I am he? And why?"

Ian wearily ran his hands through his hair. This long day's journey into night was getting longer and trickier. "Certain people, because of certain information. However, Jane is now convinced that you aren't Count Dracul. I daresay she will convince her father of the fact. Especially if you are marrying into the family to save her good name."

Asher's eyes bored holes into Ian. "And just who is her father?" His tone was full of chilling menace.

Placing his hands on the desk, tensing his body for an attack, Ian replied, "Her father is Major Edward Van Helsing."

The breath hissed out of Asher, a low growl vibrating from his throat. The vampire's eyes narrowed to ice blue slits, blazing as they were.

Dracul was a nefarious foe, but the Van Helsings were detestable enemies of every vampire in the world. The family were cunning, ruthless and fanatical about executing members of the undead, and sometimes demons too. Although Asher had no truck with demons, he had lost a few vampire friends over the centuries to a vile Van Helsing stake. It was tough to consider Jane was one of *those*.

Ian's eyes narrowed also. He sat in preternatural stillness, appraising the situation. Tensed, he waited for Asher's rage either to dissipate or escalate. He was at a disadvantage: Although he was a werewolf, he could only change form on nights when the moon was full. He was much stronger several days before and after a full moon, but only slightly stronger than a human at other times. This was one of those other times.

"How long have you known?" Asher ground out,

leaping to his feet. Having forgotten his injury, he let out a startled gasp.

Stiffly he turned his back on Baron Huntsley and ferociously paced the room. He was furious enough to destroy anything in his path, not to mention still wounded by Clair's betrayal. He snarled, "I'm furious enough to throw back my head and howl to the heavens, and I'm not even a werewolf!" Only centuries of aristocratic breeding and vampire stoicism kept him from doing so.

"I only learned who Jane is tonight," Ian reminded him.

"And Clair?" Asher's question was edged with fury.

"They have been friends for quite some time," Ian admitted.

"So, your wife invited a vampire murderer here to your estate with me as a guest as well," Asher said. He turned his face away, hiding the intense pain he felt, a taste of bile so bitter he thought he would choke. Asher had loved Clair and she had betrayed him. It was unforgivable, even if it was most likely one of her preposterous plans turned upside down.

Ian could sense the waves of hurt. Though he didn't like Asher's interest in his wife, he felt a stirring of pity. He explained, "If it makes you feel any better, Clair was trying to play matchmaker. You see, she had this plan . . ."

Asher snorted loudly, his expression grim.

"I know," Ian went on, "Clair and her plans usually go astray. But Clair truly believes that you and Jane are the perfect pair. That you and Jane will find great love together—once-in-a-lifetime kind of love. For an immortal that's pretty significant."

"Perhaps she should have told Jane of this plan," Asher snapped. "Your wife is a menace to society. She is as wildly demented as her friend! They're two mad hatters, hopping around, creating havoc, pandemonium, mayhem and attempted murder!"

Ian grimaced. He didn't like slurs on Clair, but this time his wife had outdone herself. When the vampire was right, the vampire was right. "Clair cares for you as a dear friend," he said. "She would never willingly see you hurt. She only wants your happiness."

Asher halted abruptly. "I truly think your wife has run mad. I'll be a pincushion in less than a week. Damnation, Huntsley! My supposed bride-to-be a bloodthirsty Van Helsing, the scourge of vampire kind?"

"Not after she marries you. She will be an Asher, the Countess of Wolverton."

Asher's usual savoir faire having long deserted him, he violently shook his head. "What an utterly horrifying thought. I shall wear mourning clothes for the rest of my life." If he had to marry the treacherous, conniving, vicious vixen, he would make her pay dearly for as long as she lived—which in the mood he was in right now, would be until just before sunrise.

"A wife's duty is to her husband," Ian remarked, "and Jane is a stickler for duty. She intensely disliked being a vampire hunter, but the major left her no choice."

Again, Asher shook his head. More slowly this time. "A Van Helsing by any other name would still be a Van Helsing."

Ian waited, silent.

"I cannot marry her. I'll be the laughing stock of vampires everywhere. A master vampire married to a bloody butcherous Van Helsing?"

Ian raised both hands imploringly. "You have to marry her. Imagine the consequences. Besides, being married to a mortal is only until death do you part. It's quickly over. Why, it will be a drop in the bucket to you, the years speeding by on your way to eternity."

"Ha! Every night will seem like an eternity shackled to that monstrous menace!" But he found himself a bit swayed. If she quickly died . . . But, no! He steeled himself. "Besides, her father will never agree. He loathes vampires. He wants us all to bite the dust. I presume he would rather see her dead first than married to me." Realizing what he'd said, Asher quickly added, "Not '*then* married to me.'"

"Major Van Helsing thought you were Dracul. You're not. Jane can dissemble and maybe say you aren't even a vampire. If the Van Helsing spies got the identities of you and the count confused, they could also be wrong about what you are. Right? Besides, Major Van Helsing has little choice."

Asher glowered. "How surprising. I would never peg you as an optimist. Do you really think Jane would lie for me? She staked me, Ian!"

"And she's terribly upset about the whole thing," Baron Huntsley volunteered.

"She's 'terribly upset'?" Asher mocked. "I have a hole in my arse, and not where one should be! Bloody hell!"

Ignoring the vampire, Ian explained his plan of action. "I'll send two messengers out early in the morning. One will carry a note requesting Major Van Helsing come here immediately. The other will be for your man of business to attend to the special license, since you can't possibly ride in your condition." Ian's lips twitched. "Besides, you couldn't make it to London before first light anyway." He was glad to see that Asher's fangs had retracted.

"How thoughtful you are," Asher mocked him.

"Clair says Jane has cried herself sick. And . . . Jane remarked that if you hadn't scared her by trying to give her a little love bite, she probably wouldn't have staked you at all."

"Ha! Measure for measure it's a lie. Jane is a blood-thirsty wench. She's a bloody backstabbing betrayer. I can see myself introducing her to my vampire friends: 'My good fellows, meet my wife—she or her family have probably slain one of your kin'." Asher shook his head slowly. His anger was gone, leaving him curiously detached. He felt all alone, afloat in the vast dark universe, where stars and events spun crazily out of control. He hated Miss Paine in the Ass; she was his enemy, an enigma and an eccentric. But, then, what could one expect from such a lineage? And to think, his exalted personage and hers would be linked in unholy matrimony. His ancestors would turn over in their graves, then rise and come yell at him.

"What a farce this all is. A tempest of dire proportions."

Baron Huntsley smiled grimly. "You made your coffin. Now you have to lie in it with Jane," he said.

Asher glared intensely at the man who was neither his foe nor really his friend. "You know, Ian, you always had a morbid sense of humor. But if you make sport of me right now, I feel I will have to do murder. Then Clair would despise me—if my beloved fiancée didn't stake me first."

Ian coughed, covering his chuckle.

Asher clenched his fists, longing to choke the breath out of the man. But that would start a vampire and shape-shifter war. Clair would never forgive him.

Honor was now a suit of armor so heavy he was afraid he'd come crashing to earth, right into a muddled puddle. Such was his look.

Resigned to the frightening, fantastic farce his life had suddenly become, he said morosely, "I guess what

Shakespeare said is true. 'Some Cupid kills with arrows, some with traps.'"

And it's all a pain in the butt, Ian agreed mutely. Wisely he kept his amusement to himself.

Father of the Vampire's Bride

Knowing that a gathering of eagle-eyed Van Helsings awaited her filled Jane with trepidation as she sought out the Huntsleys' sun filled parlor. The messenger sent for her father had returned early, with both the major and her brother, Brandon, in tow. The major had departed London before the messenger had even reached there, meeting him along the way and riding hell-bent for leather to reach Huntsley Manor. As for why, both Jane and Clair were in the dark.

Jane hadn't seen either her brother or her father yet. Not twenty minutes earlier, Asher and the major had been closeted in the library with Baron Huntsley. Their voices had been raised, yet their remarks were undistinguishable. Jane and Clair had tried listening at the door, but to no avail; they could only make out a word here and there, but not sentences.

Girding herself for one of her father's tirades, Jane straightened her spine, lifted her chin and entered the large room. She found the major sitting on the rose brocade settee in the corner before the fire. His right leg, slightly swollen with gout, was resting on a stool cushion of matching rose and green hues. His expression was indignant, his face ruddy, his eyebrows arched in blatant disapproval.

Brandon, Jane's brother, stood to his father's right, in one hand a glass of brandy, the other hand on the mantel. In spite of the terror and shame she was feeling, Jane was glad to see he looked his usual handsome self. His brown hair, the color of polished walnuts, was longer than usual, tied back in a queue. His eyes were almost the same shade as her own, except his held more green and they stared at her in sympathy. His smile was fleeting but heartfelt.

Jane started toward her brother to welcome him back from the continent with an animated hug, but he solemnly shook his head, his eyes darting to their father. Abruptly she halted, tormented contemplation tightening her chest further, making her want to run screaming from the room. With great resolve and trepidation, she held her ground, ready for the dressing-down that was soon to come.

"Well, Jane, what dustup have you gotten into now?" the major asked grimly. "What am I to do with you? How could you bungle such a simple stratagem? If I didn't know your mother, I'd think you were born on the wrong side of the blanket."

Jane blanched, moving apprehensively to her father's left side. The major was going to ring a peal over her head that would put the great St. Paul's Cathedral bells to shame. Not that that was unwarranted, just unwanted. Her future hung in the balance. Her whole life was turned upside down. She needed a sympathetic shoulder to cry upon—someone to tell her all would be right with the world. Someone to hold her tight and offer the comfort of knowing she was loved in spite of all the bad and scary things that would happen.

She lowered her head, hiding her tears since the major despised watering pots. Besides, she had spent the past day and night crying her eyes out. She was surprised that there was a single drop of water left in her overwrought body.

"I told you to pretend to seduce the earl, not for you to let the earl seduce you! I told you to stake him, not to be caught alone with him in the wee hours of the morning. I am deeply astounded and ashamed that a daughter of mine would act like a Covent Garden doxy!" The major snorted derisively.

Jane gasped, her cheeks burning. Anger flared inside her. Her nerves were tootling like a cavalry troop's call to battle.

Brandon's expression became one of anger. "Father! *You* sent Jane into this whole ramshackle affair. She's no seductress—anyone can see that," he said. He shook his head vigorously. His father never should have sent Jane to do a man's job. Er, not that seducing the earl was a man's job.

Jane gasped. She knew she was no femme fatale, but really! A brother should take up for his sister, not disparage her lack of sensuality.

Brandon glanced at her apologetically. "Sorry, Jane. But Father has no right to berate you."

"Right? Right? I am her father! If I can't point out her flaws, who can?" The major gave both his unruly children withering glances.

Brandon nodded fiercely. "And 'tis a good thing she did. If Jane had succeeded, she would have been tried for the murder of an earl!"

"Murder?" Jane peeped.

Brandon nodded. "Didn't you wonder why we made such good time? The messenger found us en route to Huntsley Manor."

"I know," she said. "Why?" She was so nervous, her queasy stomach was doing somersaults. She was about to cast up her accounts all over Clair's Persian rug. It was only with a supreme effort of will that she forced the nausea to recede. Did Clair have any brandied bonbons lying around?

"Father got his information wrong. The Earl of Wolverton may be many things, but he is not our foe Count Dracul," Brandon announced, giving his father an annoyed look. Then he added wrathfully, "Although, it's apparent that Wolverton is a seducer of innocents!"

Jane ignored the latter comment. She hadn't really been all that innocent. She was the one who'd instigated the whole rotten scenario, although with a great deal of help from her father.

"How did you discover the case of mistaken identity?" Jane asked, wondering if they knew Asher was a vampire with big, nasty, pointy white teeth.

His forehead bunched, clearly tense, Brandon answered. "Our spies were wrong. I found and followed Dracul in Transylvania, but lost his trail in Paris. So I came home in hopes that he might turn up in London. He used to live here over a century ago, for nearly forty years, but was forced to flee for his life. Now I believe he *has* returned, secretly, in spite of we Van Helsings who live here. Lady Veronique has not run off with her lover since he returned to Town yesterday from a brief trip to the country. The widow is definitely missing, and I have word that some ladies of the evening from White Chapel are missing as well. Although one was found with two holes in her neck, very much dead."

Jane shook her head grimly. This was not good news at all. Returning to her own problems, she grimaced, her foot tapping a sharp beat on the hardwood floor. "I could have killed an innocent man," she scolded her father. Her instincts had told her that Asher wasn't the Prince of Evil, and Clair had also championed the earl. If events had turned out differently, she would have dispatched an innocent vampire. Well, she amended, no vampire was innocent, but Asher certainly wasn't the Prince of Depravity.

Furious with herself and her sire, she wanted to stomp her feet and scream curses. If she wasn't such a lady, she would have. Her cursed father! He had sent her on her merry doomed way to destroy a Peer of the Realm on faulty information. Asher probably thought she was touched in the head. He had a case.

"Innocent? How do you know he's innocent? Just because my spies were wrong about who he was doesn't mean they're incorrect about *what* he is," the major argued.

Jane let that comment slide. "How could your spies have been so mistaken?"

"Well, if you've seen one vampire, you've seen them all. They all look alike," the major said with a dismissive hand wave. "A simple case of mistaken identity."

"Not so simple, Papa," Jane reprimanded him bitterly. She sank into a rose-hued chair near where her brother stood resting his foot against the fireplace grate. "It has quite changed my life. Now I am ruined. Ruined." She and Orville could go and hide their heads in the giant sandbox she had ordered especially for him.

Glancing down, Jane sighed bleakly. "Ruined."

"Not quite. Your reputation may be slightly tarnished, but it's not damaged beyond repair," her brother said, leaning down to pat her on the shoulder. Jane knew he loved her dearly and hated seeing her so disheartened. He above all people knew her life had not been an easy one, most especially with the death of their mother.

"Your brother's right, Jane. The earl has asked for the honor of your hand, and I have accepted," the major pronounced. His voice was strained.

Jane smothered her gasp. She had been talked into

expecting the offer of marriage by what little Clair had explained of Ian's conversation with the earl, but still it came as a shock. Even more shocking was her father's permission.

She took a deep breath, trying to calm herself. If she didn't marry Asher, she was doomed to spinisterhood and shunning from society. If she did marry the hoity-toity earl, she would be doomed to a lifetime with a husband who despised her. Not to mention his fetish for blood. And his age! He was way too old for her, and way too experienced. Although, he did make her heart go *pitter-pat* whenever he was near.

Tears welled in her eyes, and Jane furiously blinked them back. Her life was never to be the same again. Yet, wasn't that what she longed for, a different life? But, what would the proud earl think of her lineage? Her antecedents had killed his.

Her tears dried up as she reasoned that being married to a vampire would have certain advantages. First and foremost, she would never again have to hunt the walking dead. Rather, married to the Earl of Wolverton, she would only have to watch out for the walking wed—the terrifying wives of other nobles. Second, there would be no more vampire training in the rain, sleet or snow. Third, the earl was handsome and very wealthy. She could buy as many pretty new gowns as she wanted, and jewelry. She did so love emeralds. And maybe they could travel—to the Dark Continent, perhaps—so that she could go exotic bird-watching. And perhaps she could have those delicious chocolates from Paris imported. Fourth, Asher probably didn't have a speck of silver anti-vampire paraphernalia in the house. Never again would she polish silver chains or crosses as punishment.

Intrigued with the possibilities, she cautiously asked her father, "If the earl was a vampire would you let me marry him?"

GET UP TO 4 FREE BOOKS!

You can have the best romance delivered to your door for less than what you'd pay in a bookstore or online. Sign up for one of our book clubs today, and we'll send you **FREE* BOOKS** just for trying it out...**with no obligation to buy, ever!**

HISTORICAL ROMANCE BOOK CLUB

Travel from the Scottish Highlands to the American West, the decadent ballrooms of Regency England to Viking ships. Your shipments will include authors such as CONNIE MASON, SANDRA HILL, CASSIE EDWARDS, JENNIFER ASHLEY, LEIGH GREENWOOD, and many, many more.

LOVE SPELL BOOK CLUB

Bring a little magic into your life with the romances of Love Spell—fun contemporaries, paranormals, time-travels, futuristics, and more. Your shipments will include authors such as LYNSAY SANDS, CJ BARRY, COLLEEN THOMPSON, NINA BANGS, MARJORIE LIU and more.

As a book club member you also receive the following special benefits:

- **30% OFF all orders through our website & telecenter!**
- **Exclusive access to** special discounts!
- **Convenient** home delivery **and 10 day examination period to return any books you don't want to keep.**

There is no minimum number of books to buy, and you may cancel membership at any time. See back to sign up!

YES! ☐

Sign me up for the **Historical Romance Book Club** and send my TWO FREE BOOKS! If I choose to stay in the club, I will pay only $8.50* each month, a savings of $5.48!

YES! ☐

Sign me up for the **Love Spell Book Club** and send my TWO FREE BOOKS! If I choose to stay in the club, I will pay only $8.50* each month, a savings of $5.48!

NAME: _____

ADDRESS: _____

_____

TELEPHONE: _____

E-MAIL: _____

☐ **I WANT TO PAY BY CREDIT CARD.**

☐ VISA ☐ MasterCard ☐ DISCOVER

ACCOUNT #: _____

EXPIRATION DATE: _____

SIGNATURE: _____

Send this card along with $2.00 shipping & handling for each club you wish to join, to:

Romance Book Clubs
20 Academy Street
Norwalk, CT 06850-4032

Or fax (must include credit card information!) to: 610.995.9274. You can also sign up online at www.dorchesterpub.com.

JOIN NOW!

The major waved his hand dismissively. "If he is a vampire, and if Dracul has come to London as your brother suspects, you will be our ears and eyes to the plans of those bloodsucking fiends."

Brandon let out an exasperated sigh, shaking his head.

Unaware of his tactlessness, the major continued. "Of course, if he's a vampire, then after you have gathered the information we seek and Dracul has been exterminated like the crawling vermin he is, then I imagine the earl will have an unfortunate accident. That will leave you free of the heinous, hideous creature, and you'll be left a wealthy widow free to continue vampire-slaying."

Once again, her autocratic father had insulted Jane. He did not care for her welfare, nor for her personal code of honor. All he cared about was slaying the great Count Dracul before his brother did. Her father had windmills in the head, but not the least clue what ill winds he was blowing.

Jane stood, her hands clenched so tight that her fingernails dug into the tender flesh of her palms. "I see! You will sacrifice me on the altar of family duty. I am to marry a man who might possibly be a vampire in order to spy on him. This man, who has offered me the honor of marriage and saved my good name as well as your honor—when his use to us is at an end, you will end him!"

"Jolly good, Jane. For once you have quickly grasped the situation," her father congratulated her, his gruff voice booming through the room.

Jane counted to ten. She could hear her brother counting to twenty. She wanted to slap her father silly and kick him in the shins.

Seeing his sister's grim expression, her eyes sparkling with rage, Brandon took her hands and asked apprehensively, "Jane, when you were alone with him last night, did he try to bite your neck? *Have* you found any proof that he's a vampire?"

As much as Jane loved her brother and hated telling him an untruth, she knew if she was honest, she'd be in widow's weeds before the month was out. On the other hand, as soon as she was pronounced Asher's wife, she would be at the mercy of a vampire. Jane was no idiot. She knew Asher's mercy would be miniscule; and yet she owed him her loyalty. He was kindly saving her from a life of social ostracism when she'd been the one to instigate the whole situation.

"No," Jane lied. If the earl later proved vindictive, she would tell the truth to her brother then. But her first loyalty was now to her soon-to-be husband. A refreshing change . . . if only he was alive. Which made her think of last night's debacle and almost-debauching, and Asher's very alive-seeming and magnificent chest.

Pursing her lips, she wondered if the earl slept au naturel? Did he sleep with a pillow? Would he expect her to share his coffin? She made a moue of distaste. She would slam the lid on that idea, and quickly. Even for more of the man's deadly sweet kisses, Jane wouldn't share a cramped casket in a dark, damp mausoleum. No way, no how.

"No, I have seen no evidence of the earl being a vampire," Jane replied, her eyes studying the hunter green Persian rug on the floor. She would take a page from Clair, who wrote the book on telling little white fibs to save other people's feelings—or their very lives, as it was in this case.

"No. Asher is most definitely not a vampire," Jane said, smiling weakly. She put Asher's big, white fangs and red eyes out of her mind.

Relief flashed across her brother's face. "Good, good," he said. "Since the information was wrong about him being the Prince of Darkness, I was most devoutly hoping the earl was not even one of the undead. I have been worrying since we left London."

"No need," Jane lied stiffly, studying her brother's boots.

"Damnation!" the major cursed. "If the earl is not a vampire, then we lose our inside track. You can be bloody well sure that my brother, Jakob, will be hot on Dracul's trail if he gets a whiff that the gruesome who-some is on the island." He pounded on the end table beside him, upsetting his glass of brandy. "This whole jumbled mess is for nothing! Once again, Jane has put herself in the brambles, and has put a stain on the Van Helsing pedigree with her actions."

Brandon stood straighter, his expression outraged. "By gawd, Major! Jane is in this mess because of your dubious orders. As her commander," he suggested, "doesn't the buck stop with you, father?"

"D'oh! Oh dear. Yes, well," her father blustered, his pinkered face now scarlet. "I am just disappointed in losing a possible connection to that vicious vampire. I was counting on Jane's eyes and ears."

"We'll find a way, father. We always do," Brandon remarked pensively. "Besides, this time it's personal."

Noting that her brother's anger had faded, sorrow taking its place, Jane gently stood and patted his arm. "What's happened, Brandon? What occurred in Transylvania that has you so down?"

"Dracul is what happened. He killed a friend of mine in Bulgaria."

She reached up and kissed his check. "I am so sorry. Can I do anything to help?" she asked, but she already knew what she would do. Suddenly, living with a vampire had a fifth good reason. As her father suggested, vampires often flocked together in nests. Surely living in the same residence as Asher would enable her to gather information on whether Dracul was come to

Town. Once she had gathered this information, she would relay it to her brother in the form of an anonymous tip. She didn't want to harm Asher, but she wasn't her father's daughter for nothing.

Married to the Monster

The vicar of Huntington parish surveyed the dour wedding party with a twinge of unease. He much preferred morning weddings to these late-night affairs. In the past month he had presided over four weddings and a funeral. This wedding reminded him more of the funeral. The vicar knew that this ceremony was being rushed. In point of fact, the groom had only proposed the night before. But what could you say when the nobility were involved?

The vicar sighed and glanced over at the father of the bride. The man's expression was bordering on petulant. The bride's brother wore a look of woe. Baron Huntsley, who was seated next to his wife, appeared resigned, while the earl's man of business had a solemn demeanor. Worst of all was the groom, who for all his exalted personage looked as if he wanted to bite somebody's head off.

The bride entered the chapel. She was pale, her mouth was pursed in a tight line and the bouquet of flowers in her hands was shaking, scattering petals here and there, which made the vicar feel that there was definitely more going on than a case of bridal nerves. To be honest, the vicar decided that the only person who appeared happy at this supposedly joyous occasion was the baroness Clair Huntsley—she was smiling merrily.

The vicar shook his head slightly. There was just no judging the Quality. They were a breed unto themselves. And the Huntsleys and their peers more than most.

Clair turned around in her front-row pew and waved dramatically at Jane. Then, turning to her husband she remarked, "Oh dear, Ian, look at Jane. Why, she is beyond pale, and she's not even undead."

Ian nodded. "She would have been beyond *the* pale if the earl hadn't married her." Glancing over at the groom, he added, "Asher isn't in much better shape. I can't tell which of the two is whiter."

Clair patted her husband's thigh. "They'll be fine. I give them two months, and they'll be madly in love."

"Mad, I concede, but love is a pipe dream. This time that Frankensteinian brain of yours has conceived a plan that's scientifically doomed to failure."

"Never," Clair argued. "But speaking of mad, the major looks like he could spit nails. Or Neils," she added as a joke.

Ian grinned.

Unaware that he was under discussion, Major Edward Van Helsing raised his arm to escort his daughter down the aisle, his pudgy face somber. Glancing down, he noticed Jane's extreme pallor. "Come now, girl. Buck up. Remember, neither rain nor sleet nor hail nor snow can stop a Van Helsing from his duty. Besides, you are marrying an earl—quite a coup, Jane. Your mother would be proud."

Jane straightened her spine and laid her trembling fingers upon the man's arm. Then, turning toward

Clair, she managed to nod stiffly, physically restraining herself from running screaming from the church.

Tonight was an ending for her, as well as a beginning. From the ashes of her old life, she would begin a new life with Asher.

Regrets beat at her mind like a trapped bird in a too-small cage: Regrets that by this marriage she would be leaving her brother, whom she dearly loved, and her father, who had never seen who she really was or what she wanted to be. Regrets that her father would have used her as a spying tool if he had known she was really marrying a monster. Regrets that she and her groom were being forced to wed at all. So many regrets, they were fighting each other in her mind for attention.

Scrunching her eyes, Jane recalled that she needed to speak to Clair about the fur in the settee leg. She would also hint that a better carpet might be bought for this church.

Looking up from her study of her shoes and the awful brownish red carpet in the aisle, her eyes sought out the groom. He would have taken her breath away, if she'd had any left to give. Asher was dressed entirely in black, with the exception of a red waistcoat, trimmed in jet. Anger radiated from him in waves. She guessed the old adage was true, and she muttered, "Hell hath no fury like a vampire made to marry."

"What did you expect, daughter? The earl is renowned for his dalliances with *beautiful* women."

She missed a step at her father's words. Anger overcame some of her panic. But glancing at the groom, Jane swallowed hard at the frosty look in his eyes. There was no welcoming smile to soften his stern features. And she couldn't really blame him for detesting her; not after her foiled attempts on his undead life and this forced trip to the altar.

She felt like crying. Her groom was not only cold-blooded, but he also had very cold feet. And not because he was undead, but about her! Even discounting the fact that the earl didn't want to be wed to a woman he detested, he was also marrying beneath him. Her father was a mere knight, and her uncle only a baron. The Earl of Wolverton could have married any lovely lady in the land. Any other woman on this day would be merrily singing, thrilled to wed such a handsome, wealthy earl; overjoyed to marry up in status, not fearful. But, then, they wouldn't know that the groom might pop up in bed (his casket?) at any time and bite her neck—in a bloody way.

Feeling Asher's scornful gaze upon her, Jane returned to her intense scrutiny of the ugly rug and her pale green slippers. She was afraid. In less than an hour she would belong to a man who was not a man, and he would have absolute control over her life. And this man was a vampire in love with her bosom chum, which was a fact impossible to ignore.

Despite her groom's obvious disgust, Jane felt her eyes drawn to Asher once again. Tonight he was wearing dignity and a new suit of clothes, standing stiff and starched and unfriendly. Jane breathed deeply, trying to calm her nerves. She had *not* forced Asher into the misalliance of the century.

No matter the earl's feelings, Jane intended to do all she could to be a good and loyal wife. She had a fine example in her mother. Thinking back to childhood, Jane recalled how her mother often used to wait for the major to come home from his nightly forays in vampire-staking. The woman often had a hot bath prepared, cold water too, to soak his jacket and shirt, and a glass of brandy for her husband. She'd never scolded the major for the dusty ashes or blood on his clothing.

Would Asher want a hot bath and brandy, or would he want a blood bath? That particular thought made Jane twist her lips in an expression of pure distaste, and her stomach grew queasy.

"Buck up," Jane mumbled to herself under breath. She intended to be a solicitous wife, even regarding her groom's blood fetish. She just wasn't quite sure how. There was so much about her new husband she didn't know. Did Asher have any mirrors in his house? If not, how would she do her hair and dress for balls? Did he mind sleeping in such close quarters night after night? Perhaps he'd had an oversized coffin made. She hoped so. Did he have a silver tea service and if not, what did he use when entertaining? All the best tea services were silver. Did he track in mud from the graveyard at night? Did he rise at sunset all grumpy and ill-tempered, as her father did upon his morning wake-up call? Would her husband expect her to entertain large nestings of vampires? If so, what was the social etiquette? Did one offer them wine, brandy—your blood?

As she passed the Huntsleys in their pew, Jane took a shaky breath and managed a faint smile for Clair, who was grinning ear to ear. At least someone was enjoying the wedding, she thought morosely. Too bad it wasn't her. At least she would never have to polish her father's silver again.

Where were her chocolates when she needed them? Her life was spinning out of control. Her thoughts were tripping over each other. Would the major discover Asher's secret? She sincerely hoped not. She did look so dreadful in black. What did she really know of the groom besides that he was a notorious womanizer and vampire? Did he like to walk barefoot in the grass, or did he reserve that solely for his crypt? Were monsters' balls solely for monsters? Would Asher keep a mistress now that he was joined in the holy state of matrimony? Probably, she answered herself, since a rake was a rake, even if he had fangs instead of teeth.

Somehow the thought of Asher's mistresses irritated Jane; she realized that she couldn't bear to conceive of him being passionate about another woman. Jane wasn't sure what her feelings were for this tall, handsome vampire; they were feelings she would rather not take out and examine in the naked light of day. But despite her best intentions, her childhood training, and her lack of ability to draw and keep the attention of such a remarkable catch, Jane had felt strong emotions about Asher from the first. He'd called to her in a way no man or creature of the night had ever done. It was as if he had her destiny written upon his face.

Her father had taught her to put her heart into her objectives—an easy feat with Asher as her husband. She intended to cherish him until the day she died, and to one day make him proud that he had married and saved her from ruin. Despite his pompous airs and neck-biting tendencies, her groom stirred a deep pool of emotion that had been tightly dammed inside her.

Finally, the long walk down the aisle was done. She glanced up as her father handed her over to the groom. Asher was a lighter shade than his usual color, and Jane wondered if his injury was bothering him. She managed a weak smile.

"Your bride, Wolverton," the major said curtly. "Take good care of her, if you can."

Asher glared bitterly at his soon-to-be father-in-law and noted the man's stiff posture and sour features. "I will do my duty, Major," he retorted contemptuously. Ian had explained that the Van Helsings knew they had a case of mistaken identity. They also believed he was innocent of being a vampire. Ha! Asher thought morosely—he wouldn't take the Van Helsings at their word. They were a bloodthirsty, vicious, murdering lot. And he was to be related to the whole untrustworthy group. It was a sorry state of affairs that a master vampire should be made to suffer such a horrendous misalliance.

Yes, he could see his future going up in smoke. Married to a Van Helsing, that was certainly a very real possibility. If she didn't stake him one day in his sleep, she might burn him up in his coffin. How could he ever trust her to see to his health and hearth? And look how clumsy she was, scattering orange blossoms from her bridal bouquet as she stood next to him, visibly trembling.

Jane Van Helsing was to wear his name and share a small portion of his undead life. He, who appreciated beauty in all its forms, would be married to a diamond of the . . . fifth water? He, who had sworn never to marry except for love, was bound to a detestable, vampire-slaying Van Helsing. This was irony at its worst. The Fates must be dancing a merry little jig on his ancestors' graves.

"We are gathered here today to join this man and this woman," the vicar began.

With a gesture of indignant tribulation, Asher grasped Jane's hand. Dimly he was aware that it was colder than his own. Perfect, he thought maliciously. The harridan was afraid. And she *should* fear for her very life, for she had caused disaster with her moronic folly. He would make her short mortal life a misery. In fact, he would make it his duty to make her life miserable for cutting him down in his undead prime.

Glaring down at her bent head, he observed the crown of orange blossoms she wore, interwoven with the short veil that covered her face. The flowers gave off a lush, rich smell. And also was the scent of Jane's essence—fresh and spicy, like her blood. Unconsciously he licked his lips. Unaware, he tightened his grasp on her hand, causing Jane to wince.

179

Again Asher glanced down at his unwanted bride, abstractly appreciating how the pale green color of her gown emphasized her eyes. The neckline of her dress was low and round, pushing her abundant breasts upward. He recognized that Jane's breathing had increased with her anxiety, causing her bosoms to rise and fall like lush fruits waiting to be sampled. He wondered if the tips were coral hued or rose. He wondered what they would taste like.

Catching himself admiring his soon to be wife, Asher bit back a snarl. Hellfire! It would be a cold day in hell and elephants would fly before he touched this venomous vampire slayer! He hadn't survived this long by underestimating his foes. He would also have to talk to his bride about wearing gowns that revealed too much of her body. Just because he was not going to enjoy two of her finest assets did not mean he wanted other men or monsters to ogle them.

Observing the silent but ominous byplay between the groom and bride, the vicar continued the ceremony. His voice filled the pews. Secretly he prayed that the bride wouldn't faint and the groom wouldn't burst the throbbing blood vessel in his forehead before the *I do*s were spoken.

Nervously he hesitated, his gaze fearfully searching the small assemblage. "If any man can show just cause why these two should not be lawfully joined in holy matrimony, let him speak now or forever hold his peace."

After several tense moments of silence, the vicar, along with several members of the wedding party, breathed loud sighs of relief.

The bride had also held her breath, half fearing her brother would protest—or worse, the groom would. She wished that circumstances could have been different. Yet, Jane was well content with the husband destiny had provided. It didn't matter that he was another species. Lord Asher made her blood rush to her head. He made her breathless. Even when he was at his most pompous and sneering, she found him enthralling. Whenever he was near, Jane felt more alive than she ever had. Odd, she thought, that an undead could make her feel so un-dead—and how much joy she now felt in just drawing breath.

Stealing a sideways peek at Asher, Jane longed to hold him close and listen to his heartbeat. To feel his strong, cold arms around her. She wanted to ease his burdens and warm his pale, icy body. Although Asher would never be the prince of her dreams, he very well could be the earl of them.

After the vicar hesitated and no one protested, Asher stifled a growl, desiring to shout to the heavens. But centuries of good breeding kept him mum. For all his wealth and power, he was held helpless hostage to society's rigid conventions and rules. Both societies— English and that of the Undead. He could hear the coffin lid crashing down on his well-ordered, hedonistic lifestyle.

"For better or for worse. In sickness and in health," the vicar said in a baritone voice.

Jane glanced up at Asher, thinking wryly that the clergyman could just skip that part; the undead never got sick. She felt an uncontrollable urge to giggle. As a pair they had certainly experienced the "worse," and so now it was time for the "better." She controlled herself, knowing that if she started laughing now she would never stop.

"Till death do you part," the vicar intoned solemnly.

Jane nodded. But they could skip that part too. Asher was already dead.

The churchman's words pierced Asher's morose thoughts. *Till death do you part?* That wasn't soon enough for him, he seethed, piercing his bride with his icy glare.

Unfortunately for Jane, she knew actually what her soon-to-be husband was thinking. She sighed again. It seemed that they were still on the "worse" part of their marriage after all, and might be for some time to come. But at least she could give up her dubious and unsuccessful career as a vampire hunter. That gloomy part of her life was over, except for the possible hunt for Dracul in October. Never had she felt more relieved. Her loyalty and allegiance were now to her husband, as she had just vowed before God, man, werewolf and vampire.

"I now pronounce you man and wife. You may kiss the bride."

Silence filled the church. Asher stood glaring at his bride. When he made no move toward her, Jane bravely stretched up on her tiptoes to bestow a kiss on his stubborn mouth. His lips were cold, firm and sweet, like her favorite bonbons.

Jane kissed him harder, feeling the silken smoothness of his lips begin to melt under her not-so-tender mercies. When her tongue sought entrance to his mouth, he growled.

Suddenly she felt his strong arms grab her, drawing her close, pressing her tightly to him. His lips became warm, his mouth opened and he swirled his tongue in a wicked caress, a dance that was both angry and hungry.

Tingling waves of heat shot throughout Jane's body. Her toes curled and her knees began to give way. Only Asher's embrace kept her from falling flat on her back. Her hands combed through his hair, passion flaring hot and bright between them.

In the background Ian teased, "Hear, hear. We

Huntsleys have a wild reputation, but we never consummated our marriage in the church!"

Clair hit her husband stoutly on the arm with her fan, but his words brought Asher slamming back to reality. The wretched wolfman was married to the lady of his dreams, while he, the superior being, was married to this inferior vulgar, vile, venomous Van Helsing. Even if she did kiss like she was an angel.

Jerking back, he shoved his bride away from him, and only centuries of breeding kept him from exposing his fangs in a hiss. His bloody bride was not delicate and lovely. His bloody bride was an unfit, unreliable, butcher of his kind! His bloody bride could not be trusted. Yet, he wanted her with a fervor he hadn't felt in centuries.

Asher stalked away down the aisle. Jane hurried to keep up with him. At the door, they joined together to wave to those gathered outside to wish them well.

Glancing up at her husband, Jane whispered, "I imagine you are wishing me to the very Devil right now."

"How astute," Asher replied, a mocking curl to his lips. "In fact, I'll take you to meet him with all due speed, or we can stay right here and wait for his well-wishes. Surely he's the one behind this farce of a marriage!"

Tears filling her eyes, Jane stepped outside the chapel into the cold, brisk air. Fortunately that revived her senses. Above, the stars glittered in the heavens—like Asher's eyes glittered with icy disdain as he walked out to stand beside her.

She could see his carriage in the distance, waiting out in the cobbled courtyard with his piebald stallion. He would ride outside the carriage, while Jane remained inside, Asher informed her frostily as he gave her another withering glance.

"We will be arriving at my hunting lodge later tonight. It is twenty miles from here, and forty more on to London," he managed with a bare semblance of civility.

Bleakly Jane nodded to show she had heard; then Ian and Clair hurriedly approached to offer their congratulations.

Clair swiftly led Jane away from the other guests to a quiet corner beside the church, and Ian took Asher in the other direction.

He shook Asher's hand. "I would offer you my heartiest congratulations," the baron said.

Asher shook his head. "Don't. It's more like condolences. Besides, if you wish me a long and prosperous married state, I might just have to tear your throat out."

Across the way, Clair held Jane's hands tightly, saying, "I wish to offer you my felicitations."

Her face a mask of gravity, Jane arched her brow.

"Am I out of line?" Clair asked.

"I shouldn't have tried to stake Asher. I should have gone for the matchmaker of this whole mess," Jane grumbled. She was feeling very discouraged. "My not-so-esteemed husband has insulted me, sending Ian to do everything. Your husband proposed to me, not Asher," she complained bitterly. "My groom has barely addressed two words to me. When he does speak, he addresses me with chilly disdain."

Jane sniffed, her heart aching, and she added, "I hate to admit it, but Asher does chilly disdain better than anyone I know, including my father. And that's saying quite a lot."

Clair nodded. "Of course. Asher has had centuries to practice. Your father's a beginner."

Jane would have giggled, if her heart weren't breaking.

Noting her friend's forlorn expression, Clair's smile faded. "Just remember this: Life is like a box of bonbons," she advised, knowing Jane's fetish for chocolate. "Sometimes the bonbons are sweet. Sometimes they're sticky. And sometimes you just end up with big brown smears on your gloves."

Jane blinked.

Clair smiled cheerfully. "You two were meant for each other," she encouraged.

Not wishing to take her hurt feelings out on her best friend any further, Jane added a trifle stiffly, "Thank you for your good wishes. I have a feeling we will need them. Each and every one." She loved Clair dearly, but sometimes the girl was oblivious to the sheer chaos she created.

"As do all newlyweds," Clair replied. She knew Jane had an inner core as strong as iron. She would have had to develop such strength, or else be destroyed by her father's tyrannical reign. In time Jane would do well with Asher, and the couple would be happy—or her name wasn't Clair Frankenstein Huntsley!

Drawing Jane to her, Clair hugged her friend. "All will be well. Neil will come around sooner rather than later, I suspect."

"Humbug," was Jane's only response.

Clair escorted her to the carriage amidst all the guests, who were shouting congratulations. Asher followed behind, raking a hand through his immaculate hair. Ian Huntsley pulled his wife into his arms and grinned. This was the second time in his life that he had seen the vampire looking less than his usual distinguished self—and he rather enjoyed it.

Asher glanced back as he mounted his huge piebald stallion and caught the amusement on Baron Huntsley's face. He shot the man a glance of pure threat. Where were silver bullets when one needed them? For once and probably the only time in their marriage, Asher agreed with his wife: Humbug!

It Didn't Happen One Night

Asher's hunting lodge was set back in a beautifully wooded area. The moonlight highlighted the ivy-covered walls and large French balconies on the second story of the house. Jane thought it was quaint, and had started to remark on this to Asher, but he had brushed her comments aside and delivered her rudely to the maid. The maid was terribly quiet, answering only two of Jane's questions, and had quickly left after depositing Jane in the yellow-and-lilac bedchamber where Jane now sat alone with her thoughts.

Her feelings were bruised by her husband's brisk behavior. As she sat brushing her long brown hair, her face was an expression of intense study. She was also nervous about what would occur in the large four-poster bed in the corner of the room tonight.

Clair had once hinted at the wild delights and ravenous hungers that could be found in the marriage bed. Of course, she was married to a werewolf.

Still, being married to a vampire might be a similar experience. Jane's husband was certainly a fine specimen of a male. But angry as he was with her right now, she didn't know what kind of experience under the bedcovers might be in store for her. Surely he wouldn't want to drink her blood while doing it? If he did, then what? Would she pass out? The thought of him drinking from her was disgusting.

"Can I actually let him?" she wondered aloud. Would it hurt like the time that mouse bit her finger after she'd rescued the poor thing from her grandfather's trap? Would she bring up everything in her heart (and stomach!) if her husband went for her neck?

Asher was her spouse, and her duty was to him; but letting him suck her life away seemed a bit beyond the call. If only her mother's lectures on wifely duty had included a course in making love to a vampire.

Pouring herself a small glass of brandy, she wondered what she should offer Asher. She stifled a nervous giggle. In spite of all the problems behind and before them, Jane had great hopes for this marriage—and for tonight, besides wanting to be alive at the end of it.

As Asher made his way up the stairway to his wife's chamber, he too had great expectations. Expectations of being poked in the back if he ever dropped his guard to his spouse. He shuddered. His situation made his blood run cold. Colder than normal. What he needed was hot, wet sex, and a midnight snack. What he was going to get was a course of a different color. . . .

Opening the door, he entered the room, and his attention was captivated in spite of himself by the sight of his bride brushing her hair. Before tonight, Asher had only seen her hair in braids, braids that had hid the small golden highlights. Now her locks hung long and free past the curve of her generous bottom. It looked like a wave of cascading silk. He had the strongest urge to touch it. His arm started to lift, but he caught himself quickly and quelled the urge.

Placing both hands firmly behind his back, Asher took in the picture of his unwanted bride. She stood by the bed, the fireplace highlighting her silhouette, revealing her curvaceous frame. She was wearing a white lace nightgown, cut deliciously low around the neck, exposing a great expanse of beautiful, pale bosom. Her rose-hued nipples were clearly visible through the fabric.

Asher could feel his mouth watering. No doubt, the gown had been a gift from Clair, the intention to whet his appetites. How he wished Clair were before him, for if it were she, he understood clearly how differently the night would end. But he clenched down angrily on his hurt and his carnal urges, driving them far away, his expression hardening like that other part of his body that was betraying him.

When her husband entered the room, Jane turned to him, then rose, unaware of the feelings she was engendering. Slowly she started toward him, feeling a great need to touch his body. His deep blue dressing gown was open to the waist, revealing a long expanse of pale yet muscular flesh.

"Hello, husband," she said softly, her eyes greedily traveling over him. Neil Asher was the most beautiful creature in the world. And he was hers! She noted vaguely that his fangs were exposed ever so slightly, but that was not all.

"I would prefer you not address me that way," he said.

"But we are married."

"To my eternal and utter disbelief and disgust."

"That's rather good. Keep it up and you'll be in your coffin long before sunrise," Jane remarked curtly, hiding the hurt his words caused.

Ignoring her, Asher went on, "I never thought to get caught by the parson's mousetrap—especially not by a slice of Van Helsing cheese." Glaring at her, he leaned against the bedpost, but the movement caused his dark blue robe to fall open. Revealed was a fleshy stake, much like the Van Helsing model six.

Jane gasped in stunned and curious amazement. Her eyes flew upward to her husband's face and caught a flash of fury there. Instantly, as if someone had wiped a cloth down his features, all hint of emotion on Asher's features was wiped away. He became still, deadpan. But, then, her husband did deadpan better than anyone she knew; he had a leg up on them by being dead to begin with.

"Madame. I came to announce what will happen tomorrow," Asher stated tersely, snapping his robe closed and belting it. It was amazing; it did appear that his wife's breasts might be even larger than Clair's, although he had never seen Clair's in this type of a situation.

Jane stepped back. With her groom in the room, it seemed immeasurably smaller. He was so large, and his energy so intense, the chamber had narrowed considerably as if by magic. And that portion of him was certainly quite big—big and interesting.

"Yes, what about tomorrow?" she asked.

"You will leave for the Wolverton town house tomorrow at first light. I want you to prepare the house for my return late tomorrow. Is that clear?"

"I know my duty," Jane retorted. But she winced, stung by his icy tone. This was her wedding night—a night Jane had feared would never come to pass as the years slowly did. Asher should be holding her close and kissing her with his wondrous lips!

Asher caught her small wince, and that her smile had faded completely. Satisfied he had wounded her, he pressed on. "Do you?" he asked with a contemptuous smile. "To whom is your duty: the grand and glorious Van Helsings? Or to your dearly beloved husband?"

His bitterness filled the room like a gathering storm, causing Jane to despair. They could have a comfortable life together, if Asher would only relent a little.

"Tonight, I became your wife," she said. "I took a solemn oath before God to you and no one else. My past is just that. It is left in the past where it belongs now, a dead issue."

The earl cocked his head and studied her for long, tense moments. Jane had the urge to squirm, but she remained still, her eyes locked with his.

Asher finally shook his head. Jane's eyes had depths, depths he'd not been prepared to find. But she could take her rotten little Van Helsing mysteries to the grave. "And you expect me to believe you? You, a *Van Helsing!* You must think me mad to believe such balderdash." Asher spat out the family name as if it were poison.

Jane gritted her teeth and, undaunted, challenged this fire-breathing vampire. Her life was at stake here, her future happiness. She had to make him understand that she'd done what she had to do, what she'd been trained to do for the good of the world. "I apologize, Asher. But mistakes happen."

"Mistakes happen? My life is over as I know it, and all you can say is, 'Mistakes happen'?"

"I am sorry you were forced to marry beneath you, sorry you were forced to wed an enemy. Sorry I tried to stake you. But I didn't try to kill you, I just got scared when you began to bite me."

"Ian explained it all," Asher said, acute distaste lacing his tone. "You were born and bred a Van Helsing, brought up to revile vampires. And I am a vampire. Not just your run-of-the-mill vampire, either; I am the master vampire of London—a title not easily gained. It took over a century for my appointment as leader of the London Nosferatu."

Jane tried to say something, but Asher held up his long pale fingers, interrupting her. His expression was scornful and harsh.

"You were taught to hunt, to stalk and to stake us. It is

your heritage. So apologizing for your part in this stark-mad fiasco doesn't really matter, does it? It's a case of too little, too late!" Asher's manner one of total disgust, he paced the room.

"'Let me not burst in ignorance!' 'I do not set my life at a pin's fee.' 'Something is rotten in the state of Denmark'," he quoted coldly.

Hurt and wounded in her heart and soul, Jane adeptly hid her pain, curtseying slightly and quoting back, "'When I was a child, I spake as a child, I understood as a child, I thought as a child: but when I became a man, I put away childish things. For now we see through a glass, darkly; but then face-to-face: now I know in part; but then shall I know even as also I am known'."

"Corinthians?"

She nodded.

Asher said nothing for a moment, merely stared at Jane with one aristocratic brow slightly arched, impressed in spite of himself. She really was well versed in the classics, and for a Van Helsing she had some wit. Also, he couldn't help but feel a hint of admiration for his wife's adaptability and courage. In fact, if he didn't detest her so much, he might have been tempted to debate philosophies with her in bed after a long, carnal loving—virgin blood for an aperitif and a few love bites for dessert.

Jane continued: "As of tonight, I am a child no longer but your bride. I am what I am, because of who and what I was. But now all that I am, I pledge to you and yours. My loyalty, my affection and all the talents I possess."

Asher remarked ruthlessly, "Talents? Such as murdering vampires? Shall you teach me how to stake my species?"

Tears filled her eyes. "I have never personally staked anyone before. To be honest . . . I have an aversion to blood."

"The hell you say! A vampire slayer who doesn't like the sight of blood? What farce is this?"

"It's the truth. The sight of blood makes me ill."

He snorted, disbelieving. "Then it is a good thing that I am not taking you to bed. The sight of your virgin's blood might be your undoing."

Her emotions in turmoil, Jane paled, feeling his rejection of her as a wife to the very depths of her soul. "I know you need no heir, nor can you beget one being hundreds of years of age, but I thought that you would at least want to . . ." She couldn't continue, a blush putting some color back into her white cheeks.

"To have carnal relations with you? To take you to that bed over yonder and thrust into your soft, sweet body?" Asher had to repress a shiver at the image of his bride on her back with her pale thighs spread for his wanton enjoyment.

Cursing himself to Hades nine ways and back, he was incensed to admit he was indeed interested in his plain little wife. It was not even fashionable! Lust should be reserved strictly for other men's wives. That was the way it had always been in the *ton*, and the way it would always be.

"I think not. I do not trust you. Having a stake stuck in my backside during the courtship rather crimped my desire for lovemaking," he sneered. "And I give you fair warning, if you try to kill me, it will the last mi*stake* of your sorry little life."

"How droll, vicious wordplay on our wedding night," Jane retorted. "However, I gave my word before God, man, vampire and werewolves tonight in church, that I would honor, cherish and tend you. That word is my bond."

She knew Asher was outraged. She knew he was bitter. And she recognized that he was more than justified. But surely her words made some effect on the steel armor of his heart? If not, her situation would be unbearable.

Unthinkingly, she murmured her thoughts: "Will we *ever* do in the dark what husbands and wives do so duly do?" Her feet were freezing. Where had she put her slippers? Her husband loathed her. Life was certainly not much of an improvement as the Countess of Wolverton. When her husband left, she would cry.

Asher laughed, a sound which could cut glass. "I've made love to half the known beauties of the world. After all that lovely flesh, what could I possibly find in *your* bed?" he said.

Jane jerked back. "You pompous, callous monster. As if I want to share my bed with the undead. What a laugh!"

"I'll make love to you Jane, when hell freezes over and elephants fly," he vowed. And with those damning words, Asher stalked toward the door. He knew a grand exit line when he'd spoken one.

Before he escaped, Jane called out, "I didn't know that earls pouted. I thought that beneath their dignity."

Asher halted abruptly, his back ramrod straight. He turned swiftly around. His eyes were blazing with pure blue fire. "Pout? You call this a pout? What I am, woman, is enraged. Which after the month's events I have every reason to be. I could have married royalty, had I wished to be wed at all. So don't goad me!"

Her tears dried, Jane faced him squarely, her temper coming into its own. "Don't mock me, then!" she warned.

Asher ran a hand through his hair, mussing the perfect lines. Once again, his wife had caused him to lose his composure. "You don't think you deserve to be mocked? To be despised for forcing this disastrous misalliance upon us?"

Anger overwhelmed her wounded heart. Stalking forward, Jane stuck her finger in his face. "Don't say things you'll regret," she snarled.

"How can I regret the truth? Don't you ever look in the mirror?"

"What, mirror envy?" she asked. He ignored her.

"What do you have to recommend you, Jane?"

"I have *me* to offer," Jane stated proudly, patting her chest. "*Me* to recommend. What you can't see is the best of me, and you're a fool for only admiring surface beauty. I am so much more than you deserve," she realized.

Asher was taken aback by her impassioned words, her green-silver eyes flashing molten emerald fires. But she wasn't finished yet.

"You have lived a long, long time. You are a big vampire now. You know life isn't always fair. Things can be harsh, and we don't always get our way. You can take out your hatred on me nightly. But what will that accomplish besides finally resulting in me despising you? Then we will be two strangers, hating each other, stuck together until I die. Is that what you want—open warfare in your home? I know I don't!"

Asher started to speak, then halted. She was magnificent when maddened! He turned to leave again. No Van Helsing was going to make him see reason on his wedding night. If he wanted to pace and curse fate until daylight, then that was just what he was going to do. It didn't matter that his bride had luscious breasts and a swanlike neck. It didn't matter that she smelled of warm honey and sweet orange blossoms. He snorted indignantly and opened the bedchamber door to flee.

Jane again called out to him. "Lord Asher, one more thing, please. I need to ask you something important."

With one hand on the door he glanced back at her, his mouth drawn in tight lines. She looked like she hated to ask him for anything, but was driven by despair.

"Yes?"

"I need to bring my pet Orville to Town. He is causing havoc without me at the Van Helsing estate."

"Orville?"

Embarrassed, Jane explained, "My pet ostrich."

"You have an ostrich for a pet?" Asher asked, intrigued in spite of himself. That was the kind of a pet Clair Frankenstein would have.

She nodded. "My grandfather brought him to me when Orville was just a hatchling. I am his mother. But the major hates him. He said he would chop off his head and stuff him if we didn't let Orville come and live with us immediately."

"Your father is quite good at killing things, isn't he?" Asher retorted mockingly. The backstabbing bastard. Glaring hard at his small, voluptuous wife, Asher decided the fruit didn't fall far from the tree. Even if her fruits were entrancing.

"Please. Orville has done nothing to earn your enmity," Jane beseeched. She loved Orville as much as she loved Spot, her dog. She couldn't live without her two pets near her. Originally she had planned on asking this favor of her husband after they had made love, because Clair had advised her all husbands were putty in their wives' hands after a rigorous bout of lovemaking. However, since she doubted hell was going to come into an ice age anytime in the near future, and espying no flying elephants out her bedroom window, Jane had little choice but to place her request before this cruel, indignant vampire now.

Swallowing what little dignity she had left, Jane pleaded, despising herself for groveling. But love for her pets was stronger than her pride, humiliation or anger. "Please. I beg you. Let Orville come to London with his keeper, Bert."

"You have the nerve to request a favor of me? After

all you have done?" How queer, he mused, an ostrich for this silly goose. It was another surprising facet to his wife's nature. He wondered what else was in store over the long years of matrimony ahead.

"Please!"

"What utter unmitigated gall you Van Helsings have!" he snapped. And with those words, he threw open the door.

"Asher, please!"

He turned and paused, then finally nodded. Then, glancing down at her feet, he remarked with surprise, "Is that a spider I see?"

Jane screamed, and she jumped a good two or three feet off the floor. "Where? Where?" Glancing back to the door, she saw her husband disappear down the hall, chortling.

The sneaky vampire had lied to her. There was no spider. Slamming the door shut, Jane could still hear his chuckles. "Well, I guess that's that. The honeymoon is over."

Waking Neil, Divine

It was the best of times, it was the worst of times, it was the age of wisdom, it was the age of foolishness, it was the epoch of belief, it was the epoch of incredulity, it was the season of Light, it was the season of Darkness, it was the spring of hope, it was the winter of despair; we had everything before us, we had nothing before us, we were all going direct to Heaven, we were all going direct the other way.

Yes, Jane thought, as she walked down the hallway; Charles Dickens was right, and he had accurately described her first four days as the vampire's bride.

Asher had been conspicuously absent, leaving Jane to her own devices in his majestic Town home and in the massive ornamental gardens outside. Jane frowned, knowing her husband was avoiding her as though she had the coughing sickness—or that she was someone who had tried to stab him in the back.

Asher had communicated with her only twice, by note sent on a bronze platter. Jane recognized that the action was a small way to demean her. Asher was an inventive vampire. It was almost scary to think of all the small ways he could demean her in their married life to come. He was so thoroughly ignoring her now, she had began to despair of ever having a chance to set things right. Still, men liked to pout, even her brother Brandon.

She knew she could be strong in the face of adversity. Her father had taught her that lesson early. It was odd: The more things changed, the more they remained the same.

She only wished she were smarter. How could she care for a vampire who so obviously held her in contempt? Jane liked the fact that Asher was a handsome creature who knew his own worth. He was a pleasure to watch and to look upon. She admired his dignity and his loyalty, when he chose to give it. Her husband had a droll wit and a fine mind. He was interesting and exciting. She was intrigued by the mystery of him, and bound by an invisible pull that kept butterflies tickling her stomach whenever he was near, which unfortunately was rare since their abortive wedding night. She was definitely ready for the "for better" part of married life.

Yet, in spite of her recent travails, hope sprang eternal in her breast. She was finally married, a feat she had truly feared would never happen. In years of exile at the Van Helsing country estate, Jane had often envisioned herself at forty, an old maid, leaping out at strange men with large fangs, lurking about servants quarters, listening to maids gossiping about where their mistresses' love bites were strategically placed, and just who had placed them. Often, late in the night, Jane had seen the dreary years marching by, while she made endless trips to the church filling bottomless vials of holy water. Countless trips to countless cemeteries had haunted her dreams. And really, when a person had seen one big yard full of dirt holes, she had seen them all.

But now, her whole world was changed. She had a new life, and she was not going to let some pesky detail like her husband's intense dislike of her stop her from making a good marriage based on trust and affection.

Although his company was not the best, the same could not be said for Asher's London residence. The house was an imposing structure, four stories tall, with a steeply pitched gabled roof done in pale red. Large iron balconies lined the second- and third-story windows. She had wonderful times exploring her new home, to her heart's content and to Renfield's disgust.

The elaborate mansion was located on the outskirts of London, with extensive formal gardens that were well maintained. Marble statues of alabaster white and cerulean blue, with ornate flowing fountains, were placed strategically around a lovely wooded area. The area abounded with birds of all kinds, from robin red-breasts to softly cooing doves. Jane had been ecstatic upon first spying them. Not only could she traipse about and watch birds to her heart's content, but the gardens were also big enough that Orville would have plenty of room to run, play and terrorize anyone fool-ish enough to bring food anywhere near him.

All, in all, the Wolverton London home was magnifi-cent; and unbelievably Jane was mistress of the impres-sive domain. She had even caught herself pinching her arm last night to see if she was dreaming. When she was a small girl, she'd dreamed of being mistress of just such a place, and of being cherished and adored by a de-voted husband.

Passing a footman on her way down the large mar-bled stairway, Jane smiled briefly. At least she could say honestly that Asher's household was run with rigid pre-cision. His butler, two of the butler's sons, who were also footmen, the housekeeper; and three of her daugh-ters, who were maids and an assistant cook, had been with the earl since they were quite young. That was continuity in its extreme, since these same servants' great-grandparents, grandparents and parents had served the earl, the housekeeper had explained upon Jane's arrival. Although vampires kept knowledge of what they were on a strictly need-to-know basis, Jane had deduced that the earl's closest servants needed to know, and had been somehow sworn to secrecy by a blood oath. She shuddered at the bright red images that evoked in her head.

Fortunately for Jane, most of the staff seemed proud to finally have a mistress to serve, with a few exceptions being three or four buxom maids with fair hair. The maids Jane had eyed with displeasure, wondering just who and what the maids had been serving Asher. Stabbed with sharp needles of jealousy, Jane intended to find them employment elsewhere as quickly as possible.

And then there was Renfield, Asher's longtime valet. Renfield greatly resented her, barely concealing his contempt. She assumed that the man was her husband's human servant. Jane also knew that human servants lived longer than most mortals and were a little stronger due to sharing the master's blood twice every fourth year in some secret Nosferatu ritual. They were also extremely loyal; her lessons in vampire protocol had taught her that. But they had never taught her what to do if she found herself married to a roguish vampire with a human servant who sniffed in disdain whenever she gave him an order.

Besides his obvious disapproval of her, Renfield also gave Jane the shivers for other reasons. He had a smile like he was secretly eating bugs, and the valet's beady little eyes followed her around the mansion distrustfully. Due to the circumstances of her marriage, she supposed she couldn't blame him.

The way Asher was treating her didn't help matters with his trusted servant either. She wanted to befriend

Renfield, to confide in him that her loyalty was now owned by her husband alone—as well as a bud of affection. Still, she doubted anything would put a dent in the valet's pompous armor.

She glanced warily around for any sign of Renfield. "Good, it looks like I'm in the clear," she said. After four days of her husband's silent treatment, and Renfield's not-too-subtle spying, she was ready to scream. "I've got information to ferret out and an undeadline to meet. And all I've got so far are dead ends," Jane joked to herself quietly, her brow furrowed with concern. If Dracul were in London, he probably wouldn't stay long. Not with the famous Van Helsings in residence.

Yet, every time Jane tried to quiz the staff for news concerning Dracul, or to pry with wifely concern into Asher's vampiric affairs, she would spy Renfield lurking about, her human watchdog for her not-so-human husband.

Another problem regarding living with the undead was the food. The meals left much to be desired. But, then, that was no big surprise. The tea services were in gold, which was also not a surprise. Asher's coffin was nowhere to be found. (Also not a surprise). Not that Jane had been diligently searching. But she was curious. She couldn't help imagining what Asher might look like sound asleep, like a slumbering prince before his lover's kiss awakened him. In her dreams, Jane would wake him with her lips, and he would sigh and tell her how nice it was to have her near him, sharing the nightlife.

"Yes, waking Neil would be divine," she said to herself.

Knowing that she should let sleeping vampires lie, Jane still couldn't resist searching for Asher's daytime resting place once again. She truly hated unsolved puzzles, and she was curious as to what her husband's casket looked like. And while so far she hadn't been able to elude the crafty valet in order to search the cellars of the mansion, Renfield would be occupied today in finding quarters for Bert and Orville, who had both arrived earlier this morning.

The unusually gigantic bird and his keeper had created quite a stir in the Asher household. It wasn't often the earl's staff saw a six-foot-something bird with such a big beak. And Bert—with his skinny seventeen-year-old body, carrot red hair and scruffy clothes, which Orville had chewed on—was certainly of a different bent from the starchy, impeccably dressed staff of the earls. Each and every one of those looked as if they had stepped out of the plates of *La Belle Assemble*, and knew what the well-dressed servant of 1828 was wearing.

"Are you feeling lucky today?" Jane asked herself, thinking she possibly had an hour to tour below. If a casket were to be found, it was probably in the cellars. For whatever reason, Jane had learned early in her studies that the undead had an affinity for resting places below ground level—in spite of the nasty cobwebs and vicious little spiders down there.

Carefully creeping down the basement stairs, she found a large wooden door. Taking the household keys, Jane unlocked the door, laughing under her breath. She had outsmarted both Asher and his valet. It seemed that at the ripe old age of twenty-three she was gaining wisdom.

Lifting the candelabra in her hand, she peered inside. Disappointment made her sigh. She had craftily discovered . . . the wine cellar. Shaking her head ruefully, Jane closed the door, then hurried to the other end of the dank, dark corridor, conscious of the sands of the hourglass sifting away her precious hunt-and-search time.

Unlocking this door, Jane discovered that it was much easier to push open than the first. As she lifted her candles high, the shadows were dispelled, revealing discarded furniture and other household items.

"Foiled again!" she exclaimed, but as she turned to leave, a voice behind almost startled her into dropping her light.

"Lady Asher, may I inquire as to what you are doing down here in the cellars?" Renfield asked with undisguised scorn. His words positively made her cringe.

Perhaps she wasn't as wise as she thought. Guilt crept up Jane's face, as did the beginnings of a blush. She really disliked overly clever servants. She knew the valet thought she was trying to find Asher's coffin in order to stake him. But in reality, all she wanted was to see her husband peacefully sleeping. And maybe to steal a kiss. A kiss she wouldn't get when Asher was awake and kicking.

"I was going to pick a bottle of wine for dinner," she ad-libbed, thinking the answer rather clever.

Renfield glanced around the storage room. "I see. There are so many fine vintages here. How many *casks* . . ." Renfield stressed the syllable, and. Jane could hear him mentally adding *-ets*, calling her credibilty into question. "Which were you looking for?"

Jane sniffed. Good help these days was getting harder and harder to find in London. "I meant, of course, that I *thought* this was where the wines were kept. Of course I now realize it's merely for storing other items." She closed the door abruptly. "Please show me to where the wine is located."

Holding his candelabra high, Renfield led Jane back the way she had come. His light reflected on her footprints in the dust, trailing to the wine cellar door.

What rotten luck, Jane bemoaned. Every foot can tell a story.

The Prime of the Ancient Mariner

"I have told you time and time again that we dead men don't wear plaid," Asher reprimanded his valet, who was laying out a dark plaid waistcoat and a midnight blue jacket.

With a long-suffering look, Renfield disdainfully put the waistcoat back. "It would be superb with the jacket," he complained. Then he shrugged. "No matter. You are, after all, only having dinner with your wife."

Asher shot the valet an icy look. "You're dismissed for now. I believe I'll dress myself tonight."

He walked over to the balcony off his bedroom. There he stood in perfect silence, breathing deeply of the sweet fragrance of night-blooming jasmine and honeysuckle located in the gardens directly below.

Asher loved to take in these last few moments, when the sun was a hint on the horizon like a sad song. It was as close to feeling the sunshine on his shoulder that he dared.

Welcome to my life, he thought wryly. He had stood here often like this, watching the pinks and deep violets with their hints of gold, fade into the inky blackness of night. In these times, in these quiet seasons of the heart, he had thought that perhaps love would find him on some dark enchanted evening. But there was no rhyme or reason to whom one fell in love with, or when. It didn't matter that he was a wild heart looking for home. Love came when it came, and left just as silently.

A sudden movement below in the garden caught Asher's attention. His bride was playing fetch-the-stick with her ugly mutt and his butler's grandson, Dickey. He could see Spot jump after the stick. He could see Jane jump, her lush breasts bouncing. He could see Dick jump. He could feel dick jump.

"Bloody hell!" It was considerably déclassé for a vampire to lust after his wife, he admitted reluctantly, adjusting the bulge in his pants. It was even worse for said wife to be a Van Helsing. She wasn't even a diamond of the first water. In fact, his wife couldn't even be called a carat. She had freckles, for heaven's sake!

Asher shook his head. He liked his women pale, whiter than himself if he could find them that way. Yet there was something about Jane, some indomitable spirit that resided in her eyes and soul. Some mystery lurked around the corner to be solved. He had to admit that she looked quite fine standing below in his garden, as if she hadn't a care in the world.

Why should she care that she hasn't seen you in four nights? Asher thought sardonically. He certainly hadn't cared to see her. He had thought distance would clear his head, would lessen his desire. Instead, his longing for her had grown to a fierce need, an aching need, which was utterly despicable. "Lusting for a Van Helsing!" he snorted.

He scowled. He had a right to be angry about this forced marriage. He didn't want to solve anything about Jane. No, in fact, he didn't even want to have dinner with her tonight. He had been avoiding her, letting his anger ease gradually as he returned to his old haunts, feasting on sensual delights.

Just last night he had gorged himself on a five-course meal at the Birds of Paradise Club. The club was an exclusive brothel catering to the more exotic, perfect for the hedonistic supernatural predator. It was an exciting place where gentlemen both mortal and otherworldly could find plucky whores of their choice, dressed in feathers and plumes, like sitting ducks in a row—or laying ducks in a row, as the case might be. Asher had sampled a tasty black-haired warbler, a delicious brunette partridge, a delightfully redheaded wagtail, a plump feather-headed goose and a silvery-blond soiled dove.

Yes, he had filled their bodies with his hunting cock and sipped the full-bodied blend of their blood. It had been a night to remember, to reminisce about at the Dead Poets' Society: an exclusive vampire haunt where the more literate and clever of his kind met in secret, as gentlemen are wont to do. At the Dead Poets' Society vampires discussed all subjects of the night, placed bets, conversed about upcoming events, discovered who was biting whom, played cards and discussed, naturally, all the supernatural gossip of the *ton*.

Yet, the past two times he'd gone to his club, he'd been silently quoting Coleridge: *"I feel 'as idle as a painted ship upon a painted ocean.'"*

This melancholy feeling had only deepened today, causing Asher some concern. He was growing older. He had seen too many sunsets to count. He had felt too many dawns dragging him down to deathlike sleep. He had seen a score of kings come and go. He had been friends with a few, and disposed of a few others. Ennui was dogging his heels.

Changes. Many changes had come and gone, places

and people, as the centuries crept past. Inventions, like Babbage's analytical machine, and Fulton's harnessing the power of steam. Art had become more dreamlike in quality, while music became more uplifting. Everything moved toward the future, even the changing seasons. He had loved so many women that they all ran together in a formless image of red lips, slender necks and white thighs. As of late, his pleasure was harder to seek, and boredom was his ever-present enemy perched upon his shoulder.

Lately there had been a small but insistent voice in the back of his mind calling Jane's name. Asher knew he owed his unwanted wife little to nothing, certainly not his loyalty or fidelity. Yet, he had made that solemn vow in church to love and protect her. In the three-hundred-plus years of his life, he had only broken two vows. Both had been life-and-death situations.

Cocking his head, he studied Jane closely as she walked about the garden, her misbegotten mutt following her. She was certainly no beauty in the eyes of the *ton*, yet she drew him in a way he could not dismiss.

Despite the marital vow he had sworn, last night's feast of flesh and blood at the brothel had been solely to get back at his wife, and to help expunge his anger. Still, her face remained firmly lodged in his head. Suddenly every sodden jacket, freckle and sight of a swan gracefully gliding across the lake in Hyde Park reminded him of Jane. It was strangely sweet, yet disconcerting, how thoughts of his wife clung to him like twining vines of honeysuckle.

"I will not feel guilty. I will carouse at all hours of the night and sleep with whom I wish. Bite as many beautiful women as I wish," he told himself angrily. He was a male vampire in his prime, and he had every reason to seek his lusty diversions. He was the master of the un-dead of London. Other males, both dead and alive, envied him, and all manner and species of female threw themselves at him. No one could tell him what to do with his life. Certainly not a back-stabbing Van Helsing. It had been that way for centuries. So why was he feeling so downcast tonight?

Intrigued in spite of himself, Asher observed as his wife approached that enormous freak of her big bird. He arched a brow as the avian lowered its huge head to be petted. His wife stretched up on her tiptoes to carry on a conversation with it, unaware that she was being observed. It was true: She wasn't much of a vampire hunter if she couldn't feel his hungry eyes upon her.

She spoke confidently, in a tone too low for even Asher to hear, gabbing away at the bird. The big ugly beast lowered its head again, and Jane placed a kiss on its fuzzy head. The ostrich shoved her lightly, and Asher could hear Jane's laughter ring out. She had a marvelous laugh, he admitted. His breeches tightened further.

"Damnation!" he snarled to his empty bedroom. Jane was an albatross around his neck. Just because she was intelligent and witty was no reason to want to bed the wench. Lusting after her was insane! But she did have the most incredible breasts. And her eyes were fascinating, not to mention the silken waterfall of her long burnished brown hair. And her neck was to die for.

The image of Jane brushing her hair, and how Asher wanted to see it spread all around his bride as he spent himself inside her, stiffened his erection further.

"Bloody bride! Bloody breasts! Bloody hell!" he cursed. He had awakened hard in his coffin, wanting to sink his fangs into Jane's neck and his arousal into her virgin body. Yes, he had been having wet dreams about his wife, fool that he was. He wanted to take her and she wanted to stake him. No matter Jane's sweet words of loyalty, nor Clair and Huntsley's assurances, Asher couldn't trust Jane any further than he could throw her.

Well, much less than that, as he could probably throw the short mortal pretty far.

Frustrated, he cursed a red streak for several moments, venting his spleen. He apparently had a voracious hunger for his bride, yet she was oblivious to the pain he was in, walking stiffly and having trouble sitting down comfortably with the bulge in his breeches. What a breach! A good wife would show concern for her husband's pants. In his fit of pique, he didn't reason that he hadn't seen Jane recently for her to help.

Instead he grieved for Clair. For Clair, he would have been willing to be married for eternity . . . eventually.

"'Alone, alone. All, all alone, alone on a wide wide sea.'" Asher quoted Coleridge. He had been solo so long, sitting in the silence of his crypt. He had no one to share laughter or jests with, to discuss the gossip of the *ton*. He had no one to share his coffin or to pledge his scarred and bleeding heart to. He had few close friends, only acquaintances, and only one or two loves.

Part of the problem was that he was an earl. Add to that the fact that he was a creature of the night with supernatural powers. Few would interact with such a superior being.

World-weary, Asher shook his head, amazed that he had finally married after centuries of being extremely particular about who would bear his name. This was what fate had in store for him; a bizarre female who was having a one-sided conversation with an ostrich?

Below in the garden, unaware of her husband's surveillance, Jane petted Orville.

"It's a different world here," she said to the bird. "And it can be rather lonely." She glanced around at the massive gardens. "I'm glad you're here. You're a piece of home. A wonderful piece of my past. Now, we are all here together—you, Spot, Bert and me. We have a new future to make as bright and loving as we can. If only I can be strong and brave enough to storm the castle walls that hide the earl's heart. The reward would be a love that I've only dreamed of in my deepest dreams." Jane scratched Orville's beak, picturing a good life with Asher. Bringing his slippers to his coffin at night. Sharing his love and his thoughts. Laughing with him over the day's events. Waiting for him to come home from the cemetery while she worked on her bird sketches. Could she be bold enough to make such a dream come true? Could she brave the vampire's lair and survive?

Orville nudged her gently, almost knocking her over. Jane laughed, and her heart told her to reach for the stars. "I am a Van Helsing. We are used to storming walls and are rather expert on working our way into hearts. Well, in one manner of speaking," she qualified, thinking her strategy should be a little less pointed than her father's.

Finally Jane hurried away, butterflies filling her stomach. She vowed under her breath, "Tonight I will have dinner with my husband. Our very first dinner as vampire and wife."

The Prime of Miss Jane's Body

Jane hurried down the large marble staircase, her heart pounding in her chest. Her husband had agreed to have dinner with her. Smoothing back the soft wisps of hair that framed her face, she warily prepared her fortitude, uncertain what kind of greeting she would receive from the moody groom.

To say she was surprised would be an understatement. Entering the lush, massive drawing room, Jane halted abruptly. Shock made her mouth round into a perfect O. Asher was adjusting his cravat and studying his profile in a large oval mirror.

Jane gasped. Her husband was a vampire. She knew that. She had seen his fangs, felt them pressed against her neck! Yet, he had a reflection, and a very attractive reflection at that.

Observing Jane's reaction, Asher laughed—a wicked sound that sent her toes curling. "Don't believe everything you hear or read about us," he said, guessing her shock.

He couldn't help but be pleased by the surprise he

saw on her face. He had decided to put his short wife on her toes tonight and try to discover any hidden agenda she might have, such as early widowhood. He knew it wouldn't be easy, since the Van Helsings were a tricky lot. As treachery was their family middle name, Asher well knew that getting info out of a Van Helsing wife would be a slow dance, with steps cunning and cagey; he'd have to keep her off balance with wit and charm. But the end result would be Jane as butter in his hands, and he would get her pathetic plans down pat.

Staring at her husband in bewilderment, Jane blurted, "But . . . I can see you in the mirror. How can this be? Vampires don't have reflections. I learned that in vampire class."

Asher smiled wickedly, engaged in a deadly deception with his deceitful companion. Tonight his deft illusions in this daring encounter with the damnable stranger who was now his wife must be done with decided charm if he didn't want to be dead and buried. And he had no death wish.

"You can see you in the mirror. Everyone can't be wrong," Jane said, her brows furrowed.

"Yes, they can. And glad I am. What a waste it would be to miss *this*," he replied, gesturing vaguely at the face staring back at him in the gilt-framed mirror. Elegantly he turned, a small sardonic smile on his face. "What a tragedy that would be, if I couldn't see my own smiling face each sunset when I awake. How would I know if I'm getting gray hairs, or if my cravat is crooked?"

Jane smiled, her stunned reaction fading. Her husband seemed approachable tonight, even teasing her. She liked this lighter mood much better than his usual caustic self. "And how old are you? Did you help Noah with the ark?" she joked.

"You knew I was old when you married me," he replied.

"Ah, but not *how* old."

"That's a question you never ask a vampire," Asher said, making a dismissive gesture with his hands.

Jane retreated, not wanting to spoil the mood. "Then let me ask you what it's like to live forever," she said curiously. She really wanted to know. "Did you know Henry the Eighth? What was Anne Boleyn like? Did she often lose her head? Did you ever get to see a Shakespeare play in person, with the playwright in the same theatre? How exciting, to not only be able to read history, but to have lived it."

He shrugged, his expression enigmatic. "Eternity can be very long. 'Men may come and men may go, but I go on forever,'" he quoted.

"Tennyson?" Jane asked, thinking she recognized the words from a volume of poetry she had kept upon her bookshelves back home. Her husband nodded, and she could see a faint hint of approval in his eyes.

"It seems I have married a bluestocking."

"I strive to be well-read and well learned. The Van Helsing heritage, you know. Learn everything." Jane left unsaid that her ancestors believed in knowing everything about their enemies. Although she didn't think any had ever gone as far as marrying one.

"Lessons which no doubt included the killing of my race," Asher said. He couldn't seem to resist getting in a jab at her heritage, despite his plan to ferret out her deadly agenda by being witty and charming.

Jane's lighter mood dissolved. "I learned many things, my husband." Seeing a hint of disgust in his eyes, Jane tried again to reach him with words. "It is not easy being a Van Helsing, a protector of humanity. When you are a Van Helsing, the dark at the top of every staircase could be a vampire or demon hiding there to kill you. Our journeys are dark, our victories darker. Of course, we work at night," she admitted.

Asher's face remained coldly detached—a death mask, Jane thought. But why wouldn't it? He was one of the walking dead.

"You murder my species," he accused.

"Your species eat my people," Jane argued calmly, without wholesale condemnation.

"You Van Helsings judge without a trial," Asher continued.

"And you, my lord, have a hard head to match your stubborn heart."

"The better to withstand you, my dear little wife." Asher found himself speaking curtly as he stared at Jane's luscious chest. He was again envisioning his unwanted wife opening her thighs, beckoning him to have a taste. Would she have freckles on the flesh there? He would kiss them, savoring the sweet flavor.

Blinking rapidly, he realized where his thoughts were leading him: down the garden path to a dirty grave! "You Van Helsings are a menace to every blue-blooded Nosferatu around. Your ancestors have decimated whole families of us. We have learned our lessons well about you and yours. A Van Helsing does his duty through rain, sleet, snow, and the fires of hell."

"And you don't think we Van Helsings have learned lessons from you as well? We die too! Each death a hard lesson. You don't think my ancestors have suffered?" Jane pointed a finger at him. "During the French Revolution, my aunt lost her head over Count Langella and ended up as his top-off of the day. That drained the family bloodline, I can tell you. My great-great-grandfather went up in smoke when he tried to dispatch one of Lucifer's fallen angels. He forgot to give the Devil his due!"

Asher remained motionless, as still and pale as marble. He watched her with dark fascination.

But how could he stand there so stone-faced? The condemning cad, Jane mused curtly. She went on: "One great uncle got so wrapped up in his mission that he was left in a tomb in Egypt. Mummy wasn't pleased. Another uncle learned never cross the Alps with a vampire. Hannibal ate him with fava beans and a nice chianti."

"Well, you know what they say," Asher remarked, lifting up a bottle of champagne with sangfroid. "The only good Van Helsing is a—"

Jane gasped. "How rude, how crude, how contemptible."

Ignoring her but not finishing his joke, Asher poured himself and Jane glasses of wine. "I took the trouble to select something appropriate for the occasion. I trust one glass won't put you in your cups?"

Jane lifted her chin, her green-silver eyes sparking. "Hemlock?"

Asher narrowed his eyes, hiding his grin. His wife had a sharp wit—almost as sharp as her stakes. She was a complex creature, and he found himself slightly stunned to find that he wanted to know more about her—from an enemy's standpoint, of course.

"Touché," he said. "Now come have a drink and before I Socrates one to you. Tell me more about your life. Since we married in haste, I fear I know little about you except what Huntsley and Clair have informed me of."

"I don't really like to talk about myself," she hedged.

Asher took a sip of champagne. "Is your life so dull that you think you'll put me to sleep? Come now, don't be shy, little vampire hunter."

Jane arched a delicate brow. "If you insist?"

"I do," he agreed.

"If you start snoring don't say I didn't warn you," she said.

He took offense. "I don't snore!"

Jane grinned and took a drink of the bubbling liquid he'd given her. After another sip, she cautiously began. "My childhood was difficult, but it was made easier by my mother. She died when I was twelve, leaving a hole in my life that has never been filled. She was a remarkable woman, always ready with a smile or a hug. She kept me from as much of my Van Helsing lessons as she could. She was a petite woman, yet she would always stand up to my father for my sake, and he usually relented. He loved her greatly and has never quite been the same since she died. I was always a reluctant hunter. She was my touchstone, always there to tuck me in bed at night and read me stories. My mother loved to read and I inherited her love of the written word along with my love of bird-watching."

"Yes, Clair did mention something about birds," Asher said. He had known from the beginning that Van Helsings raised no fools. His wife was learned, which he viewed as one of the few high points of the marriage. It was also interesting to hear the sincerity in her tone about her abhorrence of stalking and staking the undead. Clair had told him. Ian had told him. Neither had convinced Asher. Yet Jane's words tonight seemed honestly real. What must it have been like for her to grow up with a fanatical bigot like the major? Most females would have been crushed beneath such weight. His small wife was alive and well.

"Clair said you disliked stalking through the dead of night under your father's dark command," Asher mentioned. "I know that Major Van Helsing has a dark past, and that he's known for his obsession with slaughtering the undead. Your grandfather, the colonel, is a fairer man to deal with. He gives a vampire a sporting chance. Or at least he did back in his halcyon days."

Jane nodded. "My grandfather is a good man. Gruff

sometimes, definitely eccentric. But I love him, and he understands that I truly, truly dislike the sight of blood. He doesn't push me to do anything I don't want."

"Ian mentioned that to me at Huntsley Manor—being afraid of blood." Finishing his brandy, Asher set it on the mantel, crossing in front of the mirror once more. Jane again regarded his reflection with a sense of wonder.

Noticing her distraction, he stopped and stood, letting the mirror reflect his back. "I told you—not all old wives' tales are true."

Observing how the candlelight reflected in Asher's wavy hair, she nodded and addressed his earlier comment: "Yes, it *would* be a great waste. All that beauty hidden from its owner . . ."

Asher's mouth crooked up in a small grin. "Too true. Though I hate to admit to it. What conceit you must attribute to me."

She nodded. "I am sorry to discompose you, my lord, but I really must point out that you *are* vainglorious."

"With just cause," he answered devilishly, clearly not offended. He extended his arm. "Come. Dinner is waiting."

Taking his arm, Jane let Asher lead her into the small informal dining room, studying him as he seated her. The buffet table was set up with many covered dishes.

"I thought we would serve ourselves tonight. I do so love helping myself to dinner," Asher explained. "To have my food *at hand*, so to speak." He touched her neck.

Jane arched a brow, surprised by his sense of humor. She watched Asher sit down at his place, and his long, elegant fingers picked up a plate and uncovered small pieces of lamb stewed in mushroom-and-wine sauce. She wondered idly what those hands would feel like on her skin. Then Asher picked up a piece of lamb and sensuously licked off the sauce.

The room suddenly felt extremely warm as Jane watched his tongue teasing the morsel. Fanning herself, Jane remarked, "Didn't your mother ever teach you not to act saucy?" The smell wafted upward, whetting her appetite.

"Ah, but that's the best part," Asher answered, watching her. He noted how the pale blue gown she wore revealed a tantalizing expanse of soft white flesh. His groin got hot and swelled in spite of his wishes. His wife was in her prime—virgin territory waiting to be taken. It was a sobering and seductive thought. He would be the first, if he so chose. But could he bed a Van Helsing? Looking at Jane, he rather thought he could.

After pouring them each a glass of wine so red it looked like rubies in the glow of the chandeliers, Asher seated himself. "I saw that your ostrich arrived today. I have heard it has the house at sixes and sevens."

Her wine went down the wrong way. Recovering, Jane replied with great warmth, "Thank you for letting Orville and Bert come. Orville has been dear to me ever since my grandfather Ebenezer brought him home. He used to travel abroad quite a bit for work."

I just bet he did, Asher thought, recalling a hunt on the Dark Continent for the Prince of Darkness that had been the talk of the supernatural world for decades.

Jane continued: "My grandfather always brought me something back from his travels. Knowing I loved bird-watching, he brought me the biggest bird he could find, mostly to support me in my endeavor to catalog and learn as much as I could about our feathered friends. My cousins used to tease me unmercifully about my hobby, but they were quite impressed with Orville, who is an amazing bird and quite a character."

Asher nodded curtly, not liking the warmth that curled low in his belly as he stared at his wife. He should not care that she was easy to please, since she was nothing but a villain—or a daughter of one. That was a fact he had best not forget while he watched her luminous eyes shining and the pulse beating within her swanlike neck, making his own pulse accelerate. She had been married to him less than a week, and already he knew she was spying on him.

"Your cousins? You are speaking of Jakob Van Helsing's boys," he commented.

Jane nodded.

Asher shook his head. "They are a wild, unruly bunch. I can well imagine they would have disdain for anything as sedate as bird-watching." Was that an understatement, Asher thought. The Van Helsing boys were notorious at wenching and wrenching open casket lids, playing havoc with vampires everywhere. No sane Nosferatu wanted to meet one in a light alley. Still, his small wife had stood up to her ill-mannered, capricious cousins, and had continued with her interests, such as cataloging birds.

"I saw some of your drawings yesterday in the library. You are quite talented," he admitted.

Jane blushed becomingly. "A compliment from my husband? Is this the 'for better' part of our marriage, started at last? I want to be sure and note it, if it is."

Emptying his wineglass, Asher decided that two could play at such teasing. "I am sorry that I didn't have the wine you were looking for this morning. But I prefer red, not white. Please remember in the future." He studied her closely, waiting to see guilt creep across her face.

Jane managed a faint smile. Humbug! Renfield, the bloody tattletale, had told her husband about the cellar visit. "Thank you for that sage advice. I must thank your servant also. Renfield has been so solicitous of me. It seems I can go nowhere without his helpful personage putting in an appearance."

Asher cut to the chase. "You won't find my coffin,

Jane," he warned, forgetting his plan to get her to betray her secrets. The thought of his wife searching diligently for his resting place, so that she could stake him when his back was turned and he was dead to the world, was an unforgivable breach of every etiquette there was.

His eyes glinted with fierce blue light as he warily studied his wife. He detested betrayal, especially that of a wife betraying her husband. In his pique, Asher forget the hundreds of wives of other men he had seduced into betraying their own wedding vows. But, then, the horse was a different color when it was in his stable.

With remarkable aplomb, Jane kept her expression neutral, hiding her hurt, having learned long ago that a woman's pain did no good in the world of men. She hated that Asher thought her capable of hurting him. But he did, as was evidenced by his stiff manner and the silence with which he held himself in check.

"I'm sorry. I was curious. I have never been married to a vampire before. I just wanted to watch you sleeping."

"So you could kill me?" he asked. His voice held a hint of ennui, meant to hide his true feelings, which were anything but placid.

His words struck deep into Jane's heart, but she didn't flinch. She pleaded, hoping to reach his deadened heart, "Asher, think. If I wanted you staked, I could have told the truth to my father."

Asher fingered the glass of wine in his hand and continued to study his plain wife, to look into her remarkable eyes. He could see the hurt in their green, murky depths. "I must admit, I have been curious why you didn't."

His wife looked so innocent. She was a marvelous actress. But of course she would be. The vandalous Van Helsings, who broke into crypts and staked his kind, causing the ends of many innocent vampires, were highly trained in many different arts: why should acting be excluded? No, death never took a holiday when the Van Helsings were in town.

"Would you believe I look beastly in black?" she teased. "Would you believe that I meant to make the most of this marriage? To be the very best wife I could be? I would like to make your life easier in any way that I can, if you will only let me. I know we have had a rocky beginning—"

Asher interrupted her. "A rocky beginning? Ha! More like an avalanche. And I don't intend ending buried alive."

Jane pursed her lips, straightening her spine. "Charming. Thank you for your confidence."

He arched an aristocratic eyebrow, his expression one of patent disbelief. "By a cruel twist of fate, I find myself married to one of the vigilante scourges of vampires everywhere. You are not only a source of danger to me and my friends of the supernatural world, but an embarrassment." Yet her skin looked so soft in the glow of the candlelight. Her neck begged to be tasted, savored, sipped like the finest wine.

Jane shook her head, responding emphatically. "Why, you big bag of dirt! I owe my loyalty to you after you selflessly saved my honor. Can't you believe that? If I was taught nothing else, I was taught to hold duty close to my breast. I'm hardly going to go around staking you and your friends, no matter what my last name used to be!"

"Well, I am sure my chums will be vastly relieved. As am I," Asher responded.

Jane held her temper by the barest thread, a false smile on her lips. Asher didn't believe her. But then, why should he? What was his incentive?

"I am the Countess of Wolverton now, my duties lie

221

with you. Although, I must admit, staking you in the arse right now does hold a certain appeal. Did it hurt much?"

Asher lifted his lip in a contemptuous sneer. But, studying her from the top of her head to the bottom of her slippers, the word "lie" conjured up images of Jane's naked form in bed waiting for him. Distracted and angry, he retorted, "Shall I show you? Perhaps I can return the favor too. I don't have a stake with me, but I can use my hands."

Jane held her ground. If he touched her, she would scream bloody murder. She hadn't been spanked since she was nine, and her husband wasn't going to start now. "I am the Countess of Wolverton," she repeated. "Countesses are above that sort of thing."

Asher stood and rapidly paced over to the fireplace, pointing to the large portrait above the hearth. The picture was of a beautiful woman with flowing chestnut hair, in an outdated costume of the seventeenth century. "That was the fifth Countess of Wolverton, who was married to my grandfather. She was not only a beauty, but descended from kings! You are not. Shall I tell you if she was spanked? She deserved it less than you."

Dignity in place, but her temper reaching the boiling point, Jane threw her napkin beside her plate. Enough was enough. She might not be a raving beauty; so hang her. She might not be a princess of royal blood; so chop off her head. "Bull's blooming ballocks?" she cursed, using her father's favorite phrase. Ladylike decorum be damned; Asher had just met his match.

"I am descended from a venerable, valiant line of barons and marquesses. My lineage may not be quite as exalted as yours, but it is a proud one. My family line was saving the world when you were just a gleam in your father's fangs!"

Asher seethed, lifting his glass of wine and taking a gulp, his thoughts murky and nasty. He knew her entire Machiavellian ancestry. Murderous and sly, they were. "Jane, Jane, you are treading on thin ice. Don't make me lose my temper with you," he growled.

"What will you do, play the big bad vampire, and bite me on the neck?" Jane laughed.

Asher blinked. The image of sinking his teeth into his wife's lovely neck was enticing; her blood would go to his head like bubbles in a glass of champagne. But he didn't want to do that, and he hadn't survived this many years without learning a thing or two. When all else failed, change the subject. "I heard your brother came by. What did he want?" he asked.

"Excuse me?" she replied.

"Your brother. He was here today."

"He brought Spot."

"What did you tell him about me?" Asher pried, wondering what plots Jane and her sibling had hatched while he lay sleeping like the dead.

"I lied. I said you were kind to me," Jane hissed, her eyes pools of turbulent emotion. She and her brother had talked at great length about the proposed hunt for Dracul in October, since it would be of grave importance. They had discussed Brandon's good friend's death. But she had revealed very little about her marriage, not wanting her brother to become suspicious of her husband.

"That's not what I meant. Does he know what I am?" Asher asked.

"That you're a stubborn jackass? No. I didn't tell him that. I told them you're a man. And I will continue to lie to my family about what you really are—even the jackass part."

"How very noble of you," Asher mocked, ignoring

the look of wounded dignity in his wife's eyes. "Such surprising thoughtfulness, for a Van Helsing."

"My lord, were you born such a bastard, or did that trait occur after you were given the vampire's kiss?" Jane bristled.

"Do you know you look like a hedgehog right now?" Asher confided snidely, watching her. In spite of all his good intentions, he couldn't seem to resist striking at her. He felt the need to fight, to assuage his tattered dignity by force. He knew he was being pigheaded, but no more than that wereboar friend of the Huntsleys.

"Born a bastard, I see," Jane snapped.

"I will not be spoken to like this in my own home! Bite your tongue, woman, or I will do it for you," he threatened.

"Oh!" Jane seethed with righteous indignation. "You sound just like my father. Ordering me around without so much as a by-your-leave."

"Don't insult me, Jane. My temper has been sorely tried by this misalliance. And while you may have gotten what you wanted, I didn't want a wife in a thousand years!"

"What makes you think I wanted to be your wife—especially when you insult and degrade me at every given opportunity?"

Asher looked taken aback. "Why, everyone wants to be my wife. I've been chased to ground by connubial bliss–minded females for hundreds of years."

"Oh, you arrogant blood guzzler. You're driving me batty. You're a bloody, no-good—"

"Jane, Jane, remember your new station in life. I don't believe a countess should curse," Asher interrupted.

Jane ignored him, almost weeping. "You'll never forgive me, will you? You will harp on and on about how you've been cheated. Well, my toplofty earl, I've been cheated too. I desired a marriage to a man who would willingly share his life with me, who wanted me to have his children. I wanted to cherish and be cherished. And look what I ended up with—a dead man walking always away from me. So if this marriage isn't your ideal, it isn't mine either!"

Asher snorted.

Cut to her very soul, her dignity and self-esteem shredded, Jane sighed. "You know, your tongue is sharper than any stake my family ever made." She stood up regally, fighting back tears. She wouldn't let her callous, contemptible husband see her cry. Turning abruptly toward the door, Jane hurried off, almost running to escape.

As Asher watched his prey flee, his predatory instinct came to the fore. He growled. Jane of all people should know better than to run. He wanted to feel her warm lips under his. He needed to drink in her erotic scent, to drink her virgin's blood. He longed to feel her underneath him, moaning in ecstasy.

Before she could reach the door, he leapt over his chair. Taking another leap, he reached Jane's side and yanked her into his arms, crushing her to him and pinning her against his chest. Lowering his head, he ravaged her lips.

He could taste the blood welling from a cut on her mouth. He could smell the sweet, cloying odor. It almost drove him wild. He licked at her, his tongue tasting all her honeyed essence. He groaned, his thirst begging to be slaked. She was a bloody good experience, this unwanted, plain, vampire-hunting wife of his.

His hands rose to squeeze the firm plumpness of her bosom, which overflowed his large fingers. They felt wonderful. Bloody marvelous. His cock swelled, and he began to ache with a new need: to bury himself deep in her tight, hot depths.

Jane moaned, her senses reeling. At first Asher's kiss

had scared and hurt her. But in the space of a heartbeat, the assault had changed to a fierce persuasion, a sweetness that required her response.

As her husband pressed her close, Jane felt a large hardness against her. It gave her pause. Asher was not as immune to her as he pretended. And most certainly his body felt the same way she did—maybe even more so, she thought vaguely as he rubbed it against her.

"Oh, Asher," she moaned, and pressed tighter, trying to meld her body into his. She wanted to be consumed, to burn and burn, to go up in flames like a phoenix to be reborn. She sensed that Asher could take her to places she had never been, and to walk on clouds that knew no end.

Pressing herself against him, she clung to his shoulders, her world spinning. She felt strange tinglings in her body, which began to burn. She hungered for her husband's touch, and for something she couldn't name.

Her breathing became erratic as longings of a more explicable nature swamped her. Tonight! She would finally, truly be his wife tonight; and if this kiss was anything to go on, she felt as if she might be reduced to dust by it.

Asher himself wanted Jane with a fervor that surprised him. His plain little duckling had the softest of lips, and her neck so was very, very inviting. Her scent was beyond description, calling to him in a primeval way. He had to have her *now*.

He lowered his head and placed a kiss on her breasts. She squirmed against him. Enflamed, he suckled her breast into his mouth, drawing it gently between his teeth. He could feel the nipple peaking, and waves of her heat scorched his groin. He felt as if he needed to bury himself within her in the next few seconds, or he would explode—something he hadn't done since he was a young man of fourteen.

Suddenly, the most hideous noise interrupted their passionate encounter. Asher broke away, a little dazed.

"What is that sound?" he asked, his breathing labored as he tried to crush down his desire.

It took Jane a few seconds to understand what he husband was asking, so dazed was she by his kisses.

"That noise, Jane—what is it?"

Bemused, she finally recognized the sounds coming from outside the informal dining room's open balcony window. They were coming from the garden. And only one creature in the garden—probably in all of London—could make that screeching.

"It's Orville," she answered. "Orville sometimes likes to sing at night."

Pushing her away, Asher stared at Jane in stunned disbelief. "Does he make that noise often?" He shifted uncomfortably, his pants too tight. His wife could certainly kiss. If he didn't know better, he would swear she wasn't a virgin. But he did know better. And that noise . . . "Surely not. Nothing should even ever make that noise once!"

Jane would have laughed at the look on her husband's face, if she didn't feel like crying. Her body was a riot of emotions. "No. It's just that this is a new place, and he is probably lonely for me." As she spoke, she put one hand behind her back and crossed her fingers. One small fib wouldn't hurt too much.

Asher bowed curtly. "Then you must go and comfort the infernal bird. And since the night is not getting any younger, I have places to go and people to see." He stalked icily off.

He could feel Jane staring at his back, but he breathed a long, deep sigh of relief. She was quite pretty when she was angry, and he had been stopped from taking his wife on the floor of the dining room. For that, Asher was more than grateful. Who would believe it? Saved by the bird.

Fighting Tooth and Neil

The theatre was crowded with society's elite, who were sparkling and shining in their jewels and rich clothing. With so many present, the noise was like a thousand wasps trapped in a bell jar. Now some were discussing Lady Veronique's mysterious disappearance, and the missing prostitutes that the newspaper had been writing about. Twelve were now gone, vanished. Normally newspapers wouldn't take note, but with the total so high, the public's interest had begun to stir.

Ian, Clair and Jane had discussed it in the carriage earlier, wondering if supernatural species were involved. Jane hadn't revealed that she thought it was Dracul. She'd save that for later.

They all sat in Baron Huntsley's box, waiting for the play to begin. Clair and Jane had been discussing the first week of wedded bliss—or rather, the lack thereof. Ian observed the crowd.

"Asher doesn't trust me. He doesn't *want* me," Jane complained. She didn't want to speak ill of the dead, but

Neil Asher was impossible. He made her so mad at times, she wanted to spit Neils.

Clair patted Jane's hand, commiserating. "But I've seen the way Asher looks at you. He wants you, all right. He's just too stubborn to act. But he will. Men like to sulk a bit. I imagine the earl will sulk a bit longer."

"If I were a man, I'd never sulk and treat my wife shabbily," Jane declared. "I'd be free to do as I please. And I'd punch Asher in the mouth."

Clair laughed.

Jane sighed. After a week of marriage, she was still a virgin. And the way things were progressing, she just might die one. Imagine, being married to one of the biggest rakes in London, being the envy of all women, and yet she slept alone, untouched and unwanted.

There were good things, however. For the first time in her life, Jane was free not to be a Van Helsing. She was free to do the things she enjoyed, to be herself and not have to tote stakes, formulate battle strategies or be around blood and gore. For the first time in her life, Jane was mostly happy. And she was falling in love. She felt excited, agitated, hurt and a little sick. Shaking her head, she wondered why people raved about the experience.

"I just know everything will turn out well. I believe when Asher comes to his senses, he will realize what a wonderful wife you will make. He will fall down on his knees and declare utter love and devotion to you," Clair confided confidently.

"I wouldn't hold my breath, Clair. I rarely even see my husband. He has quite the aversion to me," Jane said. "He didn't want a wife. And if he did have to marry, he would have much preferred someone else."

Clair shook her head regretfully. "Who? Jane, you have a beauty that shines forth from your lovely eyes, a brave heart, a good nature and a bright wit. You have a beautiful neck, the envy of any woman, and especially desirable to a vampire. And your bosom is large—larger than my own!" Sneaking a peak at her husband, Clair blushed, adding, "Believe me, the bosom being big is a big thing for men, be they mortal or immortal."

"I wouldn't know," Jane remarked despondently. She glanced down at the plump fullness of her breasts, displayed quite deliberately and prettily by her low décolletage. "But I could be the very loveliest lady and Asher wouldn't care. You know he is in love with you." Jane said the last with a hint of jealousy in her voice. She couldn't help it; she loved Clair dearly, but some small part of her resented her friend's hold on her husband. It made her feel small, but she felt it just the same.

"He *thinks* he is, or was. But you love many people and many things in life," Clair stated firmly. "The heart is a most wondrous organ. It is big enough to love deeply and passionately more than once in a lifetime. Asher will realize that. He has loved before me, and he will love you. I know this, Jane. I know this with all my soul."

Jane's eyes misted, and her misery lessened just a tad. She gripped Clair's hand, giving it a firm squeeze. "Yet . . . we have so much against us, Clair, for him to love me."

"You, my dear Jane, are well worth loving. Never let a little thing like you having been a vampire-slayer and him being a vampire spell the end. Such small things in a marriage can set it on a rocky course, but you have the power to overcome."

Jane hid her smile. Only Clair Frankenstein Huntsley would think that their problems were small things, easily overcome. "So, do you take your own advice?" she asked, her tone light. "Ian being a werewolf doesn't bother you at all?"

Clair laughed. "Of course not! It's bloody marvelous.

My supernatural research has never gone so well. And never has it been so much fun. Having your own private specimen to study in the flesh . . . it's quite invigorating."

Jane blushed, a quick visual of what Clair meant flashing through her mind. But it was a dark visual. It was so unfair! She had been married a week and still was ignorant of what went on in the bedchamber at night.

"I've quite given up my Bunsen burners," Clair said slyly. "Ian was tired of getting singed."

Jane laughed this time, but the laughter died abruptly as she saw her husband enter a box directly across the theater. On his arm was a stunning woman with dark hair piled high upon her head. Her scarlet gown was daringly cut, revealing a large cluster of rubies and a rather impressive bosom. Jane frowned, thinking that the so-called lady looked as if she knew exactly what went on behind closed doors between a woman and a vampire.

Seeing the distress on her friend's face, Clair turned her attention to the box. "Drat! Drat! And double drat!" she exclaimed. Nudging her husband none too gently in the ribs, she indicated that he look across the crowded theatre.

"What the bloody hell is Asher doing with that wicked bitch of the west?" Ian asked.

"I thought she was being punished," Clair retorted.

"She is supposed to be locked in her coffin," Ian agreed in a bewildered tone. "I like this not."

Regaining her composure, her hands fisted in her skirts, Jane asked, "Who is she?" But she knew: The woman was an encroaching tart, and her husband was a contemptible cad.

"An old friend of Asher's," Clair answered. "Lady Montcrief." Her lack of elaboration spoke volumes.

Jane read between the lines. "You mean his old mistress."

Clair remained silent, but Ian nodded.

"She is very beautiful. And, I take it, she is one of the undead?" Jane recognized the pallor and predatory look that some vampires could not hide from her expertly trained eyes.

"Yes," Clair said, her eyes blazing. "And at one time she tried to kill Ian, Asher and myself. What the fool is doing with her now is beyond me."

Glancing in the direction of Asher's box, Jane saw her husband leaning over the voluptuous lady, staring down her gown. "He appears to be looking into her heart," she remarked, hoping her droll wit would cover the sound of her own heart breaking into a thousand pieces.

Ian gave a sharp bark of laughter, but quieted when Jane and Clair glared at him.

"He also appears to be trying to humiliate me before the *ton*," Jane went on coldly. And he had. She was hurt, humiliated and angry that Asher would bring his old lover to such a public place where all eyes would be upon them. Especially since he was so newly wedded.

She wanted to pull out the brunette's hair by the roots. She wanted to claw her tooth and nail. She wanted to wipe that lascivious smile off her arrogant face. She wanted to plant a fist in his.

Frowning, she looked away. Lady Montcrief and Asher made a very handsome pair. The vampiress was very beautiful. Again, jealousy raged through Jane's system, making her want to kill her opponent. It wasn't fair for the vampiress to be so lovely, while she was nothing more than plain. Where was a Van Helsing model-four when you needed one?

Breathing deeply, she fought the feelings of betrayal, anger and jealousy that made her want to screech like a fishwife and act like a true Van Helsing. But just because she was married to a monster didn't mean she had to act like one. One soulless fiend per family was more than enough.

"Perhaps I should go to Edinburgh and buy a love potion from Dr. Jekyll," Jane muttered morosely.

"All the way to Scotland for a love potion is a bit extreme—even if Henry Jekyll is quite brilliant with magic potions," Clair said. "Besides, you don't need magic potions to win Asher's love. All you need is your big heart and a lot of patience. The idiot."

Just then Asher threw back his head, laughing at something his companion said. Jane gritted her teeth. She was so furious, she could chew Neil. She wanted to scratch out his leering eyes. She wanted to lock him in his coffin for a month.

Taking another deep breath, she tried to calm herself, to recall her mother's lessons in deportment. If she were a true lady, she could pretend that nothing had happened. If she were a better Van Helsing she would go home and make good on her threats.

"Smile," Clair warned, glancing around the theatre and noting that the members of the *ton* were craning their necks for a better view. They looked from this box to Asher's and back again.

Taking Clair's advice, Jane managed a passable smile. She couldn't let society know how hurt she was; they would rip her to shreds. She couldn't let her husband know how much his actions had done to wound her, either. She bravely faced Ian and Clair, whose eyes held a wealth of sympathy as well as anger.

"I am fine," she stated firmly.

Across the theatre, one of Lady Montcrief's followers, Sir Rowton, had joined Asher and Lady Moncrief in the box. "I say, Asher, isn't that your wife over there?—the Van Helsing chit?" he asked with his usual hint of ennui.

Asher nodded curtly.

Sir Rowton shook his head. "She isn't your usual style. Pity."

If Asher hadn't spent the last two centuries being civilized, he would have snapped Sir Rowton's fat neck. Instead he gave the man a glare filled with fires of hell. No one insulted his wife. "She is Lady Wolverton to you!" he snarled.

Turning toward the box where his wife sat, Asher regarded her closely. She was dressed in a gown of deep green. He knew that up close it would enhance the beauty of her eyes. The gown fit to perfection and displayed her great assets. He scowled. Her breasts were exposed to the view of other men of the *ton*. He made a mental note to himself to have some new gowns made up for her, with the neckline raised at least several more inches.

His wife seemed oblivious to his scrutiny, looking around the rest of the theatre. He would have the dressmaker raise her neckline a good three inches. No, make that four.

Seeing Ian Huntsley, Asher nodded in the man's direction. Briefly and stiffly the baron acknowledged the gesture, then quickly turned back to the two ladies he escorted. But Asher had seen disgust in the werewolf's eyes.

Slightly chagrined, Asher admitted he deserved it. He had seen his wife the moment he sat down. He berated himself for not asking what her plans for tonight had been.

Despite what Ian obviously thought, Asher would not have escorted Lady Montcrief here if he had known the Huntsleys and Jane were coming. He could easily have taken the scheming tart someplace else to work his seductive wiles upon her, to find out just who had released her months early from the silver-chained coffin into which he had forced her after her attack on Clair. He had to know who was brave enough, or foolish enough, to release Lady Montcrief from her just punishment. There were few vampires strong enough to break the spell placed upon the coffin, and none of them should be in London—not without letting him know that they were visiting his territory. It was a serious breach of etiquette, and a deadly one, that he'd only discovered last night upon spying Lady Montcrief out feeding.

He feared he knew who the dark intruder was. It was his archenemy, Dracul.

At that moment, Lady Montcrief broke into his dark thoughts by stroking his thigh, her long red fingernails tracing erotic patterns on his leg. Asher ached to remove her treacherous hand, but knew he must play the part of devoted lover to entice her into revealing the name of her rescuer. It was a delicate game of cat and catty mouse, one which Asher had played a hundred times before.

"I really can't believe you married that creature," Lady Montcrief commented, pertly pursing her lips. "She is so common. And then there is her unfortunate heritage. But perhaps she is good enough in bed to compensate. I would not have thought it, but then Van Helsings would make strange bedfellows."

Asher smiled, hiding the blow she'd dealt to his pride. "I find special delights in my wife that you might not understand."

Lady Montcrief leaned closer, her breath whispering on his face. She smiled. "She could certainly not be better than me in the bedchamber, *mon ami*? Or perhaps you play those games with whips, stakes and silver chains. That would explain why you married one of those horrid Van Helsings. Strange, that type of bedsport was not to your taste before."

"You know I like pleasure more than pain," he agreed

coolly, hiding his anger. How he hated this scheming jade!

Unconsciously, he searched the other side of the theatre with his eyes, watching his wife become paler as Lady Montcrief caressed his arm. But he had no choice except to ignore the brief flash of hurt he saw—just as he ignored the slight pain in his stomach that felt like guilt. He was probably just hungry; he hadn't fed tonight. Why should he care what his wife felt or thought? She was a burden forced upon him.

Yes, he should feel relieved and proud that he had humiliated his wife by not presenting her to society before being seen with his ex-paramour, he told himself. She would be on the tongues of all the gossips tonight, and tomorrow too the vicious tongues would be wagging, all making sport of the new Countess of Wolverton. Just as the few vampires he had encountered recently had spurned or made sport of him. One of those vampires was still at home recuperating, while the other two had fled to Paris, intending to wait until Asher's temper had cooled.

Jane deserved this treatment, he argued silently. She, her dog and her big bird were albatrosses around his neck. Yet, he couldn't help but admire her fortitude. She was laughing with Clair and Ian now, ignoring him completely, and acting as if he were no more than a fly upon the wall. She was magnificent, not showing the *ton* any hint of vulnerability.

Surprising himself, he leaned over and whispered something to Lady Montcrief. Angrily, her red lips clenched tight, and she got to her feet and followed him from the box, leaving a trail of whispers in their wake.

"Well, I'll be damned," Ian said to Clair.

"Never," Clair teased, watching her husband watch Asher exit. "Why?"

Noting that Jane was also watching, Ian whispered, "I concede that you might be right about Asher's feelings toward Jane. He has left the theatre tonight before the play even started. I might also add, he had a slightly guilty expression on that arrogant face. Asher *never* feels guilt. I wasn't even aware he knew what the word meant."

"Good!" Clair stated harshly. "I hope he drowns in guilt." Then, thinking on her words, she asked her husband curiously, "Can vampires drown?"

Jane answered. "Only in their own blood," she said, clenching the highly polished wooden armrests of her chair like she would a Van Helsing model-three stake.

If only she had a real one.

Snow White, the Vampire

Sleepy and grumpy were only two of the things Jane was feeling as she shut the seventh drawer of her large oak chest. Sneezing softly, she doctored her red nose with a handkerchief.

Walking back over to her dressing table, she sat down, slowing unbraiding her long brown hair. She frowned, wondering if Asher was coming home, and if not, just whose coffin he was sharing. Her mind was poisoned by visions of her husband cuddled up with the beautiful Lady Montcrief, their snow-white bodies locked in carnal acts—acts Jane had only bashfully dreamed about, never experienced. Envisioning the two vampires entwined, Jane hoped the coffin lid came crashing down on their heads in the middle of whatever men and woman did in the privacy of their caskets.

"I would kill him myself, if he weren't already dead," she muttered to herself.

Briskly she began to brush her hair, staring into the oval gilt-framed mirror. She knew she wasn't pretty. She knew she could never match the sly, seductive vampiress. But she, not Lady Montcrief, was married to Asher. She should be the one receiving his soulful looks and scorching smiles, not his ex-paramour, who was now his paramour again and no longer an ex.

Once again, someone was rejecting her. He was placing her in a preconceived box upon a shelf, without really coming to know her.

Her childhood had been spent knowing she was not what her father wanted. Now she'd found herself a man who felt the same way. What Asher had done tonight cut deeply, ripping open old wounds that had barely begun to heal.

"I can't believe he's with that vamp," Jane muttered indignantly. Tonight Asher had not only rejected her; he had humiliated her as well. Tomorrow everyone in the *ton* would know that he preferred his ex-mistress to his wife. It was unfair and cruel. The only saving grace was that Asher had had the decency to leave the theatre before the play began. That was something for which to give her cad of a husband credit.

Still, speculation in the theatre had run rampant, forcing Jane to wear an emotionless mask when all eyes turned upon her. Fortunately Ian and Clair had fended off the worst of the gossipmongers. Jane had made it home before she burst into tears in the privacy of her room.

Staring at the ravages of her face, she could still see the results of her crying binge in her puffy eyes and red nose. No, she would never be a beauty.

"'Mirror, mirror, on the wall, who's the fairest of them all?'" Asher's voice echoed from the doorway into her bedchamber, startling Jane, who hadn't even heard him approach.

He could tell that Jane had been crying. A stab of

guilt pierced him. Scowling, he brushed a piece of lint from the cuff of his jacket. He hadn't felt guilt in at least a century. It was an uncomfortable feeling, and one he seemed doomed to experience since meeting and marrying this infernal Van Helsing chit.

Staring at her husband's reflection in the mirror, her green-silver eyes hard, Jane retorted, "Fairest? Why, you of course. Or Lady Montcrief, if she were here." She turned. "Certainly not me. My looks could curdle milk to hear you tell."

Her words hit Asher square in the heart, worse than a well-aimed stake. "Jane, I never said your looks would curdle milk. You . . . mistake my words."

"I mistake nothing. How could you escort your former fling for all the *ton* to see? How could you so humiliate your wife in a public setting?"

"*Unwanted* wife," he reminded her.

"And now all society knows it," Jane spat. "I could box your ears—or box you in your box! How could you prefer that predatory, murderous creature? I thought you had better taste."

"I have excellent taste," Asher retorted. He hated feeling guilty! He was a superior being, far above such petty emotions, being both vampire and one of the most highly titled men in the realm. And if he couldn't be married to Clair, he hadn't wanted to be married at all. He certainly hadn't wanted to be married to a Van Helsing. It made him cruel. "Except in wives. So, Lady Montcrief is none of your business."

Her temper ignited, Jane stood abruptly, shoving her husband back with a strength that surprised him. "You find *her* interesting even after she tried to kill you and Clair. Tell me what she possesses that could make you find her attractive after such a betrayal? I want to emulate her, so that you might condescend to take *me* to the theatre. Perhaps I can dance a jig around the room naked, a rose in my teeth. No, it would have to be blood, wouldn't it? I shall kiss and nibble around your man thing like a goldfish. Or bite your thigh."

Asher's eyes widened in stunned shock, the image of her dancing around the room naked making his blood heat. "You're being vulgar, Jane. And the word isn't 'man thing'—it's 'cock,' or 'rod,' or 'phallus.' Not 'man thing.' That's so demeaning."

"So your cock is demeaned and that concerns you, but not your wife? How touching!"

"Are you practicing to be a harridan?" Asher questioned tartly. "I must remind you that the Countess of Wolverton should be more careful."

"Why, you bloodsucking bastard. Dare you criticize my conduct when you have made me a laughingstock by your insensitivity?"

"Mind your manners, backstabber," he replied frostily. But he couldn't help staring at her heaving bosom, and at the pulse beating rapidly in her neck. Just a little sample, he thought as he stepped closer, in awe of her fire. She was so pretty when enraged.

"Coldhearted corpse!" Jane glowered, and she raised her hand to slap him. Asher caught her palm and threw it aside.

"Vicious vampire murderer!" he replied. And yanking her to him, he kissed her fiercely, savoring the hot spice of her lips, listening to the blood beating in her heart. His erection came to life. He wanted her—it was that simple and that complex.

Infuriated beyond words, Jane jerked away from her husband, her fists clenched, wanting to pound on Asher's chest and at the same time to run her hands all over that smooth sweet skin. "I hope you cock up your toes," she gasped.

Asher shuddered, trying to stem the tide of pure lust he felt. He was cocked up all right. "Thank you for your kind wishes," he said.

"I hope you rot in your grave!" she seethed. "It's bad enough that you ignore me all the time, but now I can add humiliation to the myriad list of your faults. And not just private humiliation, which you supply daily, but public. In front of all society. You're nothing but a debauched fiend. And I deserve better than to be imprisoned with you for life."

"What a charming sentiment. Now I know how you really feel. All those earlier words of wifely devotion and loyalty, they were merely words. Words without honesty. But then, why I should expect honesty from a Van Helsing is beyond me," Asher sneered. Surprisingly, Jane's venom hurt. He had thought his heart long frozen over.

But as he glared at his wife, he knew he couldn't trust her. He just wouldn't give her that power or satisfaction, for she would betray him as surely as she was a Van Helsing.

"Humbug! You wouldn't know honesty if it bit you on the neck." And with those words, Jane turned and fled the room, her long hair trailing loose behind her like a glorious brown-gold cloak.

Asher yelled after her, "Or staked me in the ass! Oh, sorry, you already did that!" It was childish, but no Van Helsing alive was going to get the last word on him. Not if he had anything to say about it.

Her husband's words made Jane even angrier then she already was—not an easy feat to accomplish. But her horrid hubby did it with such polished ease. So she had made a tiny mistake and poked him in the fanny; it wasn't the end of the world. Or even his own end,—at least, not the end of his life. It *had* been his hind end.

Reaching the hallway, Jane furiously realized that she was leaving her own bedchamber. Slapping her hand against her forehead, she grumbled, "Stupid, stupid, stupid."

Chagrined, she stormed back inside, pointing a finger at the door and saying, "Take your stubborn distrust and your rotten, rakish, vainglorious vampire ways out of here."

"You're quite pretty when you're mad." He bowed curtly, a sardonic smile on his lips, his anger obviously simmering as he stalked from the room.

As he closed the door behind him, Asher heard the sound of glass exploding against it. In spite of himself, he laughed. His feisty little wife had stood up to him in a fine fit of temper. She was a virago, but she was *his* virago. And somehow the sound of the word "his" began to feel right.

Shaking his head in disgust at his momentary lapse, Asher went to find his valet. He had to impart the dangerous news he had discovered. The disappearance of so many prostitutes and Lady Veronique had him deeply concerned that vampires were the cause. Vampires with no moral concerns, no concern for the rest of the species. Vampires who drew attention to the nest in London. Asher could think of only one vampire despicable enough: Dracul. Yes, Asher's nemesis. He must be alive and well, and living in London. Where, Asher wasn't sure yet. But he would find out as if his life depended on it—because it very well could.

Dracul was many things, and all of them were very, very bad. The Prince of Darkness was . . . well, just that. There wasn't even a flicker of light in his blackened soul. He inspired fear and terror. But most importantly, the count detested him with a burning intensity which did not bode well for any of Asher's close friends.

Opening the library door, Asher found Renfield having his nightly brandy. Renfield glanced up worriedly at his long-time master.

"You have news?"

Asher nodded solemnly, seating himself before the fire. "It's not good. Although, I must say that the performance I put on tonight would have rivaled Keene's. Ferreting out information from Lady Montcrief was rather an odious task, despising the tart and her heinous betrayal as I do, but I think she doesn't suspect my plot or her place in it."

"Of course not, my lord. You are a master of hiding your emotions, and Lady Montcrief is vain enough to believe you just want her."

"True, Renfield. I am a master of deception when needs be," Asher agreed.

"My lord, the news about the Prince of Darkness?" Renfield probed.

Asher sighed. "You know, Renfield, sometimes you are such an old fuddy duddy. No joy in you at all." But with those words, Asher began to explain what had occurred, and the information he had gleaned most brilliantly about his archenemy.

Jane hid outside. Her husband was so aminated, the sound of his voice carried out into the corridor beyond the hall where she crouched in deep shadow, listening avidly to anything she could discern.

It had not been her intent to eavesdrop. She had only meant to yell one or two more things she thought up immediately after he left—a development that made her even more enraged, having come up with such pithy and witty comebacks to his taunts after he left the room. This happened to Jane often with her father or cousins. With her cousins, she generally gave as good as she got; with her father, she remained mute. Not so

with her husband. He was going to get his comeup-
pance tonight!

But she'd quickly discovered that Asher was not in
his bedchamber changing. Knowing of the valet's pen-
chant for a late-night glass of brandy, she'd found him
in the library with Renfield. Unfortunately the words
were muffled, and all Jane heard was: "Dracul is my
enemy . . . danger."

Then came the useful words, which would help change
Jane's life forever: ". . . the Birds of Paradise Club, two
nights from now. I have other places . . . tomorrow."

Smiling to herself, Jane crept furtively away. So, her
husband did know Dracul, possibly even where Dracul
was hiding. But more importantly, her husband wasn't
on good terms with the fiendish, unprincipled Prince of
Darkness. This eased her soul.

Tomorrow she would let it slip to Renfield that she
was going to a dinner party at the Huntsley household,
but in reality she would hide by the stables and follow
her husband on his search. If tomorrow night didn't net
Dracul, then she would visit this bird club Asher had al-
luded to. Once inside, perhaps she could determine if
Dracul was a frequent visitor. It shouldn't be too difficult to wing it inside a bird club. After all, she was a
member of the Hummingbird and Parrot Society herself; this Birds of Paradise Club shouldn't be all that
different. She was a little surprised that she hadn't heard
of the club, since she was familiar with most of the
bird-watching societies of London and the surrounding
countryside, but there was nothing to be done about it.

As she opened the door to her bedchamber, Jane
smiled. Her father would be proud of her. She was finally taking the vampire by the fangs—and the *right*
vampire. She would lead her brother to Dracul's lair,
and she could hardly wait to see her cousins' faces when

she and Brandon returned victorious. She could even envision her husband thanking her for ridding him of his deadly foe. He might even begin to trust her then!

Her smile grew wider. Yes, life was going to be good once all this blood and gore was behind her. Perhaps Brandon wouldn't even need her help in the staking. Then she wouldn't have to ruin anyone's cape by throwing up all over it.

The Cemetery Club

The night breeze was cool almost to the point of being chilly. The day before, it had rained in London, leaving a slight smell of damp earth wafting in the wind. The rain had packed the fallen leaves into a spongy cushion, and Jane's feet were silent as she walked. She was dressed to the nines in her fashionable ebony velvet spencer and skirt; if her wily husband did end up spotting her, she wanted to look her best.

Curling mists of gray gave the night a depressing sameness as Jane walked. She followed her husband with a natural grace from years of strict training, flowing from shadow to shadow just as she'd been taught. (This was easier said than done, loaded down with her vampire kit and long skirts.) But her training paid off, as always. She had hated her lessons when she was thirteen, hated the funny little men from the Orient dressed all in black who taught the Van Helsing children in silent stalkings and intricate swordplay. But they were worth it.

She even appreciated some of the later things she'd

247

been taught, the weirder stuff. At age nine, her mother had made her walk with a book on her head for ladylike deportment, while her father made her walk with eggs in her pockets.

Jane smiled suddenly, remembering another of her mother's lessons. But she already had on her best chemise and clean petticoats, just in case the night turned ugly and she was injured.

Her smile faded. There was one thing to count on with the count: He was devious. Jane knew that Dracul had slaughtered much better vampire hunters than herself. And what if he hurt Asher? she wondered. Even though still angry with Asher, she cared deeply for him. Stupid, perhaps, but true. He had stolen into her heart and someday she would steal into his—even if it killed her. But if he was hurt . . . ? She remembered a case where a distant cousin found Dracul's daytime resting place. His head had been sent home in a hatbox. Shuddering, Jane knew she did not want to be face-to-face with her husband in *that* way.

She lifted her chin, strengthening her resolve. Asher had his wife to back him up, even if he was unaware of the fact.

Watching the gaslights dancing about the figure of her moonlit husband, Jane concentrated on pretending that she was the fog, flowing forward unnoticed. So far, she had followed Asher from his favorite club to another less savory club in the East End. So far there had been no sighting of Dracul, but she knew her husband well enough to know that he would leave no gravestone unturned.

Asher walked along the cobblestone streets, his attention on the darkness before him. Few people were out. London had begun growing quieter in direct proportion to the lateness of the hour, and no longer were merchants hawking their wares or dozens of carriages crowding the lanes. His mind was distracted . . . focused on Jane.

He couldn't help but think about her, and about the way she looked last night. Her smile, rare and fleeting, had been filled with warmth for him alone. Until he had mocked and hurt her. Yet his feisty wife had borne the weight of his cruelty like Atlas. That was a rare ability in his exalted world, where everyone seemed so cruel and evil to one another.

She had called him an ass, and had been correct. He'd behaved callously to this woman who now bore his name. He shook his head with real regret. He would make it up to her. At times he found the strange tenderness growing inside him for Jane overwhelming. His plain Jane was neither plain, nor so ordinary. She might not be the usual catch of the day, but perhaps her own rare loveliness was more priceless.

What was he to do with her? He laughed, the sound harsh. He knew exactly what he wanted. He would do it from dusk until dawn's first light, and the next night and the next one after that. If only Jane were Clair. But then, Clair didn't have Jane's magnificent neck or marvelous green-silver eyes. Clair wasn't Jane.

"I'll be double deuced," he muttered. He was going insane. "To think, I prefer a Van Helsing to a Frankenstein!" One family created monsters, the other family killed them.

Jane hurried to catch up. All at once, Asher had turned off the beaten cobblestone street onto a gravel path with heavily foliaged trees, leaving Berkeley Square. His long legs ate up the ground, his black cape flowing behind him. Jane, with her short legs, was hardpressed to maintain speed. Her breath came faster as she concentrated on not tripping.

Suddenly, bird song caused Jane to halt. The beautiful notes . . . Jane would bet her last chocolate that the bird who was warbling was indeed a nightingale. Yet how could that be? The species had not been heard in London for over thirty years.

Jane scanned the darkness, trying to discover the source of the sound. To her left she saw a white owl rise like a plume of smoke and become a faint hint of white against the glittering stars as it winged upward. For an instant she longed to fly free with it, to feel the night breeze in her face.

Scanning the tree line, she tiptoed to a stand of large oaks where the notes might have originated. Once there, she realized that the nightingale must be farther away than she'd thought.

Cocking her head and listening intently, she was disappointed when the notes suddenly vanished. Worse, Jane realized that she was alone—the bird had flown the coop, and so had her husband!

The notion of her husband *flying* away suddenly struck her. She wondered if that were possible. Had Asher just turned into a big rodent and soared off?

"Curses! Foiled again! He's driving me batty," Jane griped. She had always longed to see the transformation of a vampire into a bat. Everyone in the Van Helsing family had laid odds on which of them would be first. Jane's name was always last. Still, so far none of the illustrious Van Helsings had witnessed the mysterious feat.

"How could I be so stupid?" Jane asked herself morosely. Not only had she lost the nightingale, but her husband as well. He might have to face Dracul alone!

"I should have known that a vampire bat in hand is worth some bird in a bush! What a fowl mistake," Jane grumbled as she walked along the deserted path.

Suddenly she caught sight of a wrought iron arch among the trees, and she grinned as she recalled what it signified. "Of course! It's the Rest in Peace Cemetery. Well, Dracul, I think I may have just found your daytime resting place, you crafty old count. Your peace will be anything but restful from now on, if I know my brother."

Her steps considerably lighter, Jane hurried along the pathway into the cemetery. Halting abruptly, she shook her head—it was trouble ahead. Here were the proud and the profane, the glory brigade: her Van Helsing cousins.

"Curses and double curses! Foiled again!" she muttered, taking in the sight before her. Digging in the dirt about five feet away was the dirty half dozen. They were covered in grime, with their cravats askew and mud on their faces. They looked like little boys playing in the sandbox, but then her cousins had always liked having mud on their faces—and getting it on hers. And as they'd matured, their tastes hadn't changed; playing in graves was not only a duty for them, but a joyous hobby.

Jane knew she should make her great escape, run silent, run deep before her cousins discovered her behind enemy lines at the cemetery. But the sight of all her brave-hearted cousins so focused on that one hole gave her pause. Worriedly, she wondered whose grave they were digging up. Had they too unearthed the fact that Dracul had come to Town?

She wanted to kick herself, knowing that cemeteries were one of the top three spots her cousins liked to play, even topping the gaming hells. Of course, their all-time favorite remained brothels.

Her frustrated sigh alerted Jane's cousins to her presence. Her eldest cousin, Dwight, waved her over. Reluctantly Jane obeyed. She really disliked Dwight, with his bullying ways and bulging eyes.

"Well, well, little Ethel Jane," he said. "What are you doing out and about? Or should I call you Countess?"

Jane eyed her cousin's portly figure. Apparently he'd

lost the battle of the bulge since she'd had seen him two years before. His waistcoat had popped two buttons, his protruding stomach a clear winner.

Dwight, as eldest of all the cousins, had lorded over them mercilessly in the nursery days, and he still did now. But since Jane was a female, he was more ruthless to her. As a child, he had put spiders in her bed and caused her to go into fits. Frogs had gone into the fake coffins where she was to stake vampire mummy dummies. She had given those to Clair's uncle for experiments.

"Well, well, it's just one big happy family," Jane retorted. She knew she needed to keep on her toes. Dwight wasn't the quickest guy around, but her third eldest cousin, George, was. She couldn't let any of them know why she was out lurking in the cemetery. She couldn't let them realize that Asher was a vampire, either. Dwight, the toadeater that he was, would take great delight in staking a noble.

"Of course," George spoke up. "Jane, what are you doing out here alone?"

"I was bird-watching. Following the song of a nightingale," she answered primly.

Dwight grabbed her arm and yanked her to him, while the youngest and smallest, Jemeny, chortled. His nickname was Cricket, due to his large bug eyes and his habit of popping his joints. If Jane could wish upon a star, she would wish herself well away from here—far, far away.

"Try again," George ordered coldly, moving to Jane's right while Dwight held her fast. George was bright, and loyal to the Van Helsing name, but had little compassion for the weak. He would die for her, if asked, but he could also be ruthless. Most times Jane admired George's intensity. Tonight was not one of those times.

"I find it highly suspicious that a new bride would be

out in a cemetery at night. Where is your husband, the
earl? Why aren't you with him?" George questioned.

Dwight laughed. "If I were married to Jane, I'd be
out and about too."

Jane, George and Jemeny all glared indignantly at him.

"Well, I would," Dwight said. "Besides, you didn't
answer the question. Are you hunting? Is there a vampire you're seeking? Perhaps the one we think is taking
the prostitutes? The one who no doubt made Lady
Veronique one of his own?"

"Why are you so sure it's vampires?" she asked.

"Who else? Some Nosferatu nest must have moved
into London," Dwight answered. "But we Van Helsings
will show them what's what." He finished, squeezing
Jane's arm tighter, pinching her flesh in his strong grip.

Jane jerked her arm back with all her strength, dis-
lodging Dwight's grip, but she tumbled back into the
opened grave with a muffled shriek. With a loud bump,
she landed on the coffin inside. Luckily for her tailbone,
there was a thick pad of dirt.

Feeling the casket underneath her, Jane began to
panic. What if her uninvited visit had alerted or awakened a vampire within?

"Get me out of here now!" she cried.

Throwing her arms upward toward the yawning
opening above, she leapt; listening to her cousins' guf-
faws. Once again, she had provided her barbaric cousins
amusement at her expense. Just once she wished she
could see pride in their eyes instead of derision.

Hopping up and down, she managed to see four of
her cousins. They were lying on the ground, rolling
about with tears of mirth streaking down their faces.
George, the least dirty of the half dozen, was still on his
feet. He stood near Douglas, the second youngest, who
was braying like a jackass.

"Don't look now, Ethel Jane, but you fell into a grave," Douglas mocked.

"Wonder what will pop up this time?" Steven Ray added.

Jane was beginning to feel like a bouncing ball. "Please, please, give me a hand and get me out of here."

"Tell us the truth and we will," George advised, his laughter fading as he bent over the grave. Soon Douglas joined his brother. To Jane, they were silhouettes in black against the soft glow of the moon. "You see, Jane, we've heard a rumor that something wicked this way is coming. Something big with big, white fangs. Have you heard anything to that effect?"

"I am a new bride. The only big thing I've heard about is Orville. Asher let him come live with us."

Douglas shook his head. "Jane, Jane, your nose grows when you tell a lie."

"It's really long right now," Jemeny added, his face a dark blob at the top of the grave.

"Quit pulling my strings. I'm not lying. I know nothing of any rumors," Jane managed, crossing her fingers behind her back. "I'm your cousin, a blood relation. Get me out of here. It wouldn't do the Van Helsing name any honor if I were found frozen to death in this grave. Or worse." Worse being, having her throat torn out. The thought made her queasy, and she leaned against the cold dirt wall of the hole.

"It's not that cold," George argued pragmatically.

"Well, it wouldn't do my reputation any good if I was found *not frozen* in the graveyard, either. I don't think my husband, the earl, would countenance all the gossip that would ensue."

Dwight seemed to consider. He wouldn't relish the Earl of Wolverton being angry with him.

"Come on, Dwight, George, help me up," Jane begged. She wiped her dirty hands on her gown. Realizing that she had once again ruined dress, she muttered, "Humbug!" At this rate, she would be naked by January.

Frowning, she tried and failed to tuck her hair back into its elegant French twist. Her dress was ruined, her hair was a mess, she was stuck in a grave, her cousins brayed like jackasses—this was not the way to spend a happy night. This was certainly not one of her finer moments.

"We probably should let her out," Jemeny advised.

"Yes, you should," Jane agreed. She had always liked Jemeny. He had a sweet disposition, except when he was playing a prank.

Encouraged, Jane continued, "Uncle Jakob might wonder why his gentlemen sons were less than gallant to their female cousin, even to the point of endangering her. And my husband might call one or two of you out to a duel." He probably really wouldn't, since he could care less about her. However, her barbaric cousins didn't know that, Jane decided ruefully.

"When Jane is right—which isn't often—she is right," George conceded.

Jane sighed. Her calves were beginning to cramp from jumping up and down and she had hurt her leg slightly when she fell. She let out a shout. "All right, my fine fellows, I'm warning you that I've had enough. I don't intend to spend the night in the cemetery with whatever or whoever is or was in this grave. By the way, whose grave is it?" Hopefully it was someone of a cheerful disposition, if they were undead—a good-natured vampire or ghost who wouldn't be upset about her stepping on his home or her cousins' invasion of it.

"The casket you're standing on belongs to a vampire fledgling. A babe in the tomb, so to speak. A prostitute—one of those prostitutes," George informed her. "We were going to stake her, but nobody was at home."

"We were covering the grave back up when you dropped in," Jemeny stated.

Jane exclaimed, "That's right. They found one of the prostitutes with holes in her neck."

Dwight leaned over the grave, smiling smugly. "My connections are superior to yours. They found one prostitute with holes in her neck, drained, and one dismembered. Definitely the work of vampires."

"Yuck," Jane said, her face paling. "Get me out of here now." It had to be Dracul who was doing these heinous deeds. And they had to stop him.

Reaching down, Jemeny gave Jane a hand up. They had apparently teased her enough.

She smiled brilliantly at her bug-eyed cousin. "Thanks." She turned in a circle, glaring at the rest of her rambunctious relatives. "You should be ashamed of yourselves," she chided.

"Do you think?" George asked.

Jane shook her head. "Oh, never mind. I need to be getting myself home."

"Do you need an escort?" George asked.

"No, thanks. I'll be fine," she replied. And she turned and headed toward the cemetery gates, as dignified and ladylike as she could be with her gown torn and her hair hanging in tangled wisps around her face.

Glancing up at the star-studded night, Jane made a wish. "I wish my cousins would all turn into frogs." The thought made her smile. Then, glancing back up at the heavens, she added silently, *I wish my husband would love me*, and that Dracul would die with a horrified frown on his fanged face.

Now, if only her dreams could come true.

Birds of a Feather

"Curses! Foiled again!" Some wonderful subterfuge I planned, Jane thought sardonically as she eyed the overdone interior of the bedroom where she'd been forcibly placed. "A brothel by any other name would sell ass, teats."

She had wondered at Asher's interest in bird-watching when she'd heard him and Renfield discussing this club. She had been so excited to think that they shared a love of feathered friends; they would have something in common to discuss over the upcoming years. But . . .

"Humbug! Bird-watching, my aunt Fanny," she groused. "What a silly goose I am."

Because of her husband's comment, Jane had come unescorted and in disguise to scout out this so-called bird club. And when Madame Saunders and her husband, the henpecked colonel, had asked if she was experienced, Jane had answered briskly, "Of course." After all, nobody knew birds better than she. However, it wasn't avian experience Madame Saunders was inter-

ested in. More like, experience in all kinds of cocks—
large, small, fighting cocks or placid cocks, a veritable
birdhouse full of cocks.

Yes, unfortunately Jane's assumptions had been quite
wrong. The Birds of Paradise Club was a brothel that
catered to gentlemen with an appalling lack of taste, she
thought critically, surveying the scarlet and gold fur-
nishings of the bedchamber she was in. A huge bird-
cage, empty for the moment, hung from the ceiling. It
had bright scarlet cushions and was large enough to ac-
commodate Orville.

"Yes, definitely no sense of class," Jane mumbled to
herself. And these would be gentlemen, if they could be
called that at all, who had strange taste in bedfellows. As
Jane was unceremoniously dragged into the room, she'd
caught a glimpse of a few of the soiled doves, who were
probably in this line of work because they didn't have a
feather to fly with. Although . . . one tart was actually
dressed as a dove, and the others wore various skimpy
costumes that resembled birds, plumage included.

Jane had spied a Madagascar cock, a form of lovebird,
dressed up in white, green and yellow feathers. To the
right of her, Jane had seen a robin redbreast—and what
breasts she displayed in her tight red costume! Jane next
swallowed a gasp upon glimpsing a darkwing duck
whose few feathers barely covered her chest and the
area just below. The plucky duck's jaunty little costume
also revealed long white legs, showcased by the thigh-
high cut in her gown, and two gentlemen followed her
like it was hunting season.

Pouring herself a glass of wine, Jane scrunched up her
brow. Due to her concern for Asher, Dracul and her
brother, she now found herself stuck in a house of dodos,
with herself possibly being the biggest birdbrain of all.

She shook her head and glanced around her, com-
menting, "Madame Saunders's decorator must have

kicked the bucket. How can she use bright purple pillows with a red-and-gold wall and bedspread?"

Taking a rather large sip of wine, Jane grimaced. The ruby-colored drink had a strange sweet taste. Actually, it was too sweet even for her, who had a sweet tooth. But since Jane was thirsty, she drank more and pondered her regrettable situation.

She knew exactly what the major would say of her mistake, and it wouldn't be complimentary; he'd be off and running, calling her bird-witted. And this time, he would be absolutely right. She should have realized what this club really was when Madame Saunders smiled that lecherous smile, looking her over from top to bottom. She should have noticed the woman's feathered bonnet and gray down slippers. But no, Jane berated herself, she had continued blindly on when the madam asked her if she was interested in work.

"Of course. I am quite knowledgeable about these things," Jane had said, thinking that, while working at night, she might find out something more about Dracul. She'd figured she could handle any questions about birds, or even clean out a few cages if that was the type work needed for the vulgarly dressed, over-rouged mistress of the society. "And I'm not afraid to get my hands soiled," she'd added.

Colonel Saunders had laughed lewdly, saying, "I imagine more than your hands will get soiled, my quaint little pigeon."

Jane had wondered about that comment at the time. More the fool was she, for on the way to the bedchamber Jane realized exactly where she was. And although she had never seen a brothel in person, it appeared as if she was being held captive in one now. She was stuck here; her chickens had come home to roost.

What would happen when Asher arrived? she found herself wondering.

"He's going to wring my neck. No man wants his wife found in a house of ill repute." Although she had heard that Lord Ferguson's late wife was found in one two years ago.

"Now Asher has *another* reason to find me distasteful," Jane complained dispiritedly. How would she explain what she was doing here? Her eyes crossed as she tried to come up with a believable and plausible explanation, but it looked like her husband would roast her alive when he found her cooped up here.

Perhaps, if she was lucky, when they finally let her out of this room to ply her trade, or to do whatever these ladies—or rather birds—of the evening did, she could silently sneak away. Sneak away long before Asher even knew she had set her dainty, ladylike foot in this debauched place.

"This debacle is just like something Clair would get into. It really cooks my goose that I was so hen-witted to be taken in by those two foxes!"

Grimacing, she pondered letting Asher simply find her. Maybe it would do him some good. After all, he had been coming here for whatever married couples did behind closed doors, flocking together with all manner of plumed and beaky tarts. His infidelity hurt terribly; it made her so mad, she could actually see a red deeper than the crimson hues of the bedchamber. Jane knew that if she found out exactly which soiled doves had flown on the wings of passion with her beguiling husband, she would swiftly roast them alive.

Yes, while Jane had been dreaming of Asher's kisses, longing for him to hold her tight in the security of his arms, he had been cooing to some other bird. While she had been garnering courage to be so bold as to touch him, her husband had been flying high with the high fliers in this place. Oh, how she wanted to cry, "Foul fowl!"

The more she thought, the angrier at Asher she became. He was a cooked goose, and he didn't even know it yet. From now on, the only feathers he would pluck would be hers. Ha! The stupid, vain, pompous cock—bedding everybody in this feathery den of iniquity and leaving her cooped up at home. She poured herself another glass of wine. While she had been trying to be the perfect wife, trying to make him realize he'd wed a golden goose, he had been out cavorting with loose women.

"I should have been planting a stake right through his black heart," she remarked bitterly.

Jane drank some more wine, wishing it was brandy. "Well, once bitten, twice shy," she muttered. She hardly noticed her words beginning to slur as the drug in the wine took effect. All this time she'd been pining for his kisses, and her husband was coming to this nest of infamy. Suddenly the thought struck her as funny, and she began to giggle.

She was still giggling when the bedchamber door opened and a female of questionable repute walked in with a bright yellow costume. "This 'eres for you," the woman remarked, holding out the feathered outfit.

"Me?" Jane giggled, befuddled by the laudanum in her wine. "What is it supposed to be?" she asked. She examined the plumage of yellow and peach.

"A golden cherry lovebird," the whore replied.

Jane giggled some more. If they thought she was going to go out dressed like that, then they certainly had another think coming! "No, I don't think so. I need a costume with a little more covering," Jane said owlishly, holding up the garb. She felt very dizzy.

"Sorry, ducks," the whore replied. "This 'ere's the costume the madam said you're to wear."

Jane grinned stupidly. "No! Not enough feathers in the right places." She shook her head.

Minda Webber

The whore dismissed her protestations and helped her into the costume. The gown was cut to display Jane's ample breasts. Peach and green feathers barely covered the low-cut neckline, and it had a plunging V in the back. A peach-colored mask, along with a pale yellow wig of soft curls, covered her features.

"At least I don't look like me," Jane mused, staring dizzily at her reflection in the mirror. In spite of the shocking amount of skin the costume revealed, she couldn't help admiring the way the gown enhanced her figure. "I look like a real highflier now," she commented woozily.

"Yes, um, a real prime piece," the whore agreed.

"I should be disgusted. I should be horrified," Jane stated firmly, then giggled. "But I'm not. Why am I not?"

The whore grinned, glancing over at the wine. "Madame Saunders always gives the new chicks her special something along with the elderberry wine—to help 'em with the jitters the first few times. Madame likes the new girls not to feel no shyness."

Jane grinned stupidly. "I've been drugged, then?"

"You have."

"Well, what an amazing thing! I feel wonderfully free. Like the breeze. Like a bird flying high." She knew tomorrow she would be mad, embarrassed and quite ashamed. But right now all she hoped was that Asher liked her costume enough to pluck her feathers one by one. "Why, the colors of the room don't look so garish now," she added in amusement.

Several nonsensical minutes later, Jane found herself in a room filled with soiled doves of every type, color, size and plumage, the feathers shimmering as the women sashayed about, lifting and flying everywhere. There were short birds, stout ones, thin ones, tall ones, but all were decked out in their fine-feathered best.

Jane started to giggle, whispering, "Duck, duck, goose."

There was also a female stuffed into a quail costume, whom Jane figured had a fondness for chocolates like her own. And there was a duck who introduced herself as Ala Orange. The bright color of her feathers stood out starkly.

There was a woodpecker, a tall, lithe brunette who in the scheme of things, seemed to have first crack at the gentlemen around her. She seductively fluttered her fan and feathers, and was quickly given her pecking orders.

Another of the exotic birds was warbling a soft, high tune, swaying to the beat of her own music and one glass too many of the rich ruby wine. Two gentlemen stood nearby, ogling her.

Jane watched it all, a look of awe in her eyes. So this was seduction. She wondered if she could walk the way these ladies of the evening did. Would that attract her husband? Would he even notice?

Gentlemen of every size and shape were in the room. Some were only gaping at the fancily costumed girls, while others appeared to be sampling. Jane shuddered. She could tell that more than a few were shape-shifters; she could feel their scalding heat warming the room. She could also sense the cold of the grave coming off three of the guests; she just wasn't sure which ones, the drug having clouded her senses. However, she didn't feel as if any of the vampires was a threat.

"I can't believe the Count of Corruption isn't here. And neither is my bird-wenching husband," Jane said to herself.

In spite of the tranquility she was feeling, she still suffered a twinge of anxiety. But she was being silly. Even her own father wouldn't recognize her.

And yet, prudence would be the better part of valor,

she decided, as she gazed down at the lack of material on her costume. The Countess of Wolverton could never be caught in such a compromised situation. Asher would never forgive her. The major would never forgive her. Society would never forgive her. Her cousins would think it a great lark and never let her hear the end of it.

She sighed, the dreamlike quality of being drugged starting to make her feel melancholy, but she saw a tall blond-headed man alone, watching her. The man had come out of nowhere, slipping from the shadows in the corner of the room. His demeanor was intense and unsettling. He was very tall and slender. He wore a mask that covered most of his face, like several other gentlemen in the spacious, garish room. The stranger's eyes were very blue, and they were directed at her prominently displayed cleavage.

Jane gulped and began to wobble over to a side door she had just noted. The stranger looked like he would eat her alive, and she was positive she'd seen those cruel blue eyes somewhere before. Taking a quick glance back, she noticed he appeared to be studying robin redbreast now, rather than herself. A rush of relief hit her as she thankfully backed into a hallway, leaving behind the chattering magpies and their customers.

Weaving slightly, she made her way to a room at the far end of the twisting hall. Jane glanced inside. It was a smoking parlor. Jane peered around the corner, trying to see if the room was empty, and if it had a balcony or exit to the outside world.

The room was empty. Breathing a sigh of relief, she noted there were French doors leading to a balcony too. Giddily Jane made her way inside, and had started for the French doors when a sound behind her made her turn.

"Wait, *chèrie*. Where is my little bird flying?"

Jane reeled dizzily, almost falling over beak-first. The tall blond stranger stood there. His deep blue eyes were hard and glittering. He projected an aura of malignancy that made her skin crawl.

He approached so smoothly that it looked as if his feet barely touched the ground, and he arrived before her in all his splendid menace.

"What a rare bird you are," he said, his voice betraying a foreign accent. "Are you taken for tonight?"

Jane blushed. "I . . . I . . . y-yes," she stammered. This was even more embarrassing than she'd feared. She wished he would quit staring at her as though she was a succulent piece of fowl and he, the fox. She wished Asher would stare at her like this—without the malevolence, of course.

The stranger glanced around and then arched a brow.

"I . . . He'll be here soon," Jane finally managed to say, her heart beating furiously in her chest. This man was grilling her!

He smiled wickedly, taking her small hand into his. "Who is your protector?" he coaxed.

Jane tried to think it through. But the drugs clouded her mind, along with a black streak of terror. The man's touch was as cold as the grave. His eyes were strangely alien. Yes, he was a strange stranger. "I . . . The earl, Ash—" She gasped, cutting herself off.

Blinking her eyes shut, Jane wanted to pound her head against the wall. He was the man costumed as a dark knight at the masquerade ball. The one who had been whispering with Lady Veronique, who had left with her the night before she disappeared. She hadn't meant to say his name. With an instinct old as time, she knew the man standing before her was a danger to both herself and her husband. Could he be the Prince of Darkness; her quarry? But if he was, then why did her senses keep crying wolf? He gave off the energy of a shape-shifter, while his touch felt colder than the grave.

"Stupid, stupid," she muttered, criticizing herself. She didn't want this masked man to connect her to Asher.

It seemed the stranger took offense to her words, for he drew himself taller, and a strange animosity flowed off him, radiating to her in sinister waves. "Pardon," he said.

"No, it's nothing. I meant the Earl of . . ." Jane hesitated, her drugged mind scrambling for a name. "The Duke of Earl," she replied at last. Then she wanted to drop down dead. There was no such personage as the Duke of Earl.

The stranger ignored her, lifting her hand for a kiss. His frozen stare nearly caused Jane's heart to stop in her chest. Vampire or wolf? Vampire or wolf? Where were her stakes? Back at the Van Helsing manor. Humbug! she cursed silently. Where was a good stake when you needed one—or a silver bullet?

Jane tugged on her hand uselessly, feeling as if it were clutched in a stone vise. The man's strength was greater than a mortal's, but her senses, clouded by the laudanum, couldn't tell any more than that. Finally, as there was such a strong sense of wolf about him, she decided he was a werewolf rather than a vampire.

"I was correct," the stranger remarked, and oddly he gave a hideous smile full of both beauty and evil. He bent to kiss her hand.

Feeling a slight sting, Jane gasped as heat flowed through her. Jerking back on her hand, she tried to tear it away from this threatening predator . . . to no avail.

"No, my little one. Do not fear. You will be mine," he commented knowingly. Then he leaned in closer to Jane, staring at her neck as if fascinated by the rich blood flowing there.

He's going to eat me up in one bite, Jane thought

with horror. And there will be no one to stop him. I am at his mercy, and I doubt he even knows the meaning of the word!

But before the stranger could do more than move a step closer, a loud man with a bulbous nose entered the smoking parlor with the Madagascar cock. "I say, the Earl of Wolverton is here," he commented. "Didn't he get married to that Van Helsing chit?"

"I 'eard 'he was married, but ye couldn't tell it by me. He's been here twice this week, he has," the lovebird chirped.

The masked stranger lifted his head, his eyes shooting blue fire at the interruption. Bowing gracefully to Jane, he smiled. It was a threatening look. "Until later."

Startled, Jane found herself suddenly watching the fearsome man exiting by route of the balcony. Dressed all in black, he faded into the night as if he had never been.

Jane began to shiver, instinctively realizing that she had been the quarry of the tall, eerie stranger. The arrival of the big-nosed man and his cock had possibly saved her life. But if she weren't careful, she was going to find herself in a quandary with her husband, if she couldn't manage to sneak away before he spotted her.

Trying to gather her befuddled wits, she fled through the doorway, straight into the arms of a well-muscled gentleman. Unsurprisingly, it was the one vampire in the entire world she was hoping to avoid: her husband, the Earl of Deceit and Lechery.

"Curses!" She had definitely jumped out of the frying pan and into the fire. She wanted to crow to the heavens. This was just not her night.

The Earl held out his arms, carefully inspecting the feathered female who had run into him while hastily exiting the smoking parlor. Shaking her head, Jane deduced there was nothing to do but brazen it out, to pretend that she was what she was supposed to be and not what she really was. Maybe Asher wouldn't recognize her—if she could find a thimbleful of luck tonight.

Disguising her voice, Jane remarked, "I've got to go, me lord. I've got a protector awaitin' me."

Stunned, Neil Asher looked down at the woman in his arms.

He couldn't believe it.

He wouldn't believe it.

The Countess of Wolverton was in the Birds of Paradise Club, dressed as a feathered doxy. He ruled the roost at home, and yet here was his wife in a brothel. What else did he not know about his domestic matters? The question chilled him.

His wife!

"If you wouldn't mind letting me go, luv," Jane said, her words slurring slightly.

Dropping his hands from her shoulders before he wrung her lovely neck, Asher stepped back, getting his first full look at the total costume of this golden cherry lovebird. He narrowed his eyes in anger, yet his mouth watered. His wife was a kaleidoscope of many things:

Delicious.

Delectable.

Desirable. Utterly, maddeningly desirable.

He would feast tonight. He would dip his quill into her brightly colored ink pot, he decided lustily, his fierce desire tamping down his anger, and he would write his name on her forever.

Jane grinned giddily. She was having a bit of luck after all. Her husband didn't recognize her!

Flocking Awesome

Asher knew his wife didn't think that he recognized her, but he knew exactly who the scantily dressed female in front of him was. It was his very own calamity Jane, his impossible wife. He didn't know if he wanted to pluck her, stuff her or eat her raw. But he did know that he needed to get her someplace alone, and quickly before anyone else recognized her. Although who would ever believe that his countess would be dressed up in a bird costume in the most infamous brothel in London? Certainly not anyone sane.

Glaring at her overly exposed breasts, Asher growled, "Your bedchamber. Now!" He was going to give her more than a piece of his mind. Did she not know the dignity required of their station in life? Did she not recognize the proud lineage she was now a part of? How could his wife have ended up in a brothel? This was monstrous, even for a Van Helsing. And if he wasn't mistaken, his wife was inebriated again.

"You maddening little minx!" he growled.

Jane flinched. She could feel the old coffin lid slamming shut. She'd been wrong; her husband knew exactly who she was. Master vampires lived a long time, mainly because they weren't short on intelligence. "Would you believe I got lost on my way to the museum?" she asked.

He glowered at her.

"You'll never believe it, but a funny thing happened on the way to the bird-watching forum," Jane tried, throwing another flimsy excuse into the arena as she backed her way toward the bedchamber where she'd begun this whole escapade. But at his glowering look and growling grunts, Jane decided she would save the last of her excuses for a rainy day.

Scrunching her eyes closed, which had seemed to see double in the last few moments, she decided the truth was probably the best of all answers. She pointed to the bedchamber door, which Asher slammed open in exasperation and he shoved her inside.

Before Jane could open her mouth, Asher slammed the door shut and backed her against it. This bird-bedecked spouse was a burden he wouldn't wish on his worst enemy, no matter how seductively charming she was. He was going to give her what she deserved. He would tell her exactly what he thought of her constant folly.

But as he opened his mouth to yell, Asher took a deep breath. She looked so delicious, what with her pink mouth and feathered costume, that instead he lowered his head and kissed her. But he made the kiss hard and punishing. His hand rose to tear off her blond wig, scattering the hairpins that held it in place, letting her real hair fall loose and straight down her back, the way he liked it best.

"I don't want you, Jane," he snarled, kissing her again with a hunger so intense and greedy that it stunned him. He was supposed to be questioning her, berating her or perhaps spanking her pert fanny covered in those soft feathers. Hmm. That last part had distinct possibilities.

As her lord and master vampire, he was supposed to be raging at her. He was supposed to be making her crawl to him on her hands and knees to plead for forgiveness. The idea nearly sent him to his own knees, imagining Jane sunken down before him, his cock in her soft, pink mouth. He groaned.

"No, Jane. I don't want you one tiny bit, you wayward little witch." And with those words, he tenderly clasped her breast, palming the nipple. Too many intense emotions had been building between them; he had to let them out.

His other hand began to caress her stomach in tiny circles, and a slow heat began to build as his fingers danced across her skin. He dipped that hand lower, finding the patch of hair over her nether lips. The action caused Jane to tense in his arms, her thighs locking against his hand. He caressed her until she relaxed.

Startled, surprised, bemused and still a bit dazed from the wine, Jane felt heat shooting through her as her husband's fingers gently stroked her. She gasped, her body arching tightly against his, making them both groan. What he was doing felt so marvelously wonderful, causing a sweet ache she'd never known. She felt like warbling to the heavens. "Oh, Asher. Don't stop."

She heard a low, needy sound. Intrigued, Jane opened her eyes, looking at her husband. He was staring at her breasts with a hunger that made her blood sing. The sky was falling, but she was no Chicken Little. She would follow wherever her husband led.

"You are such a handsome vampire," she said. And for once, Neil Asher's arrogant composure looked broken. His blue eyes, which were normally so glacial, appeared to be warming. It was amazing. Asher was melting, and there hadn't been any holy water, only her silky underplumage.

"And you are driving me to bedlam, my feathery temptress," he replied.

Jane snuggled closer, pressing her bosoms further into his hand, rubbing her leg up and down his. He shivered, and Jane exalted in her womanly power.

Contact with his muscular body was all she craved at the moment; she violently searched for something she couldn't name but knew with an instinct as old as time was just beyond reach. With Asher she could not only make the journey, but could reach the shining destination as well. She compulsively kissed his neck and ran her hands over his shoulders in feathery touches. He reacted by sliding his hands over her buttocks, pulling her closer to his hard, throbbing erection.

Jane gasped, and he picked her up and in three steps reached the bed. Dropping her onto it, Asher leaned over and gripped her gown. In one powerful tug, he tore the garment in two, exposing her voluptuous body to his view. Feathers flew.

This time, Asher gasped. His wife was all round and pale perfection, with nipples the hue of rosy coral. Warning chimes sounded in the back of his head. Dimly he realized that he shouldn't be doing this. Jane was his unwanted, unlikeable, undesirable wife. But he did want her, with a fierceness he found frightening. He desperately needed to sink his oar into her pink, wet sea and row to the moon.

"Bloody hell, Jane, you're perfect!" he growled, lowering himself onto his wife's delectable body, his lips brushing the column of her neck. He nibbled and nipped, and she squirmed beneath him, clearly wanting something she had no name for. Her lower body was likely in an agony of pleasure and suspense. She was on fire. "Marvelously perfect."

"Well, cock-a-doodle-do," Jane gasped.

Asher laughed, and continued his seductive assault. Jane was amazing. What other female could make him laugh when he was so aroused that he thought he'd explode?

Her husband's hot breath made Jane feel as if she were soaring high and free, entangled with soft, puffy clouds. His questing hands pebbling her nipples made her want to cry out. Suddenly he latched onto her right breast, sucking the nipple into his mouth, laving it with his tongue. Her arms tightened around his broad shoulders, and her heart began pounding in her chest.

Her breathing became short and raspy, for his fingers had inserted themselves into her damp, hot core. She arched back, her long white neck tilted, her hair a satin waterfall on the pillow beside her. She screamed in pleasure as she flew proud and free, soaring to heaven like an eagle in flight.

"No, my dear wife, I don't want you," Asher lied, his eyes ablaze with passion's hot flame. Positioning himself between her soft, plump thighs, he undid the buttons of his pants and his sex sprang free, hardened and huge. Staring at his wife, Asher noted how becoming was the flush of desire on her skin.

In a rush of tenderness, he realized quite unexpectedly that his wife was beautiful in a way no other woman was. He couldn't describe it, but knew it to be true. Never had he seen such delicious surrender, or passion; and she was his. She was beyond ordinary—perhaps even far beyond ordinary.

"How I crave you," he gasped. The thought disturbed him at the same time it pleased him. She was his, this venal Van Helsing whom he had found in this brothel. He should be yelling at her right now.

Yelling, he took her, breaking through her virginity in one hard thrust.

"You're mine, Jane. Mine!"

Jane screamed too, causing him to halt. Using all his self-discipline, Asher forced himself to hold still inside her. He wasn't certain he could do it, since his tiny wife was so tight and hot; he felt like he was going up in flames. Staring down at her upturned face, Asher tried not to move, but his every instinct cried out for continued plundering. Jane was so tight, so wet, and for the first time in an age, everything felt . . . right. To be inside her now was like coming home to a sunlit meadow after a winter of icy despair.

"Shh. It will be fine in a few moments," he consoled, kissing her tenderly. She kissed him back, her tongue dancing with his in the most carnal experience he'd ever encountered.

The kiss grew, became hungrier as he caught the scent of her virgin's blood. His fangs extended, Asher began kissing her magnificent neck, admiring its slender beauty, its sweet, spicy taste. The pulse beating rapidly there almost drove him mad.

Jane felt a small prick, and she pushed her husband away from her neck. In spite of the torrid heat inside her, and despite the voice crying in her head for total surrender, her breeding had come to the fore.

"No biting," she managed to say, her voice coming out in a soft pant.

Asher grinned wickedly. "Come now, Jane, my bark is much worse than my bite."

Again, she shook her head. "No biting allowed." Then she moaned as Asher thrust inside her. Slowly at first—then his long, hard strokes robbed her of breath.

Suddenly he stopped. In a lightning-quick move, he went from lying atop Jane to kneeling between her legs. There he lowered his head and partook, laving and tonguing Jane until she screamed for mercy. Tiny pinpricks of white light flashed through her head, erupting into a starburst of purple. She was flying high and free like a winged bird, higher and higher than was even possible. She was soaring amongst the stars, floating there, going where eagles dared. She suddenly felt a great wetness between her legs, and a lethargy that felt quite wonderful.

Before his wife could catch her breath, Asher rose and pushed himself inside her, her muscles still clenching from her climax. How he wanted to crow to all the world! He growled instead, overtaken by lust.

Thrusting harder and harder, he made her body come alive. Straining and kissing her, he pushed deep, loving the way she fit around him. He heard her scream, and he smiled. She had screamed loud enough to wake the dead this time, and her third earthshaking climax had her bucking and pitching beneath him.

Thrusting violently, he felt the headboard move as he came. His back arched, his head thrown back, his eyelids closed tight in the throes of ecstasy, and he cried out her name. Then he collapsed at Jane's side, one arm thrown over his head, his entire body sluggish.

Glancing over at him, Jane decided her husband looked like the cat who ate the canary. He was quite beautiful, this husband of hers. "I'm so glad you don't want me," she teased impishly.

Feeling her eyes upon him, Asher opened his own. He knew he should say something. They had just made glorious bed-burning love. And her blood tasted of . . . je ne sais quoi—an undefinable something that he had never tasted before. It was almost frightening to think that his wife tasted so good. To think that a Van Helsing could make his body sing was insane.

Asher grimaced. The Fates had dealt him a cruel, cruel blow. His sparrow of a wife was really an exotic bird in disguise.

Narrowing his eyes again, he rose from the bed, turning his back on her. She deserved a scolding, not praise. "I want you to tell me the truth this time. What in the bloody hell are you doing here?"

With the aftereffects of the drugs and the lovemaking, Jane had been feeling happy, sated, befuddled and bemused. She wanted poetic words and sweet kisses; yet her bad luck of the night had resumed. Her husband was scolding her. The cheek of the man! Yet, what nice cheeks they were, she thought as she stared at the firm contours of his buttocks outlined by his skintight black breeches. "Wh-what?" she finally managed to stammer.

Throwing her his cloak, he stated coldly, "Put that on. Now, what are you doing here?"

Ignoring the cloak and her nudity, Jane stood and shoved her finger into his chest. Asher's words were stripping away her love-induced, drug-induced haze, and sobriety came hard upon her. A kaleidoscope of images flowed through her mind: Asher and feathers and cockatoos and cocks.

"You question me? After . . ." Jane fell short, her quiet well of content poisoned by anger. She tried again: "You come here to this den of sin after ignoring me on our wedding night and all the nights after. You question me, when I find that you frequent this . . ." She hesitated, enraged, glancing around at the hideous décor of the bedchamber. "This place! Really, Asher, Madame Saunders has such abysmal taste. How can you even come here when the colors are so garish? You, who are such a stickler for refinement!" Jane finished hotly, staring at him scornfully.

"It is quite beneath your dignity to flee to this perverse place. Even if the women do dress up as your bird of choice to feast upon. It is so . . . weak."

"Don't call me chicken for coming to Madame Saunders's. And don't try and turn this around on me," Asher warned, his eyes an icy blue. He shoved her finger away.

"You naughty old Nosferatu, you fornicating fiend, you rutting old roué!" Jane accused.

Asher glared at her. "I am not an old roué!" He hated the image that came to mind: an older man of the *ton*, gouty knees, a corseted waist, thinning hair, trying desperately to seduce the young and beautiful. Why, he wasn't even four hundred years old yet.

"Ha! You are older than the oldest old roué in London," she snapped.

Asher opened his mouth to argue, but she spoke the truth.

"You are a libertine. A whoremonger who has a fetish for birds!" Jane yelled. Then she added curtly, "Particularly soiled doves."

"I am a vampire with needs," he shouted back.

"Which I would be more than happy to attend," Jane responded. Then she wished she had bitten her tongue before revealing how much she longed to be his wife in every sense of the word.

Asher's eyes took on a gleam as he recalled her enthusiastic response, screaming his name as she climaxed, and the sweet-tart taste of her blood. His plan had been to ignore his unwanted wife. But plans could change. A master vampire was nothing if not mutable. "Fine," he said.

"Fine what?" Jane asked warily.

"You can attend my needs," he stated offhandedly, not wanting her to see that the fires of desire were stirring once more to life in him. He glanced at the heinous décor of the bedchamber. Jane was right; the room was garish beyond belief. Odd, that he had never noticed before. He would need to speak to Madame Saunders about redecorating. That is, if he ever decided to return. He also would give notice to his mistresses.

"No more highfliers?" Jane asked hopefully.

Asher cocked a brow. "Not as long as you attend my

needs as well as you have tonight." Yes, he would definitely give notice to his mistresses tomorrow. He would see to it that his man of affairs got them nice sets of diamonds as a parting gift. Perhaps Jane would like a set of emeralds. They would go beautifully with her eyes. "I must admit you are quite spectacular. Beyond spectacular I guess."

Jane blushed and, grabbing his cloak, she pulled it about her to hide her face from view. She didn't want Asher to see the joy his words brought her. Somehow, against all odds, she had fallen in love with her roguish vampire husband.

"Here." Asher shoved a handkerchief her way. "Wipe off that ridiculous make-up."

Jane complied.

"Now, why are you here tonight?" Asher questioned, staring imperiously at her. "I want the truth, Jane. No more prevaricating. Can you do that?"

His words hurt her deeply. Of course she intended to tell the truth.

Eventually.

Hiding her pain, Jane concisely explained how her brother was looking for Dracul and why. Her husband scowled fiercely, admonishing her with dire warnings of Dracul's black deeds. She sighed. She was a Van Helsing. She knew all about the count. There was no need to beat a dead but. After all, the Prince of Darkness hadn't earned his title by delivering Easter eggs.

After a few minutes of Asher's wrathful scolding, Jane continued, explaining to her irate husband how she had overheard his conversation with Renfield, and of her concern for him.

Asher was clenching his fists by the time his wife finished her explanation. His jaw felt hard as marble. His eyes were so icy that they actually caused chilblains to run up and down her arms. In minute detail, he lectured

Jane about listening to private conversations, although his heart had skipped momentarily when she voiced her worry about him.

Finally, Jane concluded her story with meeting Colonel and Madame Saunders, the drugged wine, and running into him. Asher's mood was as black as the night outside.

Jane tried to speak, but her husband shook his head. They exited the brothel under the cloak of darkness and secrecy. He thought he might strangle her if she said anything else. She could have been killed tonight! Or compromised. Or someone else might have tasted her passion. . . .

Asher growled. He would kill anyone who tried to taste his wife. He would not be a cuckold. He would not tolerate any man, vampire or shape-shifter sampling what was his alone to taste, touch and plunder. He spoke few words as he loaded Jane into his carriage, and as the conveyance rolled away with a clatter, he sat in brooding silence.

Jane was remembering in vivid detail the loss of her virginity. She felt like singing at the top of her lungs. She now knew what went on between a man and a woman—or a vampire and a woman—behind closed doors. It was just bloody marvelous!

Eyeing the fine figure of her husband in the deep shadows in their carriage, Jane noted he was staring out the window, a study in bleak anger. Still, even knowing this, some imp inside her made Jane comment, "Hmmm. Strange, but I see no flying elephants." She stared up at the half-full moon in the sky.

Her husband's look could have frozen over the hottest desert in the world. Jane hid her grin. After all, Van Helsings were renowned for coming out on top in every battle between vampire and mortal. Next time, she'd be sure to get some that way too.

Count Dracul, I Presume

Jane laid her head against the cool glass of her balcony window, feeling the night winds blowing gently against her face. Below, the garden was thick with a soft, grayish fog, and the stars glittered ever-distant in the blue-black night sky.

It was midnight, the witching hour, or if you were a Van Helsing, it was time to pick up your old black bag of vampire tools and go out stalking. Jane sighed thankfully. Those days were behind her.

Moving sideways, she enjoyed the breeze cooling her fevered thoughts—erotic images of Asher thrusting into her, his head thrown back in ecstasy as he poured his seed into her body. She remembered the feel of his hard thighs against hers as he penetrated her, his lips licking and nipping her nipples; and she shivered. How she longed to feel him thus again. But it had been two long nights since her husband had made fiery love to her. It seemed that, on matters of lovemaking, her husband could be quite down to earth when he wasn't actually in it. The stubborn lout was avoiding her once again.

No longer was she a virgin. Now she knew what delights awaited her in the marriage bed, and she only wanted more of the same. But Asher was remote as a marble statue, the silly vacillating vampire.

Jane had seen only a glimpse of him last night, when he had descended the stairs in his long black multilayered cape. He had glanced at her briefly, then left without a word of farewell. It was simply too much to be ignored again; she would not stand for it. She would devise a plan to seduce her husband again and again and again.

She smiled at the thought. She might not be able to have her husband in the day, or to share love's delights in the afternoon, "But I will be bloody well damned if I'm going to give up the nights."

If Asher would only trust her, open up and reveal his past. That would open the door to their future, Jane believed. Trust was essential in relationships. Love would be even better. But she would settle for what she could get. She would love Asher, and he must trust and respect her. "You neglectful Nosferatu, I won't let you win this game of vampire and mouse."

Feeling better, Jane lifted her head and let the breeze caress her face like a lover's fingers. But when her wrist began to tingle uncomfortably, Jane had an inexplicable urge to visit the gardens.

She recognized that the feeling was daft; it was midnight and she was in her nightgown. Shivering, she felt a vague sense of evil as the tingling continued, compelling her to walk downstairs and outside into the fog-shrouded night. Restlessly she stirred, beginning to pace back and forth, resisting the compulsion, until a birdcall caught her attention. The sound was unmistakable.

"The nightingale," she gasped, excitement catching her in its grip. The elusive bird was somewhere close. She had been right that first night when she'd trailed Asher to the cemetery. There was a nightingale in London, as impossible as it might seem.

Once London had abounded with the beautiful birds, but their numbers had diminished as the air grew fouler and smoke from factories had filled the winds. Now they were practically extinct in England, and were found only rarely in the North Country.

"What a discovery," Jane murmured, quickly grabbing her robe and quietly descending the long marble staircase. She could hardly wait to tell the Audubon Society about it.

Outside in the garden, she followed the sound like a siren's call from the sea. Foraging carefully between thornbushes and exotic roses, Jane examined the night sky and the dark outline of the trees, wherever the angelic singing might originate.

As she walked, the fog became thicker, a white-veiled mist among the dark shadows of the garden. Those shadows loomed menacingly, causing Jane to pause right before she entered an area clothed all in solitary blackness, a void where time ceased to exist.

To her right, she heard movement. Startled, she turned, her heart pounding and her fear escalating, leaving the taste of metal in her mouth. Someone was out here with her.

A loud "Ereek!" broke the night. The sound caused Jane to jump, then to laugh giddily. It was Orville's greeting call.

Giggling foolishly, she walked back to the gate and opened it to pet her ostrich, who leaned down to rub his head across her shoulder.

"So, we meet again."

Gasping, Jane whirled. A tall, lean figure emerged

from the shadows and fog, making a dark passage, his long black cape flowing out behind him. She could see his fangs glistening in the the moonlight. He was evil personified, the dark, soulless mirrors of his eyes a dark hazard.

"Jane Van Helsing Asher," the figure said formally with a heavy Eastern European accent. "I have been waiting for you." He bowed mockingly. "You might say that you have become my obsession."

"Dracul, I presume," Jane managed to say, her throat very dry. She recognized the voice from the night at the Birds of Paradise Club. This was the blond man who was not a man, who had frightened her when he had tried to drag her off. She had felt a strong threat from him that night. She had not been wrong in that, but he was a vampire and not a werewolf.

"You did not know me last time," Dracul bragged, his voice filled with both menace and laughter, a strange combination. "I was quite disappointed to find that a Van Helsing could be so obtuse."

"That is an unjust accusation. I was drugged. Now, what do you want?" she asked, cautiously backing away. This was the monster of nightmares, the Prince of Darkness!

"Why, you're not dark at all," she noted. In fact, he was fair, with hair as golden as the sunlight—which of course hadn't set upon Dracul's head in over six centuries. Why hadn't she told her husband of what happened to her in the smoking parlor? Lust! That's why, she thought critically. She had been so wrapped up in her husband's lovemaking, she had pushed the strange meeting with this supernatural creature to the back of her mind.

Fool! she chided herself. Foolish, lovesick female, worrying about Asher's lack of interest when she should have been worrying about Dracul's.

The evil count laughed. "Dark enough, my little Van Helsing."

Staring at him, her eyes wide with fright, Jane saw that Dracul was quite handsome—a fact she found chilling. He was a vicious monster hiding behind a mask of perfection. "What do you want?"

"Why, I want you, my dear," he replied, his voice slippery-smooth.

"Why?" she questioned, her heart beating a staccato dance, threatening to pound right out of her chest. She had no stakes with her. She was alone, with no one to step in and rescue her. No father, no cousins, no brother—not even her husband, who was probably out carousing with that overblown neck-biting hussy Lady Montcrief. Really, the man was insufferable.

"Did you kill all those prostitutes?" she asked.

"Not all."

"And what of Lady Veronique?"

"She caught the eye of my cronies."

Jane shuddered. "She's a vampire now?"

All my training was for nothing, she thought hazily, gazing into the grisly hellfire in Dracul's eyes. She was going to die, and Asher was more than likely sleeping with some tart of the walking dead.

"Of course," he answered. "And soon you will be, too. Don't you see that there is a dreadful beauty in decay?" Dracul asked, his eyes full of dark insanity. "From destruction comes rebirth. As you will see. And even better, you are a Van Helsing. The major will be most distressed to find his daughter my eternal vampire bride."

Jane shook her head, backing away. "I don't intend to follow in Lady Veronique's footsteps." She came up against Orville's large feathered back. This was even worse than she feared. Dracul wasn't going to kill her:

he was going to make her one of his infamous brides. Brides who drank the blood of little children, draining them and then throwing their small bodies into gutters or off castle walls, while the count cheered them on to new heights of depravity. She would spend eternity throwing up.

It was a black contrast to the thought of eternity with her husband. That would be a different matter, a marvelous thing as they explored the wonders of the world and each other's bodies. As they watched time pass and new inventions change the world, as new thoughts changed the values of the world, as new art changed the esoteric qualities of the world. Perhaps they would discover a new bird species, fly as vampire bats among them, soaring high and free. It would be a never-ending adventure.

Reality brought her back to the ground with a thud. Asher would never ask her to be his eternal bride. He didn't love her, she reminded herself.

"You have no choice as I can see," Dracul said, glancing around him.

"Don't you have three wives already? Wouldn't one more be a bit gauche?" Jane asked, her voice shaky. She took another small step away from the fanged fiend.

Dracul snarled, "I have only two presently."

"Have you lost one?" Jane had heard the three brides of Dracul were as famous as the Loch Ness Monster in the supernatural world.

"That is a question you must ask your husband!" the count snapped, his long white fangs glistening in the night.

As Jane stared at those sharp teeth, she felt a chill wind blow through her soul. Yes, eternity with Dracul would be a fate worse than death.

"Asher will pay for killing Yvette. She was special,

that one," Dracul flared, his eyes now a brilliant scarlet. "I owe him for that, and for the time he maimed me with holy water." The vampire ripped open his shirt, revealing row upon row of melted flesh on the right side of his body, starting just below the collarbone and ending midway down his stomach. "He will pay, and dearly!"

In the blink of an eye, Dracul crossed to Jane, yanking her into his arms and away from the ostrich. Orville took exception as Dracul lowered his head, preparing to drink his fill.

Jane screamed and, seeing those long, glistening fangs descend, the ostrich attacked, pecking viciously as only an outraged bird weighing over three hundred pounds can do.

Dracul missed Jane's neck completely, caught off guard by the back-pecking bird. In the confusion, he dropped Jane. Instinct took over and she quickly rolled away, remembering her training. Silently she thanked her father for his many lengthy drills.

Dracul's fingernails became three-inch claws and he drew back to strike the bird. Jane, realizing his intent, threw herself upon his back and stuck her fingers in his eyes. The ostrich leveled a hard blow to Dracul's nose. A shrill howling filled the night as Spot, hearing his mistress's cries, ran from the house. Joining the fray, he leapt at Dracul's privates, latching on with a vengeance.

Dracul lurched backward. The enraged vampire cried out again, slinging Jane off his back, and Spot flew through the air to land in a soft green hedge. Jane herself landed hard on her hip and left thigh. She groaned, aching. Her leg felt as if an elephant had trampled upon it. She tried to stand, knowing she needed to be ready for flight or fight, but the pain was too great. Terrified, she watched in horror as Orville backed instinctively away. The perfidious Prince of Darkness threw back his head and howled in rage.

Apoplectic, his eyes a bloody red, his long claws clicking together in a furious rhythm, Dracul turned to rip the big bird into shreds. But, seeming to notice something from the corner of his eye, a blur moving with incredible speed through the darkness and shadows, the vampire hesitated.

Catching her breath, her fingers searching desperately for some kind of weapon in the grass, Jane watched curiously as Dracul liquefied into a white mist, blending with the fog. "Where's a good stake when you need one?" she grumbled. But soon the vampire vanished, a wisp of white in the brisk winds. Weakly she began to stand, was surprised when a strong hand helped her up.

"Jane?" Asher said, concern in his deep tone. "Are you all right? I heard you scream."

Asher willed his voice to stay strong. He had felt a fear like never before when he'd heard her scream. As he'd hurried to where the sound had originated, he'd kept seeing images of his wife:

The way she held her stake. The way she sipped her tea. The memory of all that . . . The way she had spilled brandy upon his coat. The way she petted her ostrich, or spoke kindly to his staff. The way she moved beneath him when making passionate, hot love, and how she seemed to understand all without him having to explain. No, no, they couldn't take that away from him. Or at least he prayed they couldn't. He had put all his energy into speed, knowing that it might all be up to him.

Upon entering the clearing, Asher had seen the incensed ostrich, the stunned dog and his calamity-ridden wife lying on the ground, and Dracul dissolving into mist. Asher thought his heart might stop beating forever. But then, like a puff of smoke Dracul was gone, and Jane was left sitting on the ground with an adorable if idiotic look on her face. Shakily, he hauled her up and tightly enfolded her in his arms.

"Are you all right, love?" he asked.

Jane snuggled close, trying to slip inside her husband's cape as she trembled with shock. He wiped a streak of blood from a cut on her forehead with his handkerchief. She was so cold. Did Asher ever get this cold? "Yes. At least, I think so." She was safe now. Safe now in her husband's arms. Right where she wanted to be, although she'd prefer to have no audience.

Knowing now that Jane was all right, Asher cursed, looking at the spot where Dracul had vanished. Bert, Renfield and two of the gardeners hurried to his side.

"Damn that fiendish monster to hell," Asher snarled, his fangs extending. He was beyond outraged. The count had dared attack what was his—and he'd almost succeeded. He drew another deep breath to calm himself down.

"Mistress Jane, you be okay?" Bert asked, worry filling his homely features.

Jane smiled faintly, nodding at the bird keeper. Even with Asher's arms around her, she couldn't seem to quit trembling.

"What happened?" Renfield asked, his sharp eyes scouting the area.

Asher looked toward Bert and the gardeners. "It's all right. You go on back to sleep. I'll take care of everything. Bert, take Orville with you."

The men all obeyed, although Bert looked as though he wanted to argue.

"Bert," Asher called, cradling Jane in his arms. "Feed that big beautiful bird anything he wants. He saved his mistress's life."

Bert grinned a crooked grin and lovingly patted

Orville on the head. "He's a fine, big fellow, my lord. You got it. Ol' Orville will have a feast fit for a king."

Jane began to shake harder as Asher picked her up. Her husband said, "I'm taking her inside, Renfield. She's had quite a fright and a lucky escape."

The valet said shrewdly, "Dracul?"

Asher nodded. No one was going to steal his wife, even if he didn't want her. Well, if he hadn't wanted her. He did want her now. In various and sundry ways. "This means war!" he cried. Immortal warfare—a deadly, dangerous game for all involved. Oftentimes it was a real bloodbath. What fun.

Renfield shook his head, knowing this was not good news. In fact, it was the worst news he could think of. Dracul had instigated war with Asher, and vampire wars always sucked. There could be only one winner, and Dracul was stronger and more hard-bitten.

The valet sighed morosely, watching Asher carry his wife back to the mansion with Spot trailing at his heels. It had taken over thirty years to train his master in maintaining his wardrobe, and they still had a way to go, especially with Lady Jane for his wife. He shook his head—he was really too old to be starting over with some new vampire master.

Staring down at Jane, who looked so pale, pretty and vulnerable, Asher silently declared that no one would ever steal her away from him. She really wasn't so bad, as far as wives went. Over his shoulder he called, "Renfield, I want you to find Orville a mate. I owe that ostrich my wife's life, and I want to reward the big bird."

The valet shook his head indignantly. Didn't he have enough to worry about. Asher ruining his jackets, his new mistress trying to discover the master's coffin? Now he was to be a procurer of an ostrich?

You Only Live Twice

Asher laid his wife on the bed, anxiously studying her. However, his spark of concern changed to something warmer as her robe fell open, revealing her soft white thighs. She looked so pretty in the moonlight.

"Why did you go outside to the gardens?" he asked.

Jane frowned, thinking back to those moments before the attack. "I heard a nightingale. But before that I had the strangest urge to go to the garden, almost as if someone was calling me," she answered, unconsciously rubbing her wrist.

Watching her closely, Asher took her hand and examined it closely, noticing two small nicks on her wrist.

He snarled, causing Jane to jerk back, eyeing him with alarm. "What's wrong?"

"He marked you. Not fully a bite, but a mark," Asher explained, looking pointedly at her wrist. "When? Where have you met him before?" His tone was glacial, matching the icy fury in his eyes. He would dispatch Dracul just as soon as he could find the marauding cretin. No one would touch his wife but him! As a boy he had never learned to share his toys. As an adult he'd grown no better.

"I met him at the Birds of Paradise Club. He wore a mask, and I didn't know who he was. But I was terribly frightened of him. He tried to get me to go outside. Fortunately, one of the other soiled doves and her customer came upon us, and I broke away. Shortly after that I encountered you," Jane answered shakily. "I felt a small sting, but I don't remember anything like a bite."

Asher shook his head. "It was a nip. Only a vampire as old as Dracul could have done this—marked you without a full bite. Only vampires over three hundred years of age can even call someone once they have been bitten. But, with Dracul, well . . . his powers are very strong." He sank beside her on the bed. "You recognized him tonight, didn't you?"

"Yes." Jane took her husband's cold hand in hers, warming it. Basking in his concern, as well as his touch, left Jane feeling slightly euphoric. In some ways she knew Asher intimately. In other ways, he was a great, wondrous mystery. Perhaps he would always be. That thought made her feel sad. She wanted her husband to need her as she needed him. She wanted him to want her as she wanted him.

Asher placed a gentle kiss on his wife's brow. The affectionate gesture surprised both himself and Jane. "He won't stop now. He has marked you, and he can call you again at anytime."

"What will we do?" Jane asked, worried. She didn't want Asher battling the fiendish count.

"It appears I have little choice but to go to war. I doubt the ignominy of being defeated by an ostrich will halt Dracul for long."

Jane gently caressed his face, worry shrouding her soul like a damp towel. "I have brought trouble to your door. He wants to hurt my father by making me his

bride. I am so sorry, Asher. I wanted to make your undead life better, not worse. I wanted you to be happy,
not hunting someone like the dark fiend of the night!"

"No, Jane, it's not just you. Dracul wants to strike at
me. I always knew the night would come when Dracul
would take his revenge."

"Revenge for what?"

"I burned his second wife to death after she attacked
a school of children in France. He has never forgiven
me for that. Or for the scar I gave him when I attacked
him with holy water over forty years ago."

Jane nodded, remembering the count's angry words.
But then she clasped her husband's face between her
palms, pleading, "You can't fight him. It's too dangerous."

"I have no choice, Jane."

Knowing it was true, her eyes filled with tears. "Then
I will help."

Asher looked affronted. "Over my dead body."

His tone irritated her. "Your point being?" she asked
coolly.

He scowled at first, but when she smiled, he followed
suit. "Graveyard humor?" he asked.

She shrugged. "It's only appropriate. I *am* a Van
Helsing."

"Don't remind me," he said stiffly. "It's something I
seemed to have forgotten."

She wanted to be angry at his answer, but she was
merely weary, the weight of the world crushing down
on her small shoulders. "You still doubt my loyalty,"
she said.

Catching a fleeting glimpse of her pain at his callous
words, Asher relented. "Jane, you are what you are. Just
as I am. I cannot step back now and regret roads not
taken, journeys I did not travel. What you see is what I
have been. Just as Dracul is. He was born of evil, and he

has bequeathed evil to the world. We can't help being what Fate created us. You are a Van Helsing, the scourge of vampirekind, and I am a master vampire. Yet, somehow . . . as the nights pass by, the importance of that decided difference seems to matter less and less."

Jane nodded vigorously, hiding a smile. Her husband's distaste for her was lessening! "Tonight we are united in a cause, our similarities binding us. Therefore, you must use me and my family connections to help you. I am a hunter. He is a vampire."

"It's too dangerous for mortals, even Van Helsings," he replied.

He turned to leave. He had to go, and soon. His mouth was dry, his groin filling with heat whenever he saw his disheveled wife, half lying upon her bed. Her cheeks were flushed a becoming coral, and the tips of her breasts were peeking out from beneath her night-gown, a temptation for mortals and immortals alike. Her long hair had come undone and hung in a silken waterfall down her back and shoulders. Asher shuddered, his breathing becoming heavy. His voluptuous wife was made for loving, and her blood was rich and sweet.

Noting her husband's heated glance, Jane began to unbutton her gown, watching his face. She had almost been made a bride of the foul fiend of the underworld. She would have been lost to Asher forever. She wanted him now with a ferocity she had never felt. "I don't want to lose you, Asher. Never!"

Asher clenched his fists, fighting the desire that had been eating him since he'd tasted not only Jane's blood, but her passion for him. She had fired his hunger to rav-enousness, to where he desired a never-ending banquet where he would glut himself on his wife for eternity, love her night after night. For the past few days he had driven himself crazy with dreams about her pale, freckled breasts, and her thatch of curly brown hair. He had thought constantly about driving his sex, along with his fangs, deep within her.

"I must go. To track him. The trail grows cold."

Jane shoved her nightgown down past her shoulders, revealing the creamy globes of her breasts, the freckles speckling around the nipples. "Stay a while," she urged. Asher *had* to stay with her tonight. As strong and able as her husband was, she feared he was no match for the crafty, corrupt Count Dracul. Tomorrow she would enlist the help of her family without Asher's knowledge. She knew exactly how he felt about the Van Helsings: Her arrogant husband would rather drink dirt than accept her family's help. But they were the only way to ensure that Asher remained with her, not put in a coffin for good.

Again, the vampire-fighting skills she had abhorred for most of her life made her happy. She would use them to the very best of her ability to save her husband and the world from Count Dracul. She would put her whole heart into it, and she would succeed. Love would find a way.

Asher didn't know when it had happened, but he knew that he had developed an affinity for freckles. His wife had the most beautiful breasts in the world. Breasts that should be worshipped nightly, and he was just the vampire to do it.

He shook his head, full of lusty hunger. Yet he knew where his duty lay. He needed to track Dracul before the trail became cold. He should back out the doorway right this minute, ignoring the lovely, luscious feast before him. He nodded once. Yes, he could do that. He was a master vampire, and master of his fate.

"I don't want you right now," he stated, a bit too emphatically to be believed by anyone.

Jane stood on her knees and shoved her nightgown away, revealing her soft thighs and thatch of brownish curls, glistening with her body's response to his nearness.

Asher gasped, seeing that his wife was already wet for him and he hadn't even touched her yet. He growled. He wanted to devour her. To throw her onto the bed and sink into her until he lost himself. "I am a master vampire and master of my own fate," he repeated. He would leave before this tempting seductress seduced him. "No, I don't want you even a tiny bit."

"Methinks the gentleman doth protest too much," Jane replied teasingly. She lay back on the bed, her body a thing of primal beauty. She beckoned him with her pale, speckled arms.

Asher stared, mesmerized, repeating to himself over and over that he was a master vampire, but the lust within him became a beast. It raged at him to mate. With a cry of frustration, he shoved his breeches to his knees and threw himself atop his wife.

Jane moaned as she took his weight, and spread her legs wide to help him penetrate her. His heated hardness made her feel complete, and she took him tightly within her.

Inside his wife's moist, hot heat, Asher felt at home. He felt like a conqueror of worlds. His wife fit him like a glove, and she made him feel like he could move mountains. Her passion burned and warmed him, recalling to his mind long-ago days in the sun. Her breasts, so plump and firm, tempted him to partake, and he suckled and licked them, enjoying the small moaning sounds his wife made. Her body moved beneath him; her arms held him tight.

Jane cried out in sheer joy as she felt the pulsating

strength of Asher within her. He thrust and thrust again and again while his tongue and lips savored her breasts. She loved the way he moved inside her, his buttocks taut, his arm muscles rigid. She loved the way his flesh felt so slick and hard beneath her hands.

Her husband bit gently on her nipples, creating havoc below. Jane felt her stomach muscles clenching, and bright white lights streaked behind her closed eyes. The white lights were like bursting stars, and she felt her climax building like a force of nature. Soon she would soar again.

Asher felt his wife's body going rigid as she crested, tiny ripples drawing him deeper into her hot, wet depths. She screamed out his name, "Asher! Oh, Asher my love!"

Growling hungrily, he stared into her eyes, which were heavy-lidded with passion's fires. "I want to feed on you," he begged, his throat hoarse with the force of his passion. He had never wanted anything more than to mate with his wife in this ancient vampire tradition, to make her his own completely.

Enthralled, Jane nodded as Asher licked her breast and sucked it deep into his mouth. He bit down gently, and she screamed as the brief stab of pain turned to blinding pleasure. Another intense orgasm shook her. Choruses of white lightning were exploding in her brain, zinging here, there, and everywhere.

Asher drank his wife's delicious blood, reveling in its spicy uniqueness. Never before had blood been so sweet. Never before had he felt so complete as he did feeding off Jane, his body joined to hers. They were one, finally bound together as it should be.

"Mine! *Mine!*" he cried out. No one else would know Jane Van Helsing's sweet essence or her core. He might not love her, exactly, but no one else would have her. He might not have wanted what he'd got at first, but he had got what he wanted. Suddenly the waves of his desire caught him, drawing him to the razor's edge. He threw back his head and howled, pumping, climaxing violently as his hot seed filled her body.

Reluctantly he quit feeding, not wanting to take too much. Gently closing the wound on her breast, he tenderly laid his head against her forehead. Nothing must happen to his wife. He would keep her safe, no matter what.

Jane smiled faintly. What an award-winning performance, she thought. Well, she could certainly say that in the heat of the night they had set the sheets aflame, silken chariots of fire. Her husband was truly a man for all seasons. It could be the best years of our lives, she thought, if only he would give an inch—well, a mile— and admit he didn't regret their marriage now. Yes, it would be so sweet to hear terms of endearment from him. Those would be like the sound of music.

Running her fingers through his burnished hair, she sighed. Hell would freeze over first? Had it?

"I'm so glad you didn't want me even a little bit," she remarked smugly.

"Maddening minx," he responded.

"Should we buy Lucifer a heavy winter cape?"

"Jane . . ." Asher warned. He didn't like having his words thrown back in his face. "You might be pushing your luck with me."

"I could push something else," she replied impishly.

"Jane, Jane, what am I to do with you?"

"Cherish me," she whispered, suddenly serious.

Asher glanced down into his wife's silver-green eyes, feeling himself drown in their divine depths.

"Oh, Asher—how I wish I were beautiful like your other lovers were," she whispered wistfully.

Asher knew he had the power to deliver his wife an almost mortal blow. He'd done it too many times already. Tenderly, he pushed back a strand of her hair from her cheek. "'Nothing is beautiful from every point of view,'" he said.

Jane cocked her head. "Horace?" she asked.

He grinned. "Do you never miss a quote? You must be the best-read lady in England—*and* one of the most lovely," he said. He leaned back to stare at her pale naked breasts, gently rounded belly and soft white thighs. He even believed his own words.

Jane's eyes filled with tears as she laid her head on her husband's chest. Asher cared, and he thought her body was lovely—for now, that was enough. Within minutes she fell asleep, a self-satisfied, sated smile upon her face.

His wife sleeping like the dead, Asher tenderly pulled the covers over her and left to speak with Renfield. He had plans to make, and a vampire to track before dawn's early light.

The Grass Is Always Greener on the Other Side of the Graveyard

Jane awakened with a strong sense of urgency. Something was wrong; she could feel it in her bones. Dressing quickly, she hurried to find Renfield. She found him returning from the cellar, a dark frown crossing his austere features.

Forgoing formality, she quickly asked, "Is Asher in his coffin?"

Warily, the valet shook his head.

"He went out last night, didn't he?" Jane probed, clasping her fingers tightly, hoping against hope that Asher was sound asleep, dead to the world in some secret casket. "He went after Dracul."

"Yes," Renfield admitted worriedly. "And he's not back yet. He promised he would sleep at home today, due to the seriousness of the circumstances, but . . ."

"Do you think he found that horrid fiend?" Jane didn't know what she would do if anything happened to him; her husband couldn't just up and really die, leaving her all alone. Not when they'd come so close to true marital bliss. How would she ever forgive him?

Yes, her stubborn husband was just now beginning to appreciate her and their marriage. The nodcock Nosferatu had better not have gotten himself fitted permanently for his coffin. She was too young to be a widow. Besides, she had only just gotten into her new life. She didn't want to have to go back to visiting cemeteries, especially to place flowers on her dead husband's grave.

"Yes, I think he found Dracul," Renfield said.

"Do you think he's . . ." Jane stopped, unable to voice the horrifying thought.

"No!" Renfield replied, his tone grim. "I would be quite ill if my master were . . . truly dead. But I think Dracul must have captured him. I imagine he will torture him for a while."

"Bloody fiendish bloodsucking swine!" Jane swore. She wanted to stick something with a stake—preferably Dracul's black heart. "But if you're correct, then Asher's alive. For now. We must rescue him!"

"How? We don't know where Dracul's lair is located," the valet complained.

Jane smiled. "But we will by day's end." She tugged at Renfield's arm. "You're absolutely correct about the torture. Dracul will delight in prolonging Asher's agony. He won't have had much time last night. So tonight's the night we must act."

Pulling Renfield with her, she slipped up the servants' stairs and hurriedly explained, "He'll want to add to the torture, and what better way than to make me his vampire bride in front of Asher's eyes?"

Renfield was amazed at his mistress's reasoning. But, then he shouldn't be, he surmised. She was a vampire hunter. She knew vampires. While he sometimes forgot the fact, the Countess of Wolverton had a deplorable lineage. Of course, it helped in this case. "What do you think Dracul will do?" he asked.

"Why, send me a note saying he has Asher, of course. Telling me to come somewhere alone," Jane explained, grabbing her cloak and gloves, and calling for her carriage to be brought around.

"Where are you going?" the valet asked, concerned for Asher's wife for the first time. He was getting too old to be breaking in another mistress.

"To get help," she replied. She wrote a quick note to her uncle Jakob. Then, motioning for the footman, she instructed it to be delivered immediately and in person.

"So, when the note comes from Count Dracul, what will you do?" Renfield asked.

"Why, I shall go wherever he asks me to," she replied. "You see, for this plan to work, I must be the bait."

And coffin bait she would be, Jane thought as she got into the carriage and it conveyed her to her father's house. This was irony at its best, she decided. The vampire hunters rescuing the vampire. But she could do no less; she loved her fanged, blood-drinking husband.

As the carriage rapidly traversed the winding roads to her father's home, at last pulling up before the massive front steps, Jane visualized Asher's pale, beautiful face, and how much it had come to mean to her. She could wake up completely happy now, satisfied with her life and her husband. She loved to listen for the sound of his first footsteps on the stairs in the evening, and hear his warm, husky voice for the first time each night. He made her feel complete, a woman unto herself.

Before him, she had thought she would end up an old maid, alone with her thoughts, her duty and herself. Comfort and love were words she'd only dreamed about. Then the big-fanged earl had come her way. He had found a place in her heart that was waiting for him—a special place where love lived and grew.

Yes, Asher was now her shining star, blazing just as brightly in day as at night. Some might say it was a fate worse than death to be married to the undead. Well, her husband might be dead in the day, but at night there was no one more alive.

They might not have eternity together, but Asher could bloody well love her until she was sixty-four, and old and gray, she reasoned as she entered her father's study. The major stood by the fireplace, along with her brother, Uncle Jakob and four of her six cousins.

The major glared pompously at his daughter. "Just what is the meaning of summoning your uncle and cousins here, Jane?"

Taking a deep breath, she spoke, her voice steady despite her frayed nerves. "I have a proposition for you all," she said. She watched their faces, their expressions ranging from disbelief to intrigue to indignant irritation. She was banking her future on this proposition, her life with Asher undead and well.

"I know how to find Dracul," she said slowly, letting the words fall upon the room like a heavy rain.

Everyone burst into shouts, her cousins and the red-faced major questioning where and how. Holding up her hand for quiet, Jane waited impatiently for the tumult to cease. Van Helsings were always a rowdy, rambunctious bunch whenever vampires where spotted on the horizon.

"Before I tell you how you can find the Prince of Darkness, every single one of you—and my two missing cousins—must promise on your very lives that you will do no harm to my husband." Jane did not ask; she demanded.

"And why should we wish to harm your husband?" her brother asked.

"Why do you think?" Jane answered.

Brandon cocked his head and studied her. "He *is* a

vampire, isn't he? Our information might have been wrong about him being Dracul, but not about being one of the undead."

"Yes," Jane admitted.

Her father's face turned scarlet. Jane had never seen that particular shade of red on him before. "Damnation, Jane! You will tell us immediately where to find Dracul and that bloodthirsty ghoul you wed."

Resolutely, Jane shook her head.

The major advanced on her, waggling his finger in her face. "Jane, you shan't disobey me! I will not have it! I am master in my own house!" the major roared. "I want Dracul's location, and I want it now. This is war. Jane, you can't make bargains when it's war."

"Oh, but I can and shall," Jane stated firmly. Her voice was laced with derision, finding strength she had learned with her husband. "I want a sworn blood oath that Asher's good health will remain that way. None of you will ever stalk or stake him. Without this promise, I will not tell you how to find Dracul and his nest." She stood before her father unafraid, and for the first time, uncaring whether he was proud of her or not. It was a freeing experience, even as distraught as she was over her husband's captivity. She felt invincible, a true Van Helsing.

Touching her brother's arm, she looked up at him. "Will you help me, Brandon? The count has captured Asher. He means to destroy my husband, and not in an easy manner."

"You love Asher?" Brandon asked solemnly.

Jane smiled, transforming her plain features into pretty ones, displaying the love she carried in her heart and soul for her husband. "Yes."

Brandon smiled back. "Then I'll help you, Jane."

"Over my dead body," the major shouted.

Everyone ignored him.

Uncle Jakob spoke for the first time, curiosity in his pale green eyes. "Why would Dracul want to kill another vampire? Is it a territorial war?"

"No. More personal. Asher destroyed his second bride, Yvette, and attacked Dracul with holy water."

"Yvette, huh? So that's how the wicked bitch was killed," Jakob remarked. "I always wondered. Never forget that she killed Great-great-uncle Abraham over a hundred years ago."

Jakob Van Helsing rubbed his chin, considering. "So, your husband was the one who rid the world of that soulless fiend." Looking at his sons, he commanded, "We shall help. Asher destroyed a vampire who killed our ancestor, which means that we owe him a debt. Jane's husband by marriage is now tied to us with a bond of blood."

Three of her cousins accepted their father's command without complaint. Dwight scowled, saying, "I will stake whatever vampire is in front of me, Jane and her vile husband be damned."

Shoving her finger into Dwight's chest, Jane snarled, "If you harm a hair on my husband's head, then I will stake *you*, cousin or no cousin. Blood relation, no blood relation, I love my husband. And I will not have him hurt!"

Dwight drew back from her anger in surprised irritation. Jane had never been so ferocious. "If this is what comes from mixed marriages, well, then I am certainly opposed," he muttered. "Bloody female, putting on airs."

Uncle Jakob bopped Dwight up side the head, remarking briskly, "If this young pup attempts to hurt your husband, I'll have his head. Understand, Dwight?"

Dwight glared at Jane, and she pressed him: "I'll have your word that no harm will befall my husband by your hand, now or ever."

"Agreed," her cousin reluctantly spat, his father giving him the evil eye.

Resolutely, Jane locked eyes with each and every member of her family. "Agreed," she said.

Down to a vampire-hunting man they all nodded, even the major, with Uncle Jakob and Jane's brother twisting his figurative arm.

When the agreement was in place, Jane revealed her bold and brilliant strategy to rescue her husband and exterminate Dracul. As the plan unfolded, wicked joy gleamed in her relatives' eyes.

Jane smiled ruefully. They all looked like little boys waiting for their presents at Christmastime. Her family and relatives acted as if they hadn't had so much fun in a good long while. She guessed they were tired of hunting the old run of the mill English bloodsuckers; they wanted some foreign undead to chase.

She sighed, guessing that the grass was always greener on the other side of the grave.

As she left her father's residence, she could hear shouts of "Tallyho! Don't stake until you see the red of their eyes." There was definitely going to be a hot time in the old Town tonight, what with the Van Helsings hunting. And heaven help the walking dead who got in their way—with the exception of her husband, who more or less had a lifetime free pass, courtesy of the no-longer-reluctant Jane Van Helsing Asher.

Wanted Undead or Alive

It was a dark and stormy night. The shadows seemed to blend into the air, creating swirling mists of deep blue-gray. Streaks of jagged lightning lit the heavens and illuminated the grim-looking manor house. Dracul's human coachman had led Jane here to meet destiny head-on, just as she had predicted.

The count's estate was a matter of acquired taste, Jane thought with a shudder. It was tall, dark and ominous, with gargoyles lining the front gates and door. The building stood out in stark relief against the bleak landscape of gray and black, and the area clearly hid frightening things that not only went bump in the night, but bumped things off.

Gathering her quickly fleeing courage, Jane raised the gargoyle knocker on the front door and let it drop. A loud clanging echoed out. Bravely she stood her ground, while fear ate at her insides. She had to do this for Asher, though Dracul terrified her. His eyes were so ancient and evil, luring the innocent to their immortal doom.

Shivering, Jane raised her chin, trying to shore up her dwindling courage. She was a Van Helsing, a curse on vampirekind everywhere. She would face Dracul and face him with her head held high. She had no choice. She was the diversionary tactic to keep the count's deadly attention, while her family slipped bravely inside.

A tall skeletonlike butler named O'Hara opened the door. He stared coldly at Jane with dull brown eyes and motioned her forward. He led her into a vast cavernlike drawing room which was decorated in dark, harsh slashes of scarlet and black. A large tapestry was embroidered with Dante's words, which Jane repeated grimly: " 'All hope, abandon ye who enter here.' "

A massive portrait of a dark-haired woman with glowing eyes and a long pale neck was hung over a black-marbled fireplace. Her face was cold and intimidating. Before it stood the Prince of Darkness himself, dressed in a deep blue smoking jacket, his pale golden hair shining in the glow of the fire. Two other vampires sat side by side on a large black settee. One was very tall, cadaverous-looking, which meant he hadn't fed in a long time. He had long red hair that was interlaced with gray and tied in a queue. The other vampire had slightly Germanic features, and a massive burn, long scarred over, on his neck. Holy water, Jane recognized. Both bloodsuckers' malevolent and monstrous eyes bored holes into her.

"Jane, my love, what a surprise," Dracul purred, his eyes glowing. Turning to his two companies, he managed a smile that revealed a hint of fang. "We love surprises, don't we, my friends?"

The two vampires nodded in agreement, their cold, reptilian eyes studying Jane as if she were a particularly fine dessert. It made her flesh crawl. It made her heart beat a thunderous rhythm that must be deafening to the predators, Jane surmised. How she wanted to hide in the corner or stick her head in a very deep hole that totally covered up her neck. If she died tonight, she hoped Renfield would still remember to find Orville a mate. And she hoped the female ostrich would be pretty—Orville deserved the best.

"I wish I could return the sentiment," she managed to say, bold in spite of the wild beating of her heart. "Where is my husband?"

Dracul threw back his head and laughed. "Loyal to the very end," he said. "How Van Helsing of you."

The other two vampires hissed as they glared at her, continuing to dissect Jane with their gruesome stares. Jane knew they were thinking wicked thoughts of what to do to her, since her family was definitely de trop in their social circles.

Again, Dracul laughed his sharp laugh. It was enough to slice skin. "Herrs Blixen and Rudolph appear to lack proper appreciation for your heritage," he said.

Jane shrugged, trying to appear nonchalant as her knees trembled beneath her skirts. "It is a fine heritage," she argued.

Blixen hissed again, this time revealing three-inch fangs.

"Herr Blixen disagrees. Your grandfather marked him with holy water over fifty years ago. He is quite pleased to find you as my guest tonight. What delights we have in store," the count warned in a mocking tone.

At these words, a lady in a bloodred gown entered the room. Jane gasped and stared. It was Lady Veronique, who turned to her and smiled, her fangs showing.

"So this is Jane Van Helsing-Asher," Lady Veronique remarked, licking her lips, her red tongue darting out. "I am hungry, my lord. May I snack upon her a bit?"

Count Dracul laughed harshly. "No, my pet. Jane is for me."

Lady Veronique pouted prettily. "But I am hungry."

"Rudolph will take you out to London later tonight. More tasty prostitutes await in White Chapel." Dracul added, "As I said, Jane is solely for me."

Chin held high, Jane drew on her inner strength. She would be brave to save her love. "Enough of your boasts. I came here to find my husband," she demanded, if her voice was barely a squeak. I should be on the stage, she thought vaguely. No one would know that right at this moment, she was about to pass out with fear.

Dracul motioned his butler to the upstairs room. "Bring down our other guest, O'Hara. If he is unable to walk, carry him."

The butler moved to obey.

Subconsciously, Jane clenched her fists and sucked in her breath. Asher had to be all right. At least she knew that her husband was still alive—well, as alive as the walking dead could be.

Dracul turned to the taller of his two guests. "Rudolph, go help O'Hara bring down our friend the earl."

The taller vampire complied with the prince's demand, exiting the room as silently as a ghost. Even from where Jane stood, she could smell a touch of the grave about him.

"Now, my dear," the count began, turning his attention back to her. "Did you come to rescue Asher?" He moved closer. "And remember, anything you say can and will be held against you. I plan to hold quite a few things against you."

"I came to see if I could bargain for my husband," Jane lied, hiding her anxiety under a streak of bravado. Silently, she quoted, *He whose ranks are united in purpose will be victorious.*

"You aren't afraid I will destroy you as Asher destroyed my bride?"

"You can try," Jane retorted bravely—and stupidly, she decided. He could squash her like a fly.

The count laughed. "Such courage. But don't push me, or I won't compare you a summer night," he mocked. He clearly intended to insult her. "The least Asher could have done was marry a beauty."

Jane's eyes narrowed. "I've been insulted by better vampires than you," she replied. She and her family could not fail in this, their greatest mission. She would get Asher out of here alive. She swore it.

Ignoring her courageous but useless words, Dracul examined Jane from the top of her head all the way to her feet. "No, you are not Asher's usual type of woman," he said, trailing one long finger down her cheek. Jane shivered, repulsed by his touch. She felt her blood run cold. The thought cheered her up. Maybe if her blood got too cold, the Count of Nasty would be too disgusted to drink it. Did he prefer hot blood?

"No, not his usual style at all," Dracul continued, slowly studying her. "Yet, I can see the attraction. Such lovely eyes . . . and that neck." He paused and leaned closer to lay a kiss on her pale skin. She shuddered in horror at the icy touch of death. She felt the wet damp of the graveyard in his kiss. Terror filled her veins.

Jane drew back rigidly, returning Dracul's gaze with one of loathing. He stiffened as he tried to mesmerize her with his stare. Then, ungracious in defeat, he snarled, "So it is true. I had heard it, but did not believe. Van Helsings do not fall wholly under our spell. But that is because shape-shifters are immune to our vampiric gaze."

Stepping back, he circled Jane like a stalking cat. "Very dangerous to our kind. Don't you agree, Asher?"

Jane gasped as she spotted the bloody figure of her husband being dragged into the room, supported by Rudolph and O'Hara. She was just in the neck of time.

Her husband was wrapped in silver chains that had

burned partially into his chest and arms. His face was whiter than a sheet, blood covering his jacket and the left side of his face. Jane darted forward to reach him, but was jerked back by Dracul's grip on her arm.

"No, Jane. You don't belong at his side anymore. Now you are mine—my war trophy, so to speak." Dracul taunted both his captives, his eyes glowing with unholy fire. "You will become my third bride tonight with Asher as our witness." The count laughed cruelly, while Jane's husband struggled in vain to break free of the tall vampire and the butler.

Asher's cry of rage filled the air. He felt as if his heart was ripped from his chest. Dracul had Jane, *his* Jane. Dracul would make her his immortal bride, and Jane would be tied through eternity to a monster of unequaled depravity and cruelty. Her kind, courageous heart would be destroyed by living with such a monster.

Jane tried wrenching her arm free, needing to place as much distance between herself and the Prince of Evil as possible. But his grip was like a vise, holding her in place.

Lady Veronique was gazing at Dracul. "I want to be your bride," she snarled.

Dracul quickly backhanded her with his free arm. "Quiet, Veronique! You are to be Rudolph's consort—as well you know."

Lady Veronique cringed at the anger in the count's eyes. She submitted with a small tremor. "As you say, my master."

Asher's vision was blurred; he had lost too much blood to have any strength, yet still he struggled, trying to reach his wife. He had always had a weakness for lost causes. Staring at Jane, he realized that he was ashamed. This woman had come to him in his greatest hour of need, risking her life. All this after he had treated her with barely concealed contempt, humiliating her in front of society and ignoring her in private.

Suddenly Asher despised himself for his misplaced affections and liaisons. For hundreds of years he had been searching for true love, a special woman to be his eternal bride, and Jane had been placed right in front of him. Perhaps he had been living in dirt so long that he couldn't understand anything above it, but true devotion was before him now: his wife in Dracul's cunning clutches, a shining example of beauty, kindness and true good. She was one of the few in the world who listened to her heart and followed through, no matter the odds stacked against her.

The tall vampire slammed Asher against the wall, causing stars to appear before his closed eyes. Sharp pain stabbed him. He hurt, and he knew he was wounded badly. They had kept him chained and thirsty to keep him from healing.

"Jane," he whispered sadly. Why had she come? Why had she risked her life and soul? The answer hit him straight in the heart like a bolt from Cupid's quiver: His calamity-ridden wife loved him.

Asher felt bloodred tears well up in his eyes. His wife loved him! He had never felt more depressed or happier, in his whole life. Blinking back sorrow, his determination to live to see another night with Jane at his side grew and expanded within him. Nothing could happen to his wife. He wouldn't let Jane be Dracul's eternal consort. She would be his own consort, and his alone. Somehow he would get them out of this dreadful debacle, and spend eternity by her side. Although things had never looked worse, things also had never looked better, because he was in love with his wife.

If he hadn't been so stubborn and idiotic, he would have recognized that the lust he felt for Jane was much more than that. The hunger he felt for her whenever he was in her presence, or out of it, was not only a hunger for blood and to lose himself in her body, but also for conversation, for the way she cocked her head when she was troubled. He loved how she played with her big bird and spoke to Spot, and the all-aglow smile she wore after he made love to her—a smile that said she had just discovered the secrets of the universe.

If he and Jane survived this night, he would swear by the heavens and stars that, in love, he would never go hungry again. "Jane, forgive me," he uttered, lifting his head and staring into her beautiful eyes.

"I do."

Oh, how the mighty had fallen. He had been waiting forever, it seemed. Waiting in the darkness for light. Jane was that: his glowing joy, his reason to get up and rise out of his coffin each night. She would be a companion for his youth and his old age, a woman of remarkable character and generosity of both spirit and nature. And he was the lucky man she'd married. They could have a wonderful future together of watching birds and the starts of sunrises, sleeping like the dead and watching the changing of the guards, art, music, literature, inventions and customs—everything as the centuries passed by. A world of words, spectacular surprises, ships perhaps sailing underwater, men flying and not as bats. If only he could remain alive beyond this one night, with Jane as his eternal bride, wedded in undead matrimony . . .

"Jane will be a replacement for the bride you murdered," Dracul stated with fiendish delight. "After all, I have always said that revenge is a dish best served at body temperature."

"I had no choice, and you know it. Yvette was killing *children*," Asher cried, his body wracked with pain. The skin near the silver chains on him was starting to char and blacken.

Dracul shrugged. "As if I care about that. Their lives meant nothing. Small, insignificant mortal children—

they are nothing before us. You sacrificed someone I cared for because of mere human weaklings," he sneered. He was clearly enraged, his clenched jaws seemingly cut from marble. "To destroy one of us, for a mortal. Us! We are like gods. Vampirekind is the superior race. Mortals are mere food. To be toyed with, tortured, used, abused, discarded and drained."

Asher shook his head, hearing some of his own words coming back to haunt him. He knew humans were weaker, but hearing the base count spew such biased filth, he felt ashamed. His wife was human, as was Clair Frankenstein Huntsley, and both women were as remarkable as people could be.

"I enjoyed Yvette's body and mind," Dracul continued. "She always envisioned the best tortures. And you destroyed her!" Dracul spat, pointing a long, elegant finger at Asher. "For humans, who are mere insects to be squashed beneath our feet!"

Asher winced, feeling trickles of blood running down his back. They had struck him with thin, silver-barbed whips. His wrists were raw and swollen where his chains slowly ate into his flesh.

"No. They are more than that," he replied, shaking his head. He had once believed fiercely in the superiority of his race. Humans had meant little to him besides sex and food. They fought and died for greed, lust, revenge and power, killing each other much faster than his own race could cause their extinction. Yet . . . "I have met men of honor and truth. I have known both good men and bad, just as there are good and bad of our own kind. Man is as complex and as special as our own race. What gives you the right to judge? Nothing. Only a fading belief in your own omnipotence."

Asher caught Dracul's look of utter disgust and disbelief. He added, "I didn't realize it before. Not until Jane came into my life." His wife was like a breath of fresh air, stirring the dankness crypt's cold, musty air. He lifted his eyes and looked at her, love filling his eyes.

The count cursed, the ferocity of his rage revealing his profound evil. "You are a fool, Asher! Man is but a breath of shadow, while we are lords of all things. Mankind is a doomed species, and we are its rightful rulers. We shall be here long after their race is dust in the wind. It is our purpose to make them so."

"That's blind, Dracul." Asher shook his head. "Without food, how will we survive? Your vision is shortsighted at best."

The count glowered at him and motioned Rudolph to secure Asher's hands above him, to attach him to a long iron hook suspended from the ceiling beams. "You're a fool, Asher!" he snarled. "A sentimental, human-loving fool. A disgrace to our kind."

Asher struggled in vain, his strength rapidly draining. His arms were lifted high above his head, and he had to stretch out fully so that they did not bear the whole weight of his body. His back arched from the uncomfortable position.

Once he was in place, Dracul approached him, pulling Jane alongside. For one moment Asher thought he might pass out from pain and loss of blood, but gallantly he managed to shove the encroaching darkness away.

"You shall watch me make her mine," Dracul jeered, pulling Jane into his arms. "You shall go to your grave forever, knowing your wife is now my consort." He encircled her from behind, his arms locking hers as he caressed her breasts. Lady Veronique clapped her hands, smiling.

Asher growled, forgetting his chains in his anger. Unable to watch such a creature of evil touch his wife, he tried to launch himself at Dracul.

The attempt caused Asher to lose his balance. He barely managed to keep his feet beneath him as fresh blood leaked from his numerous wounds, adding to the stains already on his white shirt. He hated being helpless. He hated seeing the fear in his wife's eyes. He should be protecting her, not chained to this bloody hook.

Dracul watched with nefarious enjoyment. "Such lovely, lush breasts—and they shall be mine to suckle from this night forth," the count prodded ruthlessly. Leaning back to study Jane's profile, he added, "But no great beauty like Yvette was."

He was wrong, Asher thought. Jane was the first stirring of breath in his body when he woke from the sleep of the dead. She was the melodic music of the night wind, and the twinkling stars at deep midnight. His wife might be a calamity, but she was his calamity. She might own a great big bird that ran amok in his household, but not every earl had a real ostrich in residence who could save his wife's life. His wife's family might be the cursed Van Helsings, but at least they were successful at what they did, and she loved him despite that.

"You are quite mistaken," Asher said, gazing adoringly upon his wife. "Jane is the most beautiful woman in the world, and quite extraordinary." How could anyone alive not see that? How had he missed it for so long?

Stunned, Jane raised her eyes to meet Asher's. What she saw there made her heart sing. Her husband thought she was beautiful. He thought she was extraordinary. Jane felt something break inside her, slowly cracking open to reveal the heart of the woman she really was. Never again would she feel unattractive, for the ugly duckling had at last realized she was a swan.

She felt tears filling her eyes, and at the same time she had an insane urge to laugh. For once in her life, in this miserable, frightening struggle, she felt truly radiant.

"How droll. She must be an acquired taste," Dracul mocked, his voice laced with condescension. "Perhaps, she will be at least be tasty—a fine vintage from the age-old keg of Van Helsing."

"You wish you knew," Asher muttered, his blood heating to the boiling point, the point of explosion, as Dracul's hand's roamed over his wife's voluptuous form. He would break the count's fingers one by one. No vampire touched what was his and lived to tell the tale.

Lady Veronique retorted smugly, "I bet she won't taste as sweet as I did, Count."

Dracul laughed again. "Oh, but she will. Revenge is the sweetest taste of all."

Lady Veronique frowned at her lord and master as Jane struggled against her foe's humiliating hold, trying to break free, her hands outstretched to touch her husband. In this stronghold of fear, Asher was her protection against Dracul's dark obsessions and dangerous liaison.

The count smiled again, an expression devoid of all kindness. "Stop that, Jane. You are mine now. Soon your loyalty to him will be bestowed upon a much worthier object.

"So let the games begin. We will let Asher play with Lady Montcrief. She has confided to me that she owes your husband for four long months spent in a coffin without a hint of fresh air or blood." Dracul laughed, clearly enjoying the fear emanating off Jane and Asher's helpless bodies. "Can we guess that she was not a happy vampire, being locked in a coffin for months without being fed? Such a harsh punishment for such a trifling offense," the count mocked.

Asher spoke with a hint of his old hauteur, in spite of the gravity of his injuries. "She tried to kill me, the master of her nest. You know full well I could have put her to the death for that 'trifling offense.'"

Again the Prince of Darkness shrugged. "It is lucky

for me that she didn't succeed. I do so love torture. And I have such fine things planned for you," he added mercilessly. "Don't we, my pet?" Dracul directed the last statement to Lady Montcrief, who had just entered the room. Lady Veronique's frown grew grim with jealousy.

Jane flinched when she saw the treacherous vampiress. Lady Montcrief wore a revealing black gown, better suited to the boudoir than this place, with a décolletage that plunged nearly to her waist. The wicked vamp was accompanied by two others of clearly Slavic origin.

As the vampiress approached, Jane saw Lady Montcrief's hand rise to slap Asher. The blow knocked Neil's head to the side, and her palm left a vivid red print against his pale cheek.

"Stop!" Jane cried in terror and anger.

Ignoring her, Lady Montcrief lifted her hand and touched the blood dripping down Asher's face. He jerked back.

She laughed, a shrill sound, and turned around, slowly licking his blood off her fingers. She kept her vile gaze focused on Jane, enjoying the anguish and disgust she evoked. Raising her hand, she lifted her fingers. "Care for a taste?" she asked.

Jane's stomach rumbled in reproach. She knew she would be mortified to cast up her accounts, but all this blood was sickening, even if it was her beloved husband's.

The blood-tipped fingers moved closer and closer, and soon were a mere inch from Jane's face. She swooned, only to be revived a few moments later by Dracul's cold hand on her head and his grotesque comment: "Jane, wake up and smell the blood."

Finding herself in the count's arms, with Lady Montcrief and Lady Veronique watching anxiously, Jane shuddered. Where were the troops when you needed them? Where were her annoying, barbaric cousins? She was going to kill her entire family if they didn't arrive soon, and if this army of the undead didn't kill her and her husband first.

Stiffly, she pushed away from the Prince of Darkness. Lady Montcrief leaned in, running her fingers over Dracul's lips. He kissed the blood from them.

Becoming utterly entranced, Dracul released Jane. She immediately and with great relief eased away, moving nearer to her husband in careful, tiny steps, while Lady Veronique turned to Rudolph and ran her fingers over his chest.

Asher leaned toward Jane as Dracul continued sucking on Lady Montcrief's fingers, whispering, "Never let them see you sweat." He laughed deliriously.

Jane gave him a frosty look. "Of course not! Ladies don't sweat. And I'll have you know that I was brought up to be a lady, even in the face of death."

"In the very midst of life, we are always just a step away from death," Asher said.

"You can say that again!" Jane agreed. Looking around the room at the many frightening faces of the undead, she gave a sigh of defeat.

Asher cocked a brow. His hauteur looked ridiculous with all the blood on his face. "Oh, don't give me that look of icy disdain," Jane complained.

"I do that look best," came Asher's protest.

"How well I know. But now is not the time," Jane said, her hands on her hips. "You know, Asher, sometimes you can be a real pain in the neck."

Asher smiled, amused. Yes, for once in his depraved life, Dracul was correct. Jane was definitely an acquired taste—a bit funny, a bit spicy, a bit unsure of herself, a bit cowardly. But a lot of brave. Yes, she was a fine vintage indeed. His cup ranneth over with love for her.

"Actually, my love, I think that will soon be true of you too," he teased. "I hope when I am dead and gone, and you are out sucking down little children, you'll remember what a good guy I was," he added lightly. Then he paused to watch Lady Montcrief unbutton the count's dark breeches.

How uncouth, he thought, to copulate before an audience! But, then, Dracul was like that; whenever an urge took him, he acquiesced. Asher remembered one time the count had fornicated in front of a whole regiment of English troops. Over in the corner, Lady Veronique was sucking on Rudolph's neck while he caressed her bottom.

Jane started to seek out what had caught her husband's attention, but Asher shook his head. "Don't look now, Jane."

Accepting his words, she leaned in close, scolding her husband quietly, "If you die tonight . . ." Then, realizing what she had said, she quickly amended her comment: "I mean, really die. I will never forgive you. Never, ever."

Asher smiled. Jane meant every word. She had risked life and limb to save him. Her loyalty was to him alone. What a fool he had been! If he had tomorrow, and tomorrow, and tomorrow, he would let his dearly beloved wife know just how much she meant to him.

"For I am a dead thing," Asher said, his eyes alight with the fires of love.

"Yes, I know that," Jane replied, bewildered.

Asher shook his head, explaining, "Jane, I am quoting poetry to you."

She stared in horror at him. "Now? In the midst of all this bloody danger, you're quoting poetry to me? Are you insane from blood loss?"

Asher ignored her. " 'I am every dead thing, in whom

love wrought new alchemy. For his art did express a quintessence even from nothingness.'"

"Shakespeare?" Jane questioned, intrigued in spite of their dire situation. Her husband was not just quoting poetry; he was quoting love poetry.

Asher shook his head. "Donne."

"You're done?"

"No. John Donne," Asher said.

"John's done doing what?"

"John Donne, the poet!" Asher snapped.

"Are you sure? It sounded like Shakespeare to me."

"Of course I'm sure!" Asher retorted in a huff. No one should question his ability to recall the written word, not even his wife. Why couldn't she get it through her thick skull? "I said that it's Donne and it's Donne."

"Fine. It's done. But it sounds like Shakespeare to me," she replied. When Asher started to speak, Jane shook her head. "I can't believe we're arguing over poetry now, when Count Dracul is preparing to make me a bride and put you six feet under."

"I'm used to it," he joked.

"Not these six feet you aren't," Jane argued, glancing back at their amorous enemies, who were fondling each other. Revulsion covered her face at such behind-closed-door antics being conducted in plain view.

"I didn't know you could do that standing up," she said curiously.

Asher rolled his eyes. "Jane, pay attention here. I don't suppose you have a plan?" he asked. Then he added, "And of course you can do it standing up. I'll show you later if we make it out of here alive. Now, about that plan?"

Jane smiled. "My family is coming to rescue you."

That he would dearly like to see: a Van Helsing rushing to his rescue. "When elephants fly," he muttered.

Jane blushed a becoming pink, remembering the night she lost her virginity. "Why, I believe the elephants must be forming an air force."

She could tell from her husband's heated gaze that he was remembering as well. He tried to reach out and touch her, but the chains kept him bound.

Watching his tortured movements, Jane gently caressed his arm, frowning at the damage the silver chains were doing to him. Asher's wrists were scorched badly, the chains' links beginning to dig into the puffy, raw spots. "I'm sorry, my love, for what they have done to you," she said sadly. "But we will have you free soon. Just as soon as my family arrives. I was the diversion until the troops arrive."

Asher shook his head angrily. "Jane, why did you risk your life for me? Why did your family allow you to employ this dangerous stratagem?" If he left Dracul's alive tonight, he was going to have a long, harsh talk with the major.

"I came to save you! The Van Helsings are coming to destroy the Prince of Darkness. Well . . . Brandon actually wants to save you too—for me."

Asher glanced over at Dracul and Lady Montcrief, who had just finished copulating. "Then where are the troops?" he asked, clearly unconvinced.

"You don't believe me," Jane said.

"You, I believe, Jane. Don't you realize that my bond to you is stronger than these chains of silver? What I do believe is that I love you, in spite of this crazy world going to pieces around us. But your family is . . ." Asher halted abruptly as Count Dracul turned his attention back to them.

"Oh, Asher, I really could kill you," Jane murmured, her eyes sparkling with tears. "*Now* you tell me you love me, when death is at the door." Tenderly, she stroked his cheek.

"Kiss me, Jane, and let this memory carry me through eternity," her husband whispered softly.

She did just that, letting her lips and heart speak all the wondrous things in her heart. Things too new and special for words.

"How touching. Lovers," Dracul sneered, causing them to break apart.

"Oh, how it shall hurt when I take her with my eternal kiss, Asher. You shall know the agony of defeat, of wanting what you can no longer have. Of knowing I have taken your wife in every elemental way there is." The Prince of Evil's eyes sparkled with hate and bloodlust, and he yanked Jane back into his arms.

"I don't think so. I don't want to be a bride of someone who's always hissing at people like they're undercooked steaks," Jane snapped, her voice quavering. Why was her family so late for this very important date? Where in bloody hell were her cousins, the barbarians at the gate?

The Barbarians at the Gate

"You have no choice, you foolish creature. You're going to be my immortal bride," Dracul snarled, all semblance of humanity gone. Jane's scorn had fallen upon him like drops of holy water, burning hot. His fangs were some of the finest of all vampires, two and a half or three inches in length. A length to be proud of.

Jane yanked on her arm in vain; the count's strength was too great. Terror tore through her, ripping at her with its sharp talons.

Dracul savored her fear like a rich dessert, holding her arm tightly in his grasp. "Soon you will be my blushing bride," he warned spitefully, an evil leer on his handsome features. He motioned for O'Hara to take a firm hold on Asher. "Make sure the Earl of Wolverton enjoys the view," he commanded.

Slowly, he drew Jane adjacent to him, toying with her, enjoying her terror and Asher's rage. Pulling both of Jane's hands behind her back, he caught them in one of his hands, despite her struggles. This left him one hand free to toy with her breasts.

"Wait! Count Dracul," Jane shouted, knowing that it was a deadly thing to provoke the undead—rather like stirring a nest of hornets with a small stick. "I prefer my husband to you any day of the week," she said.

Dracul glared at her, his eyes blazing.

Jane smiled. "You know the old adage: 'A vampire in hand is worth two in chains.'" She quoted fearfully, shivering in repressed revulsion at the hungry expression on the count's face. He wrapped her in his arms, hurting her with his cruel strength.

"I'll give you another saying. 'When a Van Helsing knocks, open the door,'" he said slyly.

"I always heard it was, 'When a vampire knocks, open the coffin,'" Jane argued, her heart beating furiously against her ribs.

Dracul arched a brow. He was beauty incarnate, if very, very evil. "'To kill a Van Helsing a day keeps the stakes away,'" he taunted.

"'A vampire a day is the Van Helsing way,'" Jane replied, struggling against his vastly superior strength even though she knew it was useless. Yet fear gave her both courage and strength. Unfortunately, she only managed to hurt her foot when she kicked his leg.

He chuckled, amused by her attempt. "Such a feisty little human."

"I do believe I was feistier," Lady Veronique spoke up from the corner. Only Rudolph paid attention.

In sick horror, Jane watched Dracul's face move closer, and time seemed to slow down. "There is one pertinent adage," he remarked. "'Never look a gift vampire in the mouth.'" His fangs were glistening a deadly white in the glow from the Venetian chandeliers. Jane did not want to be the Prince of Darkness's bride in any form or fashion. She really was going to have to speak to her family about their terrible timing. The diversion she had created had become her downfall.

"Wait!" she heard herself call. "Isn't that the children of the night calling you?"

Dracul cocked his head, listening. "I hear nothing."

Jane shook her head back and forth like a rag doll. "I thought I heard wolves."

"No," Dracul said coldly. "But I like the sound of that. The children of the night. I'll have to use that little saying for my own." He bent back toward Jane, fangs extended.

"No! Halt!" Asher shouted, enraged, his eyes glowing a fierce blue. He struggled against hook, chains and the skeletal butler. In this grave moment of loss and fear, guilt seemed to extend time, causing it to slow down. So many shallow moments in his life flashed past, and he realized Jane was everything he could ever hope for in a true vampire mate. She should be by his side in eternity, not Dracul's. And if he was right about the sound he thought he'd detected a moment earlier, then the Van Helsing cavalry was at the door. He had to stall his archenemy. "The condemned man requests a last favor."

Dracul laughed, along with the other vampires of the nest.

"How touching," Lady Montcrief jeered. The sound was chilling. "And what would this last favor be?"

"I wish to give a final farewell to my wife."

Dracul released his hold on one of her arms, bowing mockingly. He said, "Yes, this makes the moment all the more terrible. You have a few moments . . . so begin."

Staring at his wife with all the love in his heart, Asher quoted, hoping Jane would understand that help was on the way—if only they could stall long enough. "Ah love, let us be true to one another! for the world which seems to lie before us like a land of dreams, so various, so beautiful, so new, hath really neither joy, nor love, nor light, nor certitude nor peace, nor help for pain; and we are here as on a darkling plain swept with confused alarms of struggle and flight, where ignorant armies clash by night.'" Asher prayed that he had bought them enough time, since he had heard footsteps and a loud thump upstairs, directly above his head.

Dracul threw back his head and laughed. "What an imbecile you are. A weakling. Your favor is to quote poetry to your wife?" He sneered in disdain. "But, then, Asher, you always were a fool for the mortal word. I remember how you used to fawn over Shakespeare, following him about, never missing one of his silly plays."

Jane gasped. Her husband had known Shakespeare and never told her? Just wait till she got him alone; she would *so* give him a piece of her mind.

Asher sheepishly noted his wife's exotic eyes turn a deeper shade of green. She was in a huff. He only hoped she—

"You knew Shakespeare personally and you never told me?" She asked, clearly furious. "Asher, how could you be so stingy? How could you keep something like that from me?"

Glancing back at Dracul, Jane went on, "My husband does have a warped sense of humor." Turning back to Asher, she shook her head. "Really, Asher, how could you not have told me? You know how I adore his plays."

Asher wanted to laugh. Here they were in a life-and-death-and-undeath situation, and all she could do was scold him? She was such a feisty, unpredictable handful. But with Jane's passion, he would never, ever grow bored.

"Enough! No more interruptions," Dracul said, gathering Jane back into his arms. From above, a loud crash reverberated. The noise halted Dracul's advance, and he gazed upward to the second floor of the Gothic manor house.

"Check out that noise," he commanded Rudolph. The tall vampire stood to leave, but another crash sounded from the back of the house, a sound that definitely demanded his full attention.

Glancing at the short Baltic vampires who had entered with Lady Montcrief, Dracul commanded, "You! See what caused that sound!"

Then he turned to O'Hara, Lady Veronique and Herr Blixen, and pointed, stepping away from Jane. "Check the back of the house too," he snarled at them. His eyes had turned a bright scarlet.

Jane wanted to weep with relief, and she quickly moved back toward Asher. The cavalry had arrived! The major was here. Her barbarian cousins hadn't let her down. She had never been gladder to see anyone in her life, for she spotted Dwight and Douglas come through the door, followed by her grandfather, crossbow in hand, yelling the Van Helsing battle cry.

Dracul turned, his fangs flashing and his eyes glowing. He raced toward the eldest Van Helsing in a movement so quick, Jane had trouble following it. She gasped in fear, knowing she was about to see her grandfather slaughtered.

But in one quick move, displaying an amazing agility for one so old, honed through years of hunting the undead, Ebenezer Van Helsing lifted his crossbow. Using it, he shot his arrow straight and true. It pierced Dracul's chest, embedding itself in his cold, black heart.

The count was so startled, he glanced for a moment in stunned silence from Jane's grandfather to Jane to Asher, and then down at the wooden arrow-stake protruding from his chest. His eyes widened as blood gushed from his mouth.

"Impossible! No human can kill me!" he muttered, sinking slowly to the floor. "For me, tomorrow never dies." He gasped, but his form began to crumble to dust as if he'd been in living daylights.

Asher watched, unmoved by the death of his foul foe. "Never say never."

Jane, who had a perfect view to the kill, added, "You should have lived and let die." Her heart was racing, her eyes wide with disbelief. Her grandfather had used the goldfinger vampire-execution move, and with remarkable aplomb.

She shook her head in shock. The world was not enough for someone like Dracul, who so craved power and destruction. His death was a gruesome sight, yet a necessary one. Everyone was again safe from the evil Prince of Darkness. Light had crept back into the shadows, erasing them. Jane sighed in relief.

The emotion was short-lived, however, as Herr Blixen and a Slavic vampire rushed to attack her grandfather for killing their prince. It seemed everything slowed down, and she watched in horror as Herr Blixen leapt to within a few feet of Colonel Ebenezer Van Helsing.

But before he could strike, Blixen was melted. He was doused by holy water that Jane's eldest cousin, Dwight, threw. And a stake through the back stopped the other evil vampire's attack, courtesy of Brandon, who'd raced into the room like an avenging angel. Jane's brother had first countered an offensive move against his grandfather with a well-practiced stake-and-shake called the Thunderball, invented by the first Jakob Van Helsing in the seventeenth century.

With vampires dying right and left around her, Lady Montcrief screamed in rage. Grabbing a chair, she swung it against the wall to break it into pieces. With one broken leg in hand, she leapt toward Asher, who was still bound in chains and hanging from the hook.

Seeing what was about to happen, Jane yelled to her

grandfather. Her Catching Flying Stakes class had come to mind immediately. In one smooth motion, her grandfather threw her a stake. Grabbing it from the air as if by magic, Jane turned and plunged it into Lady Montcrief's chest.

Heedless of anything but the fierce desire to destroy Asher, Lady Montcrief continued forward, her own momentum propelling the stake through her. The timing was perfect, and Jane recognized that the many long hours of practicing in the grass had not been in vain. She might hate the sight of blood; she might hate the thought of stabbing anything other than a vampire dummy. But this time her husband's life was at stake—and she was, after all, a Van Helsing.

With a #4 protruding from her chest, Lady Montcrief fell to the floor, crying out, "You stupid bitch! How could you?" But as she fell, her face began to disintegrate. Pieces of her skin began to turn to parchment, and she was soon left a pile of white and black ashes.

Life was odd, Jane thought, staring down at the blood on her hands. Her whole life she had been pushed and prodded toward goals that were not her own. She had shed many a tear in dismay and loneliness. The road traveled had been a rocky and difficult one. Yet, from her vampire hunting beginnings she had become who she was, and that person was strong without being aggressive, caring without being cynical. She could be sad without being melancholy and happy without being a fool.

Yes, from her past Jane had garnered a solid iron core that was strong enough for her to do her duty when it needed to be done, even if that duty was a despised one. And if not for that despised duty, Asher would now be dust, a hunk of wood through his heart. Life was filled with wonderful irony, and with tiny miracles joining together to make big ones.

In a daze, she abstractly noted that her cousins George and Jemeny were lifting Asher off the hook. Suddenly Jane began to tremble, and her knees felt shaky. She sank to her knees as tears ran down her cheeks, and she vomited. Her first true staking, and she was so sick she could die.

"There's no crying in staking, Jane," Dwight scolded. She only cried harder.

"Stop that! There's no crying in this game, Jane. No crying at all," Dwight admonished.

"My wife can cry if she wants," Asher growled, dropping to his knees beside her, concerned by the pallor of her complexion. He handed her his soiled handkerchief. "Jane, Jane, never have I known you to have a handkerchief when you need one." She smiled faintly.

He felt as if he would burst from pride, and he hadn't even had any holy water spilled on him. As the sounds of battle faded in the other parts of the house, he gazed at Jane with pride. "Wife, you saved my life. I think I am the luckiest vampire in the world."

He would never forget the way she looked tonight, with blood on her dress, her hair mussed and courage in her eyes. She was magnificent, and she was his. His lady in red. He was a very lucky vampire, he decided happily. Very lucky indeed.

She shook her head. "I know. But I have never killed a real vampire before. And I never want to do it again."

Asher leaned his head against hers. "I don't want you to, either. I like my friends just as dead as they are," he teased.

Jane managed a small smile. "Bite your tongue."

"No, I believe I will let you do that," Asher argued. "And other places as well."

She shook her head. "You are insane. We have just

been rescued from the jaws of death—" Jane began, looking over at what was left of Dracul slowly disintegrating on the Persian carpet. She shuddered at the gory mess. "—and you are thinking of bedroom matters. And to think, I used to think you were so proper and stiff."

He smiled wickedly. "I am stiff. In the mornings, nights, and in point of fact, anytime you are near."

Jane blushed. "Asher!"

He continued to grin as her grandfather came and knelt down beside him, took out wire cutters and began to cut his chains. Asher winced in pain as the silver was pulled free of his flesh.

Jane watched in silent sympathy, nausea her companion as the last of the links were pulled out. Asher gasped in pained relief, and Major and Jakob Van Helsing entered the room.

Both men took in the in the scene of destruction with cheery dispositions. Jakob grinned, saying, "Vampire total dead: seven. Plus one dead human servant. Van Helsing losses were nil, but there were some minor bruises and cuts."

"All clear above and below stairs," he went on to inform them. "Jolly good show. We got every last one of the bloodsuckers."

George laughed loudly, boasting, "We came, we saw, we kicked their teeth in!"

Jane's grandfather went over to what was left of Dracul. "Looks like I finally got the biggest vampire rat of them all," he said proudly.

"And with your crossbow too," Brandon remarked. "I guess it was all that practice on the . . . vampire rats." He hesitated over the last part, as he'd always been embarrassed by his grandfather's insane theories about the mice. He summoned up some enthusiasm to cheer: "Tallyho, Grandfather, you got him! Finally, after centuries of murder, the Prince of Darkness has been stopped by a crossbow made for mice! It's almost too perfect." He knew he would tell his grandchildren of this night in years to come.

Jakob Van Helsing patted his father on the shoulder. "Jolly good show, old man."

The major however, was not amused. His crowning achievement was to have been Dracul's death. He frowned. "I should have come in here instead of taking the cellars. It should have been me."

Both Brandon and Jane shook their heads. Their father would never change.

"At least *you* didn't do the deed," the major said brusquely as he glanced over at his brother, Jakob.

Jakob and George frowned, while Jane and Brandon both shrugged their shoulders.

"Glad to see you aren't hurt, Jane. Jolly good show, old girl," the major remarked. "Proud of you."

Jane's eyes teared up. Her father was proud of her and Asher loved her. He *really* loved her. Life was beautiful.

Asher stood, rubbing his wrists where the worst of the burns from the silver had created red ridges in his flesh. "Dracul's dead now. And the world is a safer place—thanks to the Van Helsings. All of them." He bowed formally. "I am in your debt. I owe you my life, as well as my wife's. I don't know what I would do without her."

"You love her . . ." Brandon stated thoughtfully.

"With all my heart," Asher agreed.

Looks of all kinds crossed the faces of the Van Helsings in the room. Expressions of amusement, disbelief, pride and anger.

The major was the only one in a foul temper. "What is the world coming to? A Van Helsing, riding to the rescue of a vampire?" he groused.

Jane grinned, secure in herself and Asher's love for the very first time. "Elephants are flying, and I do believe I'll need to purchase a pair of ice skates," she commented, as her husband drew her into his arms and held her tight. She felt as if she had crossed a dark and desolate continent to finally find her way home. "I guess little demons all over the underworld will be shivering tonight."

Staring down at his wife, Asher threw back his head and laughed. Yes, hell had frozen over. He had fallen deeply in love with a Van Helsing. And the future had never looked rosier.

Jane joined his laughter, much to the bewilderment and bemusement of her family.

So Many Vampire Ashes
Gone with the Wind

The next night, Asher discovered both the triumphs and tribulations of life in a large family. Jane had invited the Van Helsings—cousins and all—to a victory celebration dinner.

At first he was reserved and wary. It wasn't often that a master vampire was encircled by a room full of slayers and lived to tell the tale. But the Van Helsings quickly warmed to him. They were amazed by all the mirrors in his front rooms, and even more amazed that Asher's reflection could be seen whenever he stood near one. The Van Helsings learned that one of the many things they'd thought they knew about vampires was a myth. Which alerted them to the possibility more vampires might be hiding in London than they'd previously thought. They were grateful for that.

Yes, in spite of his being a Nosferatu, the Van Helsings had taken him into the bosom of their family—and what bosoms there were! Asher thought as he stared at Jane's décolletage. He really had to talk to her about her dressmaker and lay down a few laws. The neckline of that gown should be at least two inches higher. No, make that *three*, he decided as his wife bent slightly forward, listening to her cousin George.

Cocking his head, Asher decided that his wife looked lovely in her scarlet-colored gown. He was a vampire, and he wanted her now in a most elemental way, with blood and body, heart and soul. Thanking his lucky stars, Asher realized how fortunate he was. In a world filled with lonely people, all searching for that special someone, he had found his. And since he was a vampire, he could have her by his side forever. He smiled devilishly, his love for his wife glowing from his eyes.

Jane returned her husband's smile, happier than she had ever been. Asher truly loved her, and she loved him with an intense passion that she knew would never die.

"Jane, pay attention," George admonished. "This story really is quite humorous."

Jane sighed and pretended to listen to her cousin's recollection of the other night's trip to the cemetery as she watched Spot approach Asher to be petted and held. With a sigh of resignation, Asher picked up the little dog and began scratching under Spot's chin. Jane hid her smile. Her toplofty earl was an old softie at heart. All the while she watched her husband talking with various members of her family. It was remarkable, but the Van Helsings had declared a truce with Asher, and they were all getting along famously. At this moment, Asher was discussing the tying of the oriental cravat with her brother and cousin Jemeny, who seemed awed by Asher's know-how.

Her grandfather was scouring Asher's home for mice. Uncle Jakob was deep in conversation with Renfield about the origin of the best red wines. Her eldest cousin, Dwight, was preening before the full-length mirror in the corner, and the major was sitting in the large brocade chair by the fireplace, his knees upon a cushion, discussing deer hunting with Douglas. (Though her father hadn't been very courteous to her husband, at least he wasn't reaching for silver chains or staring at Asher's chest with bloodlust in his eyes.)

She nodded happily at something George said, thinking how fortunate she was. They were just one big happy family—Orville, Spot, vampire hunters, vampire, human servant and all. In fact, Orville was singing his nightly song, screeching happily while Dwight, the major and Asher all wore disgusted expressions. Jane laughed. They had more in common than they thought.

After dinner, the hours sped by quickly, and the Van Helsings took their leave; Brandon, Douglas and Jemeny waved and called out their good-byes.

"Alone at last," Asher whispered dryly, as he watched his butler close the door on them. "Now you are mine, and I can have my wicked way with you." He leaned close and kissed her on the neck. "Stars fade, but I linger on, dear, just craving your kiss. I will *always* crave your kiss—your smile, your love, the way you argue with me . . ."

"Why, Asher, I rarely argue with you," Jane argued.

Asher threw back his head and laughed. Then he quoted, " 'Come live with me and be my love, and we will all the pleasures prove.' "

"Christopher Marlowe," Jane said, knowing at once who had written the words. "And speaking of quotes—"

Asher cut her off with a hot, brief kiss.

Jane pulled back, staring at her husband. "I can't believe you knew Shakespeare personally, and didn't tell me."

Placing both hands on either side of her face, he said, "Jane, Jane, my most cherished wife, I love you."

"That is because you have impeccable taste," she teased. "Now, my love, stop trying to distract me. Tell me all about Shakespeare," she said, trying to ignore Asher nibbling on her ear.

"Do you know that your love was sharp enough to pierce my cold heart?" he asked. " 'I do love nothing in the world so well as you: is not that strange?' "

Jane would not be distracted. "That last part is Shakespeare—and you knew him. Were you good friends? Did he confide in you? Were any of his stories written about you?" She had a hundred questions to ask about the grand old playwright.

Asher laughed. "Wife, I believe we are at cross purposes. Give me a kiss to build a dream on. To build our *future* on."

Jane happily complied, the Bard barred for a moment as she deepened the kiss. Reluctantly both she and Asher drew back, gazing into each other's eyes.

"Do you truly love me?" Asher asked, his normal hauteur vanished. He knew she loved him, but how much? Enough to be with him forever as his consort? To be what her family had once taught her to indiscriminately despise?

"Will you let me tuck you into your coffin at daylight?" Her question was said in a teasing manner, but the answer to Jane was important. It was all about trust.

"Each and every night," he agreed solemnly. "Forever."

"Yes, Asher. I love you with all my soul."

"Forever?" Asher asked, his heart beating harshly in his chest. He had never needed anyone as much as he needed Jane. Although he had loved Clair, what he felt for his Van Helsing was more. He had never loved anyone as much as he loved her, and he blessed Clair and even her hairy husband, Huntsley, for bringing them together. For his love was as boundless as infinity, as endless as the vast heavens, for the woman he held so tenderly in his arms.

"Of course. I will love you until the day I die," Jane admitted softly.

"To your good fortune." He smiled naughtily.

She playfully bit his neck and ran her fingers through his thick, wavy hair. "You're so vain. But I love you anyway."

Asher held her hand as he looked down at her, his expression quite serious. "I want forever with you, Jane, not just thirty or forty years. I want centuries to pet and spoil you." He tensed slightly, awaiting her answer. "Be my vampire bride."

Tracing his lips, she sighed dreamily. Suddenly the world was full of possibilities. Forever was a very long time, and she intended to spend it with Asher, enjoying undeath to the fullest. It would shock her family, and she would have to overcome her thing about blood, but forever looked very good right now.

But . . . not tonight. Tonight was for affirming their love for each other. Each would luxuriate in the knowledge that they had found each other in this big, wide world, filled with a million smiling or tragic faces. Each knew now that love had filled their souls and hearts to overflowing.

"I will spend eternity by your side, but we can't do it tonight. I need to prepare my family for the deed."

"They'll never accept it," Asher replied tensely.

Jane put a finger to his lips. "Give them some time. Give *me* some time to change their minds."

"But . . . ," Asher began.

Jane caressed his mouth with her finger, cocking an eyebrow. "Asher, I am Jane Van Helsing Asher, Countess of Wolverton and retired vampire huntress. I can do anything I set my heart to." She smiled gaily. For it was true. "After all, I managed to marry the most sought-after earl in England, and he fell deeply in love with me. If I can do that, I can manage to settle down a few disgruntled Van Helsings."

Asher grinned. "All right, my love. You take as long as

you need. We have forever, after all. Clasping her tightly to him, he added tenderly, "I found you. I finally found the love of my life. Come. Let us go to bed. Where we will love and love until I have worn you near to death. The world can go up in flames around us, and we will be too busy to notice. Tonight, my adorable little wife, you are in for a night of lovemaking with no intermissions."

Jane giggled. "You, my lord, are no gentleman."

"A minor point at the moment," he conceded, nipping her neck with a bit of fang, then kissing her tenderly with all the years of unspent passion he'd stored within him.

Jane felt like weeping with delight. His lips were firm and caressing, his breath as sweet as autumn apples and fresh cinnamon. He was a part of her heart now.

The kiss ended with Asher scooping her up in his arms and carrying Jane in her scarlet gown up the wide marbled staircase. She glanced at the butler, Mr. Rhett, who was trying to hide the grin on his face. Renfield stood off to the side, also smiling—a rare treat indeed.

Blushing, Jane scolded gently, "The servants, Asher. What will they think of you carrying me off like this?"

Her husband laughed. "Frankly, my dear, I don't give a damn."

Jane howled in delight as Asher scaled the stairs rapidly. Tomorrow was another day that she'd be eating breakfast alone. But tonight . . . tonight was all hers.

Epilogue

Outside Wolverton Manor, gleaming fangs showed stark white in the fog-ridden night as a man studied Neil Asher's residence. The Earl of Wolverton's home was a massive place with a red-gabled roof.

Dracula paused in his observation as he felt a twinge of guilt. His brother Dracul would have sought revenge immediately, but he, Dracula, Dracul's twin brother, was made of smarter stuff. Asher had been a powerful force before his marriage to a Van Helsing. Now he had the backing of that vampire-slaying clan as well. Not to mention, true love always made a vampire stronger.

His twin was now dust; so many good vampires were ashes, gone with the wind. Yet, he knew instinctively that revenge would come. It was a dish best served cold, despite what his brother had believed. He could wait. Dracula knew that few mortals or immortals knew of his existence. He would keep it that way—for now. But look out, world, there was a new Prince of Darkness in Town.

Taking one last look at Wolverton manor, Dracula saluted Asher. "Your time will come," he hissed.

Shrugging his shoulders, he turned away. He had a million tomorrows to avenge the death of his brother and his brother's nest. He began to stroll in the direction of Hyde Park. Fading into the ghostly London fog like smoke, he spoke his thoughts aloud: "After all, tomorrow is another night."

The Remarkable Miss Frankenstein

Minda Webber

The problem, Clair realizes, is that she's a Frankenstein. Everyone in the family is a success, while all she's managed is a humiliating misadventure with pigs. But her spirits are rising. The Journal of Scientific Discovery promises to publish a paper on the Discovery of the Decade, and she has a doozy. She simply has to prove Baron Huntsley—man of distinction—is a vampire. With his midnight-black hair, soul-piercing eyes and shiny white teeth, what else could he be? Oh yes, the Baron wants a bite of her or she's no scientist. Pretty soon she'll expose him, and on everybody's lips will be...*The Remarkable Miss Frankenstein.*
